FICTION OF THE FIFTIES

FICTION OF THE FIFTIES
A Decade of American Writing

STORIES SELECTED AND WITH AN INTRODUCTION BY

HERBERT GOLD

Dolphin Books
Doubleday & Company, Inc.
Garden City, New York

ACKNOWLEDGMENTS

SONNY'S BLUES by James Baldwin. Copyright © 1957 by James
Baldwin. First published in *Partisan Review*. Reprinted by
permission of the author.

A SERMON BY DOCTOR PEP by Saul Bellow. Copyright 1949 by
Partisan Review. Reprinted by permission of the author.

WHAT THE CYSTOSCOPE SAID by Anatole Broyard. Copyright 1954
by Anatole Broyard. Reprinted by permission of the author.

THE PRIZE by R. V. Cassill. Copyright 1955 by *Perspective*. Reprinted by permission of the author.

THE COUNTRY HUSBAND by John Cheever. Copyright 1954 by The
New Yorker Magazine, Inc. Reprinted by permission of the
author.

THE CONDOR AND THE GUESTS by Evan S. Connell, Jr. Copyright
1951 by Evan S. Connell, Jr. From THE ANATOMY LESSON AND
OTHER STORIES by Evan S. Connell. Reprinted by permission
of the Viking Press, Inc.

AMONG THE DANGS by George P. Elliott. © 1958 by Esquire, Inc.
Reprinted by permission of the author.

LOVE AND LIKE by Herbert Gold. Copyright © 1958 by Herbert
Gold. First published in *Hudson Review*. Reprinted by permission of the author.

THE SOLITARY LIFE OF MAN by Leo Litwak. Copyright © 1959
by Leo Litwak. Reprinted by permission of the author.

THE MAGIC BARREL by Bernard Malamud. Copyright 1954, 1958
by Bernard Malamud. Used by permission of the publishers,
Farrar, Straus and Cudahy, Inc.

THE ARTIFICIAL NIGGER by Flannery O'Connor. Copyright 1955
by Flannery O'Connor. Reprinted from her volume A GOOD
MAN IS HARD TO FIND by permission of Harcourt, Brace and
Company, Inc.

THE DEVIL WAS THE JOKER by J. F. Powers. Copyright 1953 by
The New Yorker Magazine, Inc. Reprinted by permission of
the author.

CYCLISTS' RAID by Frank Rooney. Copyright 1951 by Frank
Rooney. First published in *Harper's Magazine*. Reprinted by
permission of the author.

THE DANCER by Harvey Swados. Copyright 1952 by Harvey
Swados. Reprinted by permission of the author.

DOLPHIN EDITION 1961
Printed in the United States of America

CONTENTS

FICTION OF THE FIFTIES

1. The Writer as Metaphysician

Indeed it is difficult not to live cautiously these days. There is so much to gain (car, house, rank); there is so much to lose (rank, house, car). And yet, what we are sure of gaining and sure of losing remains the same. We are sure of losing our lives. We are sure of the chance at gaining our lives. The ceremonial observances of passion and joy, regret and renewal, continue as always. Parents die, children are born, lovers meet and cling to each other, "their arms round the griefs of the ages." Days pass. Age comes. Mortality decides much and yet gives us many choices: *What are we to make of our lives?* Each step of the way, bound to instinct and accident, controlled by the past and by those others who surround us, involves a new decision: *In what direction the next step?* We are left with this peculiar good news in the shape of a question; by asking it we earn the right of eminent domain. In spite of the way of the world, we utter our hopes, we challenge our fears, we take our chances: *What next? When? Where? How? Why?*

These ultimate questions are contained within every act a man or a woman performs; they have always been contained within the act of creation which is the writing of a story. This has been true for ever and ever, and was true during the decade of the Fifties.

A fly in the metaphysics has been growing, however, until it has near reached the size of a bounding Australian kangaroo. Is it *we* who decide? Who decides under the humid breath of the mass media, psychologizing preachers, statesmen of clay and lanolin made—under that interior whisper to belong, conform, and R.I.P.? Who decides about modern war, atomic fission, mass murder? We are in the shoes of the man poised on the edge of the cliff, deciding about life and mortality, who finally sighs and turns away, resolute against suicide. He will live! There is only one chance for a man, and it is here on earth! . . . At that moment he is shot in the chest by a mad sniper.

Therefore the writer, that exemplary figure, that scapegoat with a diet of tin and hope, scampering first in the lead and then in the rear of society, must accept a complicated mission. He must bounce along with the busy-rumped kangaroo. He must celebrate and value experience. He must see clearly. He must relish what he sees. He must make sense. *And he must not forget the snipers.* Sir Graspinghands who chased the grail had no harder task. Only his armor weighed him down—no publishing fads, anonymous reviews, girls asking "Are you happy?", cocktail therapy. He had his horse, his mission, his box of See-rations; "Go!" He went.

In order to balance the impossible burden of this mid-century on his back and head, the writer must be possessed by what is called style. Style is a notion much worried these and all days. It has to do with controlled strength—the control of the nervous juggler, the strength of the very strong man. It means everything is kept in the air at once, and coherent, and ordered, and eloquent, and also actually *there* in the mind. It is not a scampering trick, a minor felicity, a small device sandpapered into life. An illustration of the power of style is that carnival game which asks you to hammer a nail into a board in three strokes in order to win the prize. The stylist does not bang the board all about; he does not splay his thumb; he hits the nail neatly and swiftly and accurately. Of course, there may be hidden obstructions in the board which deflect the nail; the nail itself may not bear the burden of his stroke; but he fails with dignity and clear sight and a sense of purposeful, directed energy. Also, with good luck in an honest show, he carries off the prize doll.

Style in a writer is a policy about life, not a stunt. It is the personal cabinet of the man who is President of Himself (or at least First Tenor of Egosdale-on-Avon). It is the package containing sealed orders, and when far at sea or in the jungle we open it, we read these terrible words: *Think about cardinal matters!* It is both the map to treasure and the treasure itself.

Aiming at the truth about life on earth, possessed of his style, what has been the special mission of the writer of fiction during the decade of the 1950's? Not absolutely different from the mission of the writer of any time, of course. One role did not leave off in 1949 when automobiles were just beginning to grow their postwar tumors and television aerials sprouted like wild asparagus on the roof tops of America. But a special kind of light has been focused, a direction marked out, and when we look at the contemporary writers who mean much to us at this end of the decade, we may see how they have responded as a group to the particular disasters and challenges of our time.

We may be made uncomfortable by looking. If we are interested in fiction, we usually want only to embrace it; we hate to see too clearly—it's like examining the piece of spinach on the teeth of the loved one whom we are about to kiss. So let's look quickly, have it over with, and be ready for the kissing. Now here is the spinach:

Writers of fiction have been taking on the role traditionally played by religious leaders, philosophers, metaphysicians. They have returned in deep need to the most primitive poetic purpose: *to know;* to try to know even when they know not; to invoke knowledge; to ransom the god within by peeling off their skin. They have been driven to asking the ultimate questions. And those who love fiction must nowadays love it partly because it concerns itself with final matters.

Where? Whither? Why?

For whom do I live?

For whom?

For what?

What is the relation between freedom and isolation? When am I free and when am I merely isolated? When am I alone and independent? When am I responsible? When am I groupy, togethered into socialized isolation? When am I selfished into insignificance, savaged into incoherence?

What is the connection between love and weakness, love and strength?

Why do I live, struggle, love, defy age and history?

Why must I die and for what?

Who am I?

This question is the spinach on all our teeth and it stinks up our breath when we utter it. It's not, either, that these concerns are unique to our time—the spinach is still visible on Dostoyevsky's teeth, and Tolstoy filled his mouth with green. The great writer always explores both his inner space and that other world outside his head, and bridges the air between. *There must be coherence,* he insists. But an aching personal concern with meaning is the exceptional by-product of our age. Where can we find the truth amid the lies which surround us? There is lassitude in our bones and an aching hope in our loins. This is not ordinary spinach; this is Spinach-90.

Naturally the other kinds of writers and readers still exist. Family novels, fat historical romances, suspense and mystery stories, and various partial talebearers still have their audiences, and why not? Spinach, harsh and gritty, is not necessarily good for us, and some make no demand for it. The impulse toward metaphysics and prophecy is not universal, and why should it be? Also religious leaders, political thinkers, philosophers, psychoanalysts, columnists in *Look,* fortunetellers, revivalists, and drug-sellers all marshal their happy (unhappy) throngs. These citizens have little need to look for thought in fiction and usually have little need of fiction at all, except for the fiction of self-help.

Having eliminated these good citizens, we are left with you and me and perhaps some cowboy in Butte, Montana, waiting in a library while his MG is repaired. We like to read, you and I and that cowboy. (He is also the child in the second balcony whom the violinist plays for.) We read. We see no way of justifying the ways of men to men except by imaginative examination of life on earth. We have looked for the strong sense of personality (mysteries, style); we have found dilemmas and problems (unsolved, unsolvable); we have found resolutions (impossible, essential); we have occasionally been wrung by that strong response which tells us, in literature and in love, in ourselves or in others, I feel! I am alive! I think; therefore I exist.

All this is not to argue that the storyteller is a mere systematic philosopher, conducting a streetcar named Reality, heading home toward the Truth after a hard day. No, no. The car barn is empty; the streetcars have all been sold to Mexico City; futile to look to tropical paradises of tequila and bee-stung lips, or to Rome, or to Moscow, or to any perfect answer in the fancy heavens of archaic simplicity. The bee-stung pair of lips or the various appointments with ritual are answers to something—to a need for rest—but not to our questions, and these questions are what count. It is not so easy. We must also beware of the lofty question-answering fury in a writer. For the crime of *hubris*—that mad pride which leads a mortal to compare himself with Aldous Huxley or William Saroyan—he should be trampled into submission by ten thousand of the top editors of *Time*, all wearing wet galoshes. The writer may be looking for Reality (abstract), but he can find it only in Real Life (concrete). That is, the abstract essence is contained only within the facts of life. The Idea of Woman can never replace the way Sally scratches her head. The Celestial Milkman can only be surmised from that clinking, clanking chap who comes to the door with a brilliant smile, a doctored bill, a teamster's button in his cap, and an opinion about Brigitte Bardot. The Ultimate Meaning of coconuts and milk remains elusive despite coconut cream pie, camembert, butter, and that bump on the head when you fall asleep under the palm tree. When the writer eats a meal for the FBI and finds God, what he really finds is the roast beef pearled with droplets of blood, the golden sweet potatoes, the stray pea in the succotash, the salad tossed with crisp moral lettuce and determined erotic vinegar. That is, he finds God. That is, he finds food and love in time of hunger.

He is not sure of anything. He is absolutely certain about everything.

Saul Bellow, an exemplary writer of this generation, expresses most clearly the philosophical and religious quest necessarily contained within an abiding sense for passing things. All his work seems to ask the question, "Why am I here?" And answers his comic mood: "Because I'm here —that's enough!" And in his mood of despair: "Because I'm here—that's not enough!" But his intensely lyrical and dramatic, onflowing participation in the life of his Chicago, his Africa, his universe, makes the underlying metaphysical question possible; and so his deepest answer seems to be: "Why? Because we are all here together on earth. It is both enough and not enough."

That is probably the only permanent answer to a question which never remains the same.

II.   The Novel and the Story—The Long and Short of It

What the novelist seems to be doing at his philosophical best is to explore possibility.[1] He cuts loose from the expected and sees another possibility for an entire life—his own, his characters', everybody's. The mystery of personality, that unheard sound, always the most heavy presence in a place, works its way to some concrete clap of existence through the tangle of growth which is a successful novel. The great novelists, hearing new sounds, building new worlds in the jungle of the real world, are also great moralists by implication—committed, before all else, to an intense valuation of human experience in the here and now. They are also dangerous and destructive moralists. With angry shouts and kicks they clear away their place in the jungle before they build. They tear down our customary ways of looking at things. They stare into the sun of alternatives. They tell us: You can choose this, you can decide that. You are free! Or if not, you must seek to be free.

In the short story, a writer does something rather different in degree and therefore different in quality. Of course, some novels are merely long stories, and some stories are merely foreshortened novels, but in general the short story is work conceived with greater rigor than the novel. The short-story

---

[1] A few sentences here are taken from the author's introduction to his stories in *Fifteen by Three*, by Cassill, Gold, and Hall (New Directions).

writer pretty much knows what he is about when he begins; he puts on the smoked glasses of a limited form before watching the eclipse of the sun. The novelist, bound to freedom, may end up blind, roasted, stupefied, and lonely. He sets out with only a hint of the end of the voyage on which he has embarked with no maps but the sealed secret orders of instinct and intelligence. He is as blind as a Secretary of State on the brink of—he knows not what. He is chronically in a bad way, dazzled and sunburned, and heading full steam up shiftless creek.

Because of this necessity of psychic confusion crystallizing out toward inexplicable and miraculous clarity in the important novel—"novel" means new, and the novel brings us unwanted news of the world—the short story is usually more reassuring both to read and to write. The agony of doubt is relieved. The destructive power of a total re-evaluation of experience is not risked. The writer can put down some of his moral baggage. In the story he *knows*—and only doubt, hope, dread, expectation infect him with that inner debate of chronic invention. Knowledge is knowledge—certain-sure. It is as present and comforting as a baked potato. It is what it is. Add butter and salt and have no fear.

Yet, a story is not quite as sure as a baked potato. (*Nota bene:* Even the potato may have a worm baked into it.) The parables of the great prophets and saints are truer than their moral conclusions because tongue-tied and tail-tied to life, which means to unending reinterpretation and reunderstanding. (The word "truth" here is defined as the product of a viable manner of looking—with energy and love—rather than as a formulated conclusion.) Like the great parables, like a novel, a story opens out into a new world, too. At its best, as someone said of something else, it "goes on going on." Sometimes it won't stop going on. The most ruthless writer has trouble putting his stories away from him. Many a novel has been pried out of a writer by a dissatisfaction with what started out to be a story. He reads and thinks: No, no, that can't be all. Those people can't stop here. Now they should . . .

And all at once he finds himself committed to a year or two of griping, sweating, typing and retyping, scratching, poking, jumping out of bed at odd hours, like a parent with a cranky child, because a scene or a character or a situation does not let him sleep. He wants to shake his finger at each new story: "Promise you'll stay put if I give you your say?"

Part of the difference between the short story and the novel is the difference between a love affair and marriage. The first is piquant, exciting, less risky, but may cause beautiful troubles, such as wedlock. The second is long, complicated, noisy, unpredictable, very often unhappy, and absolutely prime to living on earth. The total commitment of marriage is very different from the lyrical joys of love. The novel is different from the story, and not merely because it is longer and heavier. The responsibility is total. "In dreams begin responsibilities"—in stories. "In the day responsibilities end, they end in responsibilities"—so the blessed total envelopment of a novel tells us. Those who read and write both forms treasure these two modes of experiencing fiction. And of course we love either a novel or a story as we love a girl—not for intelligence or virtue—but for the way it meets our gaze.

The short story, as it has developed since James Joyce, seems to be concerned with scene and incident, striking hot, like the lyrical poem. The novel since Dostoyevsky and Tolstoy has increasingly charged itself to make the whole man face the whole world—really the metaphysical enterprise, the bedrock sense of religious thought. Therefore a wholly questing writer like Ralph Ellison, forging or attempting to forge a total view of his world in which a man can stand, is poorly served by the short-story form and unrepresented here although his *Invisible Man* is one of the fine books of the decade and a representative one in its basic philosophical purpose. When the center does not hold, we try to make new centers. Or, in stories, the man whose center does not hold relies on the celebrational hope of poetry —this deed, this moment, this passing love or hate. A man may face the world alone in a story as in a novel, but he does not try to give himself his final name. He is less likely to be Melville's Ishmael than John Cheever's country husband, troubled in love, trying to make out.

The difference between the short story and the novel can

be expressed also through another partly parallel, overlapping set of categories. The short story tends to control and formalize experience (though the expressionistic story does not); the novel tends to set forward experience in documentary detail (though the Jamesian novel does not). Fiction can be divided this way into two types: First, that which seeks the ordered ranging and mastery of ideas; second, that which seeks the mastery of experience by passionate avowal. The first writer says: "This is what I can do with it!" The second says, "This is how it is—all of it!" The writers who Avow have the virtues of weight of feeling, purgation by life, passion with its submissions and excesses. They run the risks of looseness, maudlin howling, self-indulgence. The writers who Control give the satisfactions of answering formal demands for order, of coming to an understanding of ends and causes and thus purging us of menace. They run the risks of a false, faked formalism, of giving us resolutions which do not resolve. As the Avowers may howl unnaturally, so the Controllers may build atrocious humps on their backs. One tries to go from the particular to the sublime, the other from the reticulated to the sublime.

No writer of any lasting interest is purely one thing or the other. The best writers of the Fifties have both expressed the disasters of the times and given us some tentative notions of order. And the great writer, who has the chance of producing a masterpiece, certainly combines both of these irreconcilables, the Avowed and the Controlled—just as estranged metals can finally be fused under great heat. With fire, pressure, and continued intensity, the great artist rises to the peak of emotion and the pitch of resolution in the same work—and so, as Aristotle says, we are at last purged of pity and terror. In some way, the moving image of desire has been expressed through the life of one person, that monster individual, the hero who at last represents us all.

III. The Writer as Cricken, Floozie, Elder Revolu-
tionist, Young Fogie, Beautician, Mortician, etc., In-
cluding Far-Flung Flinger into Fans (Watch Out)

Harassed, often mistaken and mistook, blessed at his best
by good hope and fruitful despair, the writer of the Fifties
played hide-and-go-seek amid the disasters of the time.

He made a characteristic kind of fiction—anxious, humorous, demanding—in the image of man's hope during years
when every thinking person had to be his own Don Quixote.
The windmills surround us for the charging. Sheep may not
safely graze, sheep in these days may not even safely gaze;
but some writers munched and nosed and threw off their
sheep's clothing. They ran against the furious windmills.

Who is the writer who gives us the strongest view of the
time?

First, who is he NOT?

Not the fabricated fakes of television, Hollywood, and
the mass magazines (not Harry Belafonte improving race
relations by playing a Chinese version of *Green Pastures*
in yellowface);

Not the Truth Trumpeters with a capital P (for Penulti-
mate Reality), who are made of the nerves left over when
Dr. Jekyll turned himself into Mr. Hyde;

Nor the Crickens (Critical Chicken-Hearts saying, "Complex it up, fellas, Russian it up a little!");

Nor the Floozies (Philosophical Oozers of Timeless Indifference);

Nor Sloan Wilson and Herman Wouk with their new
upper-middle soap opera (an easier detergent for the togethered souls of suburban lads and lassies of whatever
moribund condition);

Nor the Young Fogies queerly proclaiming a brotherhood
of gangbang and gangwhimper—real toadies in imaginary
gardens ("I'm one Hell of a Guy, Damn! A-tearin' down
society and grammar! A-preachin' of the gospel to all us
delinquent kids! Man! Zip! Zen! Wow!");

Nor the Elder Tired Revolutionists ("I have found fair

logos under the skirt of Henry James and in the handkerchief which Tom Eliot keeps up his sleeve");

Nor the Beauticians and Uglifiers like Tennessee W., Truman C., Speed L. ("It's so dreadful out here in the *world*. Lemme back, Ma!");

Nor the Morticians, those guilty refugees afflicted with severe cases of penance-envy ("I've read Kierkegaard, Simone Weil, Toynbee, Russell Kirk, Peter Viereck, and my own heart, which shrivels up inside me like the stretchsox off my foot, and I tell you, brethren, it was all a mistake. God meant us to go elsewhere, down below.");

Nor the various other crossbred jackals, bats, wood lice, small-eared asses, woolly barn owls, ferrets, and viewers with abstract alarm.

Then *who?*

Don Quixote, Jungle Jim, scapegoat, juggler, spinach-toothed President of Himself, the great writer of our times will be a person who loots the world for good reason, relishing his prize. He will not have a mediocre subject—himself. He will have a subject with grandiose boundary and tangled interior—*himself.* As a man of our time, he will sing about love, ambition, and mortality expressed through the events of days and nights, and buried within the miraculous willed accidents which move his people will be questions about the relation between freedom and isolation, independence and loneliness, love and weakness, that brutal egotism which is false personality, and the fearful abandonment of the risks of personality which is false socialization. The writer as bandit in the wide world does not know exactly what he will find, frozen shrimp or cash or a good swift kick in the assumptions, but he is bound to his life of sunny crime; he is committed to love, hate, death, and rebirth, as indeed we all are. The ophthalmologists tell us that exercise will not improve nearsightedness; the eye is not a muscle. However, it may be that the soul is a muscle and that myopia of the soul can be ameliorated by stretching the imagination.

If there is a will by the reader.

If the artist has both the will and a strong inner chart.

A Note on Choice

A number of excellent writers of the past ten years are not included here. Excerpts from novels seldom do justice to either the reader or the writer. The list of those whose short fiction does not represent them at their best includes such writers as Thomas Berger, Vance Bourjaily, Ralph Ellison, Albert J. Guerard, Jr., Alan Harrington, James Jones, M. R. Kadish, Wright Morris, William Styron, Bernard Wolfe, and others.

Some fine stories have been written by writers without a large body of work to support them. It was decided that the book should be representative of the best writing of the period—not just the best isolated stories—and so work by Wayne Carver, Philip Roth, Thomas Williams, and others is reluctantly left to another occasion.

Because of the specific character of American experience in the Fifties intended to be suggested by this book, a number of skillful story writers are omitted—Nelson Algren, Hortense Calisher, Truman Capote, James B. Hall, Carson McCullers, and others.

In all cases, the taste of the editor is to be blamed for the choices made. In one instance, that of Norman Mailer, the editor wanted to include a story, and Mailer insisted on the prologue to a novel-in-progress, and so there is nothing. J. D. Salinger is now unwilling to see his stories in collections which include other hands. The editor wishes to assure meticulous readers that the names of still other writers either clean slipped his mind or ran hurriedly in and out of mind, leaving no firm track (*chacun à son goût!*).

HERBERT GOLD

A WORD FROM WRITER
DIRECTLY TO READER

The contributors to this volume were invited to answer the following question:

"In what way—if any—do you feel that the problem of writing for the Fifties has differed from the problems of writing in other times? Do you believe that this age makes special demands on you as a writer?"

Their replies follow:

JAMES BALDWIN:

I suppose that it has always been difficult to be a writer. Writers tell us so; and so does the history of any given time or place and what one knows of the world's indifference. But I doubt that there could ever have been a time which demanded more of the writer than do these present days. The world has shrunk to the size of several ignorant armies; each of them vociferously demanding allegiance and many of them brutally imposing it. Nor is it easy for me, when I try to examine the world in which I live, to distinguish the right side from the wrong side. I share, for example, the ideals of the West—freedom, justice, brotherhood—but I cannot say that I have often seen these honored; and the people whose faces are set against us have never seen us honor them at all.

But finally for me the difficulty is to remain in touch with the private life. The private life, his own and that of others, is the writer's subject—his key and ours to his achievement. Nothing, I submit, is more difficult than deciphering what the citizens of this time and place actually feel and think. They do not know themselves; when they talk, they talk to the psychiatrist; on the theory, presumably, that the truth about them is ultimately unspeakable. This thoroughly infantile delusion has its effects: it is contagious. The writer trapped among a speechless people is in danger of becoming speechless himself. For then he has no mirror, no corroborations of his essential reality; and this means that he has no grasp of the reality of the people around him. What the times demand, and in an unprecedented fashion, is that one *be*—not seem—outrageous, independent, anarchical. That one be thoroughly disciplined—as a means of being spontaneous. That one resist at whatever cost the fearful pressures placed on one to lie about one's own experience. For in the same way that the writer scarcely ever had a more uneasy time, he has never been needed more.

SAUL BELLOW:

For the writers of the Fifties as for those of immediately preceding generations the questions have been these: Is man in this century what he was in times past? Is he worth writing about and can his actions have any interest? To be sure, all writers strongly desire to answer in the affirmative, but no one cares for empty ideologies of the sort patriotically demanded in the magazines published by Henry Luce.

For James Joyce who was the most influential novelist of the twentieth century the individual became merely a point of entry into the collective. In *Finnegan's Wake* personality and event disappear entirely.

We cannot make the final assessment of human value. What we are inclined to do, however, is to renew the inquiry, abandoning old historic and aesthetic conceptions. I cannot agree with recent writers who have told us that we are Nothing. We are indeed not what the Golden Ages boasted us to be. But we are Something.

ANATOLE BROYARD:

I think that today there may be more temptations for writers to resist: do-it-yourself syntax, rusty ironies and platitudinous paradoxes, hydrogen bombast, cinematic acrobatics and documentary flatfootedness, psychoanalytic smart-alecking, G.I. Bill erudition—to name just a few—and, above all, the dogged determination of the emancipated middle-brow not to be insulted or disgusted by anything. Still, it seems to me that the *Zeitgeist* is really just scenery, and the writer's proper subject is always people and their inexhaustibly interesting and appealing imperfection—so in this sense I guess one time is as good or bad as another.

R. V. CASSILL:

The obviously special problem for a writer of the Fifties (or an educator, parent or anyone else obligated to deal responsibly with words and ideas) is that the Cold War and the McCarthy Era have so compromised the common vision and vocabulary that honesty, even at simple levels of communication, is harder to achieve than in any other time I have heard about. The writer of fiction toils on a field where two kinds of fiction contend—the black, elaborate fictions (too artless and by now too generally internalized to be properly designated as lies) that made us good soldiers and ardent voters, and the sparse white fictions that aim at spelling the charm backward and showing how, after all, we are men.

This seems to me a time when even the stupidest are disingenuous. There are no mental virgins for the bluff, straightforward and honest writer to woo into sharing awe and delight over what he has seen with his hypothetically innocent eyes. "Have you seen cowboys, hipsters, golden girls and statists in the van?" asks the wide or narrow reader. "Why—so have I." The scene of the world, as never before, is under a camera eye that takes a look for everyone. And the camera never lies—because it never has to. It merely feeds the Moloch lie that molded the conscience of a generation.

Stephen Daedalus could hope to "forge . . . the uncreated conscience of my race." Perhaps this age demands the less grateful task of thawing a frozen conscience and softening the edges of an unhallowed certainty.

JOHN CHEEVER:

The decade began for me with more promise than I can remember since my earliest youth. The war was over. Most of its reverberations were (for me) ended. I had done some work during the war but I had done it in holes in the ground and on ping-pong tables. Now this was over and I could work in peace. However, halfway through the decade, something went terribly wrong. The most useful image I have today is of a man in a quagmire, looking into a tear in the sky. I am not speaking here of despair, but of confusion. I fully expected the trout streams of my youth to fill up with beer cans and the meadows to be covered with houses; I may even have expected to be separated from most of my moral and ethical heritage; but the forceful absurdities of life today find me unprepared. Something has gone very wrong, and I do not have the language, the imagery, or the concepts to describe my apprehensions. I come back again to the quagmire and the torn sky. One can think of this—the crudeness of this image—as a challenge to a writer, and I will leave it at that.

EVAN S. CONNELL, JR.:

In regard to the question about whether writing during the Fifties has posed problems different from other times, I suppose it has, though any sort of response would necessarily be so speculative that I am rather hesitant to attempt any reply. This age makes demands on us all; perhaps more than ever before, our very lives depend on the capacity of our nerves to withstand the thought of instantaneous annihilation, and no doubt this condition reflects itself with greater or lesser subtlety in every action, most profoundly in such action as we term creative.

WILLIAM EASTLAKE:

The problem, and the only relevant demand, is still to write well, in the Fifties or any other time. To write well. To acquire the talent and the courage to write well.

GEORGE P. ELLIOTT:

Other times have had confusions and perplexities as profound as ours, though not so many at once; nor are any of the root troubles of our time peculiar to us, not even our taproot fear, that the world is about to come to an end for no good reason. If this time has about it something special for writers, I think it is not the existence or nature of our anxieties and disequilibrium but their magnitude and pervasiveness. The main stuff of fiction is the way one knows and is connected with others, himself, his country, the world, ideas of the world; and in his way of knowing and of relating to others, each of us now is seriously troubled by the ills of the age. This is all right for characters in a story; it is not all right for the creator of those characters, for not only is he troubled in his connections with other real-life people —his prime material—but he is also troubled in his connections with his own characters. In other words, our fiction is full of impurities such as metaphysics. Myself, I like the mingling of philosophy and fiction, though it is apt to be a bit hard on characterization and often on the narrative, the sense of the story.

Philosophers mostly have given up speculating about the nature of things and of man, in favor of *p*, *q*, truth tables, intuition, and antiphilosophy; churches nowadays do not give the perturbed spirit what it most needs; not many leaders, at least in this country, are believed in as knowing a way out of the wilderness. Who is left to know, to seek, to lead the seeking? Scientists and artists. Maybe the scientists will get everything figured out in time and maybe they won't; meantime the pressure is increasing, and things are not figured out by half; further, many who used to think the scientists would get there before too late, no longer think they will ever get there at all. Artists: of all artists, writers, by reason of their material, are most heavily burdened with the necessity of speculating and allaying. This burden is by no means peculiar to our time; great writers have always assumed it, and plenty of lesser ones, too. The difference is, as I believe, that nowadays almost every writer, willy-nilly, suffers from destiny on the mind.

The hazard of this is clear enough; the temptation to propagandize truths not certainly known, to pretend to a certainty not felt, to pontificate without being in fact a bishop and to prophesy though no prophet: *A Fable; The Cocktail Party* and *The Potting Shed;* Thomas Mann's political essays; Kenneth Rexroth's *Thou Shalt Not Kill.* There is the lesser hazard that a writer temperamentally unfit to deal with philosophical matters may feel obliged to flounder toward all sorts of ontologies; he offers, not a touching and pleasant story as he might, but a vision of things not there, things which he has not seen even in hallucination but has only wanted to see: *The Dharma Bums.*

But upon those who are capable of thinking without pomp about what is on everybody's mind and who flesh their meditations in felt stories peopled by characters who think, there is a heavy obligation: to make, for themselves and for those who read them, some order out of much chaos. No writer can be ignorant of this obligation; some it ponders into solemnity, and those who would evade it jiggle into obscurantism or facetiousness. Perhaps it presses too hard on writers now, for making and enjoying art should be play, and nothing is grimmer than playing because you ought to.

Though we must make sense of the world, yet even so let us enjoy making sense of the world. An anciently honorable, now heavily pressing obligation, but also exalted play: why not?

LEO LITWAK:

Even villains believe in the virtues. Industry, courage, self-control, intelligence: could Murder Incorporated have thrived without them? We tremble at tyranny that is disciplined, that has achieved the virtues we envy. We take heart from the rumors that the enemy is corrupt. If he is immoderate, then he is vulnerable. If he is a coward, then he may be intimidated. If he lacks intelligence, he may fall victim to our superior strategy. If he is uncharitable to his cohorts, he will create enemies. If he is lazy, then industrious dissenters may breed. Any man, good or bad, concerned to defend the integrity of his Self, admits the benefit of virtue. The traditional virtues are not, in my opinion, imperiled by any course of history, and I doubt that anyone seriously opposes them. This age is like all others in that regard, and the writer still has the option of characterizing the development of virtue. For instance, how is manliness achieved shooting a bear, catching a fish, surviving combat? What exercises in courage and self-restraint are needed to be cool? What kind of training is necessary for realizing the self-abandonment of complete orgasm? There are many recipes, employing different ingredients, for cooking up virtue.

And these recipes require no moral posture. ". . . The coolness of a villain," says Kant, "not only makes him far more dangerous, but also directly makes him more abominable in our eyes than he would have been without it." But Kant was able to denigrate virtue to the status of means because he wasn't confused about his moral premises. In our time a man must be remarkably insensitive to have a similar confidence in his understanding of good and evil, justice and injustice, right and wrong. The tyrant of yesterday may be tomorrow's ally. The evil we once thought definitive subsequently loses its sharp edges as we become entangled in the complexities of motives and passions. The chain of responsibility has links made of silly putty. And few of us have the ability to recover the indignation which provoked moral responses.

Our experience provides little warrant for the moral theories that have prevailed. They have not proved effective in answering the question, "How shall I act?" There is a temptation to regard this as a methodological, rather than a moral question. It is more appropriately asked of Elia Kazan or Hemingway than of Plato and Kant. In the absence of theory, we want recipes. We want to know how, given certain conditions, we can be courageous, intelligent, self-controlled. The virtues are indispensable for preserving our Selves.

A man's Self is always in peril. But in the absence of guiding principles which are believed adequate, we become especially vulnerable to the risky consequences of our actions. Who can foresee consequences or vigorously propose objectives when there are no premises upon which to base inference? Anything may happen. No action is safe. Any decision may expose the agent to blame, to shame, to the hostility of others.

For this reason, we're interested in recipes. How do we learn to endure loss? How can we condition ourselves to withstand the defeat of what we love? How are we to act? We may want an answer which will tell us how we are to be camouflaged against unknown assailants. We may want to know how to become invisible, cool, or central. If the writer is to answer this sort of question, we expect from him an account of the method needed to achieve the appropriate virtues. For instance, what demands are made on courage and self-discipline if we are to be hip? What clothes must be worn, what vocabulary mastered, what preferences confessed, what habits acquired?

We may, however, demand something else from recipes. "How shall I act?" may be an invitation to the writer to act out possibilities, "acting out" being a kind of exploration. Instead of providing a method for camouflage, he will hunt methods which do not commit us to a posture of defense, but which free our power to maneuver.

These seem to me options confronted by all men, and not peculiarly writers. Shall our energies be committed to making ourselves invulnerable or shall they be directed to the liberation of Self from the dread of unknown consequences? Our experience can be used in the service of either objective. We can try to make virtue serve the goal of self-defense or the goal of self-realization. Whatever the choice, so long as we live on the surface of contemporaneity, insubstantially rooted by tradition, we must hunt methods, invent recipes, and hope that we will discover structures which our experience can support.

BERNARD MALAMUD:

Although the Fifties have a Cold War character, I would say that the problem of writing fiction in this decade is basically no different from writing in the past. One struggles alone to achieve art. The age makes no special demands except as it tends to devalue man; that being so, I work on the assumption that the opposite is true.

FLANNERY O'CONNOR:

I presume that writing in any age is equally a chore. I would not have found it less difficult in 250, 1350, or 5050.

J. F. POWERS:

Strictly speaking, the problems of writing in the Fifties differ in no way from those of writing in other times. As for the demands of the age on a writer, readers aren't what they used to be in, say, Thackeray's day. So being a writer—a man of letters, that is—isn't what it used to be. But the demands of art are the same.

FRANK ROONEY:

The only bad time for a writer is a time when, for whatever reason, he can't write. His problem—in any age—is to get his work done. I don't think a writer works for a time, I think he works against it—either to move it ahead or to slow it down—which is why he's likely to be puzzled and frustrated by a time of rapid change (the old god falling before he can pull it down) or turned into a reporter and a businessman (his prophetic genius is no longer needed by the solidification of what he anticipates). The artist (to cover the creative field) is less the child of his time—or master of it—than any of the basic figures; he uses the external principally to dramatize the internal; less moved by the history of an age, he is in a position to span it. This is not to say that he doesn't take part in the gory calisthenics of his time—the revolutions, the wars, the genocides—but that these are not his major concern; his concern is to find and reveal in the man himself not what is subject to change but what is subject to growth, that which may be altered by events but not destroyed by them. It might be called a hunger for light, and yet more and more light; it has been called God; as he moves out of his corner in the local system, the human entity, not so dark a horse, may have to call it something else. Whatever it is, it is always the writer's theme, his constant; what happens to it—in any age—is his material.

HARVEY SWADOS:

The problem of writing for the Fifties has differed from the problems of writing in other times because the audience has changed. The audience has changed because of the enormous growth in sophistication and impatience attendant upon the pervasive influence of the mass media. The responsibility has changed proportionately. Never having lived in other ages, I can only know at second hand their demands on writers, but in *this age* I do indeed feel torn as I do believe others must also—between playing the oracle and showing the world how it must be saved from destruction, and playing the traditional game of telling private stories about private people. Both, however, are equally important to me, and I continue to hope that at my best, one will imply the other.

FICTION OF THE FIFTIES

SONNY'S BLUES

James Baldwin

JAMES BALDWIN *was born in 1924 in New York City's Harlem Hospital. He is the author of two novels,* GO TELL IT ON THE MOUNTAIN *(1953) and* GIOVANNI'S ROOM *(1956), a book of essays,* NOTES OF A NATIVE SON *(1955), and a play,* THE AMEN CORNER. *His reviews, articles, and short stories have appeared in many magazines. Mr. Baldwin has been the recipient of a number of literary prizes—the Eugene Saxton Fellowship, the Rosenwald Fellowship, the* Partisan Review *Fellowship, the National Institute of Arts and Letters Award, and, most recently, a Ford Grant.*

I read about it in the paper, in the subway, on my way to work. I read it, and I couldn't believe it, and I read it again. Then perhaps I just stared at it, at the newsprint spelling out his name, spelling out the story. I stared at it in the swinging lights of the subway car, and in the faces and bodies of the people, and in my own face, trapped in the darkness which roared outside.

It was not to be believed, and I kept telling myself that as I walked from the subway station to the high school. And at the same time I couldn't doubt it. I was scared, scared for Sonny. He became real to me again. A great block of ice got settled in my belly and kept melting there slowly all day long, while I taught my classes algebra. It was a special kind of ice. It kept melting, sending trickles of ice water all up and down my veins, but it never got less. Sometimes it hardened and seemed to expand until I felt my guts were going to come spilling out or that I was going to choke or scream. This would always be at a moment when I was remembering some specific thing Sonny had once said or done.

When he was about as old as the boys in my classes, his face had been bright and open, there was a lot of copper in it; and he'd had wonderfully direct brown eyes, and great gentleness and privacy. I wondered what he looked like now. He had been picked up, the evening before, in a raid on an apartment downtown, for peddling and using heroin.

I couldn't believe it: but what I mean by that is that I couldn't find any room for it anywhere inside me. I had kept it outside me for a long time. I hadn't wanted to know. I had had suspicions, but I didn't name them, I kept putting them away. I told myself that Sonny was wild, but he wasn't crazy. And he'd always been a good boy, he hadn't ever turned hard or evil or disrespectful, the way kids can, so quick, so quick, especially in Harlem. I didn't want to believe that I'd ever see my brother going down, coming to nothing, all that light in his face gone out, in the condition I'd already seen so many others. Yet it had happened and here I was, talking about algebra to a lot of boys who might, every one of them for all I knew, be popping off needles every time they went to the head. Maybe it did more for them than algebra could.

I was sure that the first time Sonny had ever had horse, he couldn't have been much older than these boys were now. These boys, now, were living as we'd been living then, they were growing up with a rush and their heads bumped abruptly against the low ceiling of their actual possibilities. They were filled with rage. All they really knew were two darknesses, the darkness of their lives, which was now closing in on them, and the darkness of the movies, which had blinded them to that other darkness, and in which they now, vindictively, dreamed, at once more together than they were at any other time, and more alone.

When the last bell rang, the last class ended, I let out my breath. It seemed I'd been holding it for all that time. My clothes were set—I may have looked as though I'd been sitting in a steam bath, all dressed up, all afternoon. I sat alone in the classroom a long time. I listened to the boys outside, downstairs, shouting and cursing and laughing. Their laughter struck me for perhaps the first time. It was not the joyous laughter which—God knows why—one associates with children. It was mocking and insular, its intent was to denigrate. It was disenchanted, and in this, also, lay the authority of their curses. Perhaps I was listening to them because I was thinking about my brother and in them I heard my brother. And myself.

One boy was whistling a tune, at once very complicated and very simple, it seemed to be pouring out of him as though he were a bird, and it sounded very cool and moving through all that harsh, bright air, only just holding its own through all those other sounds.

I stood and walked over to the window and looked down into the courtyard. It was the beginning of the spring, and the sap was rising in the boys. A teacher passed through them every now and again, quickly, as though he or she couldn't wait to get out of that courtyard, to get those boys out of their sight and off their minds. I started collecting my stuff. I thought I'd better get home and talk to Isabel.

The courtyard was almost deserted by the time I got downstairs. I saw this boy standing in the shadow of a doorway, looking just like Sonny. I almost called his name. Then I saw that it wasn't Sonny, but somebody we used to know, a boy from around our block. He'd been Sonny's friend. He'd never been mine, having been too young for me, and, anyway, I'd never liked him. And now, even though he was a grown-up man, he still hung around that block, still spent hours on the street corner, was always high and raggy. I used to run into him from time to time, and he'd often work around to asking me for a quarter or fifty cents. He always had some real good excuse, too, and I always gave it to him, I don't know why.

But now, abruptly, I hated him. I couldn't stand the way he looked at me, partly like a dog, partly like a cunning child. I wanted to ask him what the hell he was doing in the school courtyard.

He sort of shuffled over to me, and he said, "I see you got the papers. So you already know about it."

"You mean about Sonny? Yes, I already know about it. How come they didn't get you?"

He grinned. It made him repulsive and it also brought to mind what he'd looked like as a kid. "I wasn't there. I stay away from them people."

"Good for you." I offered him a cigarette and I watched him through the smoke. "You come all the way down here just to tell me about Sonny?"

"That's right." He was sort of shaking his head and his eyes looked strange, as though they were about to cross. The bright sun deadened his damp dark brown skin and it made his eyes look yellow and showed up the dirt in his conked hair. He smelled funky. I moved a little away from him and I said, "Well, thanks. But I already know about it and I got to get home."

"I'll walk you a little ways," he said. We started walking. There were a couple of kids still loitering in the courtyard and one of them said good night to me and looked strangely at the boy beside me.

"What're you going to do?" he asked me. "I mean, about Sonny?"

"Look. I haven't seen Sonny for over a year, I'm not sure I'm going to do anything. Anyway, what the hell *can* I do?"

"That's right," he said quickly, "ain't nothing you can do. Can't much help old Sonny no more, I guess."

It was what I was thinking and so it seemed to me he had no right to say it.

"I'm surprised at Sonny, though," he went on—he had a funny way of talking, he looked straight ahead as though he were talking to himself—"I thought Sonny was a smart boy, I thought he was too smart to get hung."

"I guess he thought so, too," I said sharply, "and that's how he got hung. And how about you? You're pretty goddamn smart, I bet."

Then he looked directly at me, just for a minute. "I ain't smart," he said. "If I was smart, I'd have reached for a pistol a long time ago."

"Look. Don't tell *me* your sad story, if it was up to me, I'd give you one." Then I felt guilty—guilty probably, for never having supposed that the poor bastard *had* a story of his own, much less a sad one, and I asked, quickly, "What's going to happen to him now?"

He didn't answer this. He was off by himself someplace. "Funny thing," he said, and from his tone we might have been discussing the quickest way to get to Brooklyn, "when I saw the papers this morning, the first thing I asked myself was if I had anything to do with it. I felt sort of responsible."

I began to listen more carefully. The subway station was on the corner, just before us, and I stopped. He stopped, too. We were in front of a bar and he ducked slightly, peering in, but whoever he was looking for didn't seem to be there. The juke box was blasting away with something black and bouncy, and I half watched the barmaid as she danced her way from the juke box to her place behind the bar. And I watched her face as she laughingly responded to something someone said to her, still keeping time to the music. When she smiled one saw the little girl, one sensed the doomed, still-struggling woman beneath the battered face of the semi-whore.

"I never *give* Sonny nothing," the boy said finally, "but a long time ago I come to school high and Sonny asked me how it felt." He paused, I couldn't bear to watch him, I watched the barmaid, and I listened to the music which seemed to be causing the pavement to shake. "I told him it felt great." The music stopped, the barmaid paused and watched the juke box until the music began again. "It did."

All this was carrying me someplace I didn't want to go. I certainly didn't want to know how it felt. It filled everything, the people, the houses, the music, the dark, quicksilver barmaid, with menace; and this menace was their reality.

"What's going to happen to him now?" I asked again.

"They'll send him away someplace and they'll try to cure him." He shook his head. "Maybe he'll even think he's kicked the habit. Then they'll let him loose"—He gestured, throwing his cigarette into the gutter. "That's all."

"What do you mean, that's *all?*"

But I knew what he meant.

"I *mean*, that's *all*." He turned his head and looked at

me, pulling down the corners of his mouth. "Don't you know what I mean?" he asked, softly.

"How the hell *would* I know what you mean?" I almost whispered it, I don't know why.

"That's right," he said to the air, "how would *he* know what I mean?" He turned toward me again, patient and calm, and yet I somehow felt him shaking, shaking as though he were going to fall apart. I felt that ice in my guts again, the dread I'd felt all afternoon; and again I watched the barmaid, moving about the bar, washing glasses, and singing. "Listen. They'll let him out and then it'll just start over again. That's what I mean."

"You mean—they'll let him out. And then he'll just start working his way back in again. You mean he'll never kick the habit. Is that what you mean?"

"That's right," he said, cheerfully. "*You* see what I mean."

"Tell me," I said at last, "why does he want to die? He must want to die, he's killing himself, why does he want to die?"

He looked at me in surprise. He licked his lips. "He don't want to die. He wants to live. Don't nobody want to die, ever."

Then I wanted to ask him—too many things. He could not have answered, or if he had, I could not have borne the answers. I started walking. "Well, I guess it's none of my business."

"It's going to be rough on old Sonny," he said. We reached the subway station. "This is your station?" he asked. I nodded. I took one step down. "Damn!" he said, suddenly. I looked up at him. He grinned again. "Damn if I didn't leave all my money home. You ain't got a dollar on you, have you? Just for a couple of days, is all."

All at once something inside gave and threatened to come pouring out of me. I didn't hate him any more. I felt that in another moment I'd start crying like a child.

"Sure," I said. "Don't sweat." I looked in my wallet and didn't have a dollar, I only had a five. "Here," I said. "That hold you?"

He didn't look at it—he didn't want to look at it. A terrible, closed look came over his face, as though he were keeping

the number on the bill a secret from him and me. "Thanks,"
he said, and now he was dying to see me go. "Don't worry
about Sonny. Maybe I'll write him or something."

"Sure," I said. "You do that. So long."

"Be seeing you," he said. I went on down the steps.

And I didn't write Sonny or send him anything for a long
time. When I finally did, it was just after my little girl died,
he wrote me back a letter which made me feel like a bastard.
Here's what he said:

> Dear brother,
>
> You don't know how much I needed to hear from
> you. I wanted to write you many a time but I dug how
> much I must have hurt you and so I didn't write. But
> now I feel like a man who's been trying to climb up
> out of some deep, real deep and funky hole and just
> saw the sun up there, outside. I got to get outside.
>
> I can't tell you much about how I got here. I mean
> I don't know how to tell you. I guess I was afraid of
> something or I was trying to escape from something
> and you know I have never been very strong in the
> head (smile). I'm glad Mama and Daddy are dead
> and can't see what's happened to their son and I
> swear if I'd known what I was doing I would never
> have hurt you so, you and a lot of other fine people
> who were nice to me and who believed in me.
>
> I don't want you to think it had anything to do with
> me being a musician. It's more than that. Or maybe
> less than that. I can't get anything straight in my head
> down here and I try not to think about what's going
> to happen to me when I get outside again. Sometime
> I think I'm going to flip and *never* get outside and
> sometime I think I'll come straight back. I tell you
> one thing, though, I'd rather blow my brains out than
> go through this again. But that's what they all say, so
> they tell me. If I tell you when I'm coming to New
> York and if you could meet me, I sure would appre-
> ciate it. Give my love to Isabel and the kids and I was
> sure sorry to hear about little Gracie. I wish I could
> be like Mama and say the Lord's will be done, but

I don't know it seems to me that trouble is the one
thing that never does get stopped and I don't know
what good it does to blame it on the Lord. But maybe
it does some good if you believe it.

Your brother,
SONNY

Then I kept in constant touch with him and I sent him
whatever I could and I went to met him when he came
back to New York. When I saw him, many things I thought
I had forgotten came flooding back to me. This was because
I had begun, finally, to wonder about Sonny, about the life
that Sonny lived inside. This life, whatever it was, had made
him older and thinner and it had deepened the distant still-
ness in which he had always moved. He looked very unlike
my baby brother. Yet, when he smiled, when we shook
hands, the baby brother I'd never known looked out from
the depths of his private life, like an animal waiting to be
coaxed into the light.

"How you been keeping?" he asked me.

"All right. And you?"

"Just fine." He was smiling all over his face. "It's good
to see you again."

"It's good to see you."

The seven years' difference in our ages lay between us
like a chasm: I wondered if these years would ever operate
between us as a bridge. I was remembering, and it made
it hard to catch my breath, that I had been there when he
was born; and I had heard the first words he had ever
spoken. When he started to walk, he walked from our
mother straight to me. I caught him just before he fell when
he took the first steps he ever took in this world.

"How's Isabel?"

"Just fine. She's dying to see you."

"And the boys?"

"They're fine, too. They're anxious to see their uncle."

"Oh, come on. You know they don't remember me."

"Are you kidding? Of course they remember you."

He grinned again. We got into a taxi. We had a lot to
say to each other, far too much to know how to begin.

As the taxi began to move, I asked, "You still want to go to India?"

He laughed. "You still remember that. Hell, no. This place is Indian enough for me."

"It used to belong to them," I said.

And he laughed again. "They damn sure knew what they were doing when they got rid of it."

Years ago, when he was around fourteen, he'd been all hipped on the idea of going to India. He read books about people sitting on rocks, naked, in all kinds of weather, but mostly bad, naturally, and walking barefoot through hot coals and arriving at wisdom. I used to say that it sounded to me as though they were getting away from wisdom as fast as they could. I think he sort of looked down on me for that.

"Do you mind," he asked, "if we have the driver drive alongside the park? On the west side—I haven't seen the city in so long."

"Of course not," I said. I was afraid that I might sound as though I were humoring him, but I hoped he wouldn't take it that way.

So we drove along, between the green of the park and the stony, lifeless elegance of hotels and apartment buildings, toward the vivid, killing streets of our childhood. These streets hadn't changed, though housing projects jutted up out of them now like rocks in the middle of a boiling sea. Most of the houses in which we had grown up had vanished, as had the stores from which we had stolen, the basements in which we had first tried sex, the rooftops from which we had hurled tin cans and bricks. But houses exactly like the houses of our past yet dominated the landscape, boys exactly like the boys we once had been found themselves smothering in these houses, came down into the streets for light and air and found themselves encircled by disaster. Some escaped the trap, most didn't. Those who got out always left something of themselves behind, as some animals amputate a leg and leave it in the trap. It might be said, perhaps, that I had escaped, after all, I was a schoolteacher; or that Sonny had, he hadn't lived in Harlem for years. Yet, as the cab moved uptown through streets which seemed, with a rush, to darken with dark people, and as I covertly studied Sonny's face, it came to me that what we both were seeking through our separate cab windows was that part of ourselves which had been left behind. It's always at the hour of trouble and confrontation that the missing member aches.

We hit 110th Street and started rolling up Lenox Avenue. And I'd known this avenue all my life, but it seemed to me again, as it had seemed on the day I'd first heard about Sonny's trouble, filled with a hidden menace which was its very breath of life.

"We almost there," said Sonny.

"Almost." We were both too nervous to say anything more.

We live in a housing project. It hasn't been up long. A few days after it was up it seemed uninhabitably new, now, of course, it's already rundown. It looked like a parody of the good, clean, faceless life—God knows the people who live in it do their best to make it a parody. The beat-looking grass lying around isn't enough to make their lives green, the hedges will never hold out the streets, and they know it. The big windows fool no one, they aren't big enough to make space out of no space. They don't bother with the windows, they watch the TV screen instead. The playground is most popular with the children who don't play at jacks, or skip rope, or roller skate, or swing, and they can be found in it after dark. We moved in partly because it's not too far from where I teach, and partly for the kids; but it's really just like the houses in which Sonny and I grew up. The same things happen, they'll have the same things to remember. The moment Sonny and I started into the house I had the feeling that I was simply bringing him back into the danger he had almost died trying to escape.

Sonny has never been talkative. So I don't know why I was sure he'd be dying to talk to me when supper was over the first night. Everything went fine, the oldest boy remembered him, and the youngest boy liked him, and Sonny had remembered to bring something for each of them; and Isabel, who is really much nicer than I am, more open and giving, had gone to a lot of trouble about dinner and

was genuinely glad to see him. And she'd always been able
to tease Sonny in a way that I haven't. It was nice to see
her face so vivid again and to hear her laugh and watch
her make Sonny laugh. She wasn't, or, anyway, she didn't
seem to be, at all uneasy or embarrassed. She chatted as
though there were no subject which had to be avoided and
she got Sonny past his first, faint stiffness. And thank God
she was there, for I was filled with that icy dread again.
Everything I did seemed awkward to me, and everything I
said sounded freighted with hidden meaning. I was trying
to remember everything I'd heard about dope addiction and
I couldn't help watching Sonny for signs. I wasn't doing
it out of malice. I was trying to find out something about
my brother. I was dying to hear him tell me he was safe.

"Safe!" my father grunted, whenever Mama suggested
trying to move to a neighborhood which might be safer for
children. "Safe, hell! Ain't no place safe for kids, nor nobody."

He always went on like this, but he wasn't, ever, really
as bad as he sounded, not even on weekends, when he got
drunk. As a matter of fact, he was always on the lookout
for "something a little better," but he died before he found
it. He died suddenly, during a drunken weekend in the middle of the war, when Sonny was fifteen. He and Sonny
hadn't ever got on too well. And this was partly because
Sonny was the apple of his father's eye. It was because he
loved Sonny so much and was frightened for him, that he
was always fighting with him. It doesn't do any good to
fight with Sonny. Sonny just moves back, inside himself,
where he can't be reached. But the principal reason that
they never hit it off is that they were so much alike. Daddy
was big and rough and loud-talking, just the opposite of
Sonny, but they both had—that same privacy.

Mama tried to tell me something about this, just after
Daddy died. I was home on leave from the army.

This was the last time I ever saw my mother alive. Just
the same, this picture gets all mixed up in my mind with
pictures I had of her when she was younger. The way I
always see her is the way she used to be on a Sunday afternoon, say, when the old folks were talking after the big

Sunday dinner. I always see her wearing pale blue. She'd be sitting on the sofa. And my father would be sitting in the easy chair, not far from her. And the living room would be full of church folks and relatives. There they sit, in chairs all around the living room, and the night is creeping up outside, but nobody knows it yet. You can see the darkness growing against the windowpanes and you hear the street noises every now and again, or maybe the jangling beat of a tambourine from one of the churches close by, but it's real quiet in the room. For a moment nobody's talking, but every face looks darkening, like the sky outside. And my mother rocks a little from the waist, and my father's eyes are closed. Everyone is looking at something a child can't see. For a minute they've forgotten the children. Maybe a kid is lying on the rug, half asleep. Maybe somebody's got a kid in his lap and is absent-mindedly stroking the kid's head. Maybe there's a kid, quiet and big-eyed, curled up in a big chair in the corner. The silence, the darkness coming, and the darkness in the faces frighten the child obscurely. He hopes that the hand which strokes his forehead will never stop—will never die. He hopes that there will never come a time when the old folks won't be sitting around the living room, talking about where they've come from, and what they've seen, and what's happened to them and their kinfolk.

But something deep and watchful in the child knows that this is bound to end, is already ending. In a moment someone will get up and turn on the light. Then the old folks will remember the children and they won't talk any more that day. And when light fills the room, the child is filled with darkness. He knows that every time this happens he's moved just a little closer to that darkness outside. The darkness outside is what the old folks have been talking about. It's what they've come from. It's what they endure. The child knows that they won't talk any more because if he knows too much about what's happened to *them*, he'll know too much too soon, about what's going to happen to *him*.

The last time I talked to my mother, I remember I was restless. I wanted to get out and see Isabel. We weren't married then and we had a lot to straighten out between us.

There Mama sat, in black, by the window. She was humming an old church song, *Lord, you brought me from a long ways off*. Sonny was out somewhere. Mama kept watching the streets.

"I don't know," she said, "if I'll ever see you again, after you go off from here. But I hope you'll remember the things I tried to teach you."

"Don't talk like that," I said, and smiled. "You'll be here a long time yet."

She smiled, too, but she said nothing. She was quiet for a long time. And I said, "Mama, don't you worry about nothing. I'll be writing all the time, and you be getting the checks. . . ."

"I want to talk to you about your brother," she said, suddenly. "If anything happens to me, he ain't going to have nobody to look out for him."

"Mama," I said, "ain't nothing going to happen to you *or* Sonny. Sonny's all right. He's a good boy and he's got good sense."

"It ain't a question of his being a good boy," Mama said, "nor of his having good sense. It ain't only the bad ones, nor yet the dumb ones that gets sucked under." She stopped, looking at me. "Your Daddy once had a brother," she said, and she smiled in a way that made me feel she was in pain. "You didn't never know that, did you?"

"No," I said. "I never knew that," and I watched her face.

"Oh, yes," she said, "your Daddy had a brother." She looked out of the window again. "I know you never saw your Daddy cry. But *I* did—many a time, through all these years."

I asked her, "What happened to his brother? How come nobody's ever talked about him?"

This was the first time I ever saw my mother look old.

"His brother got killed," she said, "when he was just a little younger than you are now. I knew him. He was a fine boy. He was maybe a little full of the devil, but he didn't mean nobody no harm."

Then she stopped, and the room was silent, exactly as it

had sometimes been on those Sunday afternoons. Mama
kept looking out into the streets.

"He used to have a job in the mill," she said, "and, like
all young folks, he just liked to perform on Saturday nights.
Saturday nights, him and your father would drift around
to different places, go to dances and things like that, or
just sit around with people they knew, and your father's
brother would sing, he had a fine voice, and play along
with himself on his guitar. Well, this particular Saturday
night, him and your father was coming home from some
place, and they were both a little drunk and there was a
moon that night, it was bright like day. Your father's
brother was feeling kind of good, and he was whistling to
himself, and he had his guitar slung over his shoulder. They
was coming down a hill, and beneath them was a road that
turned off from the highway. Well, your father's brother,
being always kind of frisky, decided to run down this hill,
and he did, with that guitar banging and clanging behind
him, and he ran across the road, and he was making water
behind a tree. And your father was sort of amused at him
and he was still coming down the hill, kind of slow. Then
he heard a car motor and that same minute his brother
stepped from behind the tree, into the road, in the moonlight. And he started to cross the road. And your father
started to run down the hill, he says he don't know why.
This car was full of white men. They was all drunk, and
when they seen your father's brother they let out a great
whoop and holler and they aimed the car straight at him.
They was having fun, they just wanted to scare him, the way
they do sometimes, you know. But they was drunk. And
I guess the boy, being drunk, too, and scared, kind of lost
his head. By the time he jumped it was too late. Your
father says he heard his brother scream when the car rolled
over him, and he heard the wood of that guitar when it
give, and he heard them strings go flying, and he heard
them white men shouting, and the car kept on a-going and
it ain't stopped till this day. And, time your father got down
the hill, his brother weren't nothing but blood and pulp."

Tears were gleaming on my mother's face. There wasn't
anything I could say.

"He never mentioned it," she said, "because I never let him mention it before you children. Your Daddy was like a crazy man that night and for many a night thereafter. He says he never in his life seen anything as dark as that road after the lights of that car had gone away. Weren't nothing, weren't nobody on that road, just your Daddy and his brother and that busted guitar. Oh, yes. Your Daddy never did really get right again. Till the day he died he weren't sure but that every white man he saw was the man that killed his brother."

She stopped and took out her handkerchief and dried her eyes and looked at me.

"I ain't telling you all this," she said, "to make you scared or bitter or to make you hate nobody. I'm telling you this because you got a brother. And the world ain't changed."

I guess I didn't want to believe this. I guess she saw this in my face. She turned away from me, toward the window again, searching those streets.

"But I praise my Redeemer," she said at last, "that he called your Daddy home before me. I ain't saying it to throw no flowers at myself, but, I declare, it keeps me from feeling too cast down to know I helped your father get safely through this world. Your father always acted like he was the roughest, strongest man on earth. And everybody took him to be like that. But if he hadn't had *me* there—to see his tears!"

She was crying again. Still, I couldn't move. I said, "Lord, Lord, Mama, I didn't know it was like that."

"Oh, honey," she said, "there's a lot that you don't know. But you are going to find it out." She stood up from the window and came over to me. "You got to hold on to your brother," she said, "and don't let him fall, no matter what it looks like is happening to him and no matter how evil you gets with him. You going to be evil with him many a time. But don't you forget what I told you, you hear?"

"I won't forget," I said. "Don't you worry, I won't forget. I won't let nothing happen to Sonny."

My mother smiled as though she were amused at something she saw in my face. Then, "You may not be able to stop nothing from happening. But you got to let him know you's *there*."

Two days later I was married, and then I was gone. And I had a lot of things on my mind and I pretty well forgot my promise to Mama until I got shipped home on a special furlough for her funeral.

And, after the funeral, with just Sonny and me alone in the empty kitchen, I tried to find out something about him.

"What do you want to do?" I asked him.

"I'm going to be a musician," he said.

For he had graduated, in the time I had been away, from dancing to the juke box to finding out who was playing what, and what they were doing with it, and he had bought himself a set of drums.

"You mean, you want to be a drummer?" I somehow had the feeling that being a drummer might be all right for other people but not for my brother Sonny.

"I don't think," he said, looking at me very gravely, "that I'll ever be a good drummer. But I think I can play a piano."

I frowned. I'd never played the role of the older brother quite so seriously before, had scarcely ever, in fact, *asked* Sonny a damn thing. I sensed myself in the presence of something I didn't really know how to handle, didn't understand. So I made my frown a little deeper as I asked: "What kind of musician do you want to be?"

He grinned. "How many kinds do you think there are?"

"Be *serious*," I said.

He laughed, throwing his head back, and then looked at me. "I *am* serious."

"Well, then, for Christ's sake, stop kidding around and answer a serious question. I mean, do you want to be a concert pianist, you want to play classical music and all that, or—or, what?" Long before I finished he was laughing again. "For Christ's *sake*, Sonny!"

He sobered, but with difficulty. "I'm sorry. But you sound so—*scared!*" And he was off again.

"Well, you may think it's funny now, baby, but it's not going to be so funny when you have to make your living at it, let me tell you *that*." I was furious because I knew he was laughing at me and I didn't know why.

"No," he said, very sober now, and afraid, perhaps, that he'd hurt me, "I don't want to be a classical pianist. That isn't what interests me. I mean"—he paused, looking hard at me, as though his eyes would help me to understand, and then gestured helplessly, as though perhaps his hand would help—"I mean, I'll have a lot of studying to do, and I'll have to study *everything,* but, I mean, I want to play *with*—jazz musicians." He stopped. "I want to play jazz," he said.

Well, the word had never before sounded as heavy, as real, as it sounded that afternoon in Sonny's mouth. I just looked at him and I was probably frowning a real frown by this time. I simply couldn't see why on earth he'd want to spend his time hanging around night clubs, clowning around on bandstands, while people pushed each other around a dance floor. It seemed—beneath him, somehow. I had never thought about it before, had never been forced to, but I suppose I had always put jazz musicians in a class with what Daddy called "good-time people."

"Are you *serious?*"

"Hell, *yes,* I'm serious."

He looked more helpless than ever, and annoyed, and deeply hurt.

I suggested, helpfully: "You mean—like Louis Armstrong?"

His face closed as though I'd struck him. "No. I'm not talking about none of that old-time, down home crap."

"Well, look, Sonny, I'm sorry, don't get mad. I just don't altogether get it, that's all. Name somebody—you know, a jazz musician you admire."

"Bird."

"Who?"

"Bird! Charlie Parker! Don't they teach you nothing in the goddamn army?"

I lit a cigarette. I was surprised and then a little amused to discover that I was trembling. "I've been out of touch," I said. "You'll have to be patient with me. Now. Who's this Parker character?"

"He's just one of the greatest jazz musicians alive," said Sonny, sullenly, his hands in his pockets, his back to me.

"Maybe *the* greatest," he added, bitterly, "that's probably why *you* never heard of him."

"All right," I said, "I'm ignorant. I'm sorry. I'll go out and buy all the cat's records right away, all right?"

"It don't," said Sonny, with dignity, "make any difference to me. I don't care what you listen to. Don't do me no favors."

I was beginning to realize that I'd never seen him so upset before. With another part of my mind I was thinking that this would probably turn out to be one of those things kids go through and that I shouldn't make it seem important by pushing it too hard. Still, I didn't think it would do any harm to ask: "Doesn't all this take a lot of time? Can you make a living at it?"

He turned back to me and half leaned, half sat, on the kitchen table. "Everything takes time," he said, "and—well, yes, sure, I can make a living at it. But what I don't seem to be able to make you understand is that it's the only thing I want to do."

"Well, Sonny," I said gently, "you know people can't always do exactly what they want to do—"

"*No,* I don't know that," said Sonny, surprising me. "I think people *ought* to do what they want to do, what else are they alive for?"

"You getting to be a big boy," I said desperately, "it's time you started thinking about your future."

"I'm thinking about my future," said Sonny, grimly. "I think about it all the time."

I gave up. I decided, if he didn't change his mind, that we could always talk about it later. "In the meantime," I said, "you got to finish school." We had already decided that he'd have to move in with Isabel and her folks. I knew this wasn't the ideal arrangement because Isabel's folks are inclined to be dicty and they hadn't especially wanted Isabel to marry me. But I didn't know what else to do. "And we have to get you fixed up at Isabel's."

There was a long silence. He moved from the kitchen table to the window. "That's a terrible idea. You know it yourself."

"Do you have a *better* idea?"

He just walked up and down the kitchen for a minute. He was as tall as I was. He had started to shave. I suddenly had the feeling that I didn't know him at all.

He stopped at the kitchen table and picked up my cigarettes. Looking at me with a kind of mocking, amused defiance, he put one between his lips. "You mind?"

"You smoking already?"

He lit the cigarette and nodded, watching me through the smoke. "I just wanted to see if I'd have the courage to smoke in front of you." He grinned and blew a great cloud of smoke to the ceiling. "It was easy." He looked at my face. "Come on, now. I bet you was smoking at my age, tell the truth."

I didn't say anything but the truth was on my face, and he laughed. But now there was something very strained in his laugh. "Sure. And I bet that ain't all you was doing."

He was frightening me a little. "Cut the crap," I said. "We already decided that you was going to go and live at Isabel's. Now what's got into you all of a sudden?"

"*You* decided it," he pointed out. "*I* didn't decide nothing." He stopped in front of me, leaning against the stove, arms loosely folded. "Look, brother. I don't want to stay in Harlem no more, I really don't." He was very earnest. He looked at me, then over toward the kitchen window. There was something in his eyes I'd never seen before, some thoughtfulness, some worry all his own. He rubbed the muscle of one arm. "It's time I was getting out of here."

"Where do you want to *go*, Sonny?"

"I want to join the army. Or the navy, I don't care. If I say I'm old enough, they'll believe me."

Then I got mad. It was because I was so scared. "You must be crazy. You goddamn fool, what the hell do you want to go and join the *army* for?"

"I just told you. To get out of Harlem."

"Sonny, you haven't even finished *school*. And if you really want to be a musician, how do you expect to study if you're in the *army*?"

He looked at me, trapped, and in anguish. "There's ways. I might be able to work out some kind of deal. Anyway, I'll have the G.I. Bill when I come out."

"*If* you come out." We stared at each other. "Sonny, please. Be reasonable. I know the setup is far from perfect. But we got to do the best we can."

"I ain't learning nothing in school," he said. "Even when I go." He turned away from me and opened the window and threw his cigarette out into the narrow alley. I watched his back. "At least, I ain't learning nothing you'd want me to learn." He slammed the window so hard I thought the glass would fly out, and turned back to me. "And I'm sick of the stink of these garbage cans!"

"Sonny," I said, "I know how you feel. But if you don't finish school now, you're going to be sorry later that you didn't." I grabbed him by the shoulders. "And you only got another year. It ain't so bad. And I'll come back and I swear I'll help you do *whatever* you want to do. Just try to put up with it till I come back. Will you please do that? For me?"

He didn't answer and he wouldn't look at me.

"Sonny. You hear me?"

He pulled away. "I hear you. But you never hear anything *I* say."

I didn't know what to say to that. He looked out of the window and then back at me. "OK," he said, and sighed. "I'll try."

Then I said, trying to cheer him up a little, "They got a piano at Isabel's. You can practice on it."

And as a matter of fact, it did cheer him up for a minute. "That's right," he said to himself. "I forgot that." His face relaxed a little. But the worry, the thoughtfulness, played on it still, the way shadows play on a face which is staring into the fire.

But I thought I'd never hear the end of that piano. At first, Isabel would write me, saying how nice it was that Sonny was so serious about his music and how, as soon as he came in from school, or wherever he had been when he was supposed to be at school, he went straight to that piano and stayed there until suppertime. And, after supper, he went back to that piano and stayed there until everybody went to bed. He was at that piano all day Saturday and all day Sunday. Then he bought a record player and started playing records. He'd play one record over and over again, all day long sometimes, and he'd improvise along with it on the piano. Or he'd play one section of the record, one chord, one change, one progression, then he'd do it on the piano. Then back to the record. Then back to the piano.

Well, I really don't know how they stood it. Isabel finally confessed that it wasn't like living with a person at all, it was like living with sound. And the sound didn't make any sense to her, didn't make any sense to any of them—naturally. They began, in a way, to be afflicted by this presence that was living in their home. It was as though Sonny were some sort of god, or monster. He moved in an atmosphere which wasn't like theirs at all. They fed him and he ate, he washed himself, he walked in and out of their door; he certainly wasn't nasty or unpleasant or rude, Sonny isn't any of those things; but it was as though he were all wrapped up in some cloud, some fire, some vision all his own; and there wasn't any way to reach him.

At the same time, he wasn't really a man yet, he was still a child, and they had to watch out for him in all kinds of ways. They certainly couldn't throw him out. Neither did they dare to make a great scene about that piano because even they dimly sensed, as I sensed, from so many thousands of miles away, that Sonny was at that piano playing for his life.

But he hadn't been going to school. One day a letter came from the school board, and Isabel's mother got it—there had, apparently, been other letters but Sonny had torn them up. This day, when Sonny came in, Isabel's mother showed him the letter and asked where he'd been spending his time. And she finally got it out of him that he'd been down in Greenwich Village, with musicians and other characters, in a white girl's apartment. And this scared her and she started to scream at him, and what came up, once she began— though she denies it to this day—was what sacrifices they were making to give Sonny a decent home and how little he appreciated it.

Sonny didn't play the piano that day. By evening, Isabel's mother had calmed down but then there was the old man

to deal with, and Isabel herself. Isabel says she did her best
to be calm but she broke down and started crying. She says
she just watched Sonny's face. She could tell, by watching
him, what was happening with him. And what was happening was that they penetrated his cloud, they had reached
him. Even if their fingers had been a thousand times more
gentle than human fingers ever are, he could hardly help
feeling that they had stripped him naked and were spitting
on that nakedness. For he also had to see that his presence,
that music, which was life or death to him, had been torture
for them and that they had endured it, not at all for his sake,
but only for mine. And Sonny couldn't take that. He can
take it a little better today than he could then but he's still
not very good at it and, frankly, I don't know anybody who
is.

   The silence of the next few days must have been louder
than the sound of all the music ever played since time began. One morning, before she went to work, Isabel was in
his room for something and she suddenly realized that all of
his records were gone. And she knew for certain that he was
gone. And he was. He went as far as the navy would carry
him. He finally sent me a postcard from someplace in
Greece, and that was the first I knew that Sonny was still
alive. I didn't see him any more until we were both back
in New York and the war had long been over.

   He was a man by then, of course, but I wasn't willing to
see it. He came by the house from time to time, but we
fought almost every time we met. I didn't like the way he
carried himself, loose and dreamlike all the time, and I
didn't like his friends, and his music seemed to be merely
an excuse for the life he led. It sounded just that weird and
disordered.

   Then we had a fight, a pretty awful fight, and I didn't see
him for months. By and by I looked him up, where he was
living, in a furnished room in the Village, and I tried to
make it up. But there were lots of other people in the room,
and Sonny just lay on his bed, and he wouldn't come downstairs with me, and he treated these other people as though
they were his family and I weren't. So I got mad and then
he got mad, and then I told him that he might just as well

be dead as live the way he was living. Then he stood up
and he told me not to worry about him any more in life,
that he *was* dead as far as I was concerned. Then he pushed
me to the door, and the other people looked on as though
nothing were happening, and he slammed the door behind
me. I stood in the hallway, staring at the door. I heard
somebody laugh in the room and then the tears came to my
eyes. I started down the steps, whistling to keep from crying,
I kept whistling to myself, *You going to need me, baby, one
of these cold, rainy days.*

I read about Sonny's trouble in the spring. Little Grace
died in the fall. She was a beautiful little girl. But she only
lived a little over two years. She died of polio and she suffered. She had a slight fever for a couple of days, but it
didn't seem like anything and we just kept her in bed. And
we would certainly have called the doctor, but the fever
dropped, she seemed to be all right. So we thought it had
just been a cold. Then, one day, she was up, playing, Isabel
was in the kitchen fixing lunch for the two boys when they'd
come in from school, and she heard Grace fall down in the
living room. When you have a lot of children you don't always start running when one of them falls, unless they start
screaming or something. And, this time, Grace was quiet.
Yet, Isabel says that when she heard that *thump* and then
that silence, something happened in her to make her afraid.
And she ran to the living room and there was little Grace
on the floor, all twisted up, and the reason she hadn't
screamed was that she couldn't get her breath. And when
she did scream, it was the worst sound, Isabel says, that
she'd ever heard in all her life, and she still hears it sometimes in her dreams. Isabel will sometimes wake me up with
a low, moaning, strangled sound, and I have to be quick to
awaken her and hold her to me and where Isabel is weeping
against me seems a mortal wound.

I think I may have written Sonny the very day that little
Grace was buried. I was sitting in the living room in the
dark, by myself, and I suddenly thought of Sonny. My trouble made his real.

One Saturday afternoon, when Sonny had been living
with us, or, anyway, been in our house, for nearly two
weeks, I found myself wandering aimlessly about the living
room, drinking from a can of beer, and trying to work up
the courage to search Sonny's room. He was out, he was
usually out whenever I was home, and Isabel had taken the
children to see their grandparents. Suddenly I was standing
still in front of the living-room window, watching Seventh
Avenue. The idea of searching Sonny's room made me still.
I scarcely dared to admit to myself what I'd be searching
for. I didn't know what I'd do if I found it. Or if I didn't.

On the sidewalk across from me, near the entrance to a
barbecue joint, some people were holding an old-fashioned
revival meeting. The barbecue cook, wearing a dirty white
apron, his conked hair reddish and metallic in the pale sun,
and a cigarette between his lips, stood in the doorway,
watching them. Kids and older people paused in their er-
rands and stood there, along with some older men and a
couple of very tough-looking women who watched everything that happened on the avenue, as though they owned
it, or were maybe owned by it. Well, they were watching
this, too. The revival was being carried on by three sisters
in black, and a brother. All they had were their voices and
their Bibles and a tambourine. The brother was testifying
and while he testified two of the sisters stood together, seeming to say, Amen, and the third sister walked around with
the tambourine outstretched and a couple of people dropped
coins into it. Then the brother's testimony ended, and the
sister who had been taking up the collection dumped the
coins into her palm and transferred them to the pocket of
her long black robe. Then she raised both hands, striking
the tambourine against the air, and then against one hand,
and she started to sing. And the two other sisters and the
brother joined in.

It was strange, suddenly, to watch, though I had been seeing these street meetings all my life. So, of course, had everybody else down there. Yet, they paused and watched and
listened and I stood still at the window. " *'Tis the old ship of
Zion,*" they sang, and the sister with the tambourine kept
a steady, jangling beat, *"it has rescued many a thousand!"*

Not a soul under the sound of their voices was hearing this song for the first time, not one of them had been rescued. Nor had they seen much in the way of rescue work being done around them. Neither did they especially believe in the holiness of the three sisters and the brother, they knew too much about them, knew where they lived, and how. The woman with the tambourine, whose voice dominated the air, whose face was bright with joy, was divided by very little from the woman who stood watching her, a cigarette between her heavy, chapped lips, her hair a cuckoo's nest, her face scarred and swollen from many beatings, and her black eyes glittering like coal. Perhaps they both knew this, which was why, when, as rarely, they addressed each other, they addressed each other as Sister. As the singing filled the air, the watching, listening faces underwent a change, the eyes focusing on something within; the music seemed to soothe a poison out of them; and time seemed, nearly, to fall away from the sullen, belligerent, battered faces, as though they were fleeing back to their first condition, while dreaming of their last. The barbecue cook half shook his head and smiled, and dropped his cigarette and disappeared into his joint. A man fumbled in his pockets for change and stood holding it in his hand impatiently, as though he had just remembered a pressing appointment further up the avenue. He looked furious. Then I saw Sonny, standing on the edge of the crowd. He was carrying a wide, flat notebook with a green cover, and it made him look, from where I was standing, almost like a schoolboy. The coppery sun brought out the copper in his skin, he was very faintly smiling, standing very still. Then the singing stopped, the tambourine turned into a collection plate again. The furious man dropped in his coins and vanished, so did a couple of the women, and Sonny dropped some change in the plate, looking directly at the woman with a little smile. He started across the avenue, toward the house. He has a slow, loping walk, something like the way Harlem hipsters walk, only he's imposed on this his own half-beat. I had never really noticed it before.

I stayed at the window, both relieved and apprehensive. As Sonny disappeared from my sight, they began singing again. And they were still singing when his key turned in the lock.

"Hey," he said.

"Hey, yourself. You want some beer?"

"No. Well, maybe." But he came up to the window and stood beside me, looking out. "What a warm voice," he said.

They were singing *If I could only hear my mother pray again!*

"Yes," I said, "and she can sure beat that tambourine."

"But what a terrible song," he said, and laughed. He dropped his notebook on the sofa and disappeared into the kitchen. "Where's Isabel and the kids?"

"I think they went to see their grandparents. You hungry?"

"No." He came back into the living room with his can of beer. "You want to come someplace with me tonight?"

I sensed, I don't know how, that I couldn't possibly say no. "Sure. Where?"

He sat down on the sofa and picked up his notebook and started leafing through it. "I'm going to sit in with some fellows in a joint in the Village."

"You mean, you're going to play, tonight?"

"That's right." He took a swallow of his beer and moved back to the window. He gave me a sidelong look. "If you can stand it."

"I'll try," I said.

He smiled to himself, and we both watched as the meeting across the way broke up. The three sisters and the brother, heads bowed, were singing *God be with you till we meet again*. The faces around them were very quiet. Then the song ended. The small crowd dispersed. We watched the three women and the lone man walk slowly up the avenue.

"When she was singing before," said Sonny, abruptly, "her voice reminded me for a minute of what heroin feels like sometimes—when it's in your veins. It makes you feel sort of warm and cool at the same time. And distant. And—and sure." He sipped his beer, very deliberately not looking at me. I watched his face. "It makes you feel—in control. Sometimes you've got to have that feeling."

"Do you?" I sat down slowly in the easy chair.

"Sometimes." He went to the sofa and picked up his notebook again. "Some people do."

"In order," I asked, "to play?" And my voice was very ugly, full of contempt and anger.

"Well"—he looked at me with great, troubled eyes, as though, in fact, he hoped his eyes would tell me things he could never otherwise say—"they *think* so. And *if* they think so—!"

"And what do *you* think?" I asked.

He sat on the sofa and put his can of beer on the floor. "I don't know," he said, and I couldn't be sure if he were answering my question or pursuing his thoughts. His face didn't tell me. "It's not so much to *play*. It's to *stand* it, to be able to make it at all. On any level." He frowned and smiled: "In order to keep from shaking to pieces."

"But these friends of yours," I said, "they seem to shake themselves to pieces pretty goddamn fast."

"Maybe." He played with the notebook. And something told me that I should curb my tongue, that Sonny was doing his best to talk, that I should listen. "But of course you only know the ones that've gone to pieces. Some don't—or at least they haven't *yet* and that's just about all *any* of us can say." He paused. "And then there are some who just live, really, in hell, and they know it and they see what's happening and they go right on. I don't know." He sighed, dropped the notebook, folded his arms. "Some guys, you can tell from the way they play, they on something *all* the time. And you can see that, well, it makes something real for them. But of course," he picked up his beer from the floor and sipped it and put the can down again, "they *want* to, too, you've got to see that. Even some of them that say they don't— *some*, not all."

"And what about you?" I asked—I couldn't help it. "What about you? Do *you* want to?"

He stood up and walked to the window and remained silent for a long time. Then he sighed. "Me," he said. Then: "While I was downstairs before, on my way here, listening to that woman sing, it struck me all of a sudden how much suffering she must have had to go through—to sing like that. It's *repulsive* to think you have to suffer that much."

I said: "But there's no way not to suffer—is there, Sonny?"

"I believe not," he said, and smiled, "but that's never stopped anyone from trying." He looked at me. "Has it?" I realized, with this mocking look, that there stood between us, forever, beyond the power of time or forgiveness, the fact that I had held silence—so long!—when he had needed human speech to help him. He turned back to the window. "No, there's no way not to suffer. But you try all kinds of ways to keep from drowning in it, to keep on top of it, and to make it seem—well, like *you*. Like you did something, all right, and now you're suffering for it. You know?" I said nothing. "Well you know," he said, impatiently, "why *do* people suffer? Maybe it's better to do something to give it a reason, *any* reason."

"But we just agreed," I said, "that there's no way not to suffer. Isn't it better, then, just to—take it?"

"But nobody just takes it," Sonny cried, "that's what I'm telling you! *Everybody* tries not to. You're just hung up on the *way* some people try—it's not *your* way!"

The hair on my face began to itch, my face felt wet. "That's not true," I said, "that's not true. I don't give a damn what other people do, I don't even care how they suffer. I just care how *you* suffer." And he looked at me. "Please believe me," I said, "I don't want to see you—die— trying not to suffer."

"I won't," he said, flatly, "die trying not to suffer. At least, not any faster than anybody else."

"But there's no need," I said, trying to laugh, "is there, in killing yourself?"

I wanted to say more, but I couldn't. I wanted to talk about will power and how life could be—well, beautiful. I wanted to say that it was all within; but was it? Or, rather, wasn't that exactly the trouble? And I wanted to promise that I would never fail him again. But it would all have sounded—empty words and lies.

So I made the promise to myself and prayed that I would keep it.

"It's terrible sometimes, inside," he said, "that's what's the trouble. You walk these streets, black and funky and cold, and there's not really a living ass to talk to, and there's nothing shaking, and there's no way of getting it out—that storm inside. You can't talk it and you can't make love with it, and when you finally try to get with it and play it, you realize *nobody's* listening. So *you've* got to listen. You got to find a way to listen."

And then he walked away from the window and sat on the sofa again, as though all the wind had suddenly been knocked out of him. "Sometimes you'll do *anything* to play, even cut your mother's throat." He laughed and looked at me. "Or your brother's." Then he sobered. "Or your own." Then: "Don't worry. I'm all right now and I think I'll *be* all right. But I can't forget—where I've been. I don't mean just the physical place I've been, I mean where I've *been*. And *what* I've been."

"What have you been, Sonny?" I asked.

He smiled—but sat sideways on the sofa, his elbow resting on the back, his fingers playing with his mouth and chin, not looking at me. "I've been something I didn't recognize, didn't know I could be. Didn't know anybody could be." He stopped, looking inward, looking helplessly young, looking old. "I'm not talking about it now because I feel *guilty* or anything like that—maybe it would be better if I did, I don't know. Anyway, I can't really talk about it. Not to you, not to anybody." And now he turned and faced me. "Sometimes, you know, and it was actually when I was most out of the world, I felt that I was in it, that I was *with* it, really, and I could play or I didn't really have to *play*, it just came out of me, it was there. And I don't know how I played, thinking about it now, but I know I did awful things, those times, sometimes, to people. Or it wasn't that I *did* anything to them—it was that they weren't real." He picked up the beer can; it was empty; he rolled it between his palms: "And other times—well, I needed a fix, I needed to find a place to lean, I needed to clear a space to *listen*—and I couldn't find it, and I—went crazy, I did terrible things to *me*, I was terrible *for* me." He began pressing the beer can between his hands, I watched the metal begin to give. It glittered, as he played with it, like a knife, and I was afraid he would cut himself, but I said nothing. "Oh well. I can never tell you.

I was all by myself at the bottom of something, stinking and sweating and crying and shaking, and I smelled it, you know? *My* stink, and I thought I'd die if I couldn't get away from it and yet, all the same, I knew that everything I was doing was just locking me in with it. And I didn't know," he paused, still flattening the beer can, "I didn't know, I still *don't* know, something kept telling me that maybe it was good to smell your own stink, but I didn't think that *that* was what I'd been trying to do—and—who can stand it?" And he abruptly dropped the ruined beer can, looking at me with a small, still smile, and then rose, walking to the window as though it were the lodestone rock. I watched his face, he watched the avenue. "I couldn't tell you when Mama died —but the reason I wanted to leave Harlem so bad was to get away from drugs. And then, when I ran away, that's what I was running from—really. When I came back, nothing had changed, *I* hadn't changed, I was just—older." And he stopped, drumming with his fingers on the windowpane. The sun had vanished, soon darkness would fall. I watched his face. "It can come again," he said, almost as though speaking to himself. Then he turned to me. "It can come again," he repeated. "I just want you to know that."

"All right," I said at last. "So it can come again. All right."

He smiled, but the smile was sorrowful. "I had to try to tell you," he said.

"Yes," I said. "I understand that."

"You're my brother," he said, looking straight at me, and not smiling at all.

"Yes," I repeated, "yes. I understand that."

He turned back to the window, looking out. "All that hatred down there," he said, "all that hatred and misery and love. It's a wonder it doesn't blow the avenue apart."

We went to the only night club on a short, dark street, downtown. We squeezed through the narrow, chattering, jam-packed bar to the entrance of the big room, where the bandstand was. And we stood there for a moment, for the lights were very dim in this room and we couldn't see. Then, "Hello, boy," said a voice, and an enormous black man, much older than Sonny or myself, erupted out of all that atmospheric lighting and put an arm around Sonny's shoulder. "I been sitting right here," he said, "waiting for you."

He had a big voice, too, and heads in the darkness turned toward us.

Sonny grinned and pulled a little away, and said, "Creole, this is my brother. I told you about him."

Creole shook my hand. "I'm glad to meet you, son," he said, and it was clear that he was glad to meet me *there*, for Sonny's sake. And he smiled. "You got a real musician in *your* family," and he took his arm from Sonny's shoulder and slapped him, lightly, affectionately, with the back of his hand.

"Well. Now I've heard it all," said a voice behind us. This was another musician, and a friend of Sonny's, a coal-black, cheerful-looking man, built close to the ground. He immediately began confiding to me, at the top of his lungs, the most terrible things about Sonny, his teeth gleaming like a lighthouse and his laugh coming up out of him like the beginning of an earthquake. And it turned out that everyone at the bar knew Sonny, or almost everyone; some were musicians, working there, or nearby, or not working, some were simply hangers-on, and some were there to hear Sonny play. I was introduced to all of them and they were all very polite to me. Yet, it was clear that, for them, I was only Sonny's brother. Here, I was in Sonny's world. Or, rather: his kingdom. Here, it was not even a question that his veins bore royal blood.

They were going to play soon, and Creole installed me, by myself, at a table in a dark corner. Then I watched them, Creole, and the little black man, and Sonny, and the others, while they horsed around, standing just below the bandstand. The light from the bandstand spilled just a little short of them and, watching them laughing and gesturing and moving about, I had the feeling that they, nevertheless, were being most careful not to step into that circle of light too suddenly: that if they moved into the light too suddenly, without thinking, they would perish in flame. Then, while I watched, one of them, the small, black man, moved into the light and crossed the bandstand and started fooling around with his drums. Then—being funny and being, also, extremely ceremonious—Creole took Sonny by the arm and led him to the piano. A woman's voice called Sonny's name, and a few hands started clapping. And Sonny, also being funny and being ceremonious, and so touched, I think, that he could have cried, but neither hiding it nor showing it, riding it like a man, grinned, and put both hands to his heart and bowed from the waist.

Creole then went to the bass fiddle and a lean, very bright-skinned brown man jumped up on the bandstand and picked up his horn. So there they were, and the atmosphere on the bandstand and in the room began to change and tighten. Someone stepped up to the microphone and announced them. Then there were all kinds of murmurs. Some people at the bar shushed others. The waitress ran around, frantically getting in the last orders, guys and chicks got closer to each other, and the lights on the bandstand, on the quartet, turned to a kind of indigo. Then they all looked different there. Creole looked about him for the last time, as though he were making certain that all his chickens were in the coop, and then he—jumped and struck the fiddle. And there they were.

All I know about music is that not many people ever really hear it. And even then, on the rare occasions when something opens within, and the music enters, what we mainly hear, or hear corroborated, are personal, private, vanishing evocations. But the man who creates the music is hearing something else, is dealing with the roar rising from the void and imposing order on it as it hits the air. What is evoked in him, then, is of another order, more terrible because it has no words, and triumphant, too, for that same reason. And his triumph, when he triumphs, is ours. I just watched Sonny's face. His face was troubled, he was working hard, but he wasn't with it. And I had the feeling that, in a way, everyone on the bandstand was waiting for him, both waiting for him and pushing him along. But as I began to watch Creole, I realized that it was Creole who held them all back. He had them on a short rein. Up there, keeping the beat with his whole body, wailing on the fiddle, with his eyes half closed, he was listening to everything, but he was listening to Sonny. He was having a dialogue with Sonny. He wanted Sonny to leave the shore line and strike out for the deep water. He was Sonny's witness that deep water and drowning were not the same thing—he had been there, and he knew. And he wanted Sonny to know. He was waiting for Sonny to do the things on the keys which would let Creole know that Sonny was in the water.

And, while Creole listened, Sonny moved, deep within, exactly like someone in torment. I had never before thought of how awful the relationship must be between the musician and his instrument. He has to fill it, this instrument, with the breath of life, his own. He has to make it do what he wants it to do. And a piano is just a piano. It's made out of so much wood and wires and little hammers and big ones, and ivory. While there's only so much you can do with it, the only way to find this out is to try to try and make it do everything.

And Sonny hadn't been near a piano for over a year. And he wasn't on much better terms with his life, not the life that stretched before him now. He and the piano stammered, started one way, got scared, stopped; started another way, panicked, marked time, started again; then seemed to have found a direction, panicked again, got stuck. And the face I saw on Sonny I'd never seen before. Everything had been burned out of it, and, at the same time, things usually hidden were being burned in, by the fire and fury of the battle which was occurring in him up there.

Yet, watching Creole's face as they neared the end of the first set, I had the feeling that something had happened, something I hadn't heard. Then they finished, there was scattered applause, and then, without an instant's warning, Creole started into something else, it was almost sardonic, it was *Am I Blue*. And, as though he commanded, Sonny began to play. Something began to happen. And Creole let out the reins. The dry, low, black man said something awful on the drums, Creole answered, and the drums talked back. Then the horn insisted, sweet and high, slightly detached perhaps, and Creole listened, commenting now and then, dry, and driving, beautiful and calm and old. Then they all came together again, and Sonny was part of the family

again. I could tell this from his face. He seemed to have
found, right there beneath his fingers, a damn brand-new
piano. It seemed that he couldn't get over it. Then, for a
while, just being happy with Sonny, they seemed to be agreeing with him that brand-new pianos certainly were a gas.

Then Creole stepped forward to remind them that what
they were playing was the blues. He hit something in all of
them, he hit something in me, myself, and the music tightened and deepened, apprehension began to beat the air.
Creole began to tell us what the blues were all about. They
were not about anything very new. He and his boys up there
were keeping it new, at the risk of ruin, destruction, madness, and death, in order to find new ways to make us listen.
For, while the tale of how we suffer, and how we are delighted, and how we may triumph is never new, it always
must be heard. There isn't any other tale to tell, it's the
only light we've got in all this darkness.

And this tale, according to that face, that body, those
strong hands on those strings, has another aspect in every
country, and a new depth in every generation. Listen, Creole
seemed to be saying, listen. Now these are Sonny's blues.
He made the little black man on the drums know it, and
the bright, brown man on the horn. Creole wasn't trying any
longer to get Sonny in the water. He was wishing him God-
speed. Then he stepped back, very slowly, filling the air
with the immense suggestion that Sonny speak for himself.

Then they all gathered around Sonny, and Sonny played.
Every now and again one of them seemed to say, Amen.
Sonny's fingers filled the air with life, his life. But that life
contained so many others. And Sonny went all the way back,
he really began with the spare, flat statement of the opening
phrase of the song. Then he began to make it his. It was
very beautiful because it wasn't hurried and it was no
longer a lament. I seemed to hear with what burning he
had made it his, with what burning we had yet to make it
ours, how we could cease lamenting. Freedom lurked
around us and I understood, at last, that he could help us
to be free if we would listen, that he would never be free
until we did. Yet, there was no battle in his face now. I
heard what he had gone through, and would continue to go

through until he came to rest in earth. He had made it his: that long line, of which we knew only Mama and Daddy. And he was giving it back, as everything must be given back, so that, passing through death, it can live forever. I saw my mother's face again, and felt, for the first time, how the stones of the road she had walked on must have bruised her feet. I saw the moonlit road where my father's brother died. And it brought something else back to me, and carried me past it. I saw my little girl again and felt Isabel's tears again, and I felt my own tears begin to rise. And I was yet aware that this was only a moment, that the world waited outside, as hungry as a tiger, and that trouble stretched above us, longer than the sky.

Then it was over. Creole and Sonny let out their breath, both soaking wet, and grinning. There was a lot of applause and some of it was real. In the dark, the girl came by and I asked her to take drinks to the bandstand. There was a long pause, while they talked up there in the indigo light and after a while I saw the girl put a Scotch and milk on top of the piano for Sonny. He didn't seem to notice it, but just before they started playing again, he sipped from it and looked toward me, and nodded. Then he put it back on top of the piano. For me, then, as they began to play again, it glowed and shook above my brother's head like the very cup of trembling.

A SERMON BY DOCTOR PEP

Saul Bellow

SAUL BELLOW *was born in Lachine, Quebec, in 1915 and moved to Chicago at the age of nine. He attended the University of Chicago and Northwestern University and has taught at Princeton and the University of Minnesota. He is the author of four novels:* THE DANGLING MAN *(1944),* THE VICTIM *(1947),* THE ADVENTURES OF AUGIE MARCH *(1953, a National Book Award winner) and* HENDERSON THE RAIN KING *(1959), and also* SEIZE THE DAY *(1956), which contains a novella, three short stories and a one-act play. Critical pieces and fiction by him have appeared in many magazines. He has been awarded a Guggenheim Fellowship and a Ford Grant, and is currently trying his hand at a play, a farce in three acts.*

In Bughouse Square, Chicago, before the brownstone length of the Newberry Library, where he spends his days.

Before long winter will be over, dear friends. Easter isn't far away. There is still hard ice protected by ashes in the corners, but it will wash out by the same process that laid the moraines of glaciers over our great states. The old leaves are drying, and skid row is thinning out as the dead-looking are resurrected off the sidewalks and sent to be gandy-walkers in the little blue flowers of Montana, where the birds chirp like the sound of scissors and snip the air into beautiful streamers, and the butterflies drink up what is left of the porcupines who passed on happy in their sleep.

I would go myself if I were younger and had all my limbs
to go with. (*Indicates his crutch.*) But many of you know
the story of how I ransomed my body with my leg after
the Skokie Valley crash of 1923, having heard the talk I
give on Man and the Machine, which talk I do not aim to
give this evening. But if I could do it, I would take off for
Montana or the Black Hills, just from the need to refresh
my heart on ground that hasn't been coated and cased and
under feet and wheels for as long as North Clark Street.
However, I am not eligible to be a section hand. Natural
selection has been rough on me—this dog-white hair growing over my head and out of my ears. I will have to be
satisfied right here where I have done a long winter of study
and thought in the Newberry reading room, among the nuns
and antiquarians poring over walled cities and Celtic
dreams. Antiquarians and young girls getting up assignments
for Teachers' College—pale, hot-faced young girls whose
laps were never meant for notebooks. I feel for the young
woman with her thick-stuffed albatross brief case which the
word of a school board will change into the weight of *Stone-
Mills Arithmetic* and three volumes of *Literature and Life*.
Not the blessing of love to take it off her. And she will arrive in her small town for a second, deeper and worse en-
chantment and think even of the Newberry as one wall
closer to freedom and mysterious hot love. But I will stay
here and see if I can find a substitute for the little green
winds of Spring in the pages of books and will keep on
smelling White Castle hamburger-onions in place of section-
hand stew.

Now since I've mentioned hamburgers, I'll lead with them
straight into my subject of disease and health, and true and
false nourishment, out of my readings in Galen and Hip-
pocrates and even further back in time. First-off I want to
say that I'm not going to discuss anything so obsolete as the
effects of Dogstar rains or descending phlegm in humid na-
tures; nor will you hear anything from me, more recent, for
or against psyllium seeds or senna leaves for regularity, or
yogurt and the parasites of carp for old age; or any of the
stuff you get from radio doctors about health-bread or the
evil of polished grain and false, agenized bleached flour or

digging your grave with your teeth. No, it's something else
I have in mind, tonight. I recall, first of all, my old friend
Dr. Julius Widig, whom you must all remember, a frequent
speaker in this square while he lived and the author of
Reefer Rosie, the Tragedy of a Girl Bum. Generous soul,
we all respect his memory. Our old friend Dr. Widig when
he was arrested in the first war for an open anarchist and
strong-armed and given the broom-handle treatment behind
the mayor's squad, when his license was taken away from
him and he was thrown into Joliet Penitentiary, he kept up
his noble heart by healing the jailbird venerealees and came
out a lot healthier than Ponce came out of the Florida
swamps, nearly killed by his quest for elixirs. Yes, while
more robust and better fleshed, gymnastical men ran off to
embrace the sickness of Berdun, where all the bones still
have not been gathered under crosses, he was hustled off to
jail. And it was caring for the prisoners that saved his vital
economy for him in spite of the war the state made on him
with strong-arming and the hoosegow drearies. It was the
miseries of other men that did him good. Now, am I
calumnifying the mild old doctor? He didn't ask for them,
no; he was too humane. But what is his example for us?
Nothing new. Only that in health we are in the debt of a
suffering creation. With that, foremost, we have to settle.
Think of the old tale of Pharaoh bathing his leprosy in the
blood of Israel's children. If you picture him sitting evil in
his basaltic tub, see his head like the head of a swimming
snake, you are partly in error. You ought to see him sad,
as anyone is taking medicine and treatments. Any way you
want to pick this thing up you have layers and series. The
welfare of the common rests on the beasts, and as for the
greatness of the great, the perfect representations of happiness and satisfaction which we have had the get-up to make
the image of democratic everybody, it was always felt to
come from the thousands and millions underneath, the
beasts and the lowly. The ignorant poor bringing their children to be cured of scrofula by the touch of a British queen
—I see the pudgy-headed infant Sam Johnson carried all the
way from Lichfield among them—brought them in that

thought, to get back a little of their own from the heart-rich
sovereign whom they had fed.

Spring and Easter make me think of these things, dear
listeners. The slaughtered Osiris gets himself together again
and his scattered body comes to life; the grave-cold Redeemer rises up; the tadpole shucks the tallowy, pond-bob-
bing egg, and his tender feet grow scratchy, and the fat of
life begins to sizzle. The new styles have been showing since
February; we little dream of the love-raging cults that pre-
ceded when we see those sprays of cloth flowers worn in
the parade or of the legs that trembled for the touch of
panting Attis in the hobbled march of tight skirts. And
pretty soon there'll be little cake and fudge lambs in the
windows that the children will croon at and eat. Yes, eat the
lamb made to eat. Why not? Is there any real love short of
eating? Bite off the tail, the little feet, the head, and make
inarticulate love with the hungry tongue and amorous teeth,
learn biting love with the little pure divinity lamb. Have you
heard the mother tell her little Tommy, "I could eat you
up!" You have; she says it, but she does not gobble him
like the cold-blooded guppy or the indiscriminate feasting
sow. And we shudder when we read of poor Thyestes dished
up his children unsuspecting by that hateful king and have
deep horror and deep envy of his ignorant cannibal dinner
because he has the tragic true love of assimilating his own
into his own body again and returning them to the glue of
his bones and the fat of his kidneys. Or turn your thoughts
to eucharistic wine and wafers. "You shall eat my body and
drink my blood"—terrible to the blood-avoiding law of
Moses. But consider it as an order to feel no blame and
have an innocent appetite. In things like this the secret of
health and eating is to be found. A Paschal lamb. To the ancient Greek islanders, a fish. And if Christ's blood ran for
us, why shouldn't the blood of steers run, and why should
anybody flinch at the butchering of the calves or the trussed
pigs that go thrashing and squealing round on the big stock-
yard wheels in the south part of our great city? Now this is
just the appropriate place for the question, for the threads
are spun out here that led to thousands of Minotaurs a day
through pens and galleries, and if the knackers' hammers

stopped falling, there would have to be some other ground-
note to hold up the harmony. But friends, let us be careful.
There is so much prosperity and fame out of the packing
industry that we dassn't think of the awful names of the
Carthaginian or Canaanite demons or Moabitic Peors in
connection with it unless we have something to propose and
speak to a useful purpose. So remember what the subject is.
Health of the person. Original vigor. *Mens sana in corpore
sano.* And you see that I am no mock-duck vegetarian or
nature-curer or Fletcherizer urging you to chew; nor a
health-parson saying that consecration is good for the nerves
and that the saints and apostles were pole-vaulters. Nor am
I here to frighten the young men with warnings of gleet
and morning-drop and other threats and terrors of the street
guide or admonish the girls not to take drugs tampering with
their courses. No scares nor superstitions, nothing like that.
I'm talking of nutrition, plain and simple, and the deep
causes of good and bad health, and I began with hamburger
meaning to explore why the shape of the creature is ground
up—not only in hamburger but in its allies chopped steak
and Salisbury steak, and other euphemisms of the menu as
well, and in croquettes and hash—ground and hidden with
the best formal art of Thompson's and Pixley's for the noon-
hour ravenous, not to give an evidence of the living and a
hint of obligation, of reverence and indebtedness. Is that a
deep offense, the beginning of sickness? Does that make
cold tallow out of the fat which should be the grease of
love? I believe so. For there is a bad conscience somewhere
about it. The injurious part is that a reality is subtracted
along the way and something spoiling creeps in. Things have
to be accounted for in full by a demand of our nature, and
in that respect the wild Melanesian and the Kalahari dwarf
are in better state than we. The Mithraic communion of
bread and wine and the totem animal masks of the cult,
almost all we have left, are hidden in a little trimming of
St. Peter's throne. The White Tower ketchup bottle is not
enough of a symbol of the sacrifice of life, and the true fact
is that death is not farther but closer to us when we are so
perfunctory and unbeholden. The real and free presence of
life is in the necessitous drink and the hungry bite of the

man and woman who know how food is supplied and have met the debt of labor and acknowledgment.

As far as I am concerned, I know my debt. The one foot of my original two that touched the ground is shod in the hide of beasts; my coat is trimmed with the skin of them. I don't know what the fur of my collar is, wolf or badger, tickling my neck. It seems mostly like the anonymous hock-shop article that never had a parent or a birth and was never anything but the trimming on a garment. But when the thaw comes and I feel it against my skin, why it gets a little pungent of the cave and the forest from the heat of my body, and then I remember what it is. I remember the animals and that I am pieced together inside and out, from joint to strap and from liver to buttons by their favor. Because I am a prince of life, ladies and gentlemen? And the natural chief of the hierarchy, the speaking over the dumb? This I must be to deserve it. Otherwise what excuse is there? I ask you it from my heart. Am I deserving? For I have to be.

Now, friends, some of you will be thinking of the rule of nature and will ask my opinion, for instance, of the tame cat eating her way wag-headed into a mackerel with her nice needles; somebody will direct me to the Lincoln Park Zoo and the whole bar-confined congress of brute life ten minutes by car from the main stem; and he will mention for sure the wiry clinging mantis that gnaws off the head of her mate in their climax. Likewise we kill and devour. Which is all very well if you think of us only in nature. Yes, I feel the drum-bumps of the species in me, of all of them. I appreciate that I am not the star-browed Apollo measuring one noble foot of space between the eyes. I am even one leg short of the average stump of Adam. But folks, I partake of everything in my own flesh; I strum on Venus-berg and float in the swamp. I do a one-leg schottische along Clark Street and buff the friendly public with my belly. I stroll in the zoo with my colleagues and ponder the throat-digging nails of the lynx and the pillars of the elephant; I sit in the Newberry and compassionate with the tender girls who have never felt anything warmer than a washcloth upon them. And I feel that I and all these creatures and

persons are images of spirit, icons, symbols, versions and
formations.

But if you disagree, let us see for a moment how we
compare with the egg-born. You will admit, each and every
one of you, that they do not have to be guided but are
never lost anywhere. I admire how the faintest light in the
summer attic will bring the fine, secret mosquito quivering
from a long distance to the screen, just as the faintest
warmth of the gopher will fetch the rattler between the eyes
and make him strike. And I marvel at the Guiana spider
that takes the ants' disguise to perfection. But let me suggest to you, listeners, that he comes into the world instructed
in mimicry and belongs to the cast of the giant creation that
goes through a performance of days and ages without a
falter and without a rehearsal. Whereas we, fallible and in
need of instruction, train in a riot of boners and howlers;
being creatures *and* more, having hopes of brilliancy, having dread of Acheron, hankering through endless series
from the inane to the earth and around the earth from end
to end, embracing everything with infinite desire.

Infinite, infinite! Is it the desire of subject creatures any
more? No, it is not, this nonpareil longing. And, like everything else, it has its health. That is glorious. It has its disease,
too, and that is to digest itself. Yes, we are the only ones
who turn our appetite on ourselves, and the most hopeful
and outward-gentle do it most of all. Too gentle and ab-
staining to be predacious at large, with the humane eyes of
civilized self-consumption. The plans of Jerusalem are open
before them, but what haunts them is the eating mouth, the
betrayal of mercy in their own teeth and the insubordinate
part of them facing toward Moloch and his capital.

What is this being gentle? Give me a little more time,
everybody, and think of it. Ah, it's a tragic, tearful subject,
and I am stripped naked when I come to it. A billion years
of devouring are behind us; will we even them up with as
many of love and compassion before the earthly time is up?

Don't take it amiss for frivolousness if I refer to the Walrus and the Carpenter to begin with. The Walrus was sorry
for the poor oysters. The Carpenter ate without caring. But
both of them wept like anything to see such quantities of

sand. Why did they? Because civilization is never complete enough? In dead earnest, it is profound. The sand remains in spite of the maids and the mops. It creeps back. And the fish of first-times loiters offshore somewhere near our loftier thoughts. Each new generation has to be tamed to manners and tamed more than its remotest ancestor. The snakes have to be made to come and braid themselves symmetrical into the healer's caduceus, forsaking poison for benevolence, and everything lay itself out harmonious and nice.

But as the subjugation goes on and the City of Man arises, the martyrs multiply faster and faster. Such work cannot go forward without firm and earnest purpose, seriousness and hardness, and the proof of such by willingness to make sacrifices. Here the martyrs come in. There is no power without them; they must appear. The young knight Curtius who threw himself horse and all into the gap in the Forum, there is your cleanest and simplest example, as the story makes it happen by heroic consent. The boys of best breeding the Mexican priests took the hearts from, there's another; or Iphigenia under the knife of her curl-bearded father, offered up for the sake of the bedoldrummed fleet. Still not like later excess. The mops of the maids are of human hair, and still the sand gathers and gathers. Beautiful Versailles and the shaped trees of Fontainebleau fed the dream of Robespierre, prepared to murder millions of his countrymen to see it real. And were the fierce moppers of Auschwitz inspired by their squared and polished home towns and the pleasant embroidery of the regulated Rhine? Remember, Baal was the lord of cultivation and humanized land, and in the eyes of Moses he was the greatest danger to the Jews of the desert-bred generation.

But I have to give over now, for I see Dr. Johannes waiting to address you on the single-tax and interpret the message of Henry George. I have only another word on gentleness, which for me is in the patriarch Abraham ready to take the life of Isaac on the angry mountain. He was tried where he was tenderest to learn what the worst was that indulgent love had to be ready for. Inhumane, the old man? Not for me. Not he. Not when he looked at the bone-enclosed head beside him, the mysterious shape between the boy's wonders and thoughts and the free air of heaven. He knew his debt—and I can see nothing but honor in it —for the presence and continuation of life.

We can keep death too near us by secret care. It inhibits the bite, it poisons each mouthful, closes the digestion and sends us to an early grave.

I make way now for my colleague.

WHAT THE CYSTOSCOPE SAID

Anatole Broyard

ANATOLE BROYARD *was born in New Orleans, spent his boy-
hood in Brooklyn, and now lives alone in Greenwich
Village. He has worked for* The Reporter *magazine
and occasionally lectures at the New School on American foibles. "What the Cystoscope Said" is part of a
novel in progress. Other parts have appeared in* Modern Writing #2, New World Writing #10, *and the*
Hudson Review.

When I saw my father with the horse collar around his
neck, I knew immediately. I didn't admit it until much later,
but there was never any doubt in my mind.

Some people are just stopped dead in their tracks, as
though the reel had broken—their last image lingers in the
mind's eye, and they never completely die—but my father
was demoted down the evolutionary scale into nothingness.
He lost position after position in an interminable retreat.
Just as he had been at first conceived, he was at last de-
conceived, and, like a child who takes apart a favorite toy,
impelled by some insatiable love, I watched his inner work-
ings come loose and found out what made him tick. Then,
as now, I felt that this was most natural. The relation between a son and father *ought to be* barbaric.

The stiff neck came from pulling up roots. After sixty
years of deferring pleasures, he'd finally bought a little
house in the country. He was pampering it when it got him
in the neck. The irony was so pat that it made you feel he
wasn't significant enough to rate a more elaborate twist.
"You must have slept in a draft," my mother said, and she

rubbed him with liniment and wrapped his neck with flannel. "You must have strained yourself," the doctor said a week later, and he gave him heat treatments.

Everyone knew that Memorial Hospital was for cancer cases. Everyone but Peter Romain, his wife Ethel, and his son Paul. He went on the subway, but he came back in a taxi because of the collar. They said it would keep him from aggravating a possible injury in his neck. He protested, he said he could hold up his own head, but when he accepted the collar, he was harnessed to his fate.

I was visiting when he got out of the taxi. This was the first I'd heard of it, and my mother hadn't quite finished the story, so that when I saw him, the whole thing was floating loosely in my mind, ready to take any shape. It never even passed through the stage of seeming like a bad joke. The moment I saw him, I knew. I realized immediately that this pathos was beyond contradiction. He threatened to throw off the yoke, and we quickly understood our parts. "You don't really need it, but it can't do any harm." This was the kind of reasoning we were to use from then on. "You're not going, but kiss me, kiss me goodbye."

Although he was a superintendent, a full grade above a foreman, my father insisted on carrying a toolbox to every job. At the rasp of a saw, he'd pull out his tools—he would never touch theirs—and "show those monkeys how to do their job." If he saw a man choking up on the handle of a hammer, he'd snatch his own hammer out of the loop at the hip of his overalls and drive the nail home with two full-arm strokes. Now he was worried about his tools, because they were still on the job. "I don't want those monkeys fooling with my box," he said. "I better go pick it up." I tried to talk him out of it, saying that I would go and get them, but he seemed to feel that no one could conceivably move his box except under his personal supervision, so we went together.

He wouldn't wear the collar. We argued back and forth for twenty minutes, but I couldn't budge him. I was holding it out toward him as an adult holds a spoonful of medicine and tries to talk a child into swallowing it. Then, all at once,

I became so intensely aware of the feel of the collar that I almost dropped it. For the first time, I perceived it as a thing. It was a sausage-shaped pad stuffed with cotton and covered with a sort of sock made of unbleached muslin. At each end the sock terminated in a string, like an apron string. It really was nothing but a simple surgical brace, but for some reason it gave me another feeling; there was something suggestively organic about it, like a fleshy deformity, voluntarily assumed.

It disgusted me, and abruptly I decided that it was not for me to take its part, so I said, "All right, if you insist," and dropped the collar on the table. Feeling that he had gained an important victory, he refused to take a taxi, too. The idea of the job made him feel himself again. He almost had me believing it.

The job was a store on the first floor of a building on West Forty-fifth Street. When we walked in, he introduced me to the carpenter foreman, whom he had talked to on the phone. The box was locked in a small storeroom to which my father still had a key. He opened the door and walked up to the box. I saw what was in his mind, so I crossed in front of him and seized it.

All my life I'd seen him with that box on his shoulder. He balanced it lightly with one hand and tipped his hat to the ladies on our block with the other. Even back when I was a child, men had stopped carrying things on their shoulders, but he did it so naturally that he never looked out of place. The box was about two and a half feet long, eighteen inches high, and six inches thick. It was made of plywood, stained mahogany, with metal-reinforced corners, and it held a surprising number of tools, because they were all ingeniously fitted into special slots. Although, as I said, I'd seen the box all my life, I'd never picked it up. I would no more have picked it up than I would have picked up my mother, as my father sometimes playfully did. Still, now that the time had come, I approached it without thinking about it.

The handle was hard. It even seemed callused, like his hand. I bent over and wrapped my palm and fingers around it and straightened up. The tendons inside my elbow and

shoulder stretched to their full length and snapped painfully
taut. I almost lost my balance, and the tools clinked telltale
in the box. My father looked away and glanced uncom-
fortably at the carpenter foreman.

In the few steps it took to reach the street, my arm was
already tired. It was three blocks to the subway. He said
very gently, "Put it on your shoulder, Paul," so I lifted it
with both hands to my right shoulder, where it rested on a
bone and cut into the muscles at the base of my neck. Although I continued to support it with both hands, I was
drenched with sweat after the first block, and the muscles
in my stomach were cramping on an inexplicable emptiness which seemed to have usurped the place where the seat
of my strength should have been. I was more than thirty
years younger, taller and heavier, and stronger, I knew, than
he was, yet I felt that my blood vessels were about to burst.
My legs trembling, I set my will blindly on reaching the
subway. People stared at me, but I hardly noticed them,
and he looked straight ahead, walking neither slowly nor
fast, his face noncommittal. The expanding sensation in my
loins made me forget the pain in my shoulder and in my
neck. From my solar plexus to my pelvis I was ten feet long.
My head was spinning, and things were whirling around me.
At the end of the second block, I lurched off the curb and
thought I would fall on my face, when my father's hand
on my arm stiffened me and seemed to resuscitate my
strength. "Wait for the light," he said.

For a blind moment I stood there, not recognizing my
deliverance, then I put the box down. I felt so light then I
thought I could have taken my father under one arm and
the box under the other and flown home. When I picked
it up again, I knew I could make it.

At my mother's incessant urging, my father agreed to
wear the collar. After the first day he even wore it with a
certain amount of independence, like the captain of a ship
wearing a lei put around his neck by Hawaiian girls trying
to sell favors to the tourists. At times he condescended to
it so successfully that the *collar* seemed absurd. When we
went to the hospital for his second visit, he wore it willingly,

remarking that it was only to please Dr. Windelband, the chief diagnostician.

Dr. Windelband looked so much like St. Peter that he was almost comically suited for his job. Very tall, he had iron-gray hair, bushy eyebrows, and a great decisive rudder of a nose. He greeted my father very graciously, and my father introduced him to me. I thought he shook my hand rather peculiarly, as though a handshake were a very revealing form of auscultation. I felt that he had illicitly taken some knowledge of me in that brief grip. He asked my father how he felt, and under his majestic solicitude my father naturally said fine. "That's good," he said, "because we have a little surprise on the program today. We want to get the inside story on you, so we're going to give you a cystoscope. They can sometimes be unpleasant, but I don't think that will bother an old soldier like you."

I didn't think so either. I'd seen my father fish around in the fleshy part of his hand with a sharp knife to look for a glass splinter, and it was his boast that he had pulled one of his own teeth with a pair of pliers. After they went off down a corridor, I sat in the waiting room reading a picture story—not in a medical journal, but in a popular magazine —on "breastplasty," a new method of building up women's breasts by stuffing them with plastic sponges. I had already finished the article and I was turning the magazine upside down to get a better look at the patient on the operating table when a nurse came out and called my name. Taken by surprise, I shut the magazine, then I looked up and she caught my eye with the curiously direct glance that only nurses seem to have, but which, this time, was softened by an expertly disciplined compassion. There was something so professional, so authoritative, about that compassion, that a cold breath blew through my belly, and I jumped up out of my seat. Without a word, she turned, and I followed her. In the corridor she stopped in front of a door and with a brief gesture of her hand said, "Your father is in there."

But my father wasn't in there. Sprawled on a table, in-credibly out of place, lay a plaster Prometheus, middle-aged and decrepit, recently emptied by an eagle, varnished and highly glazed as though still wet. Or perhaps, when you looked closer, this was just an illusion, born of an idea, and what actually lay there was only an eviscerated old rooster, plucked white, his skin shiny with a sweat more painful than blood. . . . Whatever it was, it wasn't my father. It might have been an old man, trembling and staring into eternity, whom I helped, avoiding the puddles of his exploded bladder, to dress, and who staggered out on my arm, but he was not in the least like, bore no resemblance whatsoever, to my father, who was still a relatively young man, slim and straight, with a quick step and a dark eye.

For three days my father didn't sleep, and I didn't either. On the fourth day I presented myself at the hospital and asked for Dr. Windelband. He appeared almost immediately, wearing a white coat. Without asking me what I wanted, or why I was there, he simply walked up to me and looked at me rather speculatively, as though he were trying to guess my weight. "Come along," he said, and I followed him through the corridor to the elevator. He pressed the button and turned toward me. The elevator door opened at the same time that my mouth opened to speak, and an attendant rolled out an empty wheelchair. The doctor took my arm and drew me into the elevator. I stood beside him, facing the door, waiting for it to open on the answer. He took my arm again, and we stepped out into an empty corridor. He stopped there, looking down at me. He was so tall that he seemed to peer over every screen I might erect. "The cancer has reached his bones," he said. "I'll give him six months."

I wanted to say, "Why will you only give him six months?" but this impulse seemed to be struggling, through an immense snowdrift, to the surface, where it might take shape, so I just stood there, allowing his words to find their final location in my head without passing through the complicated machinery of recognition. They went in like a film he'd given me to develop in a darkroom, or a record to be played on my phonograph sometime when I was in a listening mood.

"Are you going to take him in as a patient?" This was all I could find to say.

He removed his pince-nez. "We don't keep incurable cases," he said.

"No, you send them packing," I said, and then I bit my lips to stop a hysterical laugh.

"There are nursing homes." He peered at an even steeper angle over the screen, so that he could see to the very bottom of me, like a man looking down a shaft. He put on the pince-nez again. "Your father's a nice man," he said, and he walked off down the corridor.

Damnation is faint praise. It's not hell-fires or a Dantesque place presided over by an indefatigable devil, nor even the more sophisticated "room with other people. . . ." It's faint praise. "A nice man!" Can that phrase, or praise, penetrate an inch of eternity? Is that all sixty-two years achieve? Is that what the cystoscope said? A nice man be damned! He's a prick! He's a saint! He's a hero, a clown, a Quixote. . . .

My mother's nice husband was not doing so nicely, and it was my job to tell her. After that, someday when she was through crying, I would try to tell myself. Not now, though, there was too much else to do.

The next day, I went over. She answered the door with a faintly beseeching look in her eye, like a dog that wants to be taken for a walk. He was upstairs in bed. I felt that this was as bad a time as any. "Mom," I said, engaging her eyes for the first time in more than twenty years. "Mom," I said again, rapidly discarding words in my mind, getting no further. She looked at me as a girl looks at her first lover the first time, her eyes shiny with fear and regret and suppressed excitement, her soul splayed open to indistinguishable joy or pain, her whole being a question that strained, strained, toward an answer. . . .

"Mom," I said again, and she burst into tears on my breast, crying so copiously that after a while I felt like a child who has wet himself.

I decided to call a nursing home. I went through the Red Book and selected what seemed to be a likely place. After several rings, a woman's voice answered the phone.

"Hello," I said. "My father is a cancer patient and I would like to place him in your care."

The voice came back dry and impersonal: "Is he disfigured?"

"*Disfigured?*" I said. "I'm calling the home for cancer patients. . . ."

"Yes," the voice came back without inflection, "I inquired whether the patient is disfigured. We do not accept disfigured patients."

"No! He's handsome!" I shouted. "He's beautiful!" and I disfigured her ear with the receiver.

I had a savage desire to nurse him myself, to keep our sorrow secret between us, to fight off his illness with tooth and nail, but we had to send him somewhere, because the groans were beginning to pry open his teeth. The family doctor gave him injections, but they lasted only an hour. I could tell when they wore off by the clenching of his jaws and the stare in his eyes as he locked his will around the pain and tried to contain it. The doctor came as often as he could, but after two days of this he advised me to send him to a hospital. I was seeing him to the door when he paused and murmured quickly, almost furtively, "He needs more than I can give him—even if I had no other patients." This sounded more like recommending his soul to heaven than his body to a hospital, and after he had said it, observing too his own despairing tone, the doctor hesitated and swallowed, trying to swallow his remark, in obedience to the unwritten law that death shall be denied until it is certified.

"Which hospital?" I asked. "Memorial won't keep him, and as for the nursing homes . . ."

"Nursing homes won't do," he interrupted quickly. "He's an emergency case." He looked at me half sadly, half uneasily, afraid I might demand that he say it.

"What do I do?" I said. "Call the police emergency squad or the fire department? Isn't there someplace in this insane city where a human being can lie still and be sick? Do I have to appeal to the A.S.P.C.A.?"

"You'll have to put him in Kings County," he said apologetically. "There's nothing else you can do. I'll declare him an emergency."

At that moment, by way of bidding the doctor goodbye, my father declared himself. We heard a cry that sounded as though it came from a creature that had just acquired a voice in the furthest reaches of pain, and was now exploring that pain and that voice simultaneously, intermittently confusing one with the other. I stood there like a singing teacher fascinated by a pupil who has just produced an unearthly sound, unable to decide whether this was the most beautiful sound I'd ever heard or the most blood-curdling. The doctor ran back into the room. My mother came from the kitchen, where she had taken a habit of retreating whenever she could, but she stopped at the threshold of the door, because she was not of the initiate, and this was a matter so serious and so strange as to be a legitimate concern only for the doctor who was a professional intimate of such mysteries, and for her puzzling son, whose own mysteries must be somehow akin to this one.

Opening his bag, the doctor spoke to me over his shoulder. "Call Kings County for an ambulance," he said.

"An ambulance!" my mother said. It was true then.

There's no use pretending that Kings County was a chamber of horrors. It wasn't—it was just a hospital with too many sick people and too few well ones to take care of them. Actually, it gave me a feeling of confidence. It impressed me as a place where everyone had gotten down to brass tacks. It was a huge factory for repairing human organisms, a factory whose commitments always exceeded its capacity, a sort of sweatshop, in fact, but one where each man did his best with whatever he had. They put in a bed for my father in a big room in a tight space which they created by shifting a dozen other beds. He fitted in like a piece in a jigsaw puzzle. There his misery had so much company that illness almost took on the aspect of a universal condition. Squeezed between the beds, their standing figures reminding me of little fences around graves, were the relatives—I felt they had to be relatives—some, their hopes already exhausted, simply looking on silently, others talking sharply, practically, daring the sick to die when there were so many chores waiting for them.

My father diverted himself by criticizing the place. He

tried to discredit his illness by discrediting the hospital. He
had only one good thing to say about it—the doctor in
charge of his case was Jewish. Although he was a half-
hearted anti-Semite, he much preferred a Jewish doctor because he believed that Jews had a better grip on life. He
regarded the doctor as a sort of pawnbroker who would
make his ticket pay off. He wasn't in this business for his
health—or for my father's health either—but to get results.

And so we settled down to wait, my father waiting for his
return to normal life, a life which he would appreciate a
little more carefully thereafter, keeping out of drafts, and
avoiding strains and overspiced foods, but one which he
never thought of leaving; my mother waiting like an ostrich,
her head buried in the sand but the rest of her offered up
quivering more helplessly than ever to the inevitable catas-
trophe; I waiting like an actor, playing straight man to a
father who was disappearing before my eyes.

There were ups and downs—the room emptied out until
there were beds only along the walls with a few feet between them for us to stand in, and then there was the arrival
of a new anesthetic which helped for a while—but mostly
it was a process of measuring each day's ravages and denying their significance with an ever more preposterous optimism. After a week or so, he couldn't use his legs any
more, and they told me that every day he got up and fell
on his face. When they gave him a wheelchair, he exhausted
himself spinning through the wards and the corridors, afraid
of becoming rooted to a spot. They threatened to take the
chair away from him, and this so offended him—he had expected them to admire his gumption—that he only used it
when absolutely necessary after that.

My mother and I relieved each other every day like sen-
tries. She came mornings, and I arrived in the afternoon.
Fifteen minutes after I'd arrive, she'd leave. It wasn't that
she couldn't stay later or I couldn't come earlier—she had
nothing to do, no one to cook or keep house for, and I had
school only three nights a week—it was because we weren't
comfortable with him together. It was harder to put on our
respective acts convincingly in the presence of someone who

really knew. Our acts didn't harmonize well, either. They only do in soap operas, where everyone is unanimous in a kind of homogenized grief. The extremity of the situation had thrown each of us into a crucial relation to him, and the finality of these individual equations had made them intensely selfish. When we were there together, we were artificial, ashamed of both our hypocrisy and our emotion.

Sometimes he slept while I was there, especially after a bad night. During these hours I let my vigilance sleep too, and observed the rest of the ward, seizing every detail with unconscious gratitude. My senses alerted by the close threat of impending insensibility, I saw everything in such sharp relief that I felt I had just discovered the third dimension. It was on one of those occasions that I discovered Miss Shannon, the nurse who came on duty at four in the afternoon. I'd seen her before, and I had even felt some surprise that first time, but I'd never had a chance to speculate on her. What surprised me was her astonishing freshness. She might have been one of those white-uniformed demonstrators at a department store cosmetics counter, except that she had no trace of hardness. She was the type you also see in Rheingold Beer ads, with an almost explosive smile, and so young-looking that I wondered how long she could have been a nurse. Her complexion was so fair, her lips so red, her eyes so blue, that she reminded me of a patriotic image in pastels, the winner of some title such as Miss American Flag. She seemed invariably in high spirits, making her rounds with an expression of almost insane glee. I found this first surprising, then incongruous, and finally obscene. Although she fascinated me, I began to detest her, and although she seemed more candy-like than carnal, I longed to bite her round, aseptic and ungirdled behind as it moved tauntingly alive beneath her silky nylon skirt. Once, when she stood silhouetted against the window, her thighs clearly outlined—as though by their own gleaming light—I felt for a dazzled moment a wild impulse, a kind of call, to seize her and fuck her in the middle of the floor, and thus by sympathetic magic to resuscitate those failing men to whom she must have seemed more mirage than oasis.

I didn't suffer as much as might have been expected during those weeks. Perhaps it was because I had so much time. I had time enough to think everything away. I remember reading about a man in prison who figured the square root of two to two thousand places. He proved analogically that even the confines of his tiny cell were capable of almost infinite extension. I analyzed my situation and my father's —which might also have been thought to be inescapable— into so many places that I lost sight of the problem. It was just like my efforts to write, which I usually describe in terms of an old Irish joke: A middle-aged Irish couple are visiting another shanty Irish pair. Presently, Mrs. O'Grady of the visiting couple asks where the toilet is. "There ain't any," replies her hostess. "Begorrah, thin where do ye go?" asks Mrs. O'Grady. "Why, it's as easy as pissin' out the winder," says the lady of the house. "Yis, but what of thim as has ter shit?" pursues Mrs. O'Grady. "Why, them'll shit on the floor and sweep it around until they loses it." When they didn't fly out the window, I swept my ideas around until I lost them. As a result, I came to know the cracks in the floor pretty well, but I didn't realize this until much later.

I remember one crack in particular. At the time, I had just begun some courses at the New School in order to get the veteran's allowance. One of them was a philosophy course given by a little German whose accent somehow clothed everything he said in a sort of pseudo profundity, so that I could never separate the platitudes from the insights. On the first night, he waited with his hands clasped on the desk and a faint smile on his lips until we were all seated and duly expectant. Then he shot out quickly, without any other introduction, "What is the meaning of your life?" The class, of course, laughed, and this was partly his intention, to create an effect of startling directness—but in my condition I was like a glass which shatters when a particular note is struck, and this question, which I had, until then, contained, spilled all over me. I was so carried away that I actually expected an answer. I bent all my attention on the little German, translating each of his words into italics as it came out of his mouth. I followed him, antici-

pated him, I urged him on, faster, faster! I shifted in my
seat from one digression to another, and then I saw what
was in the wind. Setting out full sail with "What is the meaning of your life?" he circumnavigated into "What is the
meaning of meaning?" There, in that Sargasso Sea, he be-
calmed me. I was both confused and bemused. I felt I had
been taken in by an elaborate and inappropriate prank, like
the people in Paris who were the victims of a notorious Sur-
realist gag. They went to see a famous tragedy, advertised
with the best actors. After a portentous wait, the curtain
shot up to reveal—a tremendous rusty machine, whirring
and clanking, whistling and pumping, hissing and shower-
ing dirty precipitated steam on starched shirt fronts and
bare bosoms. These people, though, had their indignation,
and the Surrealists had their joke—I, I had my father, and
he, he had not only his son but his cancer, which, in spite of
all the swords with caducei on their handles, still jealously
guarded its secret.

I wasn't ready to give up yet. I carried my question carefully away with me, and that night it was a lullaby that put
me to sleep. In the morning I had forgotten it, but when I
saw my father I remembered, and then it seemed as though
he must have—or be—the key to the secret. When he opened
his lips to greet me, I half expected the answer—a newly
coined proverb, an aphorism so apt as to seem even obvious.
I looked for a radiance to rise from his flesh, I put my ear
to the shell of his hollowed body as one listens to the murmur of a conch, waiting for the stage whisper. Could this
pain be with a program? Can a man emaciate without
meaning?

He had a thoughtful expression on his face. "You know,"
he said, "I haven't had an erection since September twelfth."

When I was not with my father, he usually disappeared
from my mind, as I said before. I rarely reproached myself, at the time, for this, I considered it a trick of repression
which he himself and my mother had taught me. It was
when I came out of the elevator on his floor, when I was
walking through the corridor toward his ward, that he became intensely actual again. From the door of the ward, six
beds away from him, I tried to get an instantaneous esti-

mate of his condition, I sniffed like a bloodhound for signs. There was nothing to see—he was either awake or asleep, supine in the bed, because after the first few weeks it hurt his back to sit up—but I became so accustomed to his outline under the sheets that I could tell even from the doorway, when he had the bedpan underneath him. And I was always as pleased as a young mother about the bedpan, I regarded it as a good sign.

I was completely unprepared then—as though I had expected him always to remain the same—to find his hands in the air that day, immobile as death, and excruciatingly cramped in the act of sculpting a likeness of his pain. And the other astonishing thing was that no one in that ward of forty people paid any attention to those hands which ought to have conducted the orchestrated empathy of every living soul in sight.

I ran to his bedside to find his eyes open. "What is it, Pop?" I asked. "What do you want?" His eyes seemed glazed, but at the sound of my voice they swiveled ever so slowly, traveling a great distance, until they pointed at me. I say pointed at me, but it was rather that they focused on one point immediately in front of me and one directly behind me, so that I was bracketed in a no man's land of his gaze. He moved his lips to speak the unspeakable, then his eyes roved away and I ran for the nurse.

She was utterly uninfected by my excitement. "My father —" I began, but she said "All right!" rather tartly, picked up a needle wrapped in gauze, and walked alongside me to my father's bed, holding herself so aloof from my excitement that no one would have guessed that we were going to the same place for the same purpose. Unceremoniously pulling down his left arm like a vandal destroying a statue with a club, leaving the other grotesquely widowed in the air, she jabbed the needle unerringly into his vein, as you would flip a switch to turn off a motor, and put him to sleep.

I stood there looking at her dumbfounded—whether with horror or admiration I still can't say. Then, as all the while, she wore that infernal smile, and it was at that moment that I resolved, at any cost, to wipe it off her face.

Suddenly my father became immune to anesthesia. He couldn't have chosen a better time, because his illness was at its fullest flowering, rotting his entire skeleton until the very marrow of his bones ran with pain. Even the new wonder drug had hardly any effect. I became a beggar, begging the nurse for needles, for anything which would help him. She gave him as many as his constitution could stand, but they didn't make any difference. In fact, he began to hate the needle, flinching under its prick as though he wasn't already hurting to the limit of his capacity. Bizarre as it may seem, I began to believe that he was *insisting* on his pain. Just as a young mother wants to feel herself give birth, he seemed to want to feel himself go back into unbeing. Or perhaps he was trying to come to grips with his pain, to recognize the power he was wrestling with.

His struggles were not beautiful to behold, but I beheld them. I felt that it was my duty not to miss a single one of his writhings. His whole body had become a tongue, addressing its message to me. He was leaving so little behind that nothing could be ignored. I wanted to make movies of him to educate my children. Watching him, I learned that the convulsions of death and the convulsions of love differ only in that these were experienced utterly alone.

Now his strength fell away faster—and, against my will, mine grew. It seemed we had only a fixed amount to divide between us: as he gave it up, I acquired it. I tried to give it back, to refuse it, to make myself small, but the smaller I squeezed myself, expelling all my breath and deflating my chest with enormous sighs, the smaller he would shrink. We were on a seesaw, a scale, and my weight was catapulting him into oblivion.

It was too much for my mother. One morning she couldn't get out of bed to go to the hospital. The doctor came and diagnosed her illness as one that would last a little longer than my father. Now I ran from the hospital to her. We became a right-angled triangle in which I lied to her about the hypotenuse. "He's resting much better, the anesthesia works again, he asked about you, etc."

By that time, I was such a familiar figure around the floor that I often ate with the ward boys. When my father was

asleep, I roved all over, talking to ward boys, patients, relatives. While I was on one of these jaunts, I passed Miss
Shannon sitting at her desk over her reports. I thought I
heard her giggle, and I turned around. This time she didn't
try to smother it, she just laughed. A rage which came from
somewhere else rose up in me, but a deep, urgent curiosity
outweighed it, so I said, "What's so funny?" She laughed
again, but my curiosity grew instead of my anger, and I
said again, "What's so funny?"

"You!" she said between giggles.

"Why?" I persisted. "Why am I so funny?"

"The way you come here," she said.

"The way I come here?"

"Go on," she said, still laughing silently. "I've got my
reports to make out."

Sitting beside my father's bed, I conceded that perhaps it
was funny after all, the comic enigma of my devotion, and
for a moment I saw myself as someone who has missed the
joke, who stands by, a lugubrious and uncomprehending
figure, amid general laughter. Still, I thought, true or not, it
was another score to settle with her.

I saw so much more of her at that time that my obscure
desire began to burn like a rash in my mind. I decided to
launch a campaign, a very carefully thought out campaign,
because it had to succeed.

"You know, Miss Shannon," I said to her the next chance
I got, "I think that your presence and your spirit does more
for these men than the doctors' medicines."

She looked at me with mild surprise behind her smile. It
was the first speech I had made her. Still, she did not seem
disinclined to accept it.

"Even the doctors admit," I pursued, "that the *will* to
live often means the difference between life and death. To
these old men in this gray ward you are an advertisement
for life. Your warm smile and your yellow hair remind them
of the sun that once seemed to shine especially for them,
your blue eyes just naturally suggest the sky on a perfect
day, and your youth calls up a picture of a girl they knew,
or married forty years ago—or perhaps even of a grand-
child today." I spoke these words with an air of wistfulness,

as though I was thinking profoundly and nostalgically of my father.

Changing pace, so as not to lay it on too thick, I shifted to a different tone: "I studied philosophy in college," I said, "and I remember a professor asking us 'What is the meaning of your life?' Well, of course, we didn't know, and neither, it turned out, did he, but I've got a notion—I can't exactly say why—that *you* know. Maybe you don't realize it, maybe you never stopped to think about it, but I think you know."

This was one of the few rare occasions when the smile left her face. When she wasn't smiling, her face seemed arrested on the brink of thought, hesitating to cross over. I leaped into the breach. "For weeks now," I said, "I've been watching you and admiring the way you carry yourself. I've wanted to talk to you, to ask you so many questions about the things you've learned, the kind of things that only intimate daily contact with life and death teaches you, the kind of feelings which a man, a doctor, wouldn't know how to receive. . . . But I was always afraid you'd think I was crazy if I asked you . . . or that you'd misunderstand."

I could see that this speech touched her, and at this knowledge a wave of guilt suddenly flushed through me—but it was half pang, half thrill, and it only whetted my appetite. "I know I'm keeping you from your work," I said hastily, as though interrupting myself, "I know you have no time to talk to me here . . . and so I wondered . . . well, I wondered if sometime, sometime we might talk afterward, I mean, after you leave here. . . ."

She still seemed to be trying to think, a child trying to decide whether she dared run across the street after her ball. She's really so unsophisticated, I thought. Without the needle in her hand, she was another person. She reminded me of Ray Robinson, the most stylized performer ever to climb through the ropes in Madison Square Garden, but just a simple Harlem boy outside them. Or a young ballet star, breathtaking on the stage and pedestrian in life. It was too easy, I would have to do it while she was shoving the needle in *my* arm, so that we could, like two scorpions, sting each other to death.

"Well," she said, the clouds in her eyes clearing up, "I guess so."

"Good!" I said warmly. "I'm very glad. Tonight?"

"No, tomorrow," she said, and the smile came back.

My father and I didn't talk much. We never had. When I was a child he wouldn't; when I reached adolescence, I wouldn't. After that, we were so far apart that we couldn't have heard each other across the distance. Beyond a few fixed general remarks, he never spoke of his illness, so I didn't either. The phrase "When I get out of here," and his use of the future tense showed that he wanted to think this way. I tried not to have to join in this, because I couldn't make it sound convincing. It's one thing for a man to choose to fool himself; as a piece of practical solipsism it has a certain reality. But when someone else chimes in, his motives being so much weaker, his contact with the lie so much less intimate and passionate, everything rings false. Besides, my presence brought him peace, and he was usually satisfied with this.

With my mother, it was just the opposite. We talked all the time, as though silence were an accusation. A thousand times, she would ask me the same questions about my father's condition, and a thousand times I would vary the same lies. If she wanted to know, she knew. If not, well then I'd lie like a broken record until she no longer demanded it. "I'm going to get up out of this bed and go and see him!" she would suddenly announce in a tragic voice. "No, you're not," I would answer, "I'm not going to have both of you in the hospital," and so on in that vein. We kept our mouths stuffed with platitudes so that there was no room for sudden blurts or ejaculations, for sobs or curses, truths or revelations, for admissions, recognitions, definitions, for candid remarks, apostrophes, ambiguities, aposiopeses, for embarrassing moments, slips of the tongue, for free associations, recriminations, I-told-you-so's, or for any other quirk of communication that might have created the impression that we were a mother and son about to lose a husband and father.

As I came down the corridor of the hospital, my mind was teeming with schemes and scenes for my rendezvous with Miss Shannon. My heart was beating too hard, and I felt I couldn't conceal my gloating, so when I passed her desk I merely inclined my head and gave her a grave nod as if to say we will speak later. To my surprise though, she beckoned to me, and her face was so unreadable that I thought it was all off. But she just said, "He's in there," and pointed to a doorway across from her desk, which was set in an alcove cut out of the corridor. That phrase "in there"—so nondescript, uttered so uninflectedly, accompanied by the brief gesture of a hand with a pen in it—I had heard that phrase before, and suddenly I wondered whether, in their training, they were taught such phrases to be used on painful occasions like drugs, or strait jackets. Expecting the worst, I went through the door.

Expecting the worst—that's another phrase for you. We *never* expect the worst. I didn't recognize him at first, he was so bad. His mouth was open and his breathing was hungry. They had removed his false teeth, and his cheeks were so thin that his mouth looked like a keyhole. I leaned over his bed and brought my face before his eyes. "Hello darlin'," he whispered, and he smiled. His voice, faint as it was, was full of love, and it bristled the hairs on the nape of my neck and raised goose flesh on my forearms. I couldn't speak, so I kissed him. His cheek smelled like wax. His hand came up, light as a feather, on my shoulder. There was a chair against the wall. I pulled it up to the bed and sat down, taking his hand in both of mine. He closed his eyes. I rose out of the chair, but a vein throbbed in his neck, so I sat down again.

Sometime later—it might have been five minutes or two hours—the doctor came in. He looked at the chart at the foot of the bed, made some notes on a clipboard, and walked out. I ran after him and stopped him in the corridor to ask the inevitable question. He was young, heavy-set, and competent-looking, the competence crowding out all other expression from his face. He looked at me for a moment, and said, "A day, two days. . . ."

I went in and sat down again, taking his hand again in

mine. His eyes were closed. "A day, two days. . . ." Here
it was. All at once, the reality of it yawned in my mind and
found me standing on a brink, like an arctic explorer looking out alone over endless fields of ice. I would have liked
to cry—a great loop curled through my being—but I could
not. I could not cry for my father, and *this* realization
brought the tears to my eyes.

My proposed encounter with Miss Shannon seemed more
incongruous than ever, but I had had enough of congruous-
ness. I let her know I would wait, and she accepted this
with her standard smile. I went out to the candy store across
the street and bought a book. Then I settled down beside
my father who was asleep and waited for one thing or the
other.

I had selected a paper-backed Western. I learned to read
them in the army, like Eisenhower. The hero was the usual
superman, but instead of being grim-jawed or tight-lipped,
he had a sense of humor. His name was Happy Jack or
something like that, and he had a homely Will Rogers kind
of philosophy. Toward the middle of the book he got off a
remark that wrenched me suddenly back to reality. In a
crisis, everything wrenches you back to reality. He said, "I
want to have so much fun that when I die I'll laugh like
hell."

I was making the obvious comparison this remark suggested when they wheeled another bed into the room. The
room was long and narrow, so they situated it below the
foot of my father's bed. Lost in the sheets and pillow, I
saw a dark spot, apparently a Negro patient to keep my
father company in death's antechamber here outside the
ward, like the exit chamber in a submarine from which you
ascend to the surface through ever-decreasing pressures.
The man was so thin that his form was wholly invisible under the sheets, even on this hard bed. As soon as the bed
was in place, the doctor wheeled in a plasma rack, hung the
plasma bottle, and inserted the tube in the dying man's arm.
A woman stopped the doctor outside the door, a little spare
woman, very dark and angular. She was dressed neatly, but
twenty years out of date, and she wore her hat pulled down
and straight across her brow. She too asked the question,

then, walking resolutely up to the bed, she looked down at the sick man the way a workman approaches his bench. "Lord!" she exclaimed, "Lord! Come down and help this man! Come down and help your child! This is your child you redeemed with your blood, Lord!" She had a strong West Indian accent which gave her speech a precise, ceremonious quality. "Lord!" she cried again, her right hand seizing the plasma rack, whose short horizontal bar formed a cross, "Lord! Come down and *take* your child! Come down and *carry* him to glory!" The plasma bottle with its translucent tube undulating Greco-like beneath was a hydrocephalic Jesus on that cross. "Lord!" she exclaimed again, "I'm praying to you, Lord! I'm praying to you to *take* your child into everlasting immortality!"

I had stopped listening to her. I was thinking, to whom can I recommend my father?— To the mortician? Where is his everlasting immortality?— In the city records? Why isn't he one of God's children?— Because he's a nice man instead? As midnight approached, I felt like a time bomb. I kept expecting her to break it off. But at twelve o'clock she was ready, with a trenchcoat over her white uniform. "Where do you live?" I asked, praying for the right answer. "West Seventy-sixth Street," she said, and it was as I had hoped, in the same direction as my place.

On the subway I plied her with talk to get her off guard, philosophical talk, to establish an atmosphere of shared irrefutability. I put the conversation on the level of values, I conjured up a fog of confused sincerity, the kind of sincerity that is behind most of the drastic, dispassionate mistakes girls make. She followed willingly enough, but very passively, as though she were tired and wanted to be carried. As the doors were opening on the Fourteenth Street station, I seized her and pulled her out of the train, exclaiming in a confidential voice, "I know a wonderful little place where we can talk in peace!"

I led her to the most deserted bar I could think of, and we took a booth in the corner. She consented to a double bourbon. I couldn't decide whether to keep leading her—it was the safer way—or to draw her out, because I wanted more of her included. But she wouldn't be drawn out, even with

the bourbons. She just smiled and nodded and answered
briefly. The smile, I noticed with some surprise, had
changed. It had changed from a meaningless, artificial ex-
plosion to an almost rueful expression with a hint of complicity behind it. I judged that it was about time. "Listen,"
I said, borrowing a tone of urgency from another source,
"I want to give you a book. A book that was written for
you, a book that belongs to you as much as your diary,
that's dedicated to you like your nurse's certificate."

I called for the check, paid it quickly, and led her out by
the arm. My apartment was four blocks away, so I bridged
the distance with talk, raving about *Journey to the End of
the Night,* the book she needed like she needed a hole in
her head. She followed me without slightest hesitation, but
so passively that she made me think of a blind person being
escorted across the street.

Going up the four flights, my eyes were so intent on the
pink beneath her white stockings—I thought I even discerned
delicate blue veins—that I stumbled and had to steady myself by seizing the banister. I had cleaned and ordered the
apartment with an obsessive devotion, and I snapped on the
lamp expecting her exclamation, but she said nothing, she
just walked three steps further into the room and stopped.
"Take off your coat," I said, and she unbuttoned it for me
to remove. I strode over to the bookshelf, still following the
script, and seized the Céline. When I turned with it in my
hand, about to hold it out, I saw the futility of the gesture
in her eyes. Confused, but undismayed, I let the book fall
and seized her in a death-grip and bore her backward to
the bed, where I took her with all her clothes on. Working
with feverish haste, I nailed the coffin, dug the grave, and
dropped my precious load.

Sometime later I woke and impatiently pulled her clothes
off under the bright light, exposing her pastel body like a
calendar painting in its inhuman healthiness. Taking up my
task again, I bore the pall, trod the tread of the dead, bowed
my head and tamped down the ruffled earth. I put all my
strength into pounding it, pounding it flat, but it remained
stubbornly round, heaving against me. I tried, I tried, but

flowers sprang up under the blade of my shovel, and I dropped it.

I was in a hospital, in bed, and a nurse was standing over me, smiling. Where was the needle in her hand? I wondered, and then, as my head began to clear, she spoke. But I couldn't make out what she said, and before I could answer she was gone.

My father broke down at last, and fear haunted his eyes for the first time. When I came in, he gave me a drowning look which told me plainly that he had been adrift in uncharted seas. His eyes sucked me in. They were twin drains in a sink down which blackish waters swiftly disappeared, suddenly widening as the tides ran out. They nursed, like infant mouths, on me. I tried to find some formula to feed them, but I felt shamefully inorganic. "Don't leave me alone," he whispered, "I'm afraid." I put my hand on his. "You're not alone, Pop," I said, "I'm here." His eyes went far away. "I wish I had a hundred of my children here, and their children," he said, "I don't want to be alone." "You're not alone, Pop," I said again. "I'm with you." "Yeah, I know, honey," he said, "I know," but there was no sense of solace in his tone, and I knew what he felt. You want everybody on earth to stop what they're doing and come to say goodbye *personally* to you. You want *humanity* to see you off, the way close friends see you off on a boat. The idea of unanimity, two billion people's sympathy, is the only commensurate condolence. I did my best. I tried to refuel him with filial devotion, to plug him into some unequivocal center or source, some socially recognized certainty, by virtue of which he could say "Therefore I am," and through which he could feel himself perpetuated. . . . I tried to radiate sunlight, to show him his way and warm him on his journey . . . but I concentrated myself so hard, so crystalline, willed myself so clearly, that I could only twinkle like a diamond. I turned my straining eyes on him like magnifying glasses with no son behind them. I tried, I tried, but the more I strained, the less was I able to make our relatedness *immediate,* the more I saw him, and made him see me—I can't say it any other way—*sub specie aeternitatis.*

The Lord had come down to take his child, so we were alone in the white oblong room, like an equation written on a piece of paper. At that moment, the imminence of emptiness was so immense that everything was reduced to a mathematical perspective, to an anxiety to introduce order into that void, to pull it into finiteness by a far-flung grapple of my will.

Miss Shannon was outside at her desk, and I knew that something lay between us, I felt some needle in me trembling on that point. Something lay between us, it was a carpet rolled out for me to walk on, but I could not, my mind was still struggling like a monkey wrench to squeeze an inconceivable space down to some possible size. Space had suddenly become tragedy to me, and I needed all my will to look out on it. Miss Shannon was millions of light years away, farther away than a star. Falling like a comet, I had passed near her, felt the pull of her gravity, but now I had plunged beyond.

The following day he fell into a coma. When I came in and looked into his face, I found no sign of recognition. His eyes stared out unfocused, like a newborn child's. I tried to engage them with my own, I tried like a hypnotist to synchronize them with my will, but they would not. I stared into them until I had to come up for air, and then on their surface I saw myself bloated almost beyond recognition, a corpse risen from their depths. His gaze cast back into his mind, far-flung, flung out of focus into an infinite space, not simply folding back on itself, but fixed on some point in inner space, as a navigator charts his course on a star, or a man with a word on the tip of his tongue casts his eyes back through the dictionary of his experience, seeking that word in a void of silence. "Pop," I said softly, letting my voice sink gently into the pool of his eye like a line, "Pop," but there was no ripple to undulate centrifugally worldward, no stir in that Coney Island mirror which had once immortalized, and now monstered, my image.

The doctor was standing beside me, his ever-present clipboard in his hands. All at once with that clipboard he reminded me of a dispatcher at an airport. I looked him squarely in the face, studying him carefully for evidence of contradiction, as though he were about to lie. He looked squarely back at me, and between us passed a tacit understanding, as in the movies one spy slips forbidden information to another. "Can he hear me?" I asked. "Yes," he said, his expression becoming competent again, impersonal, until he might have been discussing a theory of poetry. "Yes, he can hear you, but he can't answer."

Again I crouched over my father as the doctor went out. He can hear me, but he cannot answer; this coma, then, would be his coda. I stood there gathering the threads together, and as I looked down that long street I had a strong sense of *déjà vu*. I was in Pennsylvania Station, in uniform. It was my final leave before going over, and at that stage the odds were not in our favor. He knew it, and insisted on taking me to the train. We were standing in the aisle, facing each other, when the conductor sang out "All aboard!" as if he were some omnipotent arbiter dividing us into two groups destined for different fates. This cry froze us in our farewell, so that we were caught there, frozen in an instant of recognition, eternalized in a classical moment which turned us into statues kinetic with a terrific frozen impulse. Finally he put out his hand, and I gripped it with a vague force. He put his other hand on my shoulder, and now we were a modern tableau, all our tragic poise gone. "Keep punching, boy," he said, and the moment died. He disappeared down the aisle, and from my throat. I stared idly out the window, the moment thrown away like a cigarette at the entrance to a movie. I waited for the platform to move, but suddenly he was out there on it, a performer, unapplauded, ineptly come back for an encore. His lips moved, he was saying something to me. I couldn't hear through the double pane, so I nodded and smiled. He spoke again. I said aloud, "That's right, Pop," and people turned and looked at me. The train didn't move. He was going to wait. He unbuttoned his coat, and, seizing the lapel, swung it open as you would a door, at the same time bending his head sharply sidewise until he seemed to be smelling his armpit. This elaborate pantomime explained that he was drawing a cigar from his pocket. He held it up for me to see. "See,

I'm going to smoke a cigar while I wait for the train." "Yes, I see, you're going to smoke a cigar while you wait for the train." He struck a match and cupped it unnecessarily in the breezeless station. Hunched over his cupped palms, he puffed powerfully and rhythmically, like a locomotive slowly starting. It didn't start. Tilting his head back, he withdrew the cigar from his mouth, holding it at arm's length and exhaling a cloud of smoke. The train didn't move. He spoke to me again. I nodded and smiled, but something came over his face, some urgency which he had been inducing all this while like a constipated person reading a newspaper on the toilet. He began to gesticulate and move his jaws grotesquely, shaping words which before would not be molded by his mouth. The train began to move in slow spasms. He walked alongside, gesticulating and grimacing. I rose out of my seat, semaphoring through the glass. Now he was running. . . .

I took up where we had left off. "Pop," I said, "you've been a good father, just what I wanted, just what you were supposed to be. You made me into a good son, and I'll always remember. You did what you were supposed to do, you don't have to reproach yourself with anything. I'm proud of you, and you can be proud of yourself, too. I love you, Pop, just like a son loves his father, and as a man, too. God bless you, Pop."

I talked to him like this for a long time, crouched close, not because I cared whether anyone else heard, but because I wanted him to hear. As I spoke, listening to my own words as though they were the judgment of some third party, I realized with a mild astonishment that they were true.

Suddenly his eyes rolled in a wild surmise. I started, and almost lost my balance, as though I were standing on those wildly rolling orbs. What had he seen, where had his spirit careened? What was it that passed through him and spun his eyes like the spinning wheels of an overturned car?

"Pop," I said, bending nearer, "Pop," but as I opened my lips to let out this vowel, he gave a huge sigh and shot a great breath into my mouth. I caught it full, and it went all through me. I swallowed it like a toast, not knowing whether it was poison or elixir. I swallowed it full, and it inflated me until I swelled incredibly in the mirror of his eyes.

It was minutes before I realized that his heaving chest had gone quiet. Frantic, my eyes sought the vein in his neck. "Nurse!" I called, "Nurse!"

She bent over him, looked into his eyes and saw my image there, and drew the sheet over his face. For the second time, that great loop curled through me, trying to unfurl me, to shake out my length, untie my knot. I ran through the corridor to the stair. Halfway down, I folded, crouched on a step with my fists on my temples. I wanted it to come, I thrust my hand down the throat of my grab-bag being, but drew nothing out. It was like trying to start a cold motor. The last time had been in anger, eighteen years ago, at him. . . .

They wheeled him out of the land of the living, leaving only a small plastic bag in which his glasses and his false teeth rattled. Miss Shannon had it on her desk. I held it in my hand as she held me in her eyes. We stood there, the way my father and I stood in the train. "If—" I said, and then I stopped, because I knew that the next word would be "only." She smiled the way she had that morning, and that was all we could do.

The ward boys looked very carefully at me as I walked down the corridor for the last time, studying my face for the reflection of death refracted through the living, but I had nothing new to show them, not yet.

Outside, the ground was covered with ice and the wind bit at my hands, but I welcomed it. I looked at the high gates and felt like a man released from prison. Passing the psychiatric ward, I saw a gray-clad figure, staring out of a heavily screened window with a wistfulness that only a maniac could feel. Watching him, I slipped on a little icy incline. My feet slid suddenly forward and I was about to fall when, without my willing it, my right foot shot backward to brace me, and I poised there a second, one foot in front of the other, arms extended for balance like a tightrope walker, then I recovered myself. All at once I felt exhilarated. How alive I was, how quick. . . .

"The king is dead. Long live the king!" I said to my mother. She spoke the language of hysteria, which I have never learned, but which I suspect is made up of clichés. I looked over her shoulder while she wet my shirt again. What if it were she? I thought. He died drily, after all, withering like a rose pressed in a book. He is the romance, but isn't she the reality? How organic she is, how unabstract. She could not wither or crumble—she could only putrefy, or melt, like the snails I poured salt on in our back yard. That must not happen, I knew, and then and there I placed her in the refrigerator of my heart.

I decided on the least expensive funeral. He hadn't left much insurance, and the house in the country had taken most of the money in the bank. I went to one of the big funeral chains, one which always stressed "correctness" in its ads. The entire front of the place—which they called a "chapel" although it was designed like a store—was of glass, so that the reception room where I announced the death of my father was an enormous show window. The clerk who received me referred to my father as "the deceased," which jarred on my nerves each time. I would have preferred hearing him called by his name, or referred to as my father. That's who he was, not "the deceased." If that would have sounded as though we were burying him alive, why that was all right too, because it was nearer to the truth.

Paying no attention to his niceties—he looked at me very gingerly, as if I was an important personage whose fly was open in public—I questioned the clerk about prices and finally said that I wanted a funeral as inexpensive as was consonant with simple dignity. This last phrase put him on his feet again, and we agreed on a price, which he described as a "ceremony."

Two days later I went back to "complete the arrangements." I had no idea what this meant, but I went. I was received by another clerk, and I identified myself, after which he said, "Would you like to see your father?" He said it just as a private secretary would, and suddenly I felt Who were all these people intermediating between my father and me? I should have taken a shovel and buried him myself.

I allowed myself to be led into a room. I waited for the clerk to make that gesture of the nurses, but his arms seemed to be sewed to his sides. He made a slight bow and disappeared. Standing just inside the door, I looked at the deep box, painted slate gray, its cover propped open like a jewel case to reveal a satin lining. I walked up to it, and then I saw a sight for which I will hold my fellow citizens responsible to my dying day, a sight for which I will forgive them only when I have made each one see himself in that same light. They had painted my father like a picture postcard, and padded his cheeks the way they pad their shoulders and brassiéres. They had produced his death in Technicolor, with 3-D, and painted a happy ending on him the way an old whore paints her face.

I decided to have him cremated. His ashes would be closer to his essence than the thing in the coffin. Besides, I didn't want to tie his memory to a little oblong of bought ground where he would rot with thousands of strangers. I was to be the only one at the funeral. My mother was still in bed, and I had discouraged all the family friends. This was between him and me, and besides, I knew that they would feel obliged to discuss the cheapness of the coffin among themselves.

I presented myself for the third time at the "chapel," and I was led out the back door where they sneaked out the bodies. I sat next to the hearse driver, and we set out for the cemetery. Halfway there, I was struck by the obscurity, the loneliness, the lack of reciprocal stir, of visible displacement, that attended my father's death. At first, I felt inclined to take the blame, but I knew it was his own fault, so I compromised and resolved to make up—I didn't know how, but I'd make up—for it.

Most of the way we drove through ordinary streets, but for the last few miles we were on a highway. For some reason the highway seemed more appropriate to our procession, if you can call a one-vehicle funeral a procession. The streets made me feel that we were in a delivery truck or a

taxi. Finally we entered the cemetery and arrived at a stone
building. The driver led me into what I suppose they would
have called another chapel. It had several small pews, and
up in front where the altar would normally be was a single
pew, facing the wall at a distance of perhaps a yard. A
faded velvet curtain or drape covered the wall directly in
front of this pew.

A big man who looked exactly like a plain-clothes man
in the movies came in. "Do you wish a service said?" he
asked me. I said no and with that he ushered me to the
single pew facing the drape. Not understanding anything
here, but feeling resigned, I sat down. A few seconds later
I jumped up again when a muffled and discordant hurdy-
gurdy struck up behind me. I spun around—the plain-clothes
man was seated at what seemed to be a toy organ, playing
an ungainly hymn by ear. I couldn't take it in, what he was
up to, and he had me hypnotized until I heard the curtain
sliding. Turning toward the wall again, I was sure then that
I was in some askew wonderland such as I've traveled in
dreams. The parted velvet uncovered a plate-glass window,
through which I could see, a few yards away, a little elevated track about waist-high. Out of nowhere, slowly moving along the track by magic, my father's coffin appeared,
floating along like a little trolley car, painted gray like the
old maintenance type which carried not passengers but
workmen. I stared at it as I would have stared at a floating
ghost performing a feat of levitation. Suddenly at the end
of the track, in what appeared to be a solid wall, a door
yawned open, and I found myself looking into an inferno.
The organ, the window, the track, the inferno, the plain-
clothes man . . . I had lost my balance and I was as close
as I'll ever come to screaming when my father disappeared
into the flames.

In the dim hallway, I made out a box before my door,
a square box, maybe a foot deep. I was pleasantly surprised, and mentally observed that I was not expecting a
package. My birthday was nowhere near, nor any holiday,
and I hadn't ordered anything. For a moment I was angry
at the deliverer for his carelessness in leaving it there where

anyone might steal it. I picked it up, noticing with satisfaction its solid weight, but then even in the dimness I made out the cemetery's name.

Here we were again. Another encounter in our endless series. I was actually glad to see him. I remembered then that I had refused to put him in that dovecote which was lined with loving cups commemorating games lost and races run. I took the box inside, and without opening it I placed it on the bookshelf.

I'd heard that ashes were supposed to be scattered from a hilltop to the four winds, or poured into the headwaters of a river going out to sea, but as I looked at the box on the shelf, I knew that those were not our ways. We knew each other much too well for that kind of make-believe. My mind was working with an unprecedented sureness, and without going into all the details, it gave me to understand one thing very clearly. It was my job to sift those ashes, and sift them I would, until he rose from them like a phoenix.

THE PRIZE

R. V. Cassill

R. V. CASSILL *was born in Cedar Falls, Iowa, and holds B.A. and M.A. degrees from the State University of Iowa. He served in the medical department of the U. S. Army during the war, and later spent time in France as a Fulbright Fellow. Mr. Cassill has taught at the University of Washington, Columbia University, The New School and the Writer's Workshop at the State University of Iowa. In 1954 he received a Rockefeller Grant for fiction writing. He has had about thirty-five short stories published and has received an* Atlantic *"First" prize and an O. Henry Prize Award.*

The first prize in the contest sponsored by the Goodyear Tire Company early in the Depression was, I remember, an overwhelmingly large one. It was probably $25,000; at any rate it was a sum on that scale, one large enough to inspire a variety of religious experience among contestants, and the scattering of lesser prizes had been conceived with similar grandeur. Looking back from a removal of two decades and from some comprehension of the economic and political turns of those years, I am impelled to visualize the Goodyear Co. struggling with titanic anxiety to shake free of the chaos that threatened organizations as well as individuals, and willy-nilly I have to admire the scale of their effort. They knew how big a battle we were in.

And I remember with a twinge that at the time of the contest I didn't even know there was a Depression. I knew we had moved out of the city to live near Chesterfield—

where my father was to work in his cousin's grain elevator
—for reasons that were not very happy or decent. But it
seemed to me when I weighed everything that we had been
expelled because of something ugly or shameful that my
family had done or because of some shameful inadequacy
in us into which it was best not to inquire too far. When I
learned, from eavesdropping on adult conversation, that my
father had lost $380 in a bank failure, I was ashamed of
him for not having had more on deposit. We lost our car
then, too, and I was pretty sure that this need not have
happened if he had had more of the installments paid on it.

There was very little talk between my parents which
named the name of Depression. Since they were both faithful Republicans who supported Hoover to the end, it might
well have seemed traitorous to them to use such a term—I
figured then it was like not holding your breath when something very important depended on your holding it.

A big green van took our furniture to the house near
Chesterfield, and the family followed in the car borrowed
from my father's cousin. We arrived on a rainy evening
just before dark, and there was the van backed up to the
house with the moving men carrying our familiar things into
its dark interior. Our rocking chairs, the fernery, and the
radio were going in where they didn't belong. The thought
struck me that we were moving into a house that no one
lived in. That was so strange. And whatever mystery was
being enacted, I didn't want it to happen. I wanted to hold
my breath long enough to keep it from happening.

Through the rainy fall of our first year in Chesterfield,
while I was trying to get used to the tiny school, to the
overpowering skills of the farm boys who were my new
classmates, and to the big old house we now lived in, I concentrated fiercely and stupidly on the problem of our expulsion from the city and began to see it as an omen of a world
committed totally to sorrow. I learned to read the most
trivial disappointments as signs that the race itself was
doomed.

Walking home after school between the cornfields that
bordered the road, I would hear the brittle noise of rain

on the corn leaves, and the surliness inside me would cry back to it, "Yes, that's the way things are, all right." In the dripping of the rain from the porch roof outside my window I saw a melting of even my memories of the time when things had been fun, and whatever I found disheartening or miserable I cherished.

Separating myself more than formerly from my brothers, who were two and three years older than I, I cultivated an almost erotic pursuit of tokens of decay. In this I was aided by one of the rooms on the second floor that had served all the former tenants in lieu of an attic.

Books, old magazines, a sewing machine, dress forms, and trunks of many funny sorts were piled in this room. Probably there was some sort of stipulation in the rental agreement that we were to have only "the rest" of the house, for my brothers and I had been forbidden to play in there. But if I was quiet I could slip into it from my own room wtihout my mother's hearing me where she worked in the downstairs kitchen.

In the room a smell of paper decomposing welcomed me and alerted my senses to a kind of dream that was detailed by the thousand articles of use and the souvenirs I stirred out of the trunks. I found an old cane with a metal bust of Lincoln for its head, the metal bearing an inscription linking it to the Republican convention of 1884. One of the trunks was half full of arrowheads and stone knives, some of them bearing paper tags that indicated they had been found in the river bluffs east of town. There was a stack of tintypes in another trunk which included pictures of the depot and the dedication of the Methodist Church. (If I wanted to I could look up and see this church through the window, sitting shabbily at the edge of a cornfield, now arched over with the elms that appeared in the tintype as twigs stuck in the loam around it. As far as one could see in such views the half-luminous white of ripe corn floored the river valley. I'd heard my father say in one of his moments of optimism that this was the richest soil on earth except for the Nile valley, and I worked on this idea too, converting it so I could gloat on these riches strung sense-

lessly under the rains and consoling my bitterness by noting
how universal the waste of things was.)

A green trunk in that room yielded a box of nickeled in-
struments which I now realize were the old-fashioned para-
phernalia of a woman's douche, and which had for me then,
ignorant as I was of their function, some quality of terminated ferocity, like the arrowheads piled in the trunk bottom—no longer an arsenal, but something oddly more than
a mass of junk.

When my mother found out that I had been playing in the
forbidden room and asked what right I had to be there, I
told her I had been reading the old magazines and books—
which was not entirely untrue. I didn't tell her that I had
jimmied the locks on most of the trunks or that I had read
batches of the old letters I found in them. Anyway, she discovered more trespasses by finding some of the arrowheads
in my treasure box that I kept in one of my drawers and
by noting small bits of vandalism. I had broken the head
of Lincoln from the cane and for no good reason (except
to mock at earthly vanity) had rubbed its nose off on the
sharp edge of a lock.

She came after me with some determination then. She
really insisted on an explanation of why I liked that room
well enough to play there so much. "With that dirty old
stuff," she said.

"Like with the arrowheads," I told her solemnly, "it
would help me remember there used to be Indians right
around here in the olden times."

"Ah," she said, mildly impressed and placated. "I see.
With them you could sort of pretend that the Indians were
still alive and more real. I see. Then I suppose you could
understand your history better and the way things are by
using that Republican cane."

She looked at me sharply. "Why did you break the cane
then?"

"I don't know."

"You shouldn't have done that to Lincoln. He was such
a great man," she said with a faraway look that seemed to
suggest he should have been my father. "It was awfully

wrong to break him up like that, but I'm glad if otherwise you learned anything."

My pretended agreement with her was a great fraud because her optimistic interpretation was so exactly wrong in its tendency. It had not been any sense of life in these trinkets that excited me. As they went through my hands I had exulted in them because they were evidence that so many who had been alive were dead and gone.

II

Far as she was from appreciating the content of my play in the closed room, my mother must have worried about it and found it inadequate, as she found so many things in our life at Chesterfield inadequate.

She had a bundle of grievances, and I think sometimes that what carried us through that winter and marked all of us forever with a special stamp was her refusal to admit the slipping downward that obviously accompanied our move to the little town. She had to take it but she wouldn't have it. She was going to lure me out to the old storeroom into some healthy activity whatever the cost, and for a while there was talk of getting me a subscription to the *Youth's Companion* even if that meant showing favoritism to me, since nothing comparable could be afforded "just then" for the older boys.

With the same frustrated force she approached the problem of utilities. There was no electricity in Chesterfield then and no bathroom in our house. From our arrival on she set the resources of her anguish to work on getting us a Delco light plant and plumbing, though with all her emotional heave in this direction and her heckling of my father she never worked out a practical plan by which we might expect to have them. She merely made us all hate fetching water from the pump more than we might have otherwise and made us all feel we would go stone blind from reading by a kerosene lamp.

What she couldn't hold onto with a full grasp she meant to cling to, as long as necessary, with her fingernails, and the obvious pity of this was that she could get her nails into nothing solid except us.

It was her passion's refusal to admit that things had changed which swept us into the Goodyear contest with such velocity and finally made it intolerable for us not to win.

Winter had come by the time the contest was announced. The evening we heard of it my brother George and I were in the kitchen helping my mother with the dishes while my father and older brother listened to the radio in the dining room.

"Hear that?" my mother cried out all at once. I thought she'd at least heard a car stopping at our front gate. But she motioned us to be still, and we got most of the announcement, not quite all. She marched into the dining room and demanded that my father explain the details she had missed.

"I wasn't entirely listening," he said guiltily, sleepily. "Just enjoying what they had to say."

"Enjoying? I don't see what there is to *enjoy* when he's talking about a contest. You ought to be listening attentively, or I don't know what's the point of listening at all."

"I know," he agreed. "I'll tell you what. It sounded like someone was going to get a patch of money, all right. I did hear them say there was a first prize of twenty-five thousand dollars. Moreover there's a whole kaboodle of little prizes."

"Little?" my mother wailed indignantly. "Why . . . why . . . *Little!* I heard myself that there were thousand-dollar prizes."

"I meant even smaller ones. Little dee-rigibles and things."

"A thousand dollars," my mother mourned his unconcern for this. "That's not so much it would wear our brains out figuring what to do with it. I wish you'd listen at the end of the program and be sure to get the details down on a piece of paper. No. You call me in if there's any more going to be said about it."

He took off his glasses and polished them slowly. "You sit down here and listen, Mother. The boys and I can finish the dishes. You're quicker at these things than I am."

"All I asked was for you to call me. Can't you even do that?" my mother demanded. "I know you're tired from your work and I wouldn't ask any more of you today."

Since he was in our big rocker and sitting as relaxed as a man can get and since it obviously wouldn't be much trouble for him to listen to the announcement, he naturally took her comment as sarcasm. So, when she'd gone back to her work, he tuned in another program.

"You hear that, Mama?" George said, wiping away like a good fellow at the dishes. "He's turned it off."

"Well," she said, "he's tired and cranky. He worked awfully hard today. You know it's always hard work at the elevator."

Then my father appeared at the kitchen door. In those days he was still wearing some of his old business suits to work and they always had grain dust in their fibers no matter how well he brushed them when he came home. The whitish dust in his clothes gave him an air of being faded like a picture from which some of the ink has been rubbed. He made a curious gesture, half in anger, half in appeasement, like a doubter crossing himself.

"You know what these darn contests are, Sally," he pleaded. "They don't mean anyone any good. They're only done to advertise the product."

"We'll talk about it later," my mother said. This was recognized by all as a threat.

"Did you personally ever know anyone who had won his postage back in a contest like that?"

"We'll not discuss it until the boys are asleep," she warned him. I think he began making up his mind to submit right then. I saw him swallow and then nod reassurance to himself that it might not be all as bad as he feared it could be.

From that first evening on, for weeks, our family had the contest like a vocation or a disease. Of course it was easy enough for my mother to find out the details of competition once she had made up our minds, and by the end of the week she and each of us boys were working on our individual lists of words that could be made from the letters

comprised in the name GOODYEAR TIRE AND RUBBER COM-
PANY. That was the task of the contest.

You can see that the first words come easily: dog, god,
ray, rite, and so on. It is when these are all put down that
the game becomes tantalizing and demoralizing. Then the
tongue tries nonsense syllables and combinations in the hope
that some lightly hidden word will fall out to be added to
the list. And that makes quite a noise in the house.

Once at supper I began mumbling to myself, and my
father, driven beyond exasperation, slammed down his water glass and howled, "Groggy, wayorv, boogly, boogly,
woogly, arf." Then he glared around the table with the
tears of the rejected squeezing angrily out of the corners of
his eyes.

"Not at the table," my mother cautioned me. She turned
to my father. "I don't know why you're so set against what
the boys are ambitious enough to try to do. I should think
you might better want to help them."

"I don't. Great Jesus, I won't," he said helplessly. "What
in His name would I be helping them to do? Lose their
minds and jabber like apes?"

"They've been working with our dictionary, and I don't
know that *that's* bad for their education," my mother said.
"The contest gives them something to look forward to."
She satisfied herself with such explanations, and for my part
I was thinking self-righteously that my father, in his outburst, had used *f*'s and *v*'s which of course, were not per-
missible under the laws of the game.

According to my mother's first, rather easygoing plan,
each of us was to work exclusively on his own list and even
keep it partly secret from the others so there would be a
sort of intrafamily contest as well as the larger one. We
worked from the dictionary by turns. It seemed to me sometimes when I was blundering unsystematically through it,
dreaming by lamplight, that each of us might win a prize
that suited his own intelligence and deserts. My mother
would probably get one of the thousand-dollar prizes. Dave
and George might or might not get something. Maybe one
of them would get a fifty-dollar prize, since they were older
than I. For myself, I thought and felt that I should win one

of the chrome-plated models of the dirigible *Akron,* the lowest prize offered. I think probably a hundred of these models were being given away. I remember telling my mother that I didn't think I was good enough to win more than a model, but that this suited me because I would rather have it than money anyhow. Altogether I managed to make this model into an image of what I was worth and of what the world would pay me for being what I was.

"You have to work hard if that's the prize you want," my mother warned. "Don't forget there'll be people from all over the country trying to win, just like you are."

When the deadline for submitting entries was approaching, my mother decided that we needed a larger dictionary to work from and that we should borrow one from the school. The question of who should borrow it became major. One of us boys should ask our teacher, she thought, but we all balked at this as being too embarrassing. The other boys got away with this argument, but I was caught —perhaps because I had done more excited talking about the contest than they.

"There's nothing wicked about borrowing a dictionary," my mother bullied me. "We're not doing something dishonest. We're working as hard as we know how to earn something, and if more people would do that I expect our country would be better off. Just explain to your teacher . . ."

This is odd, but maybe if I had believed that we were in the contest for the sake of competition I wouldn't have minded explaining to my teacher why I wanted the dictionary. Caught as I was in the dream of certainly winning a thousand dollars and a dirigible, I couldn't face it. It seemed to me like putting on airs to go to my teacher and admit the glory my family was headed for.

So my mother finally borrowed it. I remember her coming in through the snowy yard, a little after I had come home from school, with the big dictionary wrapped in a shawl to protect it from the mist in the air. Her face before she saw me was set with a harsh intensity, as of someone who has refused humiliation by sheer refusal to recognize it. Seeing me, she smiled and said, "Look. I borrowed it from your teacher after you'd left. She was good about lending it. Now you see that she would have lent it to you if you'd only asked her. Don't you see?"

"But what's she going to think of us?" After all, it was I who had to go to school the next day and possibly face my teacher's amusement, envy, or scorn.

"I didn't tell her what we were using it for," my mother said with a sly grimace that she meant to be comforting. "I fibbed to her, so don't you worry."

When I thought this over I announced that I didn't want to do the contest any more. My mother flung her arms around me and pressed my face very hard against her side. "Of course you do," she said. "We've worked so doggone hard this far that I'm convinced we're going to win. Maybe not the grand prize, but something. There's no reason why you can't win that dirigible if you want it. Don't you see that yet?" She frightened me with her determination, and even that was a lesser thing than the sheer giant onrush of the contest, beginning to reveal its true scope.

In the last week before the deadline—and this must have been in late January, at about the time of the thaws when the three of us boys would have liked to be playing outside —my mother bore down on us all. Some one of us had to be at the dictionary all the time. There wasn't any more talk of the contest's being educational or fun. It was work, and we had to work hard enough to win. We combined our lists now, at least to the extent that our inefficient systems permitted. We had begun without much system at all and, except for my mother's our penmanship was terrible. So, whether a word discovered in the dictionary at this late date or on someone else's list could legitimately be added to ours was a matter none of us could be quite sure of. Certainly each of us had duplications in his list, and none of us ever had quite the same total as any of the others though we tried to balance them for a while. Very late my mother tried to get us to alphabetize our lists, but this only got us in more tangles.

On the last afternoon Dave went to the post office immediately after school with his list and George's—that was a nervous precaution, since they had to be postmarked that day and some act of God might demolish the post office or block the road to it if we waited until too late.

On the other two lists at my mother's insistence we were adding all kinds of nonsense combinations which earlier had been only a means of helping us find pure words. Some of these, she said, we might have missed in the dictionary, and it was the responsibility of the judges to decide if they were eligible or not. *"Reay,"* she said. "That could be a girl's name. Put it down, anyway. *Burrec.* That sounds like a kind of donkey, I guess. *Yarg.* I don't see why that shouldn't be a word if there's a word *yard.* One doesn't sound like it meant any more than the other one, does it?"

She had the clock sitting on the table where we worked —the post office closed at six—and I knew that now nothing but time running out would stop her. My father came into this intensity and stood behind us, watching us without saying anything. Pretty soon my mother spoke over her shoulder to him. "If you're not going to help, go somewhere else. Go start the fire in the kitchen. I'll get supper as soon as we're finished."

"I won't," he said; and then after a long deliberation, "God damn the Goodyear Tire and Rubber Corporation."

"Company," I said.

"I suppose you mean God damn me," my mother said.

"I don't," he said. "I mean . . ."

"Shoo. Go on. I can't think while you're staring at me."

He went into the bedroom and after some banging of dresser drawers returned to throw an envelope and two ten-dollar bills on the list of words she was working on. "There," he said in a tone that was dignified only by its slightness. "There's some money and my insurance policy. I'm leaving."

"Ha," my mother said.

"You've turned the boys against me and driven them half crazy with this contest. I warned you not to do it."

"Then leave," my mother said. *"Dooger."*

After he was gone she kept muttering more and more absurd combinations of syllables. Her face flamed, and I

could see a vein in her temple bulge with her effort, but she
was not writing down any more of her inventions.

She looked up at George long enough to say, "Follow
him and see where he goes." Then she glanced hard at the
clock and told me to get my coat and rubbers and be ready
to run for the post office. "We can't be late," she said.
"You can run part of the way or go Scout's pace. You know
how to do that."

With an attempt to cheer me, she said, "You and I have
more words than the others now."

But, giving a last look at the physical ugliness of my list,
I said I wished there were time to copy at least this afternoon's work.

"Maybe if they can't quite make out some of them that
will be a good thing," she said craftily. Her imagination
apparently had strained to cover every accident of incom-
petence, weakness, taste, or unfairness on the part of the
unknown judges, and it seemed to me that she had intended
that each of our lists be somehow corrupt to fit the imagined
corruptness of the major human types.

As I was going out with the big manila envelopes containing our two lists, George arrived back to report that my
father had started west across the cornfield, had cut back
within about a quarter of a mile, climbed the fence into the
road, and was right now hiding inside a culvert about two
hundred yards from the house.

"Ha," my mother said. Her voice crackled with unhappy
triumph. "I supposed he wouldn't go far. He'll get hungry
after a little while and come in. Now *run*," she commanded
me. "Be sure you make it to the post office."

The culvert where my father was hiding was an obstacle
in the road now. I could hardly bring myself to walk over
him like that, but I knew I had to hurry. The road was wet.
Now at sundown it was beginning to freeze, and I could feel
the delicate ice crunch under every step with a beautiful
sound and sensation of touch. The rosy light over the cornfield, reflected in a thousand puddles islanded in the loam
seemed to me too strongly and unhappily beautiful for me
to stand, and it occurred to me that I might die right then,
being so divided by feelings I had never encountered be-

fore, waking to my first realization that living was something that one must choose against hardship to do.

At the culvert I left the road, knelt in the water of the ditch bottom and looked in at my father. He was sitting right in the middle of the concrete tube. In the dim light I could only see his silhouette and the glitter of reflected light in his eyes. I am sure he saw me, but neither of us spoke.

Then I ran for the post office. I think I ran all the way, because I got there in plenty of time to put the envelopes in the letter box. Walking home afterward I felt how my knees were wet from where I had knelt in the ditch.

III

Of course none of us won anything from the Goodyear Co. In about a month the winners of prizes over a thousand dollars were announced. First prize went to someone who had over three times as many words in his list as there had been in the largest of ours.

"Three times," my mother said. "That's a lie. That can't be. They must have used foreign words like French and German, Spanish and all. And they *said* that was against the rules."

My father commented, "Maybe one of you will win a littler prize. They're going to announce more next week." After the bad day of the mailing of the lists he had relaxed, had been permitted to relax, and by this time was even displaying a mild hope that something might come from all that bother.

But then the last of the cash prizes was announced and there was nothing left to wait for except the names of the winners of the model dirigibles.

"If the others didn't get any money I'm not going to win the dirigible," I said to my father, answering one of his soft optimisms aggressively.

"You don't know," he said. "I wouldn't wonder that your list would be just right for a smaller prize. You know, it might be like having the right tool for the right job. Yes, the right tool."

My mother said, "We should have had a typewriter. I can understand that now that it's too late. Even if they didn't specify that you had to use a typewriter."

"You told me that my words they couldn't read might be a good thing," I said.

"Well, on that . . ." Her lips worked carefully while she made up her mind how to answer me. "Yes, that may be so. Don't give up hope."

From this last posture she established against defeat and from my own premonitory sense of loss I began to develop the notion that they were all demanding that I win, and I added the strain of what I considered their expectations to my own. Partly for them, partly for myself I strained all the tricks of emotional force—on the order of holding my breath, crossing my fingers, figuratively—to affect what the announcer was going to say when he came to read the last list of winners. I accepted in a subterranean agreement, that I owed it to the family to win, for if I won, that would help make up for my father's hiding in the culvert, my mother's fibbing to the teacher, and our general humiliation in prostrating ourselves before a big company that had so far ignored us.

Each name on the list of winners should have been mine and none was. I wanted to howl when the reading was over, and yet I felt that, having lost, I didn't even have the right to do that. For the first time it came to me with undeniable force that beyond our mere failure to win we had lost something that had been put at stake.

After the trial of listening my father sighed tranquilly and said it appeared to him that these last prizes had been awarded on a geographical basis. "Did you notice how there was hardly ever more than two from any state except New York? You heard how this gentleman up in Red Oak got one. Well sir, that's enough for this part of the world, they likely figured. You can't tell me these contests aren't rigged some way. Naturally you didn't have much of a chance when they did things like that," he told me.

He put out his hand to rumple my hair or pat my cheek, but I flung myself beyond his reach, behaving spitefully to cover my sense of worthlessness.

"There, there, feller," he said. "There, there now."

"I worked hard," I screeched. "I had as good a list as anybody's."

"Sure you did. I'd lay money you had a better one than some of those as got the money."

I said, "I'm going to kill someone for this."

His head jerked as though I'd burned him. Then his eyes searched beyond me for my mother, and he seemed to be crawling humbly and with awkward slowness to some complicity with her. I saw this happen, but I chose then not to understand it. I thought I understood how every man's hand was against me. From then on.

"Everything comes to he who waits," my father said. "You'll see that, because that's the way things are. You remember when we came here we had such a hard job getting along without electricity and didn't think we'd ever have any?"

He paused for me to answer and I wouldn't.

"Now they're putting a line in," he said in a hearty tone, as though I might care about *that*. "They're going to bring the wire down from Parsons to Chesterfield and we'll have it out here, too. Then we can get us an electric radio and a lot of things, maybe. They were unloading poles on the other side of Chesterfield today."

"Somebody else got my dirigible," I whined.

"It would only be a little tin thing. You couldn't have any play out of it. Your mother and I thought that when the roads dry up we'd get you boys a bicycle. Wouldn't you rather have that?"

I set up an awful racket, protesting that I didn't want a bicycle or anything else but the dirigible. To which my father replied that I only wanted what I couldn't have and if that was the way of it he couldn't help me. I believed this dictum, if nothing else he said. I heard it wailing through my dreams that night like a sentence of wrath to come. Maybe on purpose I dreamed toward morning that all my family was dead. My father was dead in the culvert where he had hidden, and I was kicking up wet grass from the ditch to cover him.

At school time I pretended to be sick so I could stay

home. As a matter of fact I sulked with such ugliness that my mother suggested on her own part that I should go play in the storeroom, where I had not been for some months. I considered her recommendation and even walked upstairs to glance in at my former retreat. The dead room would not receive me, and the chilly smell of it really nauseated me. Losing the contest had even cut me off from that.

Everything was so senseless I might as well go do it like the rest until I was dead. I would just be too smart to hope for anything again, that was all.

But they tricked me back from that state, too. I came from school one evening about a month later to find my model of the dirigible *Akron* on the dining-room table. There was a mass of wrapping paper broken back from around it and some excelsior that smelled like newly sawed lumber.

It was a very shiny model, though somewhat smaller and harsher-looking than I had imagined it would be. It said GOODYEAR TIRE AND RUBBER CO. on the side.

"What's it for?" I yelled to my mother as she came in from the kitchen to see how I was going to receive it. "Did one of us win it after all?"

She smiled her best. "Sure," she said. "Isn't it a pretty thing, now? I guess this proves that if you do your level best and really want something you'll get it, doesn't it?"

I might have accepted the moral of her comment without argument, for moral significances seemed to me at that point lighter than air, but the practical accounting worried me. "How come they didn't read our name on the radio if we won?"

"We didn't *exactly* win," my mother said. "Your father and I thought that you'd worked so hard that you *were* a winner and deserved a prize. We wrote to that man in Red Oak and bought it from him."

"Oh," I said. Why did they do that to me on top of all the rest? I couldn't stand it and I said, "Thanks a lot."

Just before suppertime my brother Dave caught me outside in the yard and said, "All right, you big jackass, you got your dee-rigible. Aren't you proud of it?"

"You leave me alone."

"I'm not going to leave you alone. They had to pay fifteen bucks for it and now maybe we can't have a bicycle this summer."

"I never asked them to do it."

"Oh no," he said. "Oh no, you didn't. Just whining like a pup that you didn't get anything in this contest. Did any of the rest of us get anything?"

"I didn't want them to buy it. I didn't know they'd be such big fools."

"I don't know," he said despairingly. "I guess they were because you're such a big fool. Listen, if you don't make them think that you're real glad to get it, I'll kill you."

It was not—or not exactly—his threat that weighed on me. When he left me I had nothing to face except—as on the evening of my father's flight—the width of sundown and spring air, empty but nonetheless resonant with things learned and half-learned, again multiplying by its beauty and silence the real threat of death if I turned away from my family and their organized ways of stinging me. I could see then that I would have to keep pretending the dirigible was fine, and I have never learned what else I could have said.

THE COUNTRY HUSBAND

John Cheever

JOHN CHEEVER *was born in Quincy, Massachusetts. At the age of seventeen he was expelled from Thayer Academy at South Braintree, Massachusetts, and promptly sold a short story about it to* The New Republic. *Since then he has written about one hundred short stories, most of which have been published in* The New Yorker. *Three collections of his stories have been published:* THE WAY SOME PEOPLE LIVE (*1953*), THE ENORMOUS RADIO (*1953*) *and* THE HOUSEBREAKER OF SHADY HILL (*1958*). *His first novel,* THE WAPSHOT CHRONICLE, *won him the National Book Award in 1957. A resident of Westchester County, New York, Mr. Cheever has received a Guggenheim Fellowship and the National Institute of Arts and Letters Award in literature.*

To begin at the beginning, the airplane from Minneapolis in which Francis Weed was travelling East ran into heavy weather. The sky had been a hazy blue, with the clouds below the plane lying so close together that nothing could be seen of the earth. Then mist began to form outside the windows, and they flew into a white cloud of such density that it reflected the exhaust fires. The color of the cloud darkened to gray, and the plane began to rock. Francis had been in heavy weather before, but he had never been shaken up so much. The man in the seat beside him pulled a flask out of his pocket and took a drink. Francis smiled at his neighbor, but the man looked away; he wasn't sharing his painkiller with anyone. The plane had begun to drop and flounder wildly. A child was crying. The air in the cabin was overheated and stale, and Francis' left foot went to sleep. He read a little from a paper book that he had bought at the airport, but the violence of the storm divided his attention. The exhaust fires blazed and shed sparks in the dark, and, inside, the shaded lights, the stuffiness, and the window curtains gave the cabin an atmosphere of intense and misplaced domesticity. Then the lights flickered and went out. "You know what I've always wanted to do?" the man beside Francis said suddenly. "I've always wanted to buy a farm in New Hampshire and raise beef cattle." The stewardess announced that they were going to make an emergency landing. All but the child saw in their minds the spreading wings of the Angel of Death. The pilot could be heard singing faintly, "I've got sixpence, jolly, jolly sixpence. I've got sixpence to last me all my life . . ." There was no other sound.

The loud groaning of the hydraulic valves swallowed up the pilot's song, and there was a shrieking high in the air, like automobile brakes, and the plane hit flat on its belly in a cornfield and shook them so violently that an old man up forward howled, "Me kidneys! Me kidneys!" The stewardess flung open the door, and someone opened an emergency door at the back, letting in the sweet noise of their continuing mortality—the idle splash and smell of a heavy rain. Anxious for their lives, they filed out of the doors and scattered over the cornfield in all directions, praying that the thread would hold. It did. Nothing happened. When it was clear that the plane would not burn or explode, the crew and the stewardess gathered the passengers together and led them to the shelter of a barn. They were not far from Philadelphia, and in a little while a string of taxis took them into the city. "It's just like the Marne," someone said, but there was surprisingly little relaxation of that suspiciousness with which many Americans regard their fellow-travellers.

In Philadelphia, Francis Weed got a train to New York. At the end of that journey, he crossed the city and caught, just as it was about to pull out, the commuting train that he took five nights a week to his home in Shady Hill.

He sat with Trace Bearden. "You know, I was in that plane that just crashed outside Philadelphia," he said. "We came down in a field . . ." He had travelled faster than the newspapers or the rain, and the weather in New York was sunny and mild. It was a day in late September, as fragrant and shapely as an apple. Trace listened to the story, but how could he get excited? Francis had no powers that would let him re-create a brush with death—particularly in the atmosphere of a commuting train, journeying through a sunny countryside where already, in the slum gardens, there were signs of harvest. Trace picked up his newspaper, and Francis was left alone with his thoughts. He said good night to Trace on the platform at Shady Hill and drove in his second-hand Volkswagen up to the Blenhollow neighborhood, where he lived.

The Weeds' Dutch Colonial house was larger than it appeared to be from the driveway. The living room was spacious and divided like Gaul into three parts. Around an ell to the left as one entered from the vestibule was the long table, laid for six, with candles and a bowl of fruit in the center. The sounds and smells that came from the open kitchen door were appetizing, for Julia Weed was a good cook. The largest part of the living room centered around a fireplace. On the right were some bookshelves and a piano. The room was polished and tranquil, and from the windows that opened to the west there was some late-summer sunlight, brilliant and as clear as water. Nothing here was neglected; nothing had not been burnished. It was not the kind of household where, after prying open a stuck cigarette box, you would find an old shirt button and a tarnished nickel. The hearth was swept, the roses on the piano were reflected in the polish of the broad top, and there was an album of Schubert waltzes on the rack. Louisa Weed, a pretty girl of nine, was looking out the western windows. Her younger brother Henry was standing beside her. Her still younger brother, Toby, was studying the figures of some tonsured monks drinking beer on the polished brass of the wood box.

Francis, taking off his hat and putting down his paper, was not consciously pleased with the scene; he was not that reflective. It was his element, his creation, and he returned to it with that sense of lightness and strength with which any creature returns to its home. "Hi, everybody," he said. "The plane from Minneapolis . . ."

Nine times out of ten, Francis would be greeted with affection, but tonight the children are absorbed in their own antagonisms. Francis had not finished his sentence about the plane crash before Henry plants a kick in Louisa's behind. Louisa swings around, saying *"Damn you!"* Francis makes the mistake of scolding Louisa for bad language before he punishes Henry. Now Louisa turns on her father and accuses him of favoritism. Henry is always right; she is persecuted and lonely; her lot is hopeless. Francis turns to his son, but the boy has justification for the kick—she hit him first; she hit him on the ear, which is dangerous. Louisa agrees with this passionately. She hit him on the ear, and she *meant* to hit him on the ear, because he messed up her china collection. Henry says that this is a lie. Little Toby turns away from the wood box to throw in some evidence for Louisa. Henry claps his hand over little Toby's mouth. Francis separates the two boys but accidentally pushes Toby into the wood box. Toby begins to cry. Louisa is already crying. Just then, Julia Weed comes into that part of the room where the table is laid. She is a pretty, intelligent woman, and the white in her hair is premature. She does not seem to notice the fracas. "Hello, darling," she says serenely to Francis. "Wash your hands, everyone. Dinner is ready." She strikes a match and lights the six candles in this vale of tears.

This simple announcement, like the war cries of the Scottish chieftains, only refreshes the ferocity of the combatants. Louisa gives Henry a blow on the shoulder. Henry, although he seldom cries, has pitched nine innings and is tired. He bursts into tears. Little Toby discovers a splinter in his hand and begins to howl. Francis says loudly that he has been in a plane crash and that he is tired. Julia appears again, from the kitchen, and, still ignoring the chaos, asks Francis to go upstairs and tell Helen that everything is ready. Francis is happy to go; it is like getting back to head-quarters company. He is planning to tell his oldest daughter about the airplane crash, but Helen is lying on her bed reading a *True Romance* magazine, and the first thing Francis does is to take the magazine from her hand and remind Helen that he has forbidden her to buy it. She did not buy it, Helen replies. It was given to her by her best friend, Bessie Black. Everybody reads *True Romance*. Bessie Black's father reads *True Romance*. There isn't a girl in Helen's class who doesn't read *True Romance*. Francis expresses his detestation of the magazine and then tells her that dinner is ready—although from the sounds downstairs it doesn't seem so. Helen follows him down the stairs. Julia has seated herself in the candle-light and spread a napkin over her lap. Neither Louisa nor Henry has come to the table. Little Toby is still howling, lying face down on the floor. Francis speaks to him gently: "Daddy was in a plane crash this afternoon, Toby. Don't you want to hear about it?" Toby goes on crying. "If you don't come to the table now, Toby," Francis says, "I'll have to send you to bed without any supper." The little boy rises, gives him a cunning look, flies up the stairs to his bedroom, and slams the door. "Oh dear," Julia says, and starts to go after him. Francis says that she will spoil him. Julia says that Toby is ten pounds underweight and has to be encouraged to eat. Winter is coming, and he will spend the cold months in bed unless he has his dinner. Julia goes upstairs. Francis sits down at the table with Helen. Helen is suffering from the dismal feeling of having read too intently on a fine day, and she gives her father and the room a jaded look. She doesn't understand about the plane crash, because there wasn't a drop of rain in Shady Hill.

Julia returns with Toby, and they all sit down and are served. "Do I have to look at that big, fat slob?" Henry says, of Louisa. Everybody but Toby enters into this skirmish, and it rages up and down the table for five minutes. Toward the end, Henry puts his napkin over his head and, trying to eat that way, spills spinach all over his shirt. Francis asks Julia if the children couldn't have their dinner earlier. Julia's guns are loaded for this. She can't cook two dinners and lay two tables. She paints with lightning strokes that panorama of drudgery in which her youth, her beauty, and her wit have been lost. Francis says that he must be understood; he was nearly killed in an airplane crash, and he doesn't like to come home every night to a battlefield. Now Julia is deeply committed. Her voice trembles. He doesn't come home every night to a battlefield. The accusation is stupid and mean. Everything was tranquil until he arrived. She stops speaking, puts down her knife and fork, and looks into her plate as if it is a gulf. She begins to cry. "Poor Mummy!" Toby says, and when Julia gets up from the table, drying her tears with a napkin, Toby goes to her side. "Poor Mummy," he says. "Poor Mummy!" And they climb the stairs together. The other children drift away from the battlefield, and Francis goes into the back garden for a cigarette and some air.

It was a pleasant garden, with walks and flower beds and places to sit. The sunset had nearly burned out, but there was still plenty of light. Put into a thoughtful mood by the crash and the battle, Francis listened to the evening sounds of Shady Hill. "Varmits! Rascals!" old Mr. Nixon shouted to the squirrels in his bird-feeding station. "Avaunt and quit my sight!" A door slammed. Someone was playing tennis on the Babcocks' court; someone was cutting grass. Then Donald Goslin, who lived at the corner, began to play the "Moonlight Sonata." He did this nearly every night. He threw the tempo out the window and played it *rubato* from beginning to end, like an outpouring of tearful petulance, lonesomeness, and self-pity—of everything it was Beethoven's greatness not to know. The music rang up and down the street beneath the trees like an appeal for love, for tenderness, aimed at some lonely housemaid—some fresh-faced, homesick girl from Galway, looking at old snapshots in her third-floor room. "Here, Jupiter, here Jupiter," Francis called to the Mercers' retriever. Jupiter crashed through the tomato vines with the remains of a felt hat in his mouth.

Jupiter was an anomaly. His retrieving instincts and his high spirits were out of place in Shady Hill. He was as black as coal, with a long, alert, intelligent, rakehell face. His eyes gleamed with mischief, and he held his head high. It was

the fierce, heavily collared dog's head that appears in her-
aldry, in tapestry, and that used to appear on umbrella handles and walking sticks. Jupiter went where he pleased, ran-
sacking wastebaskets, clotheslines, garbage pails, and shoe
bags. He broke up garden parties and tennis matches, and
got mixed up in the processional at Christ's Church on Sunday, barking at the men in red dresses. He crashed through
old Mr. Nixon's rose garden two or three times a day, cutting a wide swath through the Condesa de Sastagos, and as
soon as Donald Goslin lighted his barbecue fire on Thurs-
day nights, Jupiter would get the scent. Nothing the Goslins
did could drive him away. Sticks and stones and rude com-
mands only moved him to the edge of the terrace, where he
remained, with his gallant and heraldic muzzle, waiting for
Donald Goslin to turn his back and reach for the salt. Then
he would spring onto the terrace, lift the steak lightly off
the fire, and run away with the Goslins' dinner. Jupiter's
days were numbered. The Wrightsons' German gardener or
the Farquarsons' cook would soon poison him. Even old
Mr. Nixon might put some arsenic in the garbage that Jupiter loved. "Here, Jupiter, Jupiter!" Francis called, but the
dog pranced off, shaking the hat in his white teeth. Looking
in at the windows of his house, Francis saw that Julia had
come down and was blowing out the candles.

Julia and Francis Weed went out a great deal. Julia was
well liked and gregarious, and her love of parties sprang
from a most natural dread of chaos and loneliness. She went
through her morning mail with real anxiety, looking for invitations, and she usually found some, but she was insatiable, and if she had gone out seven nights a week, it would
not have cured her of a reflective look—the look of someone
who hears distant music—for she would always suppose that
there was a more brilliant party somewhere else. Francis
limited her to two week-night parties, putting a flexible interpretation on Friday, and rode through the weekend like
a dory in a gale. The day after the airplane crash, the
Weeds were to have dinner with the Farquarsons.

Francis got home late from town, and Julia got the sitter
while he dressed, and then hurried him out of the house.

The party was small and pleasant, and Francis settled down
to enjoy himself. A new maid passed the drinks. Her hair
was dark, and her face was round and pale and seemed
familiar to Francis. He had not developed his memory as a
sentimental faculty. Wood smoke, lilac, and other such per-
fumes did not stir him, and his memory was something like
his appendix—a vestigial repository. It was not his limitation
at all to be unable to escape the past; it was perhaps his
limitation that he had escaped it so successfully. He might
have seen the maid at other parties, he might have seen
her taking a walk on Sunday afternoons, but in either case
he would not be searching his memory now. Her face was,
in a wonderful way, a moon face—Norman or Irish—but it
was not beautiful enough to account for his feeling that he
had seen her before, in circumstances that he ought to be
able to remember. He asked Nellie Farquarson who she was.
Nellie said that the maid had come through an agency, and
that her home was Trénon, in Normandy—a small place
with a church and a restaurant that Nellie had once visited.
While Nellie talked on about her travels abroad, Francis
realized where he had seen the woman before. It had been
at the end of the war. He had left a replacement depot with
some other men and taken a three-day pass in Trénon. On
their second day, they had walked out to a crossroads to see
the public chastisement of a young woman who had lived
with the German commandant during the Occupation.

It was a cool morning in the fall. The sky was overcast,
and poured down onto the dirt crossroads a very discourag-
ing light. They were on high land and could see how like one
another the shapes of the clouds and the hills were as
they stretched off toward the sea. The prisoner arrived sitting on a three-legged stool in a farm cart. She stood by the
cart while the mayor read the accusation and the sentence.
Her head was bent and her face was set in that empty half
smile behind which the whipped soul is suspended. When
the mayor was finished, she undid her hair and let it fall
across her back. A little man with a gray mustache cut off
her hair with shears and dropped it on the ground. Then,
with a bowl of soapy water and a straight razor, he shaved
her skull clean. A woman approached and began to undo

the fastenings of her clothes, but the prisoner pushed her aside and undressed herself. When she pulled her chemise over her head and threw it on the ground, she was naked. The women jeered; the men were still. There was no change in the falseness or the plaintiveness of the prisoner's smile. The cold wind made her white skin rough and hardened the nipples of her breasts. The jeering ended gradually, put down by the recognition of their common humanity. One woman spat on her, but some inviolable grandeur in her nakedness lasted through the ordeal. When the crowd was quiet, she turned—she had begun to cry—and, with nothing on but a pair of worn black shoes and stockings, walked down the dirt road alone away from the village. The round white face had aged a little, but there was no question but that the maid who passed his cocktails and later served Francis his dinner was the woman who had been punished at the crossroads.

The war seemed now so distant and that world where the cost of partisanship had been death or torture so long ago. Francis had lost track of the men who had been with him in Vésey. He could not count on Julia's discretion. He could not tell anyone. And if he had told the story now, at the dinner table, it would have been a social as well as a human error. The people in the Farquarsons' living room seemed united in their tacit claim that there had been no past, no war—that there was no danger or trouble in the world. In the recorded history of human arrangements, this extraordinary meeting would have fallen into place, but the atmosphere of Shady Hill made the memory unseemly and impolite. The prisoner withdrew after passing the coffee, but the encounter left Francis feeling languid; it had opened his memory and his senses, and left them dilated. He and Julia drove home when the party ended, and Julia went into the house. Francis stayed in the car to take the sitter home.

Expecting to see Mrs. Henlein, the old lady who usually stayed with the children, he was surprised when a young girl opened the door and came out onto the lighted stoop. She stayed in the light to count her textbooks. She was frowning and beautiful. Now, the world is full of beautiful young girls, but Francis saw here the difference between beauty and perfection. All those endearing flaws, moles, birthmarks, and healed wounds were missing, and he experienced in his consciousness that moment when music breaks glass, and felt a pang of recognition as strange, deep, and wonderful as anything in his life. It hung from her frown, from an impalpable darkness in her face—a look that impressed him as a direct appeal for love. When she had counted her books, she came down the steps and opened the car door. In the light, he saw that her cheeks were wet. She got in and shut the door.

"You're new," Francis said.

"Yes, Mrs. Henlein is sick. I'm Anne Murchison."

"Did the children give you any trouble?"

"Oh, no, no." She turned and smiled at him unhappily in the dim dashboard light. Her light hair caught on the collar of her jacket, and she shook her head to set it loose.

"You've been crying."

"Yes."

"I hope it was nothing that happened in our house."

"No, no, it was nothing that happened in your house." Her voice was bleak. "It's no secret. Everybody in the village knows. Daddy's an alcoholic, and he just called me from some saloon and gave me a piece of his mind. He thinks I'm immoral. He called just before Mrs. Weed came back."

"I'm sorry."

"Oh, *Lord!*" She gasped and began to cry. She turned toward Francis, and he took her in his arms and let her cry on his shoulder. She shook in his embrace, and this movement accentuated his sense of the fineness of her flesh and bone. The layers of their clothing felt thin, and when her shuddering began to diminish, it was so much like a paroxysm of love that Francis lost his head and pulled her roughly against him. She drew away. "I live on Belleview Avenue," she said. "You go down Lansing Street to the railroad bridge."

"All right." He started the car.

"You turn left at that traffic light. . . . Now you turn right here and go straight on toward the tracks."

The road Francis took brought him out of his own neighborhood, across the tracks, and toward the river, to a street where the near-poor lived, in houses whose peaked gables and trimmings of wooden lace conveyed the purest feelings of pride and romance, although the houses themselves could not have offered much privacy or comfort, they were all so small. The street was dark, and, stirred by the grace and beauty of the troubled girl, he seemed, in turning into it, to have come into the deepest part of some submerged memory. In the distance, he saw a porch light burning. It was the only one, and she said that the house with the light was where she lived. When he stopped the car, he could see beyond the porch light into a dimly lighted hallway with an old-fashioned clothes tree. "Well, here we are," he said, conscious that a young man would have said something different.

She did not move her hands from the books, where they were folded, and she turned and faced him. There were tears of lust in his eyes. Determinedly—not sadly—he opened the door on his side and walked around to open hers. He took her free hand, letting his fingers in between hers, climbed at her side the two concrete steps, and went up a narrow walk through a front garden where dahlias, marigolds, and roses—things that had withstood the light frosts —still bloomed, and made a bittersweet smell in the night air. At the steps, she freed her hand and then turned and kissed him swiftly. Then she crossed the porch and shut the door. The porch light went out, then the light in the hall. A second later, a light went on upstairs at the side of the house, shining into a tree that was still covered with leaves. It took her only a few minutes to undress and get into bed, and then the house was dark.

Julia was asleep when Francis got home. He opened a second window and got into bed to shut his eyes on that night, but as soon as they were shut—as soon as he had dropped off to sleep—the girl entered his mind, moving with perfect freedom through its shut doors and filling chamber after chamber with her light, her perfume, and the music of her voice. He was crossing the Atlantic with her on the old Mauretania and, later, living with her in Paris. When he woke from this dream, he got up and smoked a cigarette

at the open window. Getting back into bed, he cast around
in his mind for something he desired to do that would injure
no one, and he thought of skiing. Up through the dimness
in his mind rose the image of a mountain deep in snow. It
was late in the day. Wherever his eyes looked, he saw broad
and heartening things. Over his shoulder, there was a snow-
filled valley, rising into wooded hills where the trees dimmed
the whiteness like a sparse coat of hair. The cold deadened
all sound but the loud, iron clanking of the lift machinery.
The light on the trails was blue, and it was harder than it
had been a minute or two earlier to pick the turns, harder
to judge—now that the snow was all deep blue—the crust, the
ice, the bare spots, and the deep piles of dry powder. Down
the mountain he swung, matching his speed against the con-
tours of a slope that had been formed in the first ice age,
seeking with ardor some simplicity of feeling and circum-
stance. Night fell then, and he drank a Martini with some
old friend in a dirty country bar.

In the morning, Francis' snow-covered mountain was
gone, and he was left with his vivid memories of Paris and
the Mauretania. He had been bitten gravely. He washed his
body, shaved his jaws, drank his coffee, and missed the
seven-thirty-one. The train pulled out just as he brought his
car to the station, and the longing he felt for the coaches as
they drew stubbornly away from him reminded him of the
humors of love. He waited for the eight-two, on what was
now an empty platform. It was a clear morning; the morning
seemed thrown like a gleaming bridge of light over his
mixed affairs. His spirits were feverish and high. The image
of the girl seemed to put him into a relationship to the
world that was mysterious and enthralling. Cars were beginning to fill up the parking lot, and he noticed that those
that had driven down from the high land above Shady Hill
were white with hoarfrost. This first clear sign of autumn
thrilled him. An express train—a night train from Buffalo or
Albany—came down the tracks between the platforms, and
he saw that the roofs of the foremost cars were covered with
a skin of ice. Struck by the miraculous physicalness of
everything, he smiled at the passengers in the dining car,
who could be seen eating eggs and wiping their mouths with

napkins as they travelled. The sleeping-car compartments, with their soiled bed linen, trailed through the fresh morning like a string of rooming-house windows. Then he saw an extraordinary thing; at one of the bedroom windows sat an unclothed woman of exceptional beauty, combing her golden hair. She passed like an apparition through Shady Hill, combing and combing her hair, and Francis followed her with his eyes until she was out of sight. Then old Mrs. Wrightson joined him on the platform and began to talk.

"Well, I guess you must be surprised to see me here the third morning in a row," she said, "but because of my window curtains I'm becoming a regular commuter. The curtains I bought on Monday I returned on Tuesday, and the curtains I bought on Tuesday, I'm returning today. On Monday, I got exactly what I wanted—it's a wool tapestry with roses and birds—but when I got them home, I found they were the wrong length. Well, I exchanged them yesterday, and when I got them home, I found they were still the wrong length. Now I'm praying to high Heaven that the decorator will have them in the right length, because you know my house, you *know* my living-room windows, and you can imagine what a problem they present. I don't know what to do with them."

"I know what to do with them," Francis said.

"What?"

"Paint them black on the inside, and shut up."

There was a gasp from Mrs. Wrightson, and Francis looked down at her to be sure that she knew he meant to be rude. She turned and walked away from him, so damaged in spirit that she limped. A wonderful feeling enveloped him, as if light were being shaken about him, and he thought again of Venus combing and combing her hair as she drifted through the Bronx. The realization of how many years had passed since he had enjoyed being deliberately impolite sobered him. Among his friends and neighbors, there were brilliant and gifted people—he saw that—but many of them, also, were bores and fools, and he had made the mistake of listening to them all with equal attention. He had confused a lack of discrimination with Christian love, and the confusion seemed general and destructive. He was grateful to the girl for this bracing sensation of independence. Birds were singing—cardinals and the last of the robins. The sky shone like enamel. Even the smell of ink from his morning paper honed his appetite for life, and the world that was spread out around him was plainly a paradise.

If Francis had believed in some hierarchy of love—in spirits armed with hunting bows, in the capriciousness of Venus and Eros—or even in magical potions, philtres, and stews, in scapulae and quarters of the moon, it might have explained his susceptibility and his feverish high spirits. The autumnal loves of middle age are well publicized, and he guessed that he was face to face with one of these, but there was not a trace of autumn in what he felt. He wanted to sport in the green woods, scratch where he itched, and drink from the same cup.

His secretary, Miss Rainey, was late that morning—she went to a psychiatrist three mornings a week—and when she came in, Francis wondered what advice a psychiatrist would have for him. But the girl promised to bring back into his life something like the sound of music. The realization that this music might lead him straight to a trial for statutory rape at the county courthouse collapsed his happiness. The photograph of his four children laughing into the camera on the beach at Gay Head reproached him. On the letterhead of his firm there was a drawing of the Laocoön, and the figure of the priest and his sons in the coils of the snake appeared to him to have the deepest meaning.

He had lunch with Pinky Trabert, who told him a couple of dirty stories. At a conversational level, the mores of his friends were robust and elastic, but he knew that the moral card house would come down on them all—on Julia and the children as well—if he got caught taking advantage of a baby-sitter. Looking back over the recent history of Shady Hill for some precedent, he found there was none. There was no turpitude; there had not been a divorce since he lived there; there had not even been a breath of scandal. Things seemed arranged with more propriety even than in the Kingdom of Heaven. After leaving Pinky, Francis went to a jeweller's and bought the girl a bracelet. How happy this clandestine purchase made him, how stuffy and comical the jeweller's clerks seemed, how sweet the women who passed at his back smelled! On Fifth Avenue, passing Atlas with his shoulders bent under the weight of the world, Francis thought of the strenuousness of containing his physicalness within the patterns he had chosen.

He did not know when he would see the girl next. He had the bracelet in his inside pocket when he got home. Opening the door of his house, he found her in the hall. Her back was to him, and she turned when she heard the door close. Her smile was open and loving. Her perfection stunned him like a fine day—a day after a thunderstorm. He seized her and covered her lips with his, and she struggled but she did not have to struggle for long, because just then little Gertrude Flannery appeared from somewhere and said, "Oh, Mr. Weed . . ."

Gertrude was a stray. She had been born with a taste for exploration, and she did not have it in her to center her life with her affectionate parents. People who did not know the Flannerys concluded from Gertrude's behavior that she was the child of a bitterly divided family, where drunken quarrels were the rule. This was not true. The fact that little Gertrude's clothing was ragged and thin was her own triumph over her mother's struggle to dress her warmly and neatly. Garrulous, skinny, and unwashed, she drifted from house to house around the Blenhollow neighborhood, forming and breaking alliances based on an attachment to babies, animals, children her own age, adolescents, and sometimes adults. Opening your front door in the morning, you would find Gertrude sitting on your stoop. Going into the bathroom to shave, you would find Gertrude using the toilet. Looking into your son's crib, you would find it empty, and, looking further, you would find that Gertrude had pushed him in his baby carriage into the next village. She was helpful, pervasive, honest, hungry, and loyal. She never went home of her own choice. When the time to go arrived, she was indifferent to all its signs. "Go home, Gertrude," people could be heard saying in one house or another, night after night. "Go home, Gertrude." "It's time for you to go home now, Gertrude." "You had better go home and get your supper, Gertrude." "I told you to go home twenty minutes ago, Gertrude." "Your mother will be worrying about you, Gertrude." "Go home, Gertrude, go home."

There are times when the lines around the human eye seem like shelves of eroded stone and when the staring eye itself strikes us with such a wilderness of animal feeling that we are at a loss. The look Francis gave the little girl was ugly and queer, and it frightened her. He reached into his pocket—his hands were shaking—and took out a quarter. "Go home, Gertrude, go home, and don't tell anyone, Gertrude. Don't—" He choked and ran into the living room as Julia called down to him from upstairs to hurry and dress.

The thought that he would drive Anne Murchison home later that night ran like a golden thread through the events of the party that Francis and Julia went to, and he laughed uproariously at dull jokes, dried a tear when Mabel Mercer told him about the death of her kitten, and stretched, yawned, sighed, and grunted like any other man with a rendezvous at the back of his mind. The bracelet was in his pocket. As he sat talking, the smell of grass was in his nose, and he was wondering where he would park the car. Nobody lived in the old Parker mansion, and the driveway was used as a lovers' lane. Townsend Street was a dead end, and he could park there, beyond the last house. The old lane that used to connect Elm Street to the riverbanks was overgrown, but he had walked there with his children, and he could drive his car deep enough into the brushwoods to be concealed.

The Weeds were the last to leave the party, and their host and hostess spoke of their own married happiness while they all four stood in the hallway saying good night. "She's my girl," their host said, squeezing his wife. "She's my blue sky. After sixteen years, I still bite her shoulders. She makes me feel like Hannibal crossing the Alps."

The Weeds drove home in silence. Francis brought the car up the driveway and sat still, with the motor running. "You can put the car in the garage," Julia said as she got out. "I told the Murchison girl she could leave at eleven. Someone drove her home." She shut the door, and Francis sat in the dark. He would be spared nothing then, it seemed, that a fool was not spared: ravening lewdness, jealousy, this hurt to his feelings that put tears in his eyes, even scorn— for he could see clearly the image he now presented, his arms spread over the steering wheel and his head buried in them for love.

Francis had been a dedicated Boy Scout when he was young, and, remembering the precepts of his youth, he left his office early the next afternoon and played some round-robin squash, but, with his body toned up by exercise and a shower, he realized that he might better have stayed at his desk. It was a frosty night when he got home. The air smelled sharply of change. When he stepped into the house, he sensed an unusual stir. The children were in their best clothes, and when Julia came down, she was wearing a lavender dress and her diamond sunburst. She explained the stir: Mr. Hubber was coming at seven to take their photograph for the Christmas card. She had put out Francis' blue suit and a tie with some color in it, because the picture was going to be in color this year. Julia was lighthearted at the thought of being photographed for Christmas. It was the kind of ceremony she enjoyed.

Francis went upstairs to change his clothes. He was tired from the day's work and tired with longing, and sitting on the edge of the bed had the effect of deepening his weariness. He thought of Anne Murchison, and the physical need to express himself, instead of being restrained by the pink lamps on Julia's dressing table, engulfed him. He went to Julia's desk, took a piece of writing paper, and began to write on it. "Dear Anne, I love you, I love you, I love you . . ." No one would see the letter, and he used no restraint. He used phrases like "heavenly bliss," and "love nest." He salivated, sighed, and trembled. When Julia called him to come down, the abyss between his fantasy and the practical world opened so wide that he felt it affect the muscles of his heart.

Julia and the children were on the stoop, and the photographer and his assistant had set up a double battery of flood-lights to show the family and the architectural beauty of the entrance to their house. People who had come home on

a late train slowed their cars to see the Weeds being photographed for their Christmas card. A few waved and called
to the family. It took half an hour of smiling and wetting
their lips before Mr. Hubber was satisfied. The heat of the
lights made an unfresh smell in the frosty air, and when they
were turned off, they lingered on the retina of Francis' eyes.

Later that night, while Francis and Julia were drinking
their coffee in the living room, the doorbell rang. Julia answered the door and let in Clayton Thomas. He had come
to pay her for some theatre tickets that she had given his
mother some time ago, and that Helen Thomas had scru-
pulously insisted on paying for, though Julia had asked her
not to. Julia invited him in to have a cup of coffee. "I won't
have any coffee," Clayton said, "but I will come in for a
minute." He followed her into the living room, said good
evening to Francis, and sat awkwardly in a chair.

Clayton's father had been killed in the war, and the
young man's fatherlessness surrounded him like an element.
This may have been conspicuous in Shady Hill because the
Thomases were the only family that lacked a piece; all the
other marriages were intact and productive. Clayton was in
his second or third year of college, and he and his mother
lived alone in a large house, which she hoped to sell. Clayton had once made some trouble. Years ago, he had stolen
some money and run away; he had got to California before
they caught up with him. He was tall and homely, wore
horn-rimmed glasses, and spoke in a deep voice.

"When do you go back to college, Clayton?" Francis
asked.

"I'm not going back," Clayton said. "Mother doesn't have
the money, and there's no sense in all this pretense. I'm going to get a job, and if we sell the house, we'll take an
apartment in New York."

"Won't you miss Shady Hill?" Julia asked.

"No," Clayton said. "I don't like it."

"Why not?" Francis asked.

"Well, there's a lot here I don't approve of," Clayton
said gravely. "Things like the club dances. Last Saturday
night, I looked in toward the end and saw Mr. Granner

trying to put Mrs. Minot into the trophy case. They were both drunk. I disapprove of so much drinking."

"It was Saturday night," Francis said.

"And all the dovecotes are phony," Clayton said. "And the way people clutter up their lives. I've thought about it a lot, and what seems to me to be really wrong with Shady Hill is that it doesn't have any future. So much energy is spent in perpetuating the place—in keeping out undesirables, and so forth—that the only idea of the future anyone has is just more and more commuting trains and more parties. I don't think that's healthy. I think people ought to be able to dream big dreams about the future. I think people ought to be able to dream great dreams."

"It's too bad you couldn't continue with college," Julia said.

"I wanted to go to divinity school," Clayton said.

"What's your church?" Francis asked.

"Unitarian, Theosophist, Transcendentalist, Humanist," Clayton said.

"Wasn't Emerson a transcendentalist?" Julia asked.

"I mean the English transcendentalists," Clayton said. "All the American transcendentalists were goops."

"What kind of a job do you expect to get?" Francis asked.

"Well, I'd like to work for a publisher," Clayton said, "but everyone tells me there's nothing doing. But it's the kind of thing I'm interested in. I'm writing a long verse play about good and evil. Uncle Charlie might get me into a bank, and that would be good for me. I need the discipline. I have a long way to go in forming my character. I have some terrible habits. I talk too much. I think I ought to take vows of silence. I ought to try not to speak for a week, and discipline myself. I've thought of making a retreat at one of the Episcopalian monasteries, but I don't like Trinitarianism."

"Do you have any girl friends?" Francis asked.

"I'm engaged to be married," Clayton said. "Of course, I'm not old enough or rich enough to have my engagement observed or respected or anything, but I bought a simulated emerald for Anne Murchison with the money I made cutting lawns this summer. We're going to be married as soon as she finishes school."

Francis recoiled at the mention of the girl's name. Then a dingy light seemed to emanate from his spirit, showing everything—Julia, the boy, the chairs—in their true colorlessness. It was like a bitter turn of the weather.

"We're going to have a large family," Clayton said. "Her father's a terrible rummy, and I've had my hard times, and we want to have lots of children. Oh, she's wonderful, Mr. and Mrs. Weed, and we have so much in common. We like all the same things. We sent out the same Christmas card last year without planning it, and we both have an allergy to tomatoes, and our eyebrows grow together in the middle. Well, good night."

Julia went to the door with him. When she returned, Francis said that Clayton was lazy, irresponsible, affected, and smelly. Julia said that Francis seemed to be getting intolerant; the Thomas boy was young and should be given a chance. Julia had noticed other cases where Francis had been short-tempered. "Mrs. Wrightson has asked everyone in Shady Hill to her anniversary party but us," she said.

"I'm sorry, Julia."

"Do you know why they didn't ask us?"

"Why?"

"Because you insulted Mrs. Wrightson."

"Then you know about it?"

"June Masterson told me. She was standing behind you."

Julia walked in front of the sofa with a small step that expressed, Francis knew, a feeling of anger.

"I did insult Mrs. Wrightson, Julia, and I meant to. I've never liked her parties, and I'm glad she's dropped us."

"What about Helen?"

"How does Helen come into this?"

"Mrs. Wrightson's the one who decides who goes to the assemblies."

"You mean she can keep Helen from going to the dances?"

"Yes."

"I hadn't thought of that."

"Oh, I knew you hadn't thought of it," Julia cried, thrusting hilt-deep into this chink of his armor. "And it makes me furious to see this kind of stupid thoughtlessness wreck everyone's happiness."

"I don't think I've wrecked anyone's happiness."

"Mrs. Wrightson runs Shady Hill and has run it for the last forty years. I don't know what makes you think that in a community like this you can indulge every impulse you have to be insulting, vulgar, and offensive."

"I have very good manners," Francis said, trying to give the evening a turn toward the light.

"Damn you, Francis Weed!" Julia cried, and the spit of her words struck him in the face. "I've worked hard for the social position we enjoy in this place, and I won't stand by and see you wreck it. You must have understood when you settled here that you couldn't expect to live like a bear in a cave."

"I've got to express my likes and dislikes."

"You can conceal your dislikes. You don't have to meet everything head-on, like a child. Unless you're anxious to be a social leper. It's no accident that we get asked out a great deal. It's no accident that Helen has so many friends. How would you like to spend your Saturday nights at the movies? How would you like to spend your Sundays raking up dead leaves? How would you like it if your daughter spent the assembly nights sitting at her window, listening to the music from the club? How would you like it—" He did something then that was, after all, not so unaccountable, since her words seemed to raise up between them a wall so deadening that he gagged: He struck her full in the face. She staggered and then, a moment later, seemed composed. She went up the stairs to their room. She didn't slam the door. When Francis followed, a few minutes later, he found her packing a suitcase.

"Julia, I'm very sorry."

"It doesn't matter," she said. She was crying.

"Where do you think you're going?"

"I don't know. I just looked at a timetable. There's an eleven-sixteen into New York. I'll take that."

"You can't go, Julia."

"I can't stay. I know that."

"I'm sorry about Mrs. Wrightson, Julia, and I'm——"

"It doesn't matter about Mrs. Wrightson. That isn't the trouble."

"What is the trouble?"

"You don't love me."

"I do love you, Julia."

"No, you don't."

"Julia, I do love you, and I would like to be as we were—sweet and bawdy and dark—but now there are so many people."

"You hate me."

"I don't hate you, Julia."

"You have no idea of how much you hate me. I think it's subconscious. You don't realize the cruel things you've done."

"What cruel things, Julia?"

"The cruel acts your subconscious drives you to in order to express your hatred of me."

"What, Julia?"

"I've never complained."

"Tell me."

"You don't know what you're doing."

"Tell me."

"Your clothes."

"What do you mean?"

"I mean the way you leave your dirty clothes around in order to express your subconscious hatred of me."

"I don't understand."

"I mean your dirty socks and your dirty pajamas and your dirty underwear and your dirty shirts!" She rose from kneeling by the suitcase and faced him, her eyes blazing and her voice ringing with emotion. "I'm talking about the fact that you've never learned to hang up anything. You just leave your clothes all over the floor where they drop, in order to humiliate me. You do it on purpose!" She fell on the bed, sobbing.

"Julia, darling!" he said, but when she felt his hand on her shoulder she got up.

"Leave me alone," she said. "I have to go." She brushed past him to the closet and came back with a dress. "I'm not taking any of the things you've given me," she said. "I'm leaving my pearls and the fur jacket."

"Oh, Julia!" Her figure, so helpless in its self-deceptions, bent over the suitcase made him nearly sick with pity. She did not understand how desolate her life would be without him. She didn't understand the hours that working women have to keep. She didn't understand that most of her friendships existed within the framework of their marriage, and that without this she would find herself alone. She didn't understand about travel, about hotels, about money. "Julia, I can't let you go! What you don't understand, Julia, is that you've come to be dependent on me."

She tossed her head back and covered her face with her hands. "Did you say that *I* was dependent on *you?*" she asked. "Is that what you said? And who is it that tells you what time to get up in the morning and when to go to bed at night? Who is it that prepares your meals and picks up your dirty closet and invites your friends to dinner? If it weren't for me, your neckties would be greasy and your clothing would be full of moth holes. You were alone when I met you, Francis Weed, and you'll be alone when I leave. When Mother asked you for a list to send out invitations to our wedding, how many names did you have to give her? Fourteen!"

"Cleveland wasn't my home, Julia."

"And how many of your friends came to the church? Two!"

"Cleveland wasn't my home, Julia."

"Since I'm not taking the fur jacket," she said quietly, "you'd better put it back into storage. There's an insurance policy on the pearls that comes due in January. The name of the laundry and the maid's telephone number—all those things are in my desk. I hope you won't drink too much, Francis. I hope that nothing bad will happen to you. If you do get into serious trouble, you can call me."

"Oh my darling, I can't let you go!" Francis said. "I can't let you go, Julia!" He took her in his arms.

"I guess I'd better stay and take care of you for a little while longer," she said.

Riding to work in the morning, Francis saw the girl walk down the aisle of the coach. He was surprised; he hadn't realized that the school she went to was in the city, but she was carrying books, she seemed to be going to school. His surprise delayed his reaction, but then he got up clumsily and stepped into the aisle. Several people had come between them, but he could see her ahead of him, waiting for someone to open the car door, and then, as the train swerved, putting out her hand to support herself as she crossed the platform into the next car. He followed her through that car and halfway through another before calling her name—"Anne! Anne!"—but she didn't turn. He followed her into still another car, and she sat down in an aisle seat. Coming up to her, all his feelings warm and bent in her direction, he put his hand on the back of her seat—even this touch warmed him—and, leaning down to speak to her, he saw that it was not Anne. It was an older woman wearing glasses. He went on deliberately into another car, his face red with embarrassment and the much deeper feeling of having his good sense challenged; for if he couldn't tell one person from another, what evidence was there that his life with Julia and the children had as much reality as his dreams of iniquity in Paris or the litter, the grass smell, and the cave-shaped trees in Lovers' Lane.

Late that afternoon, Julia called to remind Francis that they were going out for dinner. A few minutes later, Trace Bearden called. "Look, feller," Trace said. "I'm calling for Mrs. Thomas. You know? Clayton, that boy of hers, doesn't seem able to get a job, and I wondered if you could help. If you'd call Charlie Bell—I know he's indebted to you—and say a good word for the kid, I think Charlie would—"

"Trace, I hate to say this," Francis said, "but I don't feel that I can do anything for that boy. The kid's worthless. I know it's a harsh thing to say, but it's a fact. Any kindness done for him would backfire in everybody's face. He's just a worthless kid, Trace, and there's nothing to be done about it. Even if we got him a job, he wouldn't be able to keep it for a week. I know that to be a fact. It's an awful thing, Trace, and I know it is, but instead of recommending that kid, I'd feel obliged to warn people against him—people who knew his father and would naturally want to step in and do something. I'd feel obliged to warn them. He's a thief . . ."

The moment this conversation was finished, Miss Rainey came in and stood by his desk. "I'm not going to be able to work for you any more, Mr. Weed," she said. "I can stay until the seventeenth if you need me, but I've been offered a whirlwind of a job, and I'd like to leave as soon as possible."

She went out, leaving him to face alone the wickedness of what he had done to the Thomas boy. His children in their photograph laughed and laughed, glazed with all the bright colors of summer, and he remembered that they had met a bagpiper on the beach that day and he had paid the piper a dollar to play them a battle song of the Black Watch. The girl would be at the house when he got home. He would spend another evening among his kind neighbors, picking and choosing dead-end streets, cart tracks, and the driveways of abandoned houses. There was nothing to mitigate his feeling—nothing that laughter or a game of softball with the children would change—and, thinking back over the plane crash, the Farquarsons' new maid, and Anne Murchison's difficulties with her drunken father, he wondered how he could have avoided arriving at just where he was. He was in trouble. He had been lost once in his life, coming back from a trout stream in the north woods, and he had now the same bleak realization that no amount of cheerfulness or hopefulness or valor or perseverance could help him find, in the gathering dark, the path that he'd lost. He smelled the forest. The feeling of bleakness was intolerable, and he saw clearly that he had reached the point where he would have to make a choice.

He could go to a psychiatrist, like Miss Rainey; he could go to church and confess his lusts; he could go to a Danish massage parlor in the West Seventies that had been recommended by a salesman; he could rape the girl or trust that he would somehow be prevented from doing this; or he could get drunk. It was his life, his boat, and, like every other man, he was made to be the father of thousands, and what harm could there be in a tryst that would make them both feel more kindly toward the world? This was the wrong train of thought, and he came back to the first, the psychiatrist. He had the telephone number of Miss Rainey's doctor, and he called and asked for an immediate appointment. He was insistent with the doctor's secretary—it was his manner in business—and when she said that the doctor's schedule was full for the next few weeks, Francis demanded an appointment that day and was told to come at five.

The psychiatrist's office was in a building that was used mostly by doctors and dentists, and the hallways were filled with the candy smell of mouth-wash and memories of pain. Francis' character had been formed upon a series of private resolves—resolves about cleanliness, about going off the high diving board or repeating any other feat that challenged his courage, about punctuality, honesty, and virtue. To abdicate the perfect loneliness in which he had made his most vital decisions shattered his concept of character and left him now in a condition that felt like shock. He was stupefied. The scene for his *miserere mei Deus* was, like the waiting room of so many doctors' offices, a crude token gesture toward the sweets of domestic bliss: a place arranged with antiques, coffee tables, potted plants, and etchings of snow-covered bridges and geese in flight, although there were no children, no marriage bed, no stove, even, in this travesty of a house, where no one had ever spent the night and where the curtained windows looked straight onto a dark air shaft. Francis gave his name and address to a secretary and then saw, at the side of the room, a policeman moving toward him. "Hold it, hold it," the policeman said. "Don't move. Keep your hands where they are."

"I think it's all right, Officer," the secretary began. "I think it will be——"

"Let's make sure," the policeman said, and he began to slap Francis' clothes, looking for what—pistols, knives, an icepick? Finding nothing, he went off, and the secretary began a nervous apology: "When you called on the telephone, Mr. Weed, you seemed very excited, and one of the doctor's patients has been threatening his life, and we have to be careful. If you want to go in now?" Francis pushed open a door connected to an electrical chime, and in the doctor's lair sat down heavily, blew his nose into a handkerchief, searched in his pockets for cigarettes, for matches, for something, and said hoarsely, with tears in his eyes, "I'm in love, Dr. Herzog."

It is a week or ten days later in Shady Hill. The seven-fourteen has come and gone, and here and there dinner is finished and the dishes are in the dish-washing machine. The village hangs, morally and economically, from a thread; but it hangs by its thread in the evening light. Donald Goslin has begun to worry the "Moonlight Sonata" again. *Marcato ma sempre pianissimo!* He seems to be wringing out a wet bath towel, but the housemaid does not heed him. She is writing a letter to Arthur Godfrey. In the cellar of his house, Francis Weed is building a coffee table. Dr. Herzog recommended woodwork as a therapy, and Francis finds some true consolation in the simple arithmetic involved and in the holy smell of new wood. Francis is happy. Upstairs, little Toby is crying, because he is tired. He puts off his cowboy hat, gloves, and fringed jacket, unbuckles the belt studded with gold and rubies, the silver bullets and holsters, slips off his suspenders, his checked shirt, and Levis, and sits on the edge of his bed to pull off his high boots. Leaving this equipment in a heap, he goes to the closet and takes his space suit off a nail. It is a struggle for him to get into the long tights, but he succeeds. He loops the magic cape over his shoulders and, climbing onto the footboard of his bed, he spreads his arms and flies the short distance to the floor, landing with a thump that is audible to everyone in the house but himself.

"Go home, Gertrude, go home," Mrs. Masterson says. "I told you to go home an hour ago, Gertrude. It's way past your suppertime, and your mother will be worried. Go home!" A door on the Babcocks' terrace flies open, and out comes Mrs. Babcock without any clothes on, pursued by her naked husband. (Their children are away at boarding school, and their terrace is screened by a hedge.) Over the terrace they go and in at the kitchen door, as passionate and handsome a nymph and satyr as you will find on any wall in Venice. Cutting the last of the roses in her garden, Julia hears old Mr. Nixon shouting at the squirrels in his bird-feeding station. "Rapscallions! Varmits! Avaunt and quit my sight!" A miserable cat wanders into the garden, sunk in spiritual and physical discomfort. Tied to its head is a small straw hat—a doll's hat—and it is securely buttoned into a doll's dress, from the skirts of which protrudes its long, hairy tail. As it walks, it shakes its feet, as if it had fallen into water.

"Here, pussy, pussy, pussy!" Julia calls.

"Here, pussy, here, poor pussy!" But the cat gives her a skeptical look and stumbles away in its skirts. The last to come is Jupiter. He prances through the tomato vines, holding in his generous mouth the remains of an evening slipper. Then it is dark; it is a night where kings in golden suits ride elephants over the mountains.

THE CONDOR AND THE GUESTS

Evan S. Connell, Jr.

EVAN S. CONNELL, JR. *was born in Kansas City, attended Dartmouth for two years and then went through naval aviation cadet training at Pensacola. After the war, he attended the University of Kansas and later did graduate work at Stanford, Columbia, and San Francisco State College. His stories have appeared in many magazines, and he has been awarded a Eugene Saxton Fellowship, among other literary awards. He has had three books published:* THE ANATOMY LESSON AND OTHER STORIES *(1957),* MRS. BRIDGE *(1959) and* THE PATRIOT *(1960), both novels. He makes his home in San Francisco.*

In Peru a female condor was staked inside a wooden cage. Every so often a male bird would get into this trap and would then be sold to a zoo or a museum. One of these captured condors, however, was sold to an American, J. D. Botkin of Parallel, Kansas.

It cost Mr. Botkin a great deal of money to get his bird into the United States, but he had traveled quite a bit and was proud of his ability to get anything accomplished that he set his mind to. At his home in Parallel he had a chain fastened about the bird's neck. The other end of the chain was padlocked to a magnolia tree which he had had transplanted to his back yard from the French Quarter of New Orleans on an earlier trip.

All the rest of that first day the condor sat in the magnolia tree and looked across the fields of wheat, but just before

sundown it lifted its wings and spread them to the fullest
extent as if testing the wind; then with a slow sweep of
utter majesty it rose into the air. It took a second leisurely
sweep with its wings, and a third. However, on the third
stroke it came to the end of the chain. Then it made a sort
of gasping noise and fell to the earth while the magnolia
swayed from the shock. After its fall the gigantic bird did
not move until long after dark when it got to its feet and
climbed into the tree. Next morning as the sun rose it was
on the same branch, looking south like a gargoyle taken
from the ramparts of some cathedral.

Day after day it sat in the magnolia tree without moving,
but every sundown it tried to take off. A pan of meat left
nearby was visited only by a swarm of flies.

Almost a week following the bird's arrival Mr. Botkin
was eating lunch at the Jupiter Club when he met his friend,
Harry Apple, and said to him, "You seen my bird yet?"

Harry Apple was a shrunken, bald-headed man who
never had much to say. He answered Mr. Botkin's question
by slowly shaking his head. Mr. Botkin then exclaimed that
Harry hadn't lived, and clapping him on the shoulder said
he was giving a dinner party on Wednesday—a sort of anniversary of the condor's first week in Kansas—and asked if
Harry could make it.

After the invitation had been extended, Harry Apple sat
silently for almost a minute and stared into space. He had
married a tall, smoke-haired ex-show-girl of paralyzing
beauty and he understood that she was the reason for the
invitations he received.

At last he nodded, saying in his melancholy voice, "Sure.
I'll bring Mildred, too."

Mr. Botkin clapped him on the shoulder and proposed a
toast, "To the condor!"

Harry sipped his drink and murmured, "Sure."

Mr. Botkin also got the Newtons and the Huddlestuns
for dinner. He was not too pleased about the Huddlestuns;
Suzie Huddlestun's voice always set him on edge, and
"Tiny" was a bore. He had asked the Bagleys, but Chuck
Bagley was going to an insurance convention in Kansas City.
He had also asked the Gerlachs, the Ridges, and the Zim-

mermans, but none of them could make it, so he settled for Suzie and Tiny. They were delighted with the invitation.

On the evening of the party "Fig" Newton and his wife had not arrived by seven o'clock, so Mr. Botkin said to the others—Mildred and Harry Apple, and Suzie and Tiny Huddlestun, "Well, by golly, this calls for a drink!"

With cocktails in their hands the guests wandered down to the magnolia tree and stood in a half-circle, shaking the ice in their glasses and looking critically upward. The men stood a bit closer to the tree than the ladies did in order to show that they were not afraid of the condor. The ladies did not think the somber bird would do anything at all and they would rather have sat on the porch and talked.

Tiny Huddlestun was an enormous top-heavy man who had been a wrestler when he was young. His larynx had been injured by a vicious Turk during a match in Joplin, so that now his voice was a sort of quavering falsetto. He bobbled the ice in his glass with an index finger as big as a sausage and said in his falsetto, "That a turkey you got there, Botkin?"

His wife laughed and squeezed his arm. Even in platform shoes she did not come up to his chin, and the difference in their sizes caused people to speculate. She never listened to what he said but every time she heard his voice she laughed and squeezed him.

Mildred Apple said a little sulkily, "J.D., I want it to do something exciting." The cocktail was making her feel dangerous.

Mr. Botkin snapped his fingers. "By golly!" He swallowed the rest of his drink, took Harry's empty glass, and went back to the house. In a few minutes he returned with fresh drinks and a green and yellow parrot riding on his shoulder. Solemnly he announced, "This here's Caldwell."

"Caldwell?" shrieked Suzie Huddlestun, and began to laugh so hard that she clutched Tiny's coat for support.

Mr. Botkin was laughing, too, although he did not want to because he disliked Suzie. His belt went under his belly like a girth under a horse, and as he laughed the belt creaked. It was several minutes before he could pat the perspiration from his strawberry face and gasp, "By golly!"

He turned to the Apples who had stood by politely smiling, and explained, "Old Nowlin Caldwell at the Pioneer Trust."

"Caldwell," the parrot muttered, walking around on Mr. Botkin's shoulder.

Tiny Huddlestun had been hugging his wife. He released her and cleared his throat. "You going to eat that bird at Thanksgiving, Botkin?"

Mr. Botkin ignored him and said, leaning his head over next to the parrot, "Looky there, Caldwell, that condor don't even move. He's scared to death of you. You get on up there and tear him to pieces."

The parrot jumped to the ground and ran to the magnolia tree. The tree had not done well in the Kansas climate and was a stunted little thing with ragged bark and weak limbs which were turning their tips toward the ground. The parrot hooked its way up the trunk with no trouble, but at the lowest fork paused to watch the condor.

Mr. Botkin waved a hand as big as a spade.

The parrot went on up, more slowly, however, stopping every few seconds to consider. Finally it crept out on the same limb and in a burst of confidence clamped its bright little claws into the wood beside the condor's talons. Then it imitated the black giant's posture and blinked down at the guests, which caused all of them except Harry Apple to break into laughter. The chain clinked. This alarmed the parrot; it whipped its head around and found itself looking into one of the condor's flat eyes.

"Eat 'im up!" Tiny shouted.

But the parrot fell out of the tree and ran toward the house, flailing its brilliant wings in the grass and screaming.

While his guests were still chuckling Mr. Botkin pointed far to the south where thunderheads were building up and said, "That's what the Andes look like."

The guests were all studying the familiar clouds when Fig Newton's sedan squeaked into the driveway. Mr. Botkin waved to Fig and his wife and went into the kitchen to get more drinks. To the colored girl Mrs. Botkin had hired for the evening he said, "Ever see a bird like that?"

The colored girl looked out the window immediately and answered with enthusiasm, "No, sir, Mr. Botkin!" But this did not seem to satisfy him so she added, "No sir, I sure never have!"

"You bet your sweet bottom you haven't." He was chipping some ice. "Because that's a condor."

"What's he eat?" she asked, but since he did not answer she felt it had been a silly question and turned her head away in shame.

Mr. Botkin shook up the drinks, bumped open the screen door with his stomach, and carried the tray into the yard. After he had greeted Fig and Laura Newton he said, "That little darky in the kitchen is scared to death of this bird. She wouldn't come near it for the world."

Fig answered, "Generally speaking, colored people are like that." He had a nervous habit of twitching his nose each time he finished speaking, which was the reason that hundreds of high-school students spoke of him as "Rabbit" Newton.

"Make him fly, J.D.," Laura said. "I want to admire his strength!" She was dressed in imitation gypsy clothes with a purple bandanna tied around her hips and a beauty mole painted on her temple. She did a little gypsy step across the yard, shaking her head so the gold earrings bounced against her cheeks. She lifted her glass high in the air. "Oh, make him fly!"

"Yes, do," added Mildred Apple. She had finished her drink quickly when she saw Laura's costume and now she stood on one leg so that her hips curved violently.

Mrs. Botkin, an egg-shaped little woman with wispy white hair that lay on her forehead like valentine lace, looked at her husband and started to say something. Then she puckered her lips and stopped.

Fig had been waiting for a pause. Now he drew attention to himself and said in measured tones, "Ordinarily the Negro avoids things he does not understand."

There was a polite silence until his nose twitched.

Then Mr. Botkin, whose cheeks had been growing redder with each drink, said, "You know what its name is?"

"What?" cried Suzie.

"Sambo," put in Fig, imitating a drawl. A laugh trembled at his lips, but nobody else laughed so he tasted his drink.

"Sherlock Holmes?" guessed Laura. Only Suzie tittered at this, and Laura glanced at her sourly.

Mr. Botkin finally said, "Well, I'm going to tell you—it's Samson."

He waited until the guests' laughter had died away and then he told them that the name of the female in Peru was Delilah. He joined the laughter this time, his belt creaking and the perspiration standing out all over his face. When the guests had quieted down to head-wagging chuckles he said, "Well, by golly, I'll stir this Samson up!" He picked some sticks off the grass and began tossing them into the magnolia. At last one hit the condor's chest, but the huge bird seemed to be asleep.

"The damn thing won't eat, either!" he exclaimed in a gust of irritation.

"Won't *eat?*" shrilled Suzie Huddlestun, standing in the circle of Tiny's arms. "Gee, what's it live on if it don't eat?"

Mr. Botkin ignored her.

Fig cleared his throat. Pointing upward he said, "If you will look at that branch, you'll see it is bent almost like a strung bow."

Mrs. Botkin suddenly turned to her husband and laid a hand on his sleeve. "Dear——"

Everybody looked at her in mild surprise, as always happened when she decided to say anything. She pressed a wisp of hair back into place and breathed, "Why don't you let the bird go?"

There was an uncomfortable pause, which Laura Newton broke by dancing around the back yard again. The candy-stripe skirt sailed around her bony goose legs. "How many want the condor to fly?" she asked, and thrusting her glass high in the air she cried, "Vote!"

Tiny Huddlestun had been squeezing his wife, but now he held his glass as high as possible without spilling the liquor and looked around with pleasure, knowing that nobody was tall enough to match the height of his ballot. Suzie's glass, clutched in her childlike hand, came just above his ear.

Mildred Apple sulkily lifted hers and so did Fig. Mr. Botkin had been watching with a curious sort of interest. His glass had gone up as soon as Laura proposed the vote. He looked at his wife, and she quickly lifted hers.

"Harry?" Laura cried.

Harry Apple continued drinking.

Mrs. Botkin murmured, "I think dinner's ready." She fluttered her hands about in weak desperation, but nobody looked at her.

Laura asked in a different tone, "Harry?" She was still holding the glass above her head.

Harry stood flat-footed and glared at the ground. A little drunkenly he swirled the ice in his glass.

After a few seconds of silence Mrs. Botkin coughed and started toward the porch; the guests filed after her. Mildred Apple was wearing white jersey. She got directly ahead of Laura and walked as if she were about to start a hula. Suzie and Tiny swung hands. Mr. Botkin, scowling, brought up the rear.

During salad Laura Newton talked mostly to the people on either side of Harry. Burgundy wine from France was served with the steaks, and while they were beginning on that the sun went down. Then one by one the guests stopped cutting their meat and looked through the porch screen.

Fig Newton twisted the Phi Beta Kappa key on his chain as he watched the condor lift first one foot and then the other from its branch. Tiny Huddlestun leaned his hambone elbows on the table and raised himself partly out of his chair in order to see over Mrs. Botkin's fluffy white head. Of the guests, only Harry Apple did not look; he stared at his wine glass, turning it slowly with his fingers on the stem. Mr. Botkin's eyes had narrowed in anticipation; he waited for the flight like an Occidental Buddha.

The condor's wings spread, brushing the leaves of other branches, and at the size of the bird Laura dropped her fork. Nobody picked it up, so it lay on the flagstones, its tines sending out a persistent hum.

The black condor lifted its feet again. This caused the chain which dangled from its neck to sway back and forth.

The dinner table was quiet. Only some June bugs fizzed angrily as they tried to get through the screens.

Mildred Apple said abruptly, "I'm cold." Nobody looked at her, so she went on in a sharp tone, "Why doesn't somebody switch off that fan? I tell you I'm cold. I won't sit here all night in a draft. I won't!"

Mr. Botkin did not turn his head, but growled, "Shut up."

Mildred was shocked, but she recovered quickly. "Don't you *dare* tell me to shut up! I won't stand for it! Do you hear?" Mr. Botkin paid no attention to her, so she turned petulantly to Harry; he was looking at his glass.

"Switch it off yourself," murmured Laura.

Mildred's eyes began to glitter. "I will not!"

"I'm sure nobody else is going to," Laura said in a dry voice.

Fig was getting ready to say something when Suzie Huddlestun gasped, "Oh!"

The condor took off so slowly that it did not seem real; it appeared only to be stretching, yet it was in the air. When its immense wings had spread and descended a second time, its talons rose above the top branches, curling into metal-hard globes. For an instant the condor hung in the purple sky like an insignia of some great war plane, then its head was jerked down. It made its one sound, dropped to the warm ground, and lay without moving.

Laura Newton observed sourly, "What a simple bird." She looked across her tack-hammer nose at Harry.

Tiny grinned. "Now's the time to cook that turkey for Thanksgiving, Botkin." He looked all around the table, but nobody chuckled, and his eyes came back to Suzie. She laughed.

Fig took a sip of water and then cleared his throat. "Fowl," he said, after frowning in thought, "are not overly intelligent."

Twilight was ending. The guests could not see the condor distinctly, but only what looked like a gunny sack under the dying magnolia. Much later, while they were arguing bitterly over their bridge scores, they heard the condor's chain clinking and soon a branch creaked.

IN A WHILE CROCODILE*

William Eastlake

WILLIAM EASTLAKE *was born in New York City in 1917 and was brought up in New York City. He served for four years in the army, mostly in the European theater, and spent a long time in Paris after the war. Upon returning to the United States, he bought a ranch in New Mexico, his present home. His stories have appeared in leading magazines, and he is the author of two novels,* GO IN BEAUTY (*1956*) *and* THE BRONC PEOPLE (*1958*).

The Prince came to the Indian country in '34 or '35. His title was no accident of blood nor fantasy nor imaginative appellation of some trader in the area. The title had been conferred on him by all, earned by him for doing something better than anybody in the world. He blew a horn. He blew the horn better than anybody in the world. His kingdom in the South had been overrun. But the vanquished were unvanquished. They left the South, New Orleans mostly, when their world fell, when corruption rode in on a slick, facile beat infecting everywhere. They left the South but they remembered, they endured, until they died in some hovel. They endured, their gold trumpet still there, their scepter still borne in the dust, and sometimes singing.

Like The Prince who wandered to Indian country to die in an unclaimed hogan, before death The Weaver, who lived hard by, could hear the quick jerk of sweet music

flow out over the quiet land, rhythmic and gay and sometimes sad.

The Prince had been on his way to Denver, he thought,
from Albuquerque, but he was on his way to nowhere. He
was one of the dispossessed, the unwanted, the wanderers
over the unsinging land.

"One of those who had secret dreams. He would not corrupt. One of those who knew who he was," the trader said.

"Yes, of course," the city man who had come so far said.
"I don't want any philosophy. I'm paid to get the facts. Did
he die of starvation?"

"Why?"

"We're making a TV of his life," the man said.

"Maybe."

"Maybe," the man who had come so far and dressed in
city clothes said. "Maybe. The editor won't settle for maybe.
I got to get the facts. I pay well."

"That may very well be," the trader said.

"All right," the city man said. "I could pay what it's
worth."

"Maybe he did," the trader said. "Maybe he died of starvation. What would that be worth?"

"I'm going to level with you," the city man said. He wore
a pork-pie hat with a narrow brim snapped down over a
harried, small-featured baby face. "I'm going to level with
you." The baby-faced city man stared around the trading
post at the goods and the Indians against the wall. "We'll
pay what it's worth if he died of starvation, for example,
and you gave it to us, we'll send you a check for what it's
worth."

"It's worth nothing," the trader said.

"All right," the city man said. "I'm going to level with
you. I want to succeed."

The trader was dressed like the Indians in jeans with a
big Stetson pushed back above a long and slanting face. Ab-
sent-minded in back of the long counter and leaning forward, he waited for the city man to continue his sentence.

"I want to succeed," the city man repeated. "That's all. I
want to succeed. Offering you money doesn't seem to work,
so I'm giving it to you straight. I want to succeed."

"Congratulations," the trader said, and he went back to trying to figure out how an adding machine works when it's busted.

"But I've failed," the city man said.

"Congratulations anyway," the trader said.

"Listen," the city man said. "I was going to bluff it through. This is my first assignment but I was going to act like an old vet, toss some money around and things like that. Did I hurt your feelings?"

The trader shook his head no.

"I'd like to get back to Albuquerque and call the wife and say look who succeeded."

The trader was mixed up with the adding machine.

"The company flew me out here in a luxurious Constellation Transcontinental Mainliner and they put me up at the Albuquerque Hilton, rented me a Drive-Ur-Self car, no questions asked. Today I'm dead. You sure I didn't hurt your feelings?"

The trader shook his head no.

"You mind if I talk to the Indians?"

"There's no law against talking to the Indians."

"Do they speak English?"

"They speak some of all foreign languages. Yes, they speak English," the trader said. "But don't tell them you want to succeed."

"Thank you," the city man said.

"And talk to the one on the end of the bench, the one with the turquoise ring. He was his friend."

"Did you know The Prince?" the city man said to the Indian without any niceties.

"Yes," the Indian said.

"Did he die of starvation?"

"Maybe," the Indian said.

"The name is Russell," the city man said.

"Congratulations," the Indian said.

"I've come a long way," the city man with the pork hat said, "to get the scoop on The Prince. And all I get is maybe. The editors won't think much of that."

"That's too bad," the Indian said.

"The Prince is a famous man now," the city man said.

"They're playing his music again. Everyone wants to know about him. I've come a long way to find out. You might say I represent a hundred million people." The city man paused and watched the Indian for the effect. "Yes, I might say it—"

"Say it," the Indian said.

The city man got up and walked back to the trader.

"I'm not getting anywhere. I'm dead," he said. "Just tell me, did The Prince come out here and starve to death? I can build from that."

"Work on that Indian you just talked to," the trader said. "They call him The Weaver. He's an artist. They were friends, The Prince and The Weaver. They were artists."

"Yes, but I can't build on that," the city man said. "The Prince must have come in your post."

"Yes."

"Did he have anything to trade?"

"No. Nothing."

"What do the Indians trade?"

"In season, wool. Most of the year their turquoise jewelry. I keep the jewelry until they redeem it."

"He had a trumpet," the city man said. "Why didn't he pawn that?"

"Because I wouldn't take it," the trader said.

"Why?"

"Because I figure with the Indians the jewelry is their wealth, their beauty. With his trumpet—"

"It was his life," Russell said.

"Maybe," the trader said.

"But you loaned him money without taking the trumpet?"

"Some."

"Listen, I'm doing all right," the city man said.

"You always will."

"I mean I'm getting somewhere," Russell said. "Now did he finally die of starvation?"

"Maybe."

"That's no help."

"He came in '34, I think, or '35."

"We know that."

"It was a rainy night. I don't know how he got here. Some

salesman, I guess, who went back to Albuquerque. He hung around the post till it closed. I couldn't see him standing out on that muddy road with no cars. It was dirt then."

"It still is."

"No. Gravel."

"Gravel?"

"I took him to a hogan. He was a tall, bent man with small alert eyes, graying hair under a wide preacher hat. Carried a brief case with socks, new shirt and such. He was a clean old man. In the other hand he carried the instrument. It was in a black case. I knew that's what it was because when I left him there, had only gotten away maybe fifty yards, it started."

"What was that?"

"This thing he had in the case. I just stood there in the rain, maybe fifteen minutes, listening, not knowing I was soaking wet. Then I realized I was surrounded by Indians listening, too."

"Then he did die of starvation?"

"No. Not then. That is, he became a thing with the Indians—his music anyway. They fed him for months, almost years, and then he had a house—a hogan—for the first time in maybe ten years. Then one night the Indians burned it down."

"Then he didn't die of starvation. He was—?"

"No," the trader said.

"But why burn his house down? Oh, of course," the city man said. "I see."

"What do you see?"

"He was a Negro."

"No," the trader said. "I mean, the Indians didn't know that, didn't care. They thought maybe he was some new kind of a white man. They'd never seen a black before and they thought he was some new kind of a white man."

"And you never told them?"

"What was there to tell them?"

"I see," the city man said. "I'll accept that. But what did he die of? You say he didn't get burned in the house."

"No. He played on that thing while the hogan burned,

helped them start the fire, then played on that thing while the house burned. Then they built him another."

"What was wrong with the one they burned?"

"A Navaho had died in it. Evil spirits. That's why it was vacant, why it was available for him to move in and why it was burned."

"I see. Then he didn't die there?"

"No," the trader said. "He became a thing with the Indians, played at all their festivals. He was their new kind of a white man. The first white man they had discovered who was black. They knew he was a white man because that's the way he acted, dressed, the language he spoke, but they knew he was a new kind of white man because he was black——"

"And made sweet music."

"Yes," the trader said.

"He was a genius. We know that now. A little late."

"A little late."

"But the Indians knew it because they, too, were primitive, could understand the clear, simple, honest note——"

"You reach," the trader said.

"Maybe we don't reach enough," the city man said. "Anyway, they'll take care of that in the office. But what happened then? When did he die of starvation?"

"Who said he died of starvation?" The trader moved down the counter.

"You didn't deny it," the city man said, following.

"I didn't say it either," the trader said.

"You mind if I try the Indian again?"

"Go ahead," the trader said.

When the city man sat down, the Indian called The Weaver got up and went over to the window. His round dark face was without expression.

I'm dead, the city man thought. You can't approach an Indian. You can't approach an Indian or a king or a genius. You can't get anything out of those kinds of people. They got a world all of their own. Why did they have to send me on this kind of assignment to the damn Indians? I'm dead. I'll never succeed. I wonder how The Prince got close to the Indians. I guess he had something they wanted to buy. Well, they won't buy money, I found that out. What did he have, what did The Prince have they wanted to buy? Art. That covers too much. That means nothing. That's awful vague. Better, it was his music that got around all languages, all customs, all cultures, all differences. What have I got? Nothing. I'm dead. I'll never get around them. I'll never succeed.

The city man thought a bit about all the money the company had put out to send him here to the end of the world.

I must have something. The wife says I've got something. The company says I've got something. Well, it certainly isn't brains and it certainly isn't good looks. Well, what else is there? Will power. That's what I got—will power. If God forgot you on everything else, you can always pick up plenty of will power around the place. And stick-to-itness and perseverance, keeping my nose clean and hitting the line hard. That's what I got. I got nothing.

The city man turned to the Indian next to him. "Yes I have. I've got patience, that's what I've got. Patience."

"Congratulations," the Indian said.

The Weaver who had gone over to the window to avoid the city man looked out over the far country and thought: How can you tell it to a man like that? How can you tell him about the man who knew who he was? How can you tell him about The Prince? Who but another artist would understand the loneliness and the separateness of wanting to belong but needing to belong on your own terms? Who would understand? Who would understand that he had to live at the end of the world because the end of the world was the only place the people understood? Now it's different, from what the city man says some people understand now all over the world and they want to make a picture. But who understood back there? No one understood back there. That's why people have to go to the end of the world because at times people don't understand in the middle of the world. Well, why not change? Why not come down to earth? I guess it's because the earth's not right. When the earth is right, people like The Prince will come down to it. How did he say it? "I will sweat it out." That's what The Prince said. That doesn't sound much like a prince talking but he said it, just that way. He said other things too, like,

"It's got to be clean, Jackson. It's got to be true, Jackson. You got to feel it, Jackson. It's got to be right or it's not worth it. Give me some skin, Indian." The city man wouldn't understand that but the city man wanted to know about starvation. Yes, The Prince starved to death but maybe not in the way a city man would understand. He wants the facts, but what good are the facts without feeling?

"Listen," the city man said. "I got a proposition." He had joined the Indian at the window and he pulled down on his narrow-brimmed oval hat. The Indian noticed that the city man had a green and red feather in the band from no bird that ever lived.

"My proposition is this." He reached into a green leather brief case and brought out strings of bright beads. He placed the bright beads along the counter, draping some of them so they hung down over the edge in all their gaudy glass brilliance. The city man stepped back away from them to admire them and envy the ones that were going to get them and wonder whether he could afford to part with them and furrowed his brow at the terrific expense of giving away this chief's ransom. When he had used up all these expressions and more, he said: "I give you these in return for the facts about The Prince."

The trader translated to some of the Indians that did not follow, and all the Indians mumbled among themselves for a long minute.

"I'm waiting," the city man said. "Is it a deal?"

The Indians ignored him, continuing to mumble.

"I've got to have a decision," the city man said.

The Indians stopped their conference now.

"Well, what is it?" the city man said.

"They want to know where you got them."

"It's a collection formerly owned by a man named Woolworth. That's who I got them from."

The Indians mumbled again among themselves before the trader announced their decision.

"They say for you to blow the whistle on that guy Woolworth. He sold you a pile of glass."

"Well, that's what I read," the city man said. "Indians will trade anything for beads."

"Manhattan Island," the trader said. "New York City maybe, but nothing they think worth while. Not for glass."

"All right, touché. You win," the city man said. "But I've got another proposition. My proposition is this," the city man said. "I've got patience. I'll stay around here for years if necessary, badgering you people. It's the ultimate weapon. I hope you people don't make me use it."

The Indians were silent.

The city man took off his hat, examined it, flicked his feather, and put it on again. Then he watched the Indians a long moment before he went over to the counter and came back with his green cowhide brief case from which he withdrew a book with the title *Hommes et Problèmes du Jazz.*

"I've got another proposition," the city man said. "You understand that?" He held up the book. "You understand what that says?"

"Yes." The Indian nodded from a hooded glance.

"Oh," the city man said. "You're not supposed to. I was going to translate what this man said about The Prince's music in exchange for your facts."

"I learned a few words at Indian boarding school," The Weaver said. "Not too much."

"Enough probably to correct me. No, I've got another proposition." The city man took off his hat and drummed on it, then he touched the bright feather of no bird with a preening motion. "Supposing I could bring The Prince back —back to life. Would you give me the facts then?"

"Yes," The Weaver said, knowing he was risking nothing. "I buried him."

"And I shall make him rise again," the city man said.

All the silent, imperturbable Indians who looked straight ahead into infinity, seeing and hearing nothing, all smiled now. All tapped their feet and moved their eyes, and all the squaws sitting under the counter shook their heads and winked and touched each other, looked at the city man and then away again, embarrassed.

"He shall rise again," the city man repeated.

"When?" The Weaver said.

"Now," the city man said. "Follow me."

All the Indians trooped out in file after the city man with

a feather. They followed him to the car while he got another case, a red one this time. Now he had a green and a red case in either arm and a green and red feather in his hat.

"Where did he live?" he said.

The Weaver pointed to the hogan under the purple brow of a near blue mesa. The Indians followed the bright feathered hat of the city man through the gray sage and stark greasewood, the beavertail and the cholla cactus. Now they went through the piñon, clumped and huddled, the line of file of the Indians swinging with the lead of the city man. Now they were in the flat country, the land of grama and sand and infinity and occasionally this.

"What's that?" the city man said.

"Arroyo," The Weaver said. All the Indians now stood at the edge of the canyon that separated them from the hogan.

"Impossible to cross here," The Weaver said. "We can cross five miles down."

"Then it might be too late," the city man said. "Might lose the tip."

"The what?"

"The audience," the city man said. "Follow me." He crossed his green and red cases in front of him and got down on his rear and slid down the bank. At the bottom he got up running. When he reached the opposite bank, he ran right up it, full at it, then he fell and scrambled, clawed his way to the top, the red and green cases finally flung over the top and the man following, slowly pulling himself up on a greasewood root.

"There," the man hollered loud across the arroyo. "Don't just watch. Follow me."

The Indians settled for just watching, standing there along the edge of the canyon. If he was going to produce The Prince, they could see from here.

"All right," the city man said, and he turned and walked toward the hogan, entered it and soon reappeared without the red and green cases and without The Prince.

"Now," the city man said and he kicked the hogan and out came The Prince, not in the flesh but as the Indians, the world, remembered him.

The Indians piled down the bank now and ran up the other side, not even scrambling but running upright on the impossible angle. Now they stood panting, listening, in front of the city man. The city man took off his hat, drummed on it and preened the feather.

"It's a phonograph," The Weaver said.

"But it's him, The Prince." The city man put on his hat. "He's come back," he said.

The Weaver listened now to the cool, solid truth of an alone trumpet blasting clearly and rich through the long Indian country.

"Yes," The Weaver said. "It's him."

A note hung now, wavered, and then blew loud and clear.

"Yes. Yes," The Weaver said.

"That's all a man is," the city man said. "What he does. This is what he did. This is The Prince. The Prince had patience."

"Yes," The Weaver said.

The music started to walk now and sing, led by the big trumpet then hushed, muted now before it shattered brilliantly like colored glass exploding in the sun.

"A man doesn't die now," the city man said. "Not some men. They can always come back when the world is ready, when the world is right. Patience."

The music shifted now to a weird, steady beat, the trumpet sliding in and out tenderly, then suddenly clean and brave.

"Some people don't die any more." The city man took out a pack of cigarettes and offered them around, but the Indians were listening. "If he has honor and patience, he can come back. He can live forever."

"Yes, yes," The Weaver said. "But listen."

"Do I win?" the city man said.

"Man is more powerful than death. Yes. Anything. But listen."

"Thank you," the city man said.

Late that night, back at the post, the city man gave The Weaver a large album of records marked "The Prince."

"Keep these," he said. "And the machine, too. You can bring him back any time you want."

"I didn't think there were any records of his."

"Not for a long time," the city man said. "But you only have to find some busted old ones in New Orleans, piece them together and make a million copies."

"Is that what they did?"

"Two million," the city man said.

"That's nice. That's very nice," The Weaver said. "Thank you."

"And now, did he die of starvation?" the city man said.

"Yes," The Weaver said. "It was a long hard winter that winter. There wasn't much a man, an Indian, could do against such a long, hard, cold winter. But he played against it and he was winning as far as we were concerned. But he couldn't stand it. With all the hunger he had seen in his own people, he had never seen anything like what happens to an Indian in a long, hard, cold winter. He sold his trumpet to a trader from Aztec, bought food from him and fed us all. Not our trader. Our trader was out of food, but he bought food from Aztec and fed us all. Then he starved to death. You understand how a man with food could starve to death?"

"I think so."

"Without his trumpet to blow. It was his life."

"Yes."

"Is that enough?"

"I think we can build with that."

"Will you do it honestly?"

"We will try to do it honestly."

The city man rose now, put on his pork hat and proffered his hand toward The Weaver. The Weaver looked at it and then up at the ceiling. The city man pulled down on his hat then held out his hand again.

"Give me some skin, Indian."

The Weaver took his hand slowly now, but he took it. They stared into each other's eyes a brief second, the pressure between their hands increasing.

"Patience. Now I go," the city man said, turning and walking to the door. Before he closed it he said, "See you later, alligator."

The Weaver went into the back room where the sheep

hides hung and where the Indians and the trader were listening to the record. He had a whole book of the records in his arms. He walked out of the room again, conscious of his riches. He went over to the window and raised the book to his lips and kissed The Prince. Then he watched out the window as the city man's car, running beneath the big mesa became a speck soon to disappear. Now he said, toward the speck and smiling—"In a while, crocodile."

AMONG THE DANGS

George P. Elliott

GEORGE P. ELLIOTT *was born in Indiana in 1918. His family subsequently moved to California and settled in Berkeley, where he obtained his M.A. in English from the University of California. He taught at St. Mary's College for several years and in 1954 traveled to London, Paris, and New York on a Ford Foundation Fellowship, studying poetic drama in contemporary staging. He has contributed to four O. Henry collections and won second prize in 1959. Mr. Elliott is now an assistant professor of English at Barnard College. His novel,* PARKTILDEN VILLAGE, *was published in 1958.* AMONG THE DANGS AND OTHER SHORT STORIES (1960) *is his first collection.*

I graduated from Sansom University in 1937 with honors in history, having intended to study law, but I had no money and nowhere to get any; by good fortune the anthropology department, which had just been given a grant for research, decided that I could do a job for them. In idle curiosity I had taken a course in anthro, to see what I would have been like had history not catapulted my people a couple of centuries ago up into civilization, but I had not been inclined to enlarge on the sketchy knowledge I got from that course; even yet, when I think about it, I feel like a fraud teaching anthropology. What chiefly recommended me to the department, aside from a friend, was a combination of three attributes: I was a good mimic, a long-distance runner, and black.

The Dangs live in a forested valley in the eastern foot-hills of the Andes. The only white man to report on them (and it was loosely gossiped, the only one to return from them alive), Sir Bewley Morehead in 1910, owed his escape to the consternation caused by Halley's Comet. Otherwise, he reported, they would certainly have sacrificed him as they were preparing to do; as it was, they killed the priest who was to have killed him, so he reported, and then burned the temple down. However, Dr. Sorish, our most distinguished Sansom man, in the early thirties developed an interest in the Dangs which led to my research grant; he had intro-duced a tribe of Amazonian head-shrinkers to the idea of planting grain instead of just harvesting it, as a result of which they had fattened, taken to drinking brew by the tub-ful, and elevated Sorish to the rank of new god; the last time he had descended among them—it is Sansom policy to fol-low through on any primitives we "do"—he had found his worshipers holding a couple of young Dang men captive and preparing them for ceremonies which would end only with the processing of their heads; his godhead gave him sufficient power to defer these ceremonies while he made half a dozen transcriptions of the men's conversations, and learned their language well enough to arouse the curiosity of his colleagues. The Dangs were handy with blowpipes; no one knew what pleased them; Halley's Comet wasn't due till 1984. But among the recordings Sorish brought back was a legend strangely chanted by one of these young men, whose very head perhaps you can buy today from a natural science company for $150 to $200, and the same youth had given Sorish a sufficient demonstration of the Dang pro-phetic trance, previously described by Morehead, to whet his appetite.

I was black, true; but, as Sorish pointed out, I looked as though I had been rolled in granite dust and the Dangs as though they had been rolled in brick dust; my hair was short and kinky, theirs long and straight; my lips were thick, theirs thin. It's like dressing a Greek up in reindeer skins, I said, and telling him to go pass himself off as a Lapp in Lapland. Maybe, they countered, but wouldn't he be more likely to get by than a naked Swahili with bones in his nose?

I was a long-distance runner, true; but as I pointed out with a good deal of feeling, I didn't know the principles of jungle escape and had no desire to learn them in, as they put it, the field. They would teach me to throw the javelin and wield a machete, they would teach me the elements of judo, and as for poisoned darts and sacrifices, they would insure my life—that is, my return within three years—for $5,000. I was a good mimic, true; I would be able to reproduce the Dang speech, and especially the trance of the Dang prophets, for the observation of science—"make a genuine contribution to learning." In the Sansom concept, the researcher's experience is an extricable part of anthropological study, and a good mimic provides the object for others' study as well as for his own. For doing this job I would be given round-trip transportation, an M.S. if I wrote a thesis on the material I gathered, the temporary insurance on my life, and $100 a month for the year I was expected to be gone. After I'd got them to throw in a fellowship of some sort for the following year, I agreed. It would pay for filling the forty cavities in my brothers' and sisters' teeth.

Dr. Sorish and I had to wait at the nearest outstation for a thunderstorm; when it finally blew up, I took off all my clothes, put on a breechcloth and leather apron, put a box of equipment on my head, and trotted after him; his people were holed in from the thunder, and we were in their settlement before they saw us. They were taller than I, they no doubt found my white teeth as disagreeable as I found their stained, filed teeth; but when Sorish spoke to me in English (telling me to pretend indifference to them while they sniffed me over), and in the accents of American acquaintances rather than in the harsh tones of divinity, their eyes filled with awe of me. Their taboo against touching Sorish extended itself to me; when a baby ran up to me and I lifted him up to play with him, his mother crawled to me on her knees beating her head on the ground till I freed him.

The next day was devoted chiefly to selecting the man to fulfill Sorish's formidable command to guide me to the edge of the Dang country. As for running—if those dogs could be got to the next Olympics, Ecuador would take every long-distance medal on the board. I knew that I had reached the brow of my valley only because I discovered that my guide, whom I had been lagging behind by forty or fifty feet, at a turn in the path had disappeared into thin brush.

Exhaustion allayed my terror; as I lay in the meager shade recuperating, I remembered to execute the advice I had given myself before coming: to act always as though I were not afraid. What would a brave man do next? Pay no attention to his aching feet, reconnoiter, and cautiously proceed. I climbed a jutting of rock and peered about. It was a wide, scrubby valley; on the banks of the river running down the valley I thought I saw a dozen mounds too regular for stones. I touched the handle of the hunting knife sheathed at my side and trotted down the trackless hill.

The village was deserted, but the huts, though miserable, were clean and in good repair. This meant, according to the movies I had seen, that hostile eyes were watching my every gesture. I had to keep moving in order to avoid trembling. The river was clear and not deep. The unmutilated corpse of a man floated by. I felt like taking the path downstream, but my hypothesized courage drove me up.

In half a mile I came upon a toothless old woman squatting by the track. She did not stop munching when I appeared, nor did she scream, or even stand up. I greeted her in Dang according to the formula I had learned, whereupon she cackled and smiled and nodded as gleefully as though I had just passed a test. She reminded me of my grandmother, rolled in brick dust, minus a corncob pipe between her gums. Presently I heard voices ahead of me. I saw five women carrying branches and walking very slowly. I lurked behind them until they came to a small village, and watched from a bush while they set to work. They stripped the leaves off, carefully did something to them with their fingers, and then dropped them in small-throated pots. Children scrabbled around, and once a couple of them ran up and suckled at one of the women. There remained about an hour till sunset. I prowled, undetected. The women stood, like fashion models, with pelvis abnormally rocked forward; they were wiry, without fat even on their breasts; not even their thighs and hips afforded clean sweeping lines undisturbed by bunched muscles. I saw no men. Before I began to get into a stew about the right tack to take, I stepped into the clearing and uttered their word of salutation. If a strange man should walk in your wife's front door and say, "How do you do," in an accent she did not recognize, simultaneously poking his middle finger at her, her consternation would be something like that of those Dang women; for unthinkingly I had nodded my head when speaking and turned my palm out, as one does in the United States; to them this was a gesture of intimacy, signifying desire. They disappeared into huts, clutching children. I went to the central clearing and sat with my back to a log, knowing they would scrutinize me. I wondered where the men were. I could think of no excuse for having my knife in my hand except to clean my toenails. So astonishing an act was unknown to the Dangs; the women and children gradually approached in silence, watching; I cleaned my fingernails. I said the word for food; no one reacted, but presently a little girl ran up to me holding a fruit in both hands. I took it, snibbed her nose between my fingers, and with a pat on the bottom sent her back to her mother. Upon this there were hostile glances, audible intakes of breath, and a huddling about the baby, who did not understand any more than I did why she was being consoled. While I ate the fruit I determined to leave the next move up to them. I sheathed my knife and squatted on my hunkers, waiting. To disguise my nervousness I fixed my eyes on the ground between my feet and grasped my ankles from behind in such a way— right ankle with right hand, left with left—as to expose the inner sides of my forearms. Now this was, as I later learned, pretty close to the initial posture taken for the prophetic trance; also I had a blue flower tattooed on my inner right arm and a blue serpent on my left (from the summer I'd gone to sea), the like of which had never been seen in this place. At sundown I heard the men approach; they were anything but stealthy about it; I had the greatest difficulty in suppressing the shivers. In simple fear of showing my fear, I did not look up when the men gathered around; I could understand just enough of what the women were telling the men to realize that they were afraid of me. Even

though I was pelted with pebbles and twigs till I was angry,
I still did not respond, because I could not think what to do.
But then something clammy was plopped onto my back
from above, and I instantly leaped up as high as I could,
howling. Their spears were poised before I landed. "Strangers!" I cried, my speech all composed. "Far kinsmen! I
come from the mountains!" I had intended to say *from the
river lands,* but the excitement tangled my tongue. Their
faces remained expressionless, but no spears drove at me,
and then, to be doing something, I shoved the guts under the
log with my feet.

And saved my life by doing so. That I seemed to have
taken, though awkwardly, the prophetic squat; that I bore
visible marvels on my arm; that I was fearless and innerly
absorbed; that I came from the mountains (their enemies
lived toward the river lands); that I wore their apron and
spoke their language, albeit poorly; all these disposed them
to wonder at this mysterious outlander. Even so, they might
very well have captured me, marvelous though I was, possibly useful to them, dangerous to antagonize, had I not been
unmaimed, which meant that I was supernaturally guarded.
Finally, my scrutinizing the fish guts, daring to smile as I
did so, could mean only that I was prophetic; my leap when
they had been dropped onto my back was prodigious, "far
higher than a man's head," and my howl had been vatic;
and my deliberately kicking the guts aside, though an in-
scrutable act, demonstrated at least that I could touch the
entrails of an eel and live.

So I was acceptable to the Dangs. The trouble was, they
had no ceremony for naturalizing me. For them, every act
had a significance, and here they were faced with a reverse
problem, for which nothing had prepared them. They could
not possibly just assimilate me without marking the event
with an act (that is, a ceremony) signifying my entrance.
For them, nothing *just happened,* certainly nothing men did.
Meanwhile, I was kept in a sort of quarantine while they
deliberated. I did not, to be sure, understand why I was being
isolated in a hut by myself, never spoken to except efficiently, watched but not restrained. I swam, slept, scratched,
watched, swatted, ate; I was not really alarmed, because

they had not restrained me forcibly and they gave me food.
I began making friends with some of the small children,
especially while swimming, and there were two girls of fifteen or so who found me terribly funny. I wished I had
some magic, but I knew only card tricks. The sixth day,
swimming, I thought I was being enticed around a point in
the river by the two girls, but when I began to chase them
they threw good-sized stones at me, missing me only because
they were such poor shots. A corpse floated by; when they
saw it, they immediately placed the sole of their right foot
on the side of their left knee and stood thus on one leg till
the corpse floated out of sight; I followed the girls' example,
teetering. I gathered from what they said that some illness
was devastating their people; I hoped it was one of the dis-
eases I had been inoculated against. The girls' mothers
found them talking with me and cuffed them away. I did
not see them for two days, but the night of my eighth day
there, the bolder of them hissed me awake at the door of my
hut in a way that meant "no danger." I recognized her when
she giggled. I was not sure what their customs were in these
matters, but while I was deliberating what my course of wisdom should be, she crawled into the hut and lay on the mat
beside me. She liked me; she was utterly devoid of reticence; I was twenty-one and far from home; even a scabby
little knotty-legged fashion model is hard to resist under such
circumstances. I learned, before falling asleep, that there
was a three-way debate among the men over what to do with
me: initiate me according to the prophet-initiation rites, invent a new ceremony, or sacrifice me as propitiation to the
disease among them, as was usually done with captives.
Each had its advantages and drawbacks; even the news that
some of the Dangs wanted to sacrifice me did not excite me
as it would have done a week before; now, I half-sympa-
thized with their trouble. I was awakened at dawn by the
outraged howl of a man at my door; he was the girl's father; the village men gathered, and the girl cowered behind
me. They talked for hours outside my hut, men arrived from
other villages up and down the valley, and finally they
agreed upon a solution to all the problems: they proposed
that I should be made one of the tribe by marriage on the

same night that I should be initiated into the rites of
prophecy.

The new-rite men were satisfied by this arrangement because of the novelty of having a man married and initiated
on the same day; but the sacrifice party was visibly unmol-
lified. Noticing this and reflecting that the proposed arrangement would permit me to do all my trance-research under
optimum conditions and to accumulate a great deal of sexual data as well, I agreed to it. I would, of course, only be
going through the forms of marriage, not meaning them;
as for the girl, I took this vow to myself (meaning without
ceremony): "So long as I am a Dang, I shall be formally
a correct husband to her." More's a pity.

Fortunately a youth down the valley already had been
chosen as a novice (at least a third of the Dang men enter
the novitiate at one time or another, though few made the
grade), so that I had not only a companion during the four-
month preparation for the vatic rites, but also a control upon
whom I might check my experience of the stages of the
novitiate. My mimetic powers stood me in good stead; I was
presumed to have a special prophetic gift, and my readiness
at assuming the proper stances and properly performing the
ritual acts confirmed the Dangs' impressions of my gift; but
also, since I was required to proceed no faster than the ritual pace in my learning, I had plenty of leisure in which
to observe in the smallest detail what I did and how I, and
to some extent my fellow novice, felt. If I had not had this
self-observing to relieve the tedium, I think I should have
been unable to get through that mindless holding of the same
position hour after hour, that mindless repeating of the same
act day after day. The Dangs *appear* to be bored much of
the time, and my early experience with them was certainly
that of ennui, though never again ennui so acute as during
this novitiate; yet I doubt that it would be accurate to say
they actually are bored, and I am sure that the other novice
was not, as a fisherman waiting hours for a strike cannot
be said to be bored. The Dangs do not sate themselves on
food; the experience which they consider most worth seeking, vision, is one which cannot glut either the prophet or
his auditors; they cannot imagine an alternative to living as

they live, or, more instantly, to preparing a novice as I was being prepared. The people endure; the prophets, as I have learned, wait for the time to come again, and though they are bitten and stung by ten thousand fears, about this they have no anxiety—the time will surely come again. Boredom implies either satiety, and they were poor and not interested in enriching themselves, or the frustration of impulse, and they were without alternatives and diversions; and that intense boredom which is really a controlled anxiety they are protected from by never doubting the worth of their vision or their power to achieve it.

I was assisted through these difficult months, during which I was supposed to do nothing but train, by Redadu, my betrothed. As a novice, I was strictly to abstain from sexual intercourse; but as betrothed, we were supposed to make sure before marriage that we satisfied one another, for adultery by either husband or wife was punishable by maiming. Naturally, the theologians were much exercised by this impasse of mine, but while they were arguing, Redadu and I took the obvious course—we met more or less surreptitiously. Since my vatic training could not take place between sunrise and sundown, I assumed that we could meet in the afternoon when I woke up, but when I began making plans to this effect, I discovered that she did not know what I was talking about. It makes as much sense in Dang to say, "Let's blow poisoned darts at the loss of the moon," as to say "Let's make love in broad daylight." Redadu dissolved in giggles at the absurdity. What to do? She found us a cave. Everyone must have known what I was up to, but we were respectable (the Dang term for it was harsher, *deed-liar*), so we were never disturbed. Redadu's friends would not believe her stories of my luxurious love ways, expecially my biting with lips instead of teeth. At one time or another she sent four of them to the cave for me to demonstrate my prowess upon; I was glad that none of them pleased me as much as she did, for I was beginning to be fond of her. My son has told me that lip-biting has become, if not a customary, at any rate a possible caress.

As the night of the double rite approached, a night of full moon, a new conflict became evident: the marriage must be consummated exactly at sundown, but the initiation must begin at moonrise, less than two hours later. For some reason that was not clear to me, preparing for the initiation would incapacitate me for the consummation. I refrained from pointing out that it was only technically that this marriage needed consummating and even from asking why I would not be able to do it. The solution, which displeased everyone, was to defer the rites for three nights, when the moon, though no longer perfectly round, would rise sufficiently late so that I would, by hurrying, be able to perform both of my functions. Redadu's father, who had been of the sacrifice party, waived ahead of time his claim against me: legally he was entitled to annul the marriage if I should leave the marriage hut during the bridal night. And although I in turn could legally annul it if she left the hut, I waived my claim as well so that she might attend my initiation.

The wedding consisted chiefly of our being bound back to back by the elbows and being sung to and danced about all day. At sunset, we were bound face to face by the elbows (most awkward) and sent into our hut. Outside the two mothers waited—a high prophet's wife took the place of my mother (my Methodist mother!)—until our orgastic cries indicated that the marriage had been consummated, and then came in to sever our bonds and bring us the bridal foods of cold stewed eel and parched seeds. We fed each other bite for bite and gave the scraps to our mothers, who by the formula with which they thanked us pronounced themselves satisfied with us; and then a falsetto voice called to me to hurry to the altar. A man in the mask of a moon slave was standing outside my hut on his left leg with the right foot against his left knee, and he continued to shake his rattle after me so long as I was within earshot of him.

The men were masked. Their voices were all disguised. I wondered whether I was supposed to speak in an altered voice; I knew every stance and gesture I was to make, but nothing of what I was to say; yet surely a prophet must employ words. I had seen some of the masks before—being repaired, being carried from one place to another—but now, faced with them alive in the failing twilight, I was impressed by them in no scientific or aesthetic way: they terrified and

exalted me. I wondered if I would be given a mask. I began
trying to identify such men as I could by their scars and
missing fingers and crooked arms, and noticed to my distress
that they, too, were all standing one-legged in my presence.
But I had thought that was the stance to be assumed in the
presence of the dead! We were at the entrance of The Cleft,
a dead-end ravine in one of the cliffs along the valley; my
fellow novice and I were each given a gourdful of some vile-
tasting drink and were then taken up to the end of The
Cleft, instructed to assume the first position, and left alone.
We squatted as I had been squatting by the log on my first
day, except that my head was cocked in a certain way and
my hands clasped my ankles from the front. The excite-
ments of the day seemed to have addled my wits; I could
concentrate on nothing, and lost my impulse to observe
coolly what was going on; I kept humming *St. James Infirmary* to myself, and though at first I had been thinking the
words, after a while I realized that I had nothing but the
tune left in my head. At moonrise we were brought another
gourd of the liquor to drink, and were then taken to the
mouth of The Cleft again. I did, easily, whatever I was told.
The last thing I remember seeing before taking the second
position was the semicircle of masked men facing us and
chanting, and behind them the women and children—all
standing on the left leg. I lay on my back with my left ankle
on my right and my hands crossed over my navel, rolled my
eyeballs up and held the lids open without blinking, and
breathed the necessary rhythm, each breath taking four
heartbeats, with an interval of ten heartbeats between each
exhalation and the next inspiration. Then the drug took
over. At dawn when a called command awoke me, I found
myself on an islet in the river dancing with my companion
a leaping dance I had not known or even seen before, and
brandishing over my head a magnificent red and blue, new-
made mask of my own. The shores of the river were lined
with people chanting as we leaped, and all of them were
either sitting or else standing on both feet. If we had been
dead the night before, we were alive now. Redadu told me,
after I had slept and returned to myself, that my vision was
splendid, but of course she was no more permitted to tell

me what I had said than I was able to remember it. The
Dangs' sense of rhythm is as subtle as their ear for melody
is monotonous, and for weeks I kept hearing rhythmic
snatches of *St. James Infirmary* scratched on calabash
drums and tapped on blocks.

Sorish honored me by rewriting my master's thesis and
adding my name as co-author of the resultant essay, which
he published in JAFA (*The Journal of American Field
Anthropology*): "Techniques of Vatic Hallucinosis Among
the Dangs." And the twenty-minute movie I made of a
streamlined performance of the rites is still widely used as
an audio-visual aid.

By 1939 when I had been cured of the skin disease I had
brought back with me and had finished the work for my
M.S., I still had no money. I had been working as the assistant curator of the university's Pre-Columbian Museum
and had developed a powerful aversion of devoting my life
to cataloguing, displaying, restoring, warehousing. But my
chances of getting a research job, slight enough with a Ph.D.,
were nil with only an M.S. The girl I was going with said
(I had not told her about Redadu) that if we married she
would work as a nurse to support me while I went through
law school; I was tempted by the opportunity to fulfill my
original ambition, and probably I would have done it had
she not pressed too hard; she wanted me to leave anthropology, she wanted me to become a lawyer, she wanted to
support me, but what she did not want was to make my
intentions, whatever those might be, her own. Therefore,
when a new grant gave me the chance to return to the
Dangs, I gladly seized it; not only would I be asserting myself against Velma, but also I would be paid for doing research for my Ph.D. thesis; besides I was curious to see the
Congo-Maryland-Dang bastard I had left in Redadu's belly.
My assignment was to make a general cultural survey but
especially to discover the *content* of the vatic experience—
not just the technique, not even the hallucinations and
stories, but the qualities of the experience itself. The former
would get me a routine degree, but the latter would, if I did
it, make me a name and get me a job. After much consulta-

tion I decided against taking with me any form of magic, including medicine; the antibiotics had not been invented yet, and even if there had been a simple way to eradicate the fever endemic among the Dangs, my advisors persuaded me that it would be an error to introduce it since the Dangs were barely able to procure food for themselves as it was and since they might worship me for doing it, thereby making it impossible for me to do my research with the proper empathy. I arrived the second time provided only with my knife (which for some reason had not much impressed these stone-agers), some salve to soothe my sores, and the knowledge of how to preserve fish against a lean season, innovation enough but not one likely to divinize me.

I was only slightly worried how I would be received on my return, because of the circumstances under which I had disappeared. I had become a fairly decent hunter—the women gathered grain and fruit—and I had learned to respect the Dangs' tracking abilities enough to have been nervous about getting away safely. While hunting with a companion in the hills south of our valley, I had run into a couple of hunters from an enemy tribe which seldom foraged so far north as this. They probably were as surprised as I and probably would have been glad to leave me unmolested; however, outnumbered and not knowing how many more were with them, I whooped for my companion; one of the hunters in turn, not knowing how many were with me, threw his spear at me. I side-stepped it and reached for my darts and, though I was not very accurate with a blowpipe, I hit him in the thigh: within a minute he was writhing on the ground, for in my haste I had blown a venomous dart at him, and my comrade took his comrade prisoner by surprise. As soon as the man I had hit was dead, I withdrew my dart and cut off his ear for trophy, and we returned with our captive. He told our war chief in sign language that the young man I had killed was the son and heir of their king and that my having mutilated him meant their tribe would surely seek to avenge his death. The next morning a Dang search party was sent out to recover the body so that it might be destroyed and trouble averted, but it had disappeared; war threatened. The day after that I chose to vanish; they

would not think of looking for me in the direction of
Sorish's tribe, north, but would assume that I had been captured by the southern tribe in retribution for their prince's
death. My concern now, two years later, was how to account for not having been maimed or executed; the least I
could do was to cut off a finger, but when it came to the
point, I could not even bring myself to have a surgeon do it,
much less do it myself; I had adequate lies prepared for
their other questions, but about this I was a bit nervous.
I got there at sundown.

Spying, I did not see Redadu about the village. On the
chance, I slipped into our hut when no one was looking; she
was there, playing with our child. He was as cute a little
preliterate as you ever saw suck a thumb, and it made me
chuckle to think he would never be literate either. Redadu's
screams when she saw me fetched the women, but when
they heard a man's voice they could not intrude. In her joy
she lacerated me with her fingernails (the furrows across
my shoulder festered for a long time); I could do no less
than to bit her arm till she bled; the primal scene we treated
our son to presumably scared him for life, though I must
say the scars haven't showed up yet. I can't deny I was glad
to see her, too; for, though I felt for her none of the tender,
complex emotions I had been feeling for Velma, emotions
which I more or less identified as being love, yet I was so
secure with her sexually, I knew so well what to do and
what to expect from her in every important matter, that it
was an enormous, if cool, comfort to me to be with her.
Comfort is a dangerous approximation to what I mean;
being with her provided, as it were, the condition for doing;
in Sansom I did not consider her my wife, and here I did not
recognize in myself the American emotions of love or marriage; yet it seemed to me right to be with her; and her son
was no bastard. *Cool:* I cannot guarantee that mine was the
usual Dang emotion, for it is hard for the cool to gauge the
warmth of others; in my reports I have denied any personal
experience of love among the Dangs for this reason. When
we emerged from the hut, there was amazement and relief
among the women, amazement that I had returned and relief that it had not been one of their husbands pleasuring

the widow. But the men were more ambiguously pleased to
see me: Redadu's scratches were not enough, and they
doubted my story, that the enemy king had made me his
personal slave who must be bodily perfect. They wanted
to hear me prophesy.

Redadu told me afterward, hiding her face in my arms
for fear of being judged insolent, that I surpassed myself
that night, that only the three high prophets had ever been
so inspired. And it was true that even the men most hostile
to me did not oppose my re-entry into the tribe after they
had heard me prophesy; they could have swallowed the
story I fed them about my two-year absence only because
they believed in me the prophet. Dangs make no separation
between fact and fantasy, apparent reality and visionary
reality, truth and beauty. I once saw a young would-be
prophet shudder away from a stick on the ground, saying it
was a snake, and none of the others, except the impressiona-
ble, was afraid of the stick; it was said of him that he was a
beginner. Another time I saw a prophet scatter the whole
congregation, myself included, when he screamed at the
sight of a beast which he called a cougar; when sober dawn
found the speared creature to be a cur it was said of the
prophet that he was strong, and he was honored with an
epithet, Cougar-Dog. My prophesying the first night of my
return must have been of this caliber, although to my disappointment I was given no epithet, not even the nickname I'd
sometimes heard before, Bush-Hair. I knew there was a
third kind of prophesying, the highest, performed only on
the most important occasions in the Cave-Temple where I
had never been. No such occasion had presented itself during my stay before, and when I asked one of the other
prophets about that ceremony, he put me off with the term
Wind-Haired Child of the Sun; from another, I learned that
the name of this sort of prophesying was Stone is Stone. It
would be indiscreet for me to press further; obviously, I was
going to have to stay until I could make sense of these
mysteries.

There was a war party that wanted my support; my slav-
ery was presumed to have given me knowledge which would
make a raid highly successful; because of this, as well as

because I had instigated the conflict by killing the king's son,
I would be made chief of the raiding party. I was uneasy
about the fever, which had got rather worse among them
during the previous two years, without risking my neck
against savages who were said always to eat a portion of
their slain enemy's liver raw and whose habitat I knew nothing of. I persuaded the Dangs, therefore, that they should
not consider attacking before the rains came, because their
enemies were now the stronger, having on their side their
protector, the run. They listened to me, and waited. Fortunately, it was a long dry season, during which I had time to
find a salt deposit and to teach a few women the rudiments
of drying and salting fish; and during the first week of the
rains every night there were showers of falling stars to be
seen in the sky; to defend against them absorbed all energies for weeks, including the warriors'. Even so, even
though I was a prophet, a journeyman prophet as it were,
I was never in on these rites in the Cave-Temple. I dared
not ask many questions. Sir Bewley Morehead had described a temple, surrounded by seventy-five poles, each
topped by a human head; he could hardly have failed to
mention that it was in a cave; yet he made no such mention,
and I knew of no temple like the one he had described. At
a time of rains and peace in the sky, the war party would
importune me. I did not know what to do but wait.

The rains became violent, swamping the villages in the
lower valley and destroying a number of huts; yet the rainy
season ended abruptly two months before its usual time.
Preparations for war had already begun, and day by day
as the sun's strength increased and the earth dried, the war
party became more impatient; and the preparations in themselves lulled my objections to the raid, even to my leading
the raid, and stimulated my desire to make war. But the
whole project was canceled a couple of days before we were
to attack because of the sudden fever of one of the high
prophets; the day after he came down, five others of the
tribe fell sick, among them Redadu. There was nothing I
could do but sit by her, fanning her and sponging her till
she died. Her next older sister took our son to rear. I would
allow no one to prepare her body but myself, though her

mother was supposed to help; I washed it with the proper
infusions of herbs, and at dawn, in the presence of her clan,
I laid her body on the river; thank heaven it floated, or I
should have had to spend another night preparing it further.
I felt like killing someone now; I recklessly called for war
now, even though the high prophet had not yet died; I was
restrained, not without admiration. I went up into the eastern hills by myself, and returned after a week bearing the
hide of a cougar; I had left the head and claws on my
trophy, in a way the Dangs had never seen; when I put the
skin on in play by daylight and bounded and snarled, only
the bravest did not run in terror. They called me Cougar-
Man. And Redadu's younger sister came to sleep with me;
I did not want her, but she so stubbornly refused to be expelled that I kept her for the night, for the next night, for the
next; it was not improper. The high prophet did not die, but
lay comatose most of the time. The Dangs have ten master
prophets, of whom the specially gifted, whether one or all
ten, usually two or three, are high prophets. Fifteen days
after Redadu had died, well into the abnormal dry spell,
nearly all the large fish seemed to disappear from the river.
A sacrifice was necessary. It was only because the old man
was so sick that a high prophet was used for this occasion;
otherwise a captive or a woman would have served the purpose. A new master prophet must replace him, to keep the
complement up to ten. I was chosen.

The exultation I felt when I learned that the master
prophets had co-opted me among them was by no means
cool and anthropological, for now that I had got what I
had come to get, I no longer wanted it for Sansom reasons.
If the conditions of my being elevated, I said to myself,
*are the suffering of the people, Redadu's death, and the
sacrifice of an old man, then I must make myself worthy
of the great price. Worthy:* a value word, not a scientific
one. Of course, my emotions were not the simple pride and
fear of a Dang, either. I can't say just what sort they were,
but I knew they were fierce.

At sundown all the Dangs of all the clans were assembled
about the entrance to The Cleft. All the prophets, masked,
emerged from The Cleft and began the dance in a great

wheel. Within this wheel, rotating against it, was the smaller
wheel of the nine ablebodied master prophets. At the
center, facing the point at which the full moon would
rise, I hopped on one leg, then the other. I had been given
none of the vatic liquor, that brew which the women,
when I had first come among the Dangs, had been preparing in the small-throated pots; and I hoped I should be
able to remain conscious throughout the rites. However, at
moonrise a moon slave brought me a gourdful to drink without ceasing to dance. I managed to allow a great deal of
it to spill unnoticed down with the sweat streaming off me,
so that later I was able to remember what had happened,
right up to the prophesying itself. The dance continued for
at least two more hours; then the drums suddenly stopped,
and the prophets began to file up The Cleft, me last, dancing after the high prophets. We danced into an opening in
the cliff from which a disguising stone had been rolled away;
the people were not allowed to follow us. We entered a
great cavern illuminated by ten smoking torches. We circled
a palisade of stakes; the only sound was the shuffle of our
feet and the snorts of our breathing. There were seventy-
five stakes, as Morehead had seen, but only on twenty-eight
of them were heads impaled, the last few with flesh on them
still, not yet skulls cleaned of all but hair. In the center
was a huge stone under the middle of which a now dry
steam had tunneled a narrow passage; on one side of The
Stone, above the passage, were two breast-like protuberances, one of which had a recognizable nipple suitably placed.
Presently the dancing file reversed so that I was the leader.
I had not been taught what to do; I wove the file through
the round of stakes and spiraled inward till we were three
deep about The Stone; I straddled the channel, raised my
hands till they were touching the breasts, and gave a great
cry. I was, for reasons I do not understand, shuddering all
over; though I was conscious and though I had not been
instructed, I was not worried that I might do the wrong
thing next; when I touched The Stone, a dread shook me
without affecting my exaltation. Two moon slaves seized my
arms, took off my mask, and wrapped and bound me, arms
at my sides and legs pressed together, in a deer hide, and

then laid me on my back in the channel under The Stone with my head only half out, so that I was staring up the sheer side of rock. The dancers continued, though the master prophets had disappeared. My excitement; the new, unused position; being mummied tightly; the weakness of the drug; my will to observe; all kept me conscious for a long time. Gradually, however, my eyes began to roll up into my head, I strained less powerfully against the thongs that bound me, and I felt my breathing approach the vatic rhythm. At this point, I seemed to break out in a new sweat, on my forehead, my throat, in my hair; I could hear a splash; groggily I licked my chin; an odd taste; I wondered if I was bleeding. Of course—it was the blood of the sick old high prophet, who had just been sacrificed on The Stone above me; well, his blood would give me strength; wondering remotely whether his fever could be transmitted by drinking his blood, I entered the trance. At dawn I emerged into consciousness while I was still prophesying; I was on a ledge in the valley above all the people, in my mask again. I listened to myself finish the story I was telling. "He was afraid. A third time a man said to him: 'You are a friend of the most high prophet.' He answered: 'Not me. I do not know that man they are sacrificing.' Then he went into a dark corner; he put his hands over his face all day." When I came to the Resurrection, a sigh blew across the people.

It was the best story they had ever heard. Of course. But I was not really a Christian. For several weeks I fretted over my confusion, this new, unsuspected confusion. I was miserable without Redadu; I let her sister substitute only until I had been elevated, and then I cast her off, promising her, however, that she and only she might wear an anklet made of my teeth when I should die. Now that I was a master prophet I could not be a warrior; I had had enough fishing, hunting, tedious ceremonies. Hunger from the shortage of fish drove the hunters high into the foothills; there was not enough; they ate my preserved fish, suspiciously, but they ate them. When I left, it was not famine that I was escaping, but my confusion; I was fleeing

to the classrooms and the cool museums where I should be
neither a leftover Christian nor a mimic of a Dang.

My academic peace lasted for just two years, during which
time I wrote five articles on my researches, publishing them
this time under my name only, did some of the work for
my doctorate, and married Velma. Then came World War
II, in which my right hand was severed above the wrist;
I was provided with an artificial hand and given enough
money so that I could afford to finish my degree in style.
We had two daughters, and I was given a job at Sansom.
There was no longer a question of my returning to the
Dangs. I would become a settled anthropologist, teach, and
quarrel with my colleagues in the learned journals. But by
the time the Korean War came along and robbed us of a
lot of our students, my situation at the university had
changed considerably. Few of my theoretical and dispu-
tatious articles were printed in the journals, and I hated
writing them; I was not given tenure, and there were some
hints to the effect that I was considered a one-shot man, a
flash-in-the-pan; Velma nagged for more money and higher
rank. My only recourse was further research, and when I
thought of starting all over again with some other tribe—in
Northern Australia, along the Zambesi; on an African island—my heart sank. The gossip was not far from the mark
—I was not one hundred per cent the scientist and never
would be. I had just enough reputation and influential rec-
ommendations to be awarded a Guggenheim Fellowship;
supplemented by a travel grant from the university, this
made it possible for me to leave my family comfortably
provided for and to return to the Dangs.

A former student now in Standard Oil in Venezuela arranged to have me parachuted among them from an S.O.
plane; there was the real danger that they would kill me
before they recognized me, but if I arrived in a less spec-
tacular fashion I was pretty sure they would sacrifice me
for their safety's sake. This time, being middle-aged, I left
my hunting knife and brought instead at my belt a pouch
filled with penicillin and salves. I had a hard time identify-
ing the valley from the air; it took me so long that it was

sunset before I jumped; I knew how the Dangs were enraged
by airplanes, especially by the winking lights of the night
fliers, and I knew they would come for me if they saw me
billowing down. Fortunately, I landed in the river, for
though I was nearly drowned before I disentangled my parachute harness, I was also out of range of the blowpipes.
I finally identified myself to the warriors brandishing their
spears along the shore; they had not quite dared to swim
out after so prodigious a being; even after they knew
who I said I was and allowed me to swim ashore, they saw
me less as myself than as a supernatural being. I was recognized by newcomers who had not seen me so closely
swinging from the parachute (the cloud); on the spot my
epithet became, as it remained, Sky-Cougar. Even so, no
one dared touch me till the high prophet—there was only
one now—had arrived and talked with me; my artificial hand
seemed to him an extension of the snake tattooed onto my
skin; he would not touch it; I suddenly struck him with
it and pinched his arm. "Pinchers," I said, using the word
for a crayfish claw, and he laughed. He said there was no
way of telling whether I was what I seemed to be until he
had heard me prophesy; if I prophesied as I had done before I had disappeared, I must be what I seemed to be;
meanwhile, for three weeks till full moon, I was to be kept
in the hut for captives.

At first I was furious at being imprisoned, and when
mothers brought their children from miles around to peek
through the stakes at the man with the snake-hand, I snarled
or sulked like a caged wolf. But I became conscious that
a youth, squatting in a quiet place, had been watching me
for hours, and demanded of him who he was. He said, "I
am your son," but he did not treat me as his father. To
be sure, he could not have remembered what I looked like;
my very identity was doubted; even if I were myself, I was
legendary, a stranger who had become a Dang and had
been held by an enemy as captive slave for two years and
then become a master prophet with the most wonderful
vision anyone knew. Yet he came to me every day and
answered all the questions I put to him. It was, I believe,
my artificial hand that finally kept him aloof from me; no

amount of acquaintance could accustom him to that. By the end of the first week it was clear to me that if I wanted to survive—not to be accepted as I once had been, just to survive—I would have to prophesy the Passion again. And how could I determine what I would say when under the vatic drug? I imagined a dozen schemes for substituting colored water for the drug; but I would need an accomplice for that and I knew that not even my own son would serve in so forbidden an act.

I called for the high prophet. I announced to him in tones all the more arrogant because of my trepidations that I would prophesy without the vatic liquor. His response to my announcement astonished me: he fell upon his knees, bowed his head, and rubbed dust into his hair. He was the most powerful man among the Dangs, except in time of war when the war chief took over, and furthermore he was an old man of personal dignity; yet here he was abasing himself before me and, worse, rubbing dust in his hair as was proper in the presence of the very sick to help them in their dying. He told me why: prophesying successfully from a voluntary trance was the test which I must pass to become a high prophet; normally a master prophet was forced to this, for the penalty for failing it was death. I dismissed him with a wave of my claw.

I had five days to wait until full moon. The thought of the risk I was running was more than I could handle consciously; to avoid the jitters, I performed over and over all the techniques of preparing for the trance, though I carefully avoided entering it. I was not sure I was able to enter it alone, but whether I could or not, I knew I wanted to conserve my forces for the great test. At first during those five days I would remind myself once in a while of my scientific purpose in going into the trance consciously; at other times I would assure myself that it was for the good of the Dangs I was doing it, since it was not wise or safe for them to have only one high prophet. Both of these reasons were true enough, but not very important. As a scientist, I should tell them some new myth, say the story of Abraham and Isaac or of Oedipus, so that I could compare its effect on them with that of the Passion, as master prophet, I should ennoble my people if I could. However, thinking these matters over as I held my vatic squat hour after hour, visited and poked at by prying eyes, I could find no myth to satisfy me: either, as in the case of Abraham, it involved a concept of God which the Dangs could not reach, or else, as with Oedipus, it necessitated more drastic changes than I trusted myself to keep straight while prophesying—that Oedipus should mutilate himself was unthinkable to the Dangs, and that the gods should be represented as able to forgive him for it was impious. Furthermore, I did not think, basically, that any story I could tell them would in fact ennoble them. I was out to save my own skin.

The story of Christ I knew by heart; it had worked for me once, perhaps more than once; it would work again. I rehearsed it over and over, from the Immaculate Conception to the Ascension. But such was the force of that story on me that by the fifth day my cynicism had disappeared along with my scientism, and I believed, not that the myth itself was true, but that relating it to my people was the best thing it was possible for me to do for them. I remember telling myself that this story would help raise them toward monotheism, a necessary stage in the evolution toward freedom. I felt a certain satisfaction in the thought that some of the skulls on the stakes in the Cave-Temple were very likely those of missionaries who had failed to convert these heathen.

At sundown of the fifth day, I was taken by moon slaves to a cave near The Cleft, where I was left in peace. I fell into a troubled sleep, from which I awoke in a sweat: "Where am I? What am I about to do?" It seemed to me dreadfully wrong that I should be telling these, my people, a myth in whose power, but not in whose truth, I believed. Why should I want to free them from superstition up into monotheism and thence up into my total freedom, when I myself was half-returning, voluntarily, down the layers again? The energy for these sweating questions came, no doubt, from my anxiety about how I was going to perform that night, but I did not recognize this fact at that time. Then, I thought it was my conscience speaking, and that I had no right to open to the Dangs a freedom I myself was rejecting. It was to late to alter my course; honesty required me, and I resolved courageously, not to prophesy at all.

When I was fetched out, the people were already in assembly at The Cleft, and the wheel of master prophets was revolving against the greater wheel of dancers. I was given my cougar skin. Hung from a stake, in the center where I was to hop, was a huge, terrific mask I had never seen before. As the moon rose, her slaves hung this mask on me; the thong cut into the back of my neck cruelly, and at the bottom the mask came to a point that pressed my belly; it was so wide my arms could only move laterally. It had no eyeholes; I broke into a sweat wondering how I should be able to follow the prophets into the Cave-Temple. It turned out to be no problem: the two moon slaves, one on each side, guided me by prodding spears in my ribs. Once in the cave, they guided me back to the side of The Stone and drove me to climb it, my feet groping for steps I could not see; once, when I lost my balance, the spears' pressure kept me from falling backward. By the time I reached the top of The Stone, I was bleeding and dizzy. With one arm I kept the mask from gouging my belly while with the other I helped my aching neck support the mask. I did not know what to do next. Tears of pain and anger poured from my eyes. I began hopping. I should have been moving my arms in counterpoint to the rhythm of my hop, but I could not bear the thought of letting the mask cut into me any more. I kept hopping in the same place, for fear of falling off; I had not been noticing the sounds of the other prophets, but suddenly I became conscious that they were making no sounds whatever. In my alarm at this I lurched to the side and cut my foot on a sharp break in the rock. Pain converted my panic to rage.

I lifted the mask and held it flat above my head. I threw my head back and howled as I had never howled in my life, through a constricted, gradually opening throat, until at the end I was roaring; when I gasped in my breath, I made a barking noise. I leaped and leaped, relieved of pain, confident. I punched my knee desecratingly through the brittle hide of the mask, and threw it behind me off The Stone.

I tore off my cougar skin and, holding it with my claw by
the tip of its tail, I whirled it around my head. The prophets,
massed below me, fell onto their knees. I felt their fear.
Howling, I soared the skin over them; one of those on whom
it landed screamed hideously. A commotion started; I could
not see very well what was happening. I barked, and they
turned toward me again. I leaped three times and then,
howling, jumped wide-armed off The Stone. The twelve-foot
drop hurt severely my already cut foot. I rolled exhausted
into the channel in the cave floor.

Moon slaves with trembling hands mummied me in the
deerskin and shoved me under The Stone with only my head
sticking out. They brought two spears with darts tied to the
points; rolling my head to watch them do this, I saw that
the prophets were kneeling over and rubbing dirt into their
hair; then the slave laid the spears alongside the base of
The Stone with the poisoned pricks pointed at my temples;
exactly how close they were I could not be sure, but close
enough so that I dared not move my head. In all my preparations I had, as I had been trained to do, rocked and wove
at least my head; now, rigidity, live rigidity. A movement
would scratch me, and a scratch would kill me.

I pressed my hook into my thigh, curled my toes, and
pressed my tongue against my teeth till my throat ached.
I did not dare relieve myself even with a howl, for I might
toss my head fatally. I strained against my thongs to the
verge of apoplexy. For a while, I was unable to see, for
sheer rage. Fatigue collapsed me. Yet I dared not relax my
vigilance over my movements. My consciousness sealed me
off. Those stone protuberances up between which I had to
stare in the flickering light were merely chance processes
on a boulder, similes to breasts. The one thing I might not
become unconscious of was the pair of darts waiting for
me to err. For a long time I thought of piercing my head
against them, for relief, for spite. Hours passed. I was carefully watched.

I do not know what wild scheme I had in mind when I
had earlier resolved not to prophesy, what confrontation
or escape; it had had the pure magnificence of a fantasy-
resolution. But the reality, which I had not seriously tried

to evade, was that I must prophesy or die. I kept lapsing
from English into a delirium of Dang. By the greatest effort
of will, I looked about me rationally: I wondered whether
the return of Halley's Comet, at which time all stakes
should be mounted by skulls, would make the Dangs destroy the Cave-Temple and erect a new one; I observed the
straight, unindented seam of sandstone running slantwise up
the boulder over me and wondered how many eons this
rotting piece of granite had been tumbled about by water;
I reflected that I was unworthy both as a Christian and as
a Dang to prophesy the life of Jesus, but I convinced myself
that I was a trivial matter, since to the Christians it was
the telling more than the teller that counted, and to the
Dangs this myth would serve as a civilizing force they
needed. Surely, I thought, my hypocrisy could be forgiven
me, especially since I resolved to punish myself for it by
leaving the Dangs forever as soon as I could. Having
reached this rational solution, I smiled and gestured to
the high prophet with my eyes; he did not move a muscle.
When I realized that nothing to do with hypocrisy would
unbind me, desperation swarmed in my guts and mounted
toward my brain; with this question it took me over: *How
can I make myself believe it is true?* I needed to catch hold
of myself again. I dug my hook so hard into my leg—it
was the only action I was able to take—that I gasped with
pain; the pain I wanted. I did not speculate on the consequences of gouging my leg, tearing a furrow in my thigh
muscle, hurting by the same act the stump of my arm to
which the hook was attached; just as I knew that the prophets, the torches, the poisoned darts were there in the cave,
so also I knew that far far back in my mind I had good
enough reasons to be hurting myself, reasons which I could
find out if I wanted to, but which it was not worth my
trouble to discover; I even allowed the knowledge that I
myself was causing the pain to drift back in my mind. The
pain itself, only the pain, became my consciousness, purging
all else. Then, as the pain subsided, leaving me free and
equipoised, awareness of The Stone arched over me flooded
my mind. Because it had been invested by the people with
a great mystery, it was an incarnation; the power of their

faith made it the moon, who was female; at the same time it was only a boulder. I understood Stone is Stone, and that understanding became my consciousness.

My muscles ceased straining against the bonds, nor did they slump; they ceased aching, they were at ease, they were ready. I said nothing, I did not change the upward direction of my glance, I did not smile; yet at this moment the high prophet removed the spears and had the moon slaves unbind me. I did not feel stiff, nor did my wounds bother me, and when I put on my cougar skin and leaped, pulled the head over my face and roared, all the prophets fell onto their faces before me. I began chanting and I knew I was doing it all the better for knowing what I was about; I led them back out to the waiting people, and until dawn I chanted the story of the birth, prophesying, betrayal, sacrifice, and victory of the most high prophet. I am a good mimic, I was thoroughly trained, the story is the best: what I gave them was, for them, as good as a vision. I did not know the difference myself.

But the next evening I knew the difference. While I performed my ablutions and the routine ceremonies to the full moon, I thought with increasing horror of my state of mind during my conscious trance. What my state of mind actually had been I cannot with confidence now represent, for what I know of it is colored by my reaction against it the next day. I had remained conscious, in that I could recall what happened; and yet that observer and commentator in myself, of whose existence I had scarcely been aware, but whom I had always taken for my consciousness, had vanished; I no longer had been thinking, but had lost control so that my consciousness had become what I was doing; and, almost worse, when I had been telling the story of Christ, I had done it not because I had wanted to or believed in it, but because, in some obscure sense, I had had to. Thinking about it afterward, I did not understand or want to understand what I was drifting toward, but I knew it was something that I feared. And I got out of there as soon as I was physically able.

For here in Sansom, what I have learned has provided me with material for an honorable contribution to knowledge, has given me a tenure to a professorship, thereby pleasing my wife; whereas if I had stayed there among the Dangs much longer, I would have reverted until I had become one of them, might not have minded when the time came to die under the sacrificial knife, would have taken in all ways the risk of prophecy, as my Dang son intends to do, until I had lost myself utterly.

LOVE AND LIKE

Herbert Gold

HERBERT GOLD *was born in 1924 and raised in Lakewood, Ohio. He was in the army from 1943 to 1946 and holds B.A. and M.A. degrees from Columbia. He spent two years in France on a Fulbright Fellowship and a year in Haiti as a Buenos Aires Convention Fellow. Other literary honors he has received include a Guggenheim Fellowship, a* Hudson Review *Fellowship and an award from the National Institute of Arts and Letters. Mr. Gold is the author of five novels:* BIRTH OF A HERO (1951), THE PROSPECT BEFORE US (1954), THE MAN WHO WAS NOT WITH IT (1956), THE OPTIMIST (1959), *and* THEREFORE BE BOLD (1960). *His stories have appeared in many magazines, and a group of them was published in the paperback volume,* FIFTEEN BY THREE. Love and Like (1960) *is the title story for his most recent collection.*

He got to Cleveland rather late, telephoned his wife from the terminal, and asked if he could see their children early the next morning. She seemed easy and friendly and said sure thing, of course, why not? He sighed when they hung up and he stared at the telephone. Maybe his absence really could work to level things between them.

Why not? as she said. They had loved each other for ten years, or rather, for a part of those ten years impossible now to calculate. He remained sitting in the telephone booth. He was a young man with a thin, almost boyish body and a large head, heavily muscled at the jaw. On his face he

wore the haunted, eaten look of a man whose accomplice
has betrayed him. Whether his accomplice was his former
wife or his conscience was not yet clear to him. Conscience
was still talking to his wife: We didn't make it, kid! And
he was remembering one of their last quarrels before they
gave up, when he said, "We'll try! We'll try!" And paining
badly with those fragments of the past, he heard again her
quiet reviving words: "We'll try, darling."

If they had finally made out, it would all have been remembered as the progress and process of love; with failure
it could seem all bad; he was determined to hold in retro-
spect to a mixed verdict—some pretty, some unpretty, and
nevertheless the long Sunday afternoon habit of lovemaking
spoke for a true intimacy. The hardest, most essential responsibility to a dead marriage is to preserve the ripe
strength it once had. Must have had, must have! So without
love now, if that's the way it was, why couldn't they simply
like each other for the rest of time? Not just for the sake of
the children. For the sake of themselves and what they had
become through their marriage.

All this was a resolution. Done.

Then he fished for another dime in his pocket and called
Sally. Okay, it was late, but wasn't she glad to hear his
voice? She laughed sleepily and asked him how he could
doubt it. She was sleepy was all. She had been thinking of
him. All right then, dreaming. He could come right up—
would it take twenty minutes? For splashing some cold
water and getting good and waked and dressed.

"Don't bother," he said, and even in the telephone booth,
under the falsification of wires and electricity, the laughter
brought her back to him with all her soft, warm childlike
sleepiness amid the fragrant bedclothes. Sally's face was devoted to laughter, especially the very blue, waiting-to-smile
eyes—those eyes of a blue which could give him what a
strong awakening on a morning in the country gives, courage and appetite and great belief in the future. The morning
he left, she had made breakfast for him, hotcakes with butter, sweet syrup, three kinds of jam—mostly he remembered
the sweetness and much melted butter. With his mouth

stuffed, he shook his finger to warn her that he had something to say as soon as he could swallow.

"What's the matter, darling?"

"Oh it's good! It's so good, Sally!"

And the lashes fell over the brave summer-sky eyes. She was timid despite her laughter's deep abandon. "Then why do you have to leave Cleveland?" she had asked. The question cost her heavily. Without me? her paleness said. The unsmiling blue eyes were trying to force his reply: Then why don't we . . . ?

Unspoken questions were, as always, the ones he felt he had to answer and precisely could not. Therefore he had spoken in a tone of stubborn exasperation. "Because my wife lives here. Because it's too soon. Because I have to." He reached across the debris of eating to touch her more gently. If he could tell her, he would. "Now, with you here, Sally, it's all right. Right now. But I can't tell you about my wife and what she did to me. What she does! What she still does!" he cried out abruptly. His heart was pounding, and the good of the breakfast was gone. "And the children—I still can't imagine any other life than being their father——"

She was looking at his hand on hers with a curious withdrawn attention.

He said quietly, "Maybe I just haven't found the way to love them without loving their mother. Maybe that's it and there is a way."

His wife made him need Sally; if only she could free him entirely for Sally! This way, entangling him in her wrath, she hardly let him know who Sally was. He had to find her in a long history in which she had no part, past a furious, gyring woman, after outrage and love gripping each other as do alloyed metals under heat and pressure. Let Sally make him pure—as he never was—let Sally make herself felt!

But her eyes were answering nothing, were asking him: And why can't we? He realized that she had not heard him at all. Everyone is sometimes made deaf by intentions. He might as well have been brutal: And I just don't know about you, either, dollface. Seems as how I met you someplace before.

Now he shrugged and felt the damp shirt moving on his back. Every time he said the word "wife" she should interrupt and say, *"Former* wife." Shaper to Shaper—*over,* he decided, ferociously willing it as if he were passing a message by radio, and the battlefield made communication difficult: *Over!* He had just finished writing a technical manual on the care and operation of a new, improved, long-range walkie-talkie. In Cleveland he had worked for General Electric on instructions for the installation of intercoms in language any mechanic could understand; in the identical off-white New York office to which he had arranged a transfer, under the same Armstrong Cork soundproofing, with thousands of little holes conking, stunning every whisper of distraction, he had labored with a Signal Corps semantics expert on further explanations of how to keep contact open under conditions of stress. "Limited contact under conditions of vital stress. . . ." He was making mass poetry for five-stripe sergeants who don't like the word *war.* It was a career for a careful explainer. But now over to Dan Shaper, please!

Deciding: Condition of stress not total chaos if receiver flashes emergency transistor filters out static toward coded meaning (see Fig. 3). Put into heart's English. Also see resources of regret, hope, and desire for possible decoding toward good conscience.

II

At seven-thirty the next morning he was running up the stairway toward his daughters. The buzzer had admitted him; the door to the upstairs flat was open.

"Paula, honey!"

"Hello, Daddy. Mommy and Cynthia are still sleeping. I knew you were coming. I got up and took my own breakfast. Wheaties and prunes and a pickle. Mommy says I can eat what's on the bottom shelf of the fridge and that's where the pickle was. Hello, Daddy."

Exactly what he wanted always, this time Paula was a six-year-old lady sitting on the couch. First she rang the buzzer to let him in, then she returned shyly to her place to wait for him.

"And I knew you would be coming back today because I counted the days," she said. "You said thirty. You promised." She was quivering with excitement beneath the formality with which she had vain hopes of hiding herself. A month is even longer in a child's life than in her father's. He took her in his arms and she said, "I'm *glad*." Her eyelashes were wet when he kissed them.

"I'm glad to see you too, honeybear."

They whispered together gravely to keep from waking the rest of the house. He felt strong in his monthlong convalescence. He forgot that he had slept only the sleep of the recently divorced, that is, no sleep but that profitless, dreamjammed one of might-have-been and exhaustion. Paula gave him her news. Not only had she lost a tooth, but also the ragged edge of the new, grownup one had begun to appear. He looked and saw. At her command he appreciated it with his finger, too. They were interrupted by another child, running scared and barefoot to join the celebration, four-year-old Cynthia. Disappointed, Paula bravely permitted Cynthia to catch up with a minute of greeting.

Then he pulled them both onto the couch beside him, still bedwarm in their summer pajamas, and so were they three sitting when his wife came out. She had heard them, stayed a long time in the bathroom, and emerged only after satisfying herself that she was sweet and alert and nice to look at. He was very aware also of how he looked to her with the two little ones wriggling close to him.

She smiled and said, "Hello, Dan." Her hair had been cut in a new fashion and fluffed out to make a soft frame for the delicate bones of her face. Her brow, finely marked by frown lines, seemed wider now, peacefully expectant. What happens to a young woman when she divorces? Aren't her eyes puffy in the morning any more? Where does the blue lymph go? Is she no longer stringy and dismayed after the first glimpse of herself in the bathroom mirror? Not this one. Dark, slender, and cool, she was mobilized for love again.

Shaper was pleased by her greeting and—with only a

twinge of self-judging jealousy—by her appearance. He put
it down to his credit that she was not ruined for the hope of
love. His moving out of town had done them both good.
Sally last night had started the visit auspiciously. Paula was
a marvel and Cynthia a wonder. And now his wife was the
decent human being he had almost always believed in.

"Yes, thanks," he said, and they all four had breakfast
together, just like a family. Since the first years of their
marriage, his wife had barely eaten in the morning, drinking black coffee and nibbling at dry toast and then rushing
to the scales, but today she took an extra piece of toast and
covered it with butter in order to show him that she could
now enjoy food. Well, let her have that pleasure, he thought
with a fine expansive sense of tolerance. They both watched
the girls munching greedily, proving something to their
parents.

Later, while the children played with their new toys, they
sat together in the front room and talked, balancing coffee
cups on their knees. "It's all right now," she said. "You did
right to go away for a while. There were good things,
weren't there, Dan?"

"I'm glad you remember."

"I do. I do." Her narrow face with its wide brow wore a
complex expression—frowning, tender, at peace. They had
shared and not shared. They had been satisfied, unsatisfied.
She had wanted, they had both wanted another child; but
(stiff white mouth and tense, silent staring out the window)
she had needed a guarantee that this time it would be a boy.
She had found a doctor in Miami with fantastic notions
about special diets, the power of raisins and lima beans
and times of the month—litmus paper, fever charts, count
the days—and a husband to be applied as an agent when
the alchemical and astrological signs say yes. Desperate
woman! Yet a man can grow to accept a partial madness
when it is the condition of the rational universe he desires.
Desperate husband! (Aren't many people superstitious?
When she has her son, what difference by what illusion she
was comforted?) But one day he faces the obvious question: All right, there's a fifty-fifty chance, say. And if it's
not a boy? Kachoo—sneezing with boredom and despair.

And if it's *not* a boy?

As always, his besetting flaw was the one of perverse hope and pride—the crazy patience of the man who needs love too much to take the necessary risk of losing it. When this danger is not challenged, love and like both are doomed. He had feared to compel his wife to follow his lead. He would not submit to being dragged along by her frantic jittering after happiness; she could not follow his bone-tired, patience-ended assertions of will; for them it had long been too late for all but knowledge, and perhaps in love it is always too late for that. The terrible guilt which he carried with him was a hope, not an understanding: Once she might have been made to want what you want, if you had pressed hard enough, and if you had said in time, No, not that way! Follow me and come to yourself!

The enduring of wrong amounts to an acquiescence in evil, a sin of active malignance which grew on the body of their marriage like a tumor and, like a tumor, sapped its strength to proliferate in this cruel organism, divorce. When the body is dead and all health irrelevant, only then will the cancer cease. In the meantime, every joy, every lively nerve, every vein of health must supply food for the fibrillar parasite. The dying creature curses its strong heart, its tuned body, because these prolong the agony. Each motive for happiness must be bled dry.

Shaper knew that he had not acted in time.

But finally he had said *no.*

NO!

Said no to lima beans and love by astrological suggestion —and maybe, kid, you're right about wanting to see Dr. Kasdan, he's supposed to be a good one—although he believed in that cure almost as little as he believed in the efficacy of lima beans to induce suckling boy babies instead of beautiful but incomplete girls.

A nightmare. Yet this was the intelligent, accomplished woman who could charm a stick into life. Seething and plausible. She took a cigarette from the box on the record cabinet, very sure of herself, very much the fresh young divorcee, and said, "Dan, I thought about you while you were away. We both lost . . ."

"Yes, despite everything we've lost a great deal."

"We lost *control*," she said firmly.

He felt rebuked, but it did not touch his reviving humor. Often she was bad, but sometimes she was steady and knew the way. She was right! He longed to regain this old sense of his wife's rightness. He needed it to go on from where he was.

"I don't blame you any more about that . . . that," she said. "It was wrong of me to be so . . . so . . . ."

This time he did not make the mistake of supplying her words. Perhaps she was testing him.

"So angry, nervous with you," she said. *"Judgmental,"* —one of those damn labels again, he thought, but nodded encouragingly. Warily she went on with a speech that seemed almost rehearsed. He did not expect her to grant him a confession, but he thought maybe she was making it in her own way at last and that this could finally release both of them: I was jealous, and not merely jealous, also morbid and criminal and made furious by fantasies, until you had to give me justice for them because you, too, demanded someone totally committed to you, because jealousy itself is an infidelity which takes a wife from her husband. . . . But she said instead (and who would she be if she used his words? Her own were good enough): "I think I've learned something. We each learned, so it wasn't so bad. We probably couldn't have married anyone else, or anyone better, so why blame each other?"

"Right! We won't any more!"

She frowned and did not hear him. He felt her effort not to slip down and down into the despair which had driven him away. It had poisoned him—all that cleverness turned to making him out a monster—and it had poisoned her. Rage, like jealousy, is a fire which burns out the future: she apparently knew it, and the softness in her eyes, even this willed, desperate kindness at the door to the furnace, restored her to him as he needed her to be restored. Then they could both go on to love again, not merely beyond hatred, but also strong in a practical, difficult friendship. Perhaps that was too much to ask, his version of her romanticism, but at least it was a principle worth striving for.

"We had some good reasons together," he said.

"What? Oh! Of course! I know, I remember, Dan. It wasn't just our psychological set, we really liked each other—"

He grinned wryly. "So it seemed at the time."

She did not admit a poor effort at humor in his enforced grip on the past. "That's the way you remember it and maybe that's partly how it was. I suppose. Anyway,"—with great solemn effort for which he wanted to thank and thank and thank her—"whatever our motivations"—although he winced at the word—"we—yes—Dan—*we loved each other*."

"Yes!"

And again she retreated. "But it was sick."

"Okay," he said.

And she folded her hands contentedly. "That's what I've learned."

Who's been teaching you now? he wanted to ask. He resisted successfully. He wanted her to understand about the passive faithlessness of the woman who expects her husband to be what he is not, what no man can be, who lies with him locked in her lonely dream of perfection, who sees her real marriage by the strange sunless radiance of a dream marriage which is unaltered by growth and event, by this particular day on earth or that one. Absolutist! Idealist! Romantic! These had been his epithets for her. And you can't make yourself into Eleanor of Acquitaine and me into a troubador by nagging me for talking with a girl at a goddamn party! All right, so I didn't, didn't, *didn't* light your cigarette! So neither of our children were boys!

He managed. He said nothing.

The admissions she had just made were an extravagant yielding. She felt loss, they meant; relief and giving up pain could help to teach her to praise life, and when she could bear the din of pleasure once more, she might even be grateful to him. Together they had exorcized childish ways—the lesson was nearly fatal; they had also learned and practiced love. Once free of each other, they could go on with this lifelong music.

But how stiff she still was!

Nevertheless, in her own way, calmly, gently, and much sweeter than his secretly unleashed judgment, with but a slight stiffness of the mouth, she went on. He was impressed by her rapid peacemaking, so soon after the tears and threats and furious thrashing. There was a deep quiet note of loss despite the artificial speech. He listened: "It was inevitable. You were my mistake and I was yours. But neither of us is *bad,* and we could have married really bad people, real stinkers—so if we know it was inevitable. . . . Dan," she concluded rapidly, with a flush, "I said things, did things. Now I'm sorry."

She was in misery. He wanted to comfort her. Then she straightened up with a strong glance of resolution and touched her hair. "I'm sorry," she said.

"I'm sorry too, kid, for all I did wrong."

Apologies and pride and gratitude. Shaper felt a reviving flow of tenderness for her because she said *stinkers,* and maybe even thought stinkers, and not that cant of hers, *destructive personalities.* They sat very still, in a heated blush, both of them, their shame almost a courting shyness, and they listened to their children splashing in the sink and laughing. An odd music for courting. The children were his laughter and hers; her body and his were met in the children as they had been entangled in each other. All this willed and anxious sweetness between them might finally give him Sally, give her whomever she wanted, and not merely send them raging after others. It could be the final creative act of their marriage—the two of them educated by their errors, not bound to them, freed for love and not greedily clutching at it. They would always have Paula and Cynthia together.

Once, on the day when their lawyers had first met, before this resilient stupor with which he shielded himself had settled in, he had cried out in this room, after they had both put the children to bed and he was facing her, ready to say goodbye, when he was at the door with all the unfinished business of their life meeting him in her huge hot eyes: "We didn't make it, kid."

"We tried. We tried."

"We tried, honey."

And they had fallen into an adulterous passion, still un-

shaken in their will on divorce, the adultery made painfully
sweet. He remembered it with shame, his eye suddenly
prickling and aching, and saw himself again covering her
with kisses, forcing her mouth open while her body bent
backwards, arched, received him. She had given herself
without a word, moaning, and then he had fled like a thief.

Now he was merely quiet. The ache in his eye was an unheard sound, an unseen tremor of desire.

Still they would always have the children together.

He felt the day's heat already sweeping in and looked
about for the fan. In his reticence in this familiar and very
unfamiliar house, his and not his, he obeyed the stricture
she had once made in anger—don't touch anything, nothing
is yours any more! (Nothing but the children.) "Put your
hands on me and I'll get an injunction," she had said the
next day. It was her only reference to that strange, silent
last lovemaking. "I'll slap a court order on you so fast it'll
make you dizzy."

"Okay, kid, do you really think I want to touch you?" And
that time his eye had not ached, not seemed invisibly swollen. It was the end. Almost comfortably he believed in playing out the rest of their career together without the danger
of intimacy. Of course he was wrong, but something of the
comfort remained in his waiting, his planning, his cautious
observance of the new rules of tact and courtesy. It was
only the children he needed.

She had rearranged all the furniture, painted, covered,
hid, and replaced, so that the house could begin anew. He
recognized it as he recognized her, from a distance, from a
long time, from a dream of voyages. She had planned it that
way. Fastidiously he had been plucked out of her skin and
the scars dusted over, so that she could say, *Who? Who?*
She wanted him to notice how much he was not at home.
How managerial and intelligent of her to begin briskly
anew! With what a rush she had retreated from him!

He smiled at her. "You look very well, kid."

She turned and pressed her lips together tightly. In pain
she had a large mouth—childbirth, bereavement—he had
been there with her; anger was a small one which sent him
away. By the resenting white line at the corners of her

mouth, he recognized his wife, the one who had first wanted
him for pride in what he did—others wanted him, he was
not like the herd of college boys; then wanted him to do
nothing that did not include her, that might make others
covet him; and then when they were cozy in a common, including misery, rebuked and rebuked him for his failure to
be her romantic ideal. O father she lost, O son I did not give
her, how amply I was repaid for trying to replace you!
What foolish pride that thought this abstract hungering of
hers was desire for me! Impossible victories that I wanted!

Now thanks to that bloodless thin line and the stiff tremor
of her response to his word for her, *kid,* he felt entirely at
home. It was almost like the last years of their marriage
again.

She reached for an envelope in her purse. "You forgot to
pay my dental bill. It dates from before our settlement," she
said with her marvelous cool telephone voice, "so of course
you are responsible. Dr. Jonas' secretary called me about it
and I said you had probably forgot. I said I'd give it to you
personally when you got back to town."

He took the paper, put it in his pocket, and called like a
drowning man, "Paula! Cynthia! Let's go outside, would
you like that?"

They came screaming with pleasure into the room, and
he believed that, yes, he could still keep his grip on the green
feelings he had brought in from his month away.

III

He liked everyone, even his wife. Perhaps he loved no one
but the children—he was so diminished by the belly-ripping,
face-clawing final year of marriage—but he felt a reviving
and undiscriminating benevolence toward the world. Plus
desire for Sally, ah, that's important! It was recovery from
an illness. When he returned to his hotel after leaving the
children for their afternoon nap, his thoughts wheeled
around to Sally, and they were imbedded within a silly glow
of sympathy for everyone, irrelevantly, from the desk clerk
with sinus trouble to the Japs at Hiroshima. Symptom of
convalescence. "Key, please! Hot enough for you?"

He wanted to share this precarious perch on health. Sally had agreed to drive out to Chagrin Falls and go swimming with him. The first time he took a girl swimming was important to Shaper. It's a risk and rousing. You run the challenges of dirt, ants, and fatigue; he took chances on a cold noting of his skinny body in boxer trunks, the scatter of hair and the ropes of tendons and no strong rhythm of distraction. Enjoying the happy vanity of a lovely object, long used to triumphant waiting, Sally might have an eye for some tumbling beach athlete, not Dan Shaper with his glasses and his bony knees. Admire, admire me! her every movement had been saying to him for months. He had done it well. Was that a guarantee that she would love him?

No matter, he thought as he shaved in his hotel room; I don't want love now, I couldn't take it yet, what I need is just what Sally is giving me. Why worry about categories? He remembered that warning song: "Silkless silk and milkless milk! Love oh love oh loveless love. . . ."

Fully dressed, he lay on the bed, organizing himself to meet Sally, feet straight and toes up, watching the hand of the clock move down to two. These few minutes of rest were necessary, despite his driving heart, after a morning spent with his children, seeing in their faces the intermingling of his wife and himself, feeling her breath with his gesture when they talked, his forehead with her dark, thick-lashed eyes when they laughed. Their eyes when he rolled on the floor to play bus or airplane as they had during the easy evenings of their babyhood (they remembered, they demanded it)—they wanted him to bathe them again, as he used to—and their mother's eyes, the tragic pouched eye of the beauty unsuccessful in love. And then the solemn politeness all around when he turned them back to her.

One minute to two! Think of Sally—full-breasted and full-hipped, blond, frequently amused—how lucky to be all those things that his wife was not! And Sally had her own secret sources, too! He remembered the yearning of her response to his first, long-delayed kiss, when in the renewal of timidity, the return to boyishness brought on by the long illness of his marriage, he had quite simply been afraid. No, it took wisdom to be full and warm like that. Her hand on his back

was deep art, her weight on his shoulder was Plato and . . .
and . . . Sally, not Plato! No romantic ideal! She did it for
herself and for him.

Lord, ten after two already. He must have dozed. He
threw swimshorts, towel, clean clothes into the blue Air
France bag he usually carried for tennis. He took a taxi to
Sally's apartment, where she was waiting for him at the entrance. She had no need to keep him waiting; she didn't play
that game any more—she felt his need for her and forgot
to protect herself. She said: "Darling! It's such a beautiful
day for us!"

That was intelligence, wasn't it? Her own marriage had
been a revolving door, in and out with practically no noise
or loss of heat, but she probably knew more about it than
he suspected. Surely she knew more than she would tell.
And she had her own automobile, a blue Ford convertible,
to which she just automatically handed him the keys—that
too made her clever and deep. Like all American boys, he
had dreamed of girls like her with their blond heads thrown
back against the leather seats of cars like these. . . . That
it was her automobile only gave the joke a turn. Once he
got over the divorce, lawyers' fees, travel costs, the rest of
it, he, too, would have the open car which his wife had always thought too dangerous, bad for a dry skin, impractical.

"Why didn't I think of picking you up at your hotel?"
Sally asked.

"Never mind, just move over and sit close to me."

"Are you a one-arm driver?"

"Like to be."

"Then I'll put a knob on the wheel for you."

Wryly he submitted to his retreat toward college-boy
pleasures—the blonde, the convertible, the exaggerations of
flesh in erotic gaming. Well, he would tolerate himself, he
would come out of it. Let the submerged fantasies see the
light, why not? Sally was there waiting, and more than
merely *the blonde*. She was Sally. Her silent smiling said that
she was with him part of the way at least.

And they teased and played while he drove under the hot
August sun through a part of the city, a part of the suburbs,
out to the private country lake he had chosen because nei-

ther of them had been there for years. They paid to enter.
On a weekday like this, they had the short clean beach almost to themselves. When they met on the beach after
dressing, he submitted to a moment of shocked, almost unpleasant awe at her perfection of body under the blaze of
sunlight. Beauty is pitiless. She turned under his brooding
with a model's pouting half-smile, her eyes blank, self-re-
garding, retreated into vanity. This must have been an old
girlish habit. He hated the thought of her searching him for
flaws, as he was now doing to her; but he needed to be
looked at with pride, too. The different male and female
ways about bodies would protect him, no? And hadn't they
already begun the long study of each other in the close and
secret dark?

Different, different.

She was a marvel, and that they both knew it somehow
widened the space that had been closed by their first tentative lovemaking. A monument wants a pedestal.

Then she turned and ran, elbows pumping, toward the
water. He caught her, and they went in together. They
laughed and spluttered, and she began swimming, and he
caught her again. "Let's go out to the dock," she said. She
swam poorly, splashing and puffing; he swam well and easily. Sally's wisdom! When he helped her up onto the outer
dock, she was no longer a monument. She leaned on him,
gasping a little and laughing. He kissed her shoulder with its
gleaming, running beads of water. She nipped his hand with
her bared teeth.

They lay a long while under the descending late afternoon
sun, stretching against each other, talking at intervals, listening to the few shrill voices back on shore. He spoke a
little of his wife. He did not speak of the children. "Just
smile," she said sleepily, her face close to the hot white-
washed boards. "I don't want you to worry about a thing."

He stopped worrying. He put his arm on her back and
rubbed the strong articulations of her spine until his fingers
ached. She smiled, saying, "More, more, more. Ah, that's
nice."

She was very young, overproud of her body in the suburban way, just beginning to get past using it as a weapon

instead of spending herself through the splendors of flesh.
But she was learning, she was. And if her beauty alone had
frightened him, could he ever have borne that rare loveli-
ness which comes of beauty joined to a proper sense of its
being? No, thank her for limitations. And she was learning
to spend herself freely, too. And with him.

At sunset they sat up to watch. She leaned on him to
share the radiating warmth of her body. They approved of
the sky. He missed not seeing the children this evening, but
he needed Sally now; he would go to them again tomorrow.
With a fine sense of no hurry, no hurry for anything, they
waited until the sun was gone.

But the swim back to shore made them furious with hunger. She suggested buying Chinese food and eating it at her
apartment. They drank a great deal of tea and nothing else.
The sunburn began to show on her face and arms. She put
a stack of records on the machine. They made love slowly,
patiently. "Why are you smiling?" he asked her, and she
replied: "Why are you smiling?" He explored a generous
body with its slowly stirring languors and bold risings to the
touch. She explored whatever he meant to her. "Why *are*
you smiling, now tell me!" His hand had discovered, with
the sense of regaining a fine lost memory, the crisp, crinkly,
blond hairs of her secret places.

They gave up talking. They loved each other until they
both felt as light and pure as driftwood, and then all tumbled
together they slept.

IV

Paula, who was six, said to her father, "Mommy says you
don't love her any more."

Her father, who was thirty-two, replied, "No, but I like
her."

"But, but," said Cynthia, who was just four. "But can I
go out and find Gary?"

"Why don't you stay with me for a little while?" her father asked. Dismayed by his querulousness, he repeated the
remark in another voice. "Stay here with me. I have to go
back soon. Anyway," he added, "it's almost bedtime."

"Okay," said Cynthia, resigned. She was a very small child, pouting and serious, with overbusy limbs. She paced back and forth on the long, low, especially constructed, "contemporary" couch which her mother had bought partly because her father didn't want it.

"But *why* don't you love Mommy any more?" Paula insisted. "You always told me you did."

"That was b-b-before." Her father stammered for an explanation, dulled by knowing that there could be no valid one for Paula. "I tried—we did—I wanted to. We just weren't happy together. You know how that is, Paula."

"No," she said flatly and firmly.

"We have to live separately. It's like when you and Cynthia are tired and quarrel. We put you in separate rooms until you feel better."

"When are you and Mommy going to feel better?"

"It's not exactly that way with grownups." The sly innocence of Paula's question brought his hand out to touch her pleadingly; he wiped away the smudge of dirt on her cheek. She always made herself up with a stroke of dust as soon as possible when her mother washed her face. Cynthia, humming to herself, was listening with a smudge of prying watchfulness across her eyes. With a premature false security, the two girls frowned for serious discussion. The children of the divorced are engaged too soon in love as a strategy. Joy recedes before strategy; these children are robbed of their childhood. The huge brooding of possibility which human beings have at their best comes of the long passionate carnival of childhood; no fear of cost down this midway, just another and another breathtaking joyride on the great rollercoaster! and another quiet gathering-in of food and rest—it should be. It should be a storing of unquestioned certainties for the infinite risks of being a person. But instead, instead. Heavily Shaper touched the two girls as if to make them child animals again. It was not right that a father should feel this hopeless pity, and this need to enlist his daughters in the harried legions of rationality: "Here's how it is with grownups—"

"You mean Mommy and you?"

"Yes. Yes. Now listen. We feel better living in separate

places. We're going to stay like that. But we like each other, Paula, and we love you and Cynthia. We both do."

"But, but, but, but," Cynthia sang, carefully wiping her feet on the pillows. "But heigh-ho, the derry-oh, the farmer takes a wife."

"Cynthia," said her father, "you shouldn't. Take off your shoes if you're going to play on the couch. It wasn't made for children."

Cynthia looked at him silently and, scraping the fabric, slid down beside him. Paula pulled between his knees, fighting to get closer than her sister. She began to suck her thumb. Her father pressed his lips together, resisted the temptation to remove her thumb from her mouth, and instead lit a cigarette. He decided that perhaps his silence would oblige her to remove the thumb and speak. It did not. At last he said, "I want you to understand. Mommy wants you to understand, too. Even though I'm not going to be Mommy's husband any more, I'll always be your father. I couldn't change that even if I wanted to, and besides, I would never want to. Don't you want always to be my daughters?"

Sucking busily, Paula said nothing.

Cynthia announced with a grin, "But I want a daddy who loves my mommy. I think maybe Uncle Carl, he loves Mommy——" The look on her father's face told her that he was not enjoying her joke. "But I *know* you're my daddy for real."

"I am. For real."

"Okay," she said, bored with the discussion.

Paula looked at her wet and slippery thumb, considered putting it back, had another idea. "Why doesn't Mommy say hardly anything to you no more?"

"*Any* more," her father said. "I already explained. Because we don't get along—just like we don't let you and Cynthia talk to each other when you don't get along——"

"But we do anyway! But that's only for a few minutes! But it's not, not, *not* the same thing, Daddy!"

"No," he said, "you're right. It's really not."

"Then *when?*"

"When what?"

"When are you coming to sleep here again?"

"I told you, I already explained. Mommy and I——"

"When you went away you said you'd come back to live here in a few days."

"Well, we thought maybe. I hoped. But it's worked out this way instead. Now listen to me, girls, it's not really so different. I see you very often. We go out together for milkshakes. We're just like before."

Silence from Cynthia. From Paula, coldly, suddenly with her mother's precise articulation: "It's not the same, and you know it."

"Okay, you're right, it's not." Her recognition of his hollow heartiness made him flush. She cut right through what he said. She remembered very well that he had been a part of the life of the house and she did not like her new sense of the house. He said, "I guess you're right, Paula, but that's how it is. That's all. We don't have to talk about it."

Silence. Then:

"So you really don't love Mommy any more." But she was a child again. The moment when she spoke with her mother's voice had passed. "Daddy," she said.

He resolved to go through it patiently once more. "No," he said, "and she doesn't love me. But we like each other, and we love and like you, both together, and we always will. You understand that, Cynthia?"

"Okay," said Cynthia.

Paula was sucking her thumb again. Her mouth was pulled around, working and bothering, as if she were trying to pull the skin off. She might be learning to bite the nail.

From the back of the house her mother walked toward the living room where the two children and their father were talking. She said hello, picked up a book, and returned to the bedroom. This meant that she would like him to notice that his time was up. A brisk, dark young woman, she was freshly showered and very pretty, although too thin. She wore a housecoat, but a girdle under it, stockings, and high-heeled shoes. Obviously she wanted to get the girls to bed early because she was going out.

He began to say goodbye to his daughters. He reminded them that he would come to see them at noon tomorrow.

Cynthia threw her arms around his neck, laughing, and demanded: "Bring me something, maybe a surprise!"

"If you like," he said. He had a sick lonely weakness in his stomach of something not yet done, not possible.

"Do you like me, Daddy?"

"I like you and love you, Cynthia kid."

Paula was rubbing her face against his hand, the thumb still in her mouth. He lifted her to kiss her saying, "And Paula too. Now goodbye until tomorrow."

As he started down the stairs, Paula stood with her swollen thumb dripping and shouted after him: "Oh, how I'm sick of those words love and like!"

v

The next day there were fresh flowers in a new vase on the coffee table. His wife was cool and abstracted, and the familiar house could not have looked more strange to him if he had returned to find it filled with angry, overheated growth, like an abandoned greenhouse. Even not considering the flowers, the entire room spoke to him with faint whispers of disarray about how his wife (ah no! *former* wife!) had been out late and importantly that evening. A wrinkle in the carpet informed on her. The piled pillows on the couch were his witness.

"The children are having lunch," she said. "Would you like something?"

"No thanks, kid, I had a late breakfast."

She hid a small yawn behind her hand. "Me too." The yawn was excessive. It was more than required. She was putting it on with a trowel. Well, still, this was very much better than the hysteria with which she had sent their marriage into darkness, like a couple trapped forever at an abandoned Luna Park in the spinning, jolting cars of the Bug. Of course, this had its own special touch of refined cruelty, which merely went to show that she still depended on his feelings for some of her satisfactions. "Sit down, please," she said.

"Make myself at home?"

She smiled tolerantly. He wondered if she had any imag-

ination for how it disturbed him to visit the place which
had been his home, which in some way still was, which was
so mysterious, like a room dreamed of and then found and
then you're suddenly unsure of whether you really dreamed
of it or only now think you did. Of course she understood;
she had worked the house out for herself, and had a right
to; but any imagination past this redecorating, working-it-
out variety requires sympathy. When he looked up at her,
she was still dressed in that social smile. Excessive!

"Some coffee?"

"No thanks, really. How do you think the children are
taking things? My being away. Visiting. I was wondering
if maybe I shouldn't see them too much when I'm in town.
You can't make up for the normal daily——"

"Yes, overstimulating them."

"Too exciting," he said, giving up his thought by agreeing
with her.

"They don't show it, of course. It's funny," she remarked,
smiling patiently, as if it really were funny, while she explained the joke. "At their age they can't express it, they're
too well behaved, they don't have the vocabulary for dis-
cussions. . . ."

He gave up listening. He was trying to place himself in
this room. Sometimes they had pulled the shades and made
love on the floor. He heard her despite the noise of memory.
Her mania for psychology had always annoyed him. Jar-
gonizing. And yet, and yet, once when she could not sleep
he had held her in his arms on the couch while they quietly
talked all night about her father and brother—she could talk
English when she wanted to—and she spoke of love and violated need and loneliness. Then they had talked about each
other and their own children and how different it would be.
Then they had gone out on the porch to hold hands in the
chill spring dawn and watch the lights go on in kitchens
and bedrooms down the street. See, we didn't need that
sleep, we've gained a night on everyone, he had said, and
she had answered: Yes, yes, yes, we have something they
don't have. I'll even make you a better breakfast!

"But," she was saying, "I'm afraid they will express what
they're feeling about us now when they get to adolescence."

Another time, after a terrible quarrel—thinking that maybe with the guidance of their bodies which wanted to give to each other . . . —more than hopeful, prayerful, they had spread a quilt on the floor just below where she was now sitting. They had helped each other down as if crippled, slowly, slowly, and then safe on the floor, had flung all their strength into the cruel struggle to possess, a lurching grinding grasping assault on tenderness, and her head thrown back and her mouth open so that he could not see her teeth, only a dark place and a pulsing groan issuing deeply from within it, and then fiercely she closed and bit his shoulder and the cry, *You did it—you did it—you did it.*

What?

Oh love, love, love.

Would the rock be there the next day for rolling up the mountain?

He blinked and straightened his shoulders in the heavy inert grip of sweated clothes. Now was now, and his former wife was talking. Now was also then, but his former wife was speaking. It was now ten summers for them. She had something to tell him about their children.

"—with sibling rivalry," she was saying. "They're beginning the latency period."

"Oh yes, yes." Didn't she remember how he disliked those words? What was she trying now? He went into the kitchen for a glass of water. The children made him rehearse what they would do together after lunch. The park and the swings and a milkshake. All the milkshakes they could drink.

When he returned she was sitting calmly in her chair, hands folded together, with a subdued half-smile on her face. He recognized her analyzed smile, the one she reminded herself to slip into when she talked psychology. That little smile cost me a year's pay. Okay, go easy, he told himself, it's only a year's pay. A convertible plus gas and insurance. A while in Europe. It's a funny nice little darling of a smile, really—all sympathy and comprehension and let's-be-mature-about-the-infantile-phase. No joy, no teeth either, but it's still better than the screams, much easier on the neighbors and a good deal easier on me.

"Did you visit Pete and Ellen last night?" she asked.

It gave him a little malicious pleasure in his turn to let her know that he had not been lonely, that he had not even gone to see his best friends in Cleveland. "No, I had something else to do. I'll see them in a day or so. I called them."

They were both silent. All the maneuvering and rivaling warned him. He was doing nicely, but better get the kids out soon, get out quickly. If she felt his strength of distance, if she sensed Sally and stopped being nourished by whatever it was in the room, the flowers, whatever it was, things might go poorly again. He followed her eyes. Three novels by Evelyn Waugh, new in their jackets, were piled on an endtable. A quick twitch of grin crossed his face. He had never liked Waugh, neither had she; ever since college they had taken literature passionately and together, even after she had begun her long crush on the bound volumes of *The Psychoanalytic Quarterly*. Now the little pile of Waugh was a roadmark meant to state: See, I've come under someone else's influence. I'm reading the books *he* recommends, doing the things he . . . It amused Shaper, but when he finally spoke his voice was husky and he had to swallow and it still didn't clear. "I talked with Pete," he said. "I suppose I should go out there."

"Yes, if you're not too busy. Really, Dan, you don't have to be afraid about our friends. I wouldn't spite you for the world—"

"I'm not worried. They know me. I mean to see them, but you know how it is, things come up, I'm only here a few days."

With a thrill of satisfaction, he felt the balance swing over: I'm giving her now! She's getting it! This while he knew how much she pained only by how she goaded him —so rusted together are the ways of untying man and wife. And this all the while that his eye began to ache, that he asked himself a fleeting, trespassing question about how he could expect to hold his job while committed to this continuous deep marital work, that he suddenly saw a tiny receding Sally fretting and scowling and making up her eyes and mouth three times over because she was jealous of his quarrel with his wife. Sally's moods were reflected in heavy

ways with her lipstick. His own lip was sore inside where
he had bit it. That was his wife's habit which he had borrowed. Divorce, divorce! he thought. Let us be divorced in
the flesh as we are by law!

She was watching him shrewdly. She knew him. He could
keep the bitten lip from her, there was no way she could
palp it. It was a contest to hold secret the hurt eye with its
invisible throbbing. And then Cynthia ran up and put her
hands in his pockets to see if he had gum.

"Get out, Cynthia! Go wait for your daddy in the other
room. Paula has enough sense. Can't you see I'm talking to
him?"

Like successive waves of fever and chills, chills and fever, his tenderness for the children, who resembled both his
wife and him, gave way to hatred, hatred, cold disdain for
this woman who forgot so much, who destroyed so much.
And then a sharp new ache in his eye, flicking all the way
up into his brain, no, just the sinuses, no, cruelly into the
brain: Maybe I should just have given in. Maybe I should
have taken it on her terms.

No, no! He wanted to turn off one whole side of his head.
The eye had a furious life of its own. He warmed it, comforted it with his palm. Bent to it for an instant, he looked
up again strictly. "You don't have to sit here if you're busy,"
he said.

"Oh I don't mind, Dan. And besides, there really are some
little things we have to straighten out."

"Well, thank God most of that is over." And he added
meaningfully, "We don't have to quarrel any more. We can
concentrate on the children. We can be friends."

"Yes, of course, but turns out there are some other expenses—"

"Oh please, no, kid."

"Yes."

"What do you mean?"

"Some other little things. It's complicated raising children
under these circumstances, all alone—well, never mind that.
Let me see. Not just Dr. Jonas, but——"

"What? That again? I won't bother pointing out about

that one bill, but as to any others, you know very well——"

"You know very well!"

"Please don't be sarcastic. Let me finish." But she was staring at him with her enormous eyes turning black—as with anger, as with love—the pupils dilating, and thick congested hate squirting like black arterial blood from a deep wound over the thin face. He struggled to be without memory. He thought again (how many times like this?) that if he could keep calm, keep easy, maybe she, too, would make the effort. He said in a low, forced, effortful voice, "You know very well that our agreement states that you meet all expenses out of the check I send you every month. There's no other way to do it, kid——"

"Don't call me kid! I never liked it! Your idea of an endearment!"

He went on stubbornly, quietly, "You know what my income is. I don't even— Well, I'm not complaining. But there's nothing more to discuss about money unless I fail to send you the check some month."

"Kid! Kid! You still want to call me kid, but if one of your children needs some special care, what's it to you——?"

"What's the matter?" he interrupted, frowning. *"What* special care?"

She mimicked him with ungainly, ferocious sarcasm. "It's not in the agreement. . . ."

"Are you going to tell me? Or is this all nonsense again?"

"I want to send Paula to the Bainbridge School."

"What for? We—*you* can't afford a private school like that. Anyway, what does she need it for?"

"A fatherless child!"

"Is that my fault? Did you want me? Did you *want* me?" —and he felt the harsh sting of self-pity like dust at his eyes and he shook it out angrily. "Didn't I fight to keep us together long after any other man would have run off or gone batty?"

She tapped her foot and did not answer. He had a suspicion that he could peel off her skin now and find a genuine, very satisfied smile, but with a forced calm—like his— she began patiently to explain. "I've discussed this with several people. The Bainbridge School——"

"I'll tell you just one thing: I don't have the money."

"—is oriented toward difficulties, special problems, broken homes——"

"Oriented, oriented!" He called out the word as if it were a verdict brought down upon her. He stood up, shaking. He had a throbbing frontal headache just behind his eyes. "Please let me get out of here, I've got to get out," he said. "Let me take the children and get out for a while. The little thing we should orient ourselves to is orienting ourselves toward not talking like this when they're watching."

And they both turned and admitted the presence of the two, very quiet, very thoughtful little girls. "We were just talking," Shaper said weakly.

Shrunken and bent, all the pleasant civilizing of their time of separation scraped away, his wife managed to wipe the children's faces for their walk. At the door she turned to him and said severely, "When you come back, please leave them downstairs to play for a few minutes. I want to talk with you alone."

Blackmail! In order to see the children, in order to keep her from trying to rip him out of their lives as she had ripped him bleeding out of hers, he had to find some way of settling into a decent habit with her. The headaches that were already a tradition of their arguments made him almost blind in his left eye. He counted on her not interfering with the children—at least for this her psychology supported him—but he suspected that she wanted to think of him as an ideal monster, and then she could reason that for their own good they should *relate, transfer, orient* to some other man. Her words! That damn vocabulary! Lousy blackmail! He tried to soothe his eye by cupping the palm of his hand over it. Blackmail!

Within the dynamics of her romantic, absolutistic passion for the ideal, each failure between them had to be complete and each small difference total war. Symbols had become reality, reality had become a great abstract, timeless, and predetermined sign; her energy was bent furiously on making reality over in the image of her idea about it, even at the cost of destroying its value as reality. (She could not measure the cost. Cost is not a part of heavenly systems.) This way of life has a kind of internal logic, perfect and unaffected by experience; there was no opposing it. Once her husband was defined by her needs ("It happened to me when I was immature"), there was nothing he could do to become human again. Even yielding to her—that most human of acts—enraged her because it violated her idea about him. She hurt herself, and could not stop, and threw herself and the husband she once loved and anyone else in the way (including their children) under the clanking treads of the interlocking syllogisms by which she lived: Good and Evil are pure; the ideal exists only in heaven; my husband is here below with me, on earth; therefore he is evil. I must have perfection; I do not have perfection; then this is hell I live in and I am damned and I will destroy, destroy, destroy. . . . Still, someday, O someday I will find pure virtue in a man! He must exist because I can imagine him. I need him right now! I deserve him, I call him, I insist on him! I am pure, I have waited for him, this other creature has no value because see the way he shrivels, vanishes, like a bad idea! I will prove that he does not exist by making him recognize it himself.

And so silly, smart novels. And bouquets of roses in a cut-glass vase. Well, if he knew how she was getting at him, he should be able to get out of the way. And he didn't have to display Sally, either.

VI

Fortified by wry self-congratulation at his assent to whatever she now needed in order to do away with him, he could turn his back on her judgment and go to another. He did not believe in magic; her eyes could no longer make love to him, make harm for him, uncover into life that which was only recently buried but quite dead, and down the dust came sifting fast. It was done. There were the children left, for ever and ever the heirs. He would shower again and scrub hard.

But always there returned the tangled memories which dragged him off the straight road leading from life into the violent death of divorce and back into life again. Their children were not the only heirs, the only judges. It would be useful simply to hate her until he forgot her. It would be fine to despise her. Pride! But when he had almost succeeded (for example, in a sweet moment of fuel and money while having the oil checked in Sally's car), abruptly his greedy feeding on resentment came back to him, his joy and suspense before what she would do if she discovered that, for almost a year, there had been another girl. She needed the lesson; he had almost told her himself to let her know how he, too, might be lonely. . . . But recognized his cruelty. And remembered that the night before she found him out, she had risen to his grief and guilt to comfort him in what she took for a passing depression; there had been a miraculous access of tenderness and gratitude, and she had said, "We have the best little kids in the world, I know it, Dan. I'm sorry about the boy, I know it's foolish. Be patient with me. Care for me."

And then the next day the gossip came round and she had confronted him and he had thought, Let her learn, let her burn awhile. We've tried everything else.

Divorce time, wake up! It was time to move past his malice and her answering sweetness, past his yearning and her vindictiveness, past their other swinging meetings and partings, and years of it, common efforts, successes, bitter ultimate failure. While she talked, talked, talked, harassed him, practiced meanness, he could still find the silent regret faraway—deep in her eyes—apology, helpless apology—and yet the two of them could not settle together into firm admission of it. Her regret and her ancient willingness to love were resin-soaked roots. She consumed them. She refused to look at them. So be it, she seemed to have decided, abandoning her will with relief, and threw the uncured wood on the fire; and the destruction of what she most needed to grow from gave a wild hissing edge to her sarcasm, "I do wish that you would please stop calling me *kid*. Customarily that's for the children of goats. I seem to recall that I have a name."

Arson. She still remembered something more than that from him. On her face—as the lover in the morning finds on his darling's face the marks of their excess together during

the night—he saw the brand of her secret self-appraisal, secret wish that it might be otherwise. It was like that thickness
and slight purpling of eyelids in the morning after the flesh
has made fantastic avowals that moments do not die (even
as the moment is dying), that what the intentions of lovers
have brought together no God shall sunder (even as spirit
and life notify us of matter and death). Who desires what
they had now earned? She had wanted to want only him.
To him she had cleaved for everything, rest, trust, energy,
hope. "But I need a son, too," she had said. "Lots of women
have sons. No one is perfect. I want *your* son, Dan, no one
else's. Why can't I have the one thing I need?"

For everything, for too much.

As he recalled his chill judgment of her fever, the summer and the city spun crazily around him and he thought:
It is as she says—all my fault, all! I was bored with her because I could not admit my need of her, because I feared
that her weakness excluded me and she could do nothing
for me. I took for boredom my dull despair of touching her
without the qualification of a son, of receiving what a husband asks *without qualification,* so that I determined to need
nothing at all from her and to build a life which did not
depend on her. I sought to harden myself by freezing. Monstrous!

"You're a monster," she had shrieked when he admitted
that his strength to indulge her had come from a little student at the Institute of Music.

"It didn't make any difference then. You were thinking
about your skin, your waistline, your father, your analyst,
your fantasies about a son—you didn't really care what
I——"

The war again. Go! He leapt from the transport. His
parachute was tangled. Other bodies hurtled free, mouths
open, teeth bared, roaring with effort. They relished the free
tumble into space; for him it was death. "Monster!" He
plummeted. Didn't he have the same rights as others? No.
He would be a sickness of gore on the earth below. "Monster, monster!" And then it came back to him, first with a
belly-jerking violence, earth and life crashing up toward him
as the parachute caught, opened, and he gasped, and then he

lazily swung like a pendulum on a great clock: I am not a
monster. Nor is she. But I am not, either.

He went to Sally that evening with something which he
knew was not love, but she thought it was. Surely she was
not really deceived; his need of her was what she needed,
and love an irrelevance. Nevertheless she showed her doubt
in ways that made it harder for him—her anxious trick of
brushing and rebrushing her eyelashes with mascara, her
rather heavy step into the kitchen, giving him a glimpse of
the thickened waist to come, the overbright, slightly foolish,
false glee of her smile, responding to uneasiness by an
American piece of advice, *Keep smiling!* She came back
with coffee, a glare of teeth, blond eyelashes on which he
made out tiny beads of blacking.

He asked her to take off her make-up, and she did. His
chill calculation shocked him. He wondered if his wife had
so shot his nerves that all he could bear now would be a
sweetly boring girl, worried only about pleasing him and
getting the shine off her nose with the right shade of powder, a lover of musicals and of her beauty sleep—and
of pleasing him! That quintessence of desirability! She
watched, frowning. He grew tender and regretful. What
could he ever do for her? She meant to be good to him.
She studied him silently, unreproaching, with the pallor of
the blond girl without make-up under bad light, and she
suddenly seemed very beautiful, the most lovely woman in
creation. He switched off the lamp and they moved toward
each other in the dark.

When they lay down together, she said something which
surprised him. It was trivial and familiar, like the breathless
delicacies of undressing, and yet it was a trouble that she
should cry out to him with words that seemed merely taken
from a popular song: "Oh put yourself close to me baby."

How he wished for her silence then!

Afterwards he realized that the shock of vulgarity came
not from her words but from his considering and judging
her without interruption. He stroked her hair gently and felt
sorry for her, for him. Someone was using someone. Somebody was somebody's weapon. There, there. "Sally, darling,

I'm not good these days," he said. "I used to be, I want to be, but I'm in trouble."

"You are, you are, don't worry, you are good."

"I'm in bad trouble. I'm afraid. Nothing's clear any more."

"It will be, don't worry. You just need time, Dan. You make *me* happy."

"Do I?"

She put her finger on his mouth, shh. She wanted to sleep. He dozed too, asking himself, Why don't I ever think of her until I have to? That first day and the swimming was an accident, the false health of fever. Not right, not right, though I take my breath from her hair.

Then he slept.

In the middle of the night he woke with a start, with a sense of flapping inconsequential interruption, as if a cat had jumped onto his back. He lay staring into the murmurous dark and fearful of the dream he could almost remember which had awakened him. Oh yes, yes. Forget about it. He had been falling without a parachute for years and years. He did not crash to earth; he diminished. The starving man could not take food—even the thinnest broth was an agony to his constricted body.

The air conditioner threw its chill breeze into the room. Gradually, very slowly, reluctant to disturb the fine integrity of her sleep, he began to stretch against Sally for ease and new rest. She was warm, spreading, slightly curled as she lay. He pressed against the softly sleeping girl. He put his hand over her back and moved it down through slopes and valleys. She stirred, and their mouths were breathing and feeding into each other. In a few minutes he heard a hoarse voice, his own, saying, "Oh come to me baby." She gathered him in.

VII

The last day of the visit. Shaper wanted to store up memories of his children so that, like a camel, he could survive away from them through a season of drought. Yellow-eyed, lurching, he was still not a camel; he could not live for oases; he could not carry Paula and Cynthia in a hump. Still he had hope. Although it was already several days past the end for his wife and him, he believed that perhaps they could manage one more meeting for the sake of the children.

Sally gave him her automobile to drive out to the house. This time the mild luxury, moving through traffic in the sun with the top down, failed to reassure him. He found himself singing an old Louis Armstrong blues tune:

> *From milkless milk*
> *And silkless silk*
> *Love oh love oh loveless love*

On an impulse he stopped at Peter's, found him home, and asked him to come along. "My wife and I will both be on good behavior with a third party present." And he looked away. "That's the way it is, Pete. Sorry."

The children were shy; they knew he was going. They had no practice in goodbyes. For them he was already gone. Paula gave him a drawing of flowers and the sun to put on his wall—"where you live, Daddy." The sun was sticking out its tongue.

As the subdued and uneventful visit ended, it occurred to Shaper that Pete might find his insistence on having a witness somewhat melodramatic.

"Goodbye," he said to his wife.

"Goodbye," she said.

"I hope everything goes well."

"Have a good trip back."

They shook hands. Peter looked embarrassed. They went downstairs. Shaper glanced back from the driveway and at the same moment two things happened: The children came out to stand on the upstairs porch, and his wife came running down the stairs. She paused, breathing shallowly, before Shaper and Peter near the door of the automobile. She put out her hand with a slip of paper in it. "I enrolled Paula at that school," she said softly. "I forgot to mention it. Here's the bill."

He drew back and tried to look merely puzzled. "You

know I'm not supposed to. . . . I can't pay these bills. We already decided about that."

She held to the low tone, but there was a stir and hiss in her voice. "Who decided? Who? Who decided?"

"Look"—and he was pleading although he knew this was the wrong way to move her. He had only found a steady right way when he was sick and needed her out of helplessness. It was the only way he could count on for sure. It was no way by which he could live. "Look, I sent a check for that dentist's bill, although you were wrong about the date. It came after our agreement. Now please try to understand, there's got to be a stop."

"A stop to what?"

"We have to start living the way things are. We have to adjust. You've said it yourself. Money shouldn't get in the way now. Our lawyers——" And he watched the pinched face and the black, swollen eyes replacing that bright young divorcee which was her pleasant role. He had hoped, but once more he misjudged her. Through those inky eyes, through the cloud of hate with which she blinded herself and poisoned him, she would not see what they had sometimes been for each other—she never saw that any more; she would not see the neighbors, she would not see Peter, she would not see the children. "Kid! Listen to me, please!" And he had no words to force her to remember how they had held hands and strolled in parks, and tenderly made up many quarrels, and congratulated each other that the girls were a fine combination of the best in both of them.

A stop? Her lips were saying, working within, white and diminishing.

"Listen, please, *please,*" he said, "you have to understand how things are with me now. I live in a room, don't you understand? One room. I'm not a college kid, I'm not used to it any more. One furnished room, do you hear me? I save my money so I can fly in to see the children——"

"Then don't do it."

"What did you say, kid?" He leaned forward, trying to see her. "I'm sorry, I didn't understand."

"I said stay there. Get yourself a kitchenette. Don't bother coming in."

He held his breath. He was peering into a night, and his
eye was tired. It throbbed, and he wanted to comfort it
with his palm. It seemed very important this time not to let
her know about the ache in his eye. He straightened up and
said, "Look at me. Look at us, kid." His eye wanted an
eye to return its gaze.

"Just don't bother," she said, as if her mind were far
away with household thoughts. "Stay away. I could spend
the money. Who needs you here? Don't bother."

She drew closer to him with a little smile on her face.

"And I may as well give you one other bit of information. Why not? Since you're leaving again." She spoke this
last phrase slowly, as if it were particularly important. He
recognized the angry wenchy smell which her body gave up
when she could no longer hold on. She said: "Now I feel
like a woman. I've found a man who knows how."

In the first moment of almost prudish shock, he felt his
face being fixed in a skeletal grin. "That had to come. The
list is complete. Okay. All right." But the grin spread un-
controllably, attacking his bones, dissolving the sockets of
his eyes.

"It was no good with you. Your fault. It was never any
good."

"All right," he said, "congratulations." He turned to
Peter. "You hear? My wife was a virgin all along."

"Yes," she said, "that's about it. I told Carl, too, how I
was never touched. Since you're going away again, you
might as well have this to take with you. Nothing. Never
anything, though I tried to make you believe. . . ."

Their children were leaning over the railing to peer down
on them. His hand flew toward his eye; he stopped it midway and put it down. He said: "All right, there's no point
in discussing this either, is there? Our lawyers have it all
settled now. We paid the lawyers to do this job for us."

"Lawyers!" And it was done. Something new had been
released, and in public, in the summertime, with people
coming out on their porches or peering through the screens
to listen and saying *a shame* and smiling to themselves.
"You want lawyers to raise our children?" she shouted.
"That's your idea of a father?"

"All right, all right," he said in a low hoarse voice. He held himself stiffly, shaking with fury and disappointment. "Can't you control it? All this nonsense. There are people. You're doing it on purpose, kid, don't you see?"

She screamed as if he had struck her. "Don't call me kid! Just get out of my life!"

"Okay, okay." He turned to climb into the car. Peter was already huddled miserably on the seat. As he moved behind the wheel, he felt an almost physical eruption, a brutal crack in his throat, and the word came out, "Fishwife!"

"Corrupt! Corrupt!" she was shrieking at him. "Get out of my driveway! Go! Corrupt! You never cared for me or your kids—*children*"—and desperately she sobbed the correction. "Or anyone but yourself! Get out of my life!"

That was how, standing silently together on the porch, the children saw him last. He was being chased by their mother's rage.

At the corner he pulled over to the curb and asked Peter to drive. "I'm not in control," he said, shivering, and went on as if this were the total explanation. "It was what broke us up. I had to stop, I couldn't be run by her temper. Once I saw Paula watching me back down like a fool just because of that look she gets in her eyes—you saw it, Pete—when she can't be reached. When I saw my daughter judging me. . . . It didn't even help to slap her, I tried that once or twice. . . ."

Peter turned and drove through the long park along East Boulevard. He was explaining, comforting, merely talking. "Well, she has to feel better about what she's doing. She's not the kind of woman who can take ambiguity. You have to be all good or all bad, and you're *it*, man. Once you could do no wrong; now. . . . Well, women are like that. Don't think she's going to be nice for the sake of the past."

"What about the kids?"

"The past has got to be wiped out. Women have their feet on the ground—anyway they call it the ground, sometimes it's our faces—and one thing she thinks she can do for the next man—whoever he is, I don't know if she's telling the truth," he added hurriedly, "is just wipe you out. That way she gets to be a girl again. She said it plain enough.

For her you've got to be pure mistake, friend, and nothing else. Evil Dan the Bad Young Man."

"No kindness at all? That's how I'd like to be. Let me tell you something: When we first decided to separate we both wept."

Peter shook his head. "She told Ellen *you* cried. She said you're maudlin. She said you held her hand until it ached. Make up your mind to take it. Women—" Did Peter believe what he was saying? No, he was tuckered out and embarrassed and his mouth was uttering for him the cynical clichés about women which men in club cars tell each other. It was what he thought Dan wanted to hear. He may even have believed it true at that moment, true because it sounded familiar, and with a deep breath of fatigue (he thought this was sympathy) he again spoke what he took to be comfort to his friend: "Women," he sighed.

"But doesn't she look all yellow, sick? Her skin that color and those enormous black eyes. Yellow, sick, and mean. She used to be so pretty. She still is. Oh she hates me!"

They both fell silent. When Peter felt that he had done his duty, he asked to be dropped at home. He needed to get away. He loved his own wife; he felt as disconnected, tired, and jittery as if he had been casually unfaithful to her. Naturally he resented his old friend for bringing him to this possibility, and also—because his wife was surely his best friend—he resented Dan for eliciting his jovial male cynicisms. And within, too, he felt a thrill of pride: not for him this failure! This is the pleasure we are said to feel at funerals. And at a still deeper, more solemn place, because he was a good and kind man, he felt regret for his friend and also knew something of what was happening to him. This sense came up through the barriers as discomfort, as a desire to squirm: I can't take it, I want to do my duty by you, Dan; I want to get away. He had his own wife and children to play with on a fine dry summer afternoon. Ellen had asked him to do some shopping.

VIII

I held her hand until it hurt her! And what a bore she was with her whining and her headaches and her suspicions! Suspicions!

Better. He used his old ritual for remembering himself into gratitude for freedom: her nagging, her picking at her face in the mirror, her stiff jealous mouth with the white lines. Sure, finally he had given her cause for jealousy, why not? But first he had warned her that she was making him lonely when she stood before the mirror, plucking, squeezing, hating herself, dreaming of miraculous sources of happiness—her father fantastically restored to life, a baby boy instead of girls, an analyst who really understood and *said* something.

> *With dreamless dreams*
> *And schemeless schemes*
> *Love oh love oh——*

It was fine to be driving Sally's car with the top down. She was waiting for him, and she would be all health and dazzling smiles, unskilled in moping, untrained for meanness.

But don't you have to take a woman from strength, not weakness, if you are to give her anything important and receive anything worth taking?

And after his ten-year marriage, wasn't he too distant from Sally to bring her anything but that cheating desire, the need for comfort? He had loved his wife despite everything, he knew he had, they had been young and unmarked together, he insisted on remembering—and he did not love Sally. He made too much of the hot pity of bodies. He had thought to find love by loving, but instead, at length, filled with crazy pride, he had discovered sex. The solution was as ineffective as the discovery was unoriginal. Like his wife, he made too much of things.

When what he needed to save his life was simplicity, a bare white room and sleep, restoring sleep, how long could greater and greater complication soothe him?

Didn't that mean only trouble to come?

Perhaps. He parked Sally's automobile on the street before the massive, teeming apartment building—luxury circa 1928—in which she lived with her closets full of clothes, her mirrors, her pink-feathered slippers, and her music-to-dream-by. But if he couldn't allow himself Sally, that beautiful and perhaps silly girl—yes, he should say it out, maybe it's true—he might be unable to prevent doing what he had too often already considered. He had stood caught in the middle of his furnished room and thought it through. He had first been indulgent, then shocked by the persistence of the idea. Apparently it was one to reckon with.

He went up the long walk to the stuffy, overdecorated entrance, found her bell, and rang it. Could Sally stop his idea?

As he often did, he tried to think of what would happen to the children. That was a puzzler.

THE SOLITARY LIFE OF MAN

Leo E. Litwak

LEO E. LITWAK *was born in Detroit and attended Wayne and Columbia Universities. He spent three years in the army, is married and has one child, a daughter. He is currently teaching philosophy at Washington University in St. Louis. His stories have appeared in* Partisan Review, Midstream, Esquire, *and* Nugget, *and he is completing a novel to be published next year.*

Melford Kuhn had done his duty and with courage. He had received a Silver Star for carrying a wounded buddy a thousand yards while under fire from a pillbox. He mocked the decoration. He cursed brass hats. He disdained all that was rear echelon. He was judged to be the most effective platoon sergeant in the company. This judgment was the buttress of his pride.

There were a few truths that had so affected him that all else seemed irrelevant. A shell fragment has a trajectory defined by its initial velocity and direction and the successive forces impressed upon it. Flesh and bone were not impressive forces. The fragment could act as bullet, knife, cleaver, bludgeon. It could punch, shear, slice, crush, tear. It could be surgical in its precision or make sadistic excess seem unimaginative.

And what happened to brass-hat zeal when the brain was exposed, when guts unfolded, when a flayed stump drooled blood? Didn't the lieutenant turn away from Morgan's shredded stump, mumbling, "I can't. Oh, no!"? Kuhn fixed the tourniquet. Yet they became zealots again when the dying was a few days past and they were in the company of their brother officers and they could begin the falsification of history which proposed heroes and cowards and right action and blunders.

He had learned that the dread of dying is a knife that hacks at all sentiments and kills those which have no validity. He scorned those who approached combat from the perspective of honor, ambition, and the other sentiments of gallantry which flourish when there is no risk of dying.

He felt that ignorance had been pared away from him until only the core of truth was left. The more imminent death became, the narrower was his focus, until now, after two years of combat, he had reached hard fact. Not country, not family, not buddies, but only he himself was relevant. And as his focus narrowed, he became more taciturn, less concerned with the vanities which depended on a wider community.

He loathed Solomon. Solomon was a supply sergeant, assigned to battalion headquarters, who had no reason for being at the front. He should have been two miles back, in a village already secured, nicely housed, nicely fed, profiting from the German obsequiousness which made everything available to acquisitive hands. Solomon was forty-five, a swarthy, big-nosed man, his face creased, tall, gaunt, with a gentle manner. He was dressed like a soldier, yet Kuhn regarded him as a caricature of a soldier. His clothes were glistening new issue, and he used all the tricks of dressing which the combat soldier learns through necessity. He wore a field jacket over his wool sweater, OD trousers tucked into combat boots, a knit wool cap under his helmet liner and steel helmet. Solomon, with his pious talk, his admiration for heroes, his fear of cowardice, his flagrant sympathizing, had become intolerable to Kuhn. Solomon used the sanctimonious language which charmed officers back in battalion headquarters, but he had no flair for the bitter invective which the GI recognized as the language of a friend.

The platoon was assembled, ready to mount the truck. The company jeep arrived with a galvanized can filled with hot coffee. The men lined up and dipped into the coffee with their canteen cups. It was a chill morning, and Solomon stood at the rear of the line, his arms wrapped around his chest, his hands tucked into his armpits.

"Solomon—" Kuhn waved him over to his side and walked him out of earshot of the others. "What are you doing here, Solomon?"

Solomon smiled, misunderstanding Kuhn's intention. "I think I should take my chances with the rest of the boys, Mel. Let them have their coffee first."

"That's damn nice of you. You could be sitting down to breakfast back in battalion."

"It weighs on my conscience, Mel, that I should be safe while the boys up here take all the risks."

"This isn't a club for healthy consciences. I'm not interested in your conscience. There isn't one of us who wouldn't be back in battalion if he had the chance. All you're doing up here, Solomon, is taking someone's coffee."

Solomon shivered. He pulled one arm free and shrugged with it. "You're right. I'll go without coffee."

"Solomon! We're going to take a village this morning. Suppose we have trouble? What do you do, Solomon?"

"What I can do I don't know. But whatever you want I should do, I'll try."

"I've got no job for you." He wanted to snarl, "Stop cringing, Stupid!" Instead he glared his dislike. "Rodansky tells me you bother him with your kraut pitying. How come you're giving Rodansky trouble?"

Solomon rubbed his eyes. He wore OD wool gloves with leather palms. He was more than twenty years older than Kuhn. "Rodansky is bothered by the German boy. I know he's bothered. So he didn't offend me."

"I don't care if you're offended. You're no problem of mine. I care about my platoon. And you're just trouble for me. I don't want you around, Solomon."

Solomon nodded. "I'll ride back with the jeep. I apologize, Mel."

Kuhn walked away from him.

Rodansky had been on guard duty the day before. He had heard a noise in the bushes at the edge of the platoon area. He had challenged, then had fired, and Kuhn had found him standing beside the dying man. The German lay behind a bush, his arms extending through it. He wore a great-coat. His wool cap had fallen off. His hair was in the midst of the bush, an abundant, dirty yellow. He wasn't armed, and Kuhn rolled him over. The German wheezed through his chest.

"I told him to put up his hands. *'Hands auf,'* I said."

"What a mess. He's a kid."

The boy was already soggy gray. The slug had hit at an angle, swerved within the compass of the chest, and his heart was bared. *"Warum hast du—"* Neither Kuhn nor Rodansky understood German and they did not respond to the boy's muttering.

Kuhn straightened up as others in the platoon joined them. "He won't last till the aid station. Leave him here. Is the medic around? It doesn't make any difference."

Then Solomon came up, gasping with fear, blanching when he heard the moans. He fell to his knees beside the boy and touched his face. He listened to the muttering. "He wants to know why did we shoot." Solomon looked up, asking the question in his own right. "He says he wanted to surrender. *'Wir haben nicht gewissen,'* " he explained to the boy, his voice trembling with compassion. "He wants to know if he's dying."

"He's dead, Solomon! Tell him he's dead. *Tot,*" Rodansky shouted at the boy. "Kraut *tot!*"

"Nein," Solomon said in turn. He told the boy they would soon have him in a hospital. *"Wir haben nicht gewissen,"* he concluded in hopeless apology.

A few weeks before, twelve men from the platoon had been killed in front of a pillbox. There had been considerable variety in their deaths. They'd been zeroed in by eighty-eights. The GIs had swallowed these deaths as part of the nourishment of combat whose grotesqueries provisioned their daily fare.

Rodansky caught Solomon's arm as they left the boy to the medic.

"What the hell you doing in the army, Solomon—an old man like you? Why aren't you back with the girls, getting the dough, saluting the flag? What are you here for, Solomon?"

Solomon was still shocked by the sight of the naked heart beating in a sheath of slime. His face mirrored the open-mouthed pallor of the dying German.

He raised his arms waist high and let them flop. He repeated this gesture several times before answering Rodansky. "He asked is he dying. He came to surrender. Why did we shoot, he wants to know. He's maybe only sixteen. The poor boy!"

"Poor boy!"

"It doesn't matter to me all of a sudden that he's German. His chest was breathing, Harry. Did you hear it? Ah! I wish we didn't shoot. It's a pity, a pity, Rodansky."

Though they had recently come from a reserve area where shower facilities were available, Rodansky hadn't washed or shaved. His helmet was set low on his forehead, and he peered from under it like a man taking a cautious look in the midst of a barrage. He released his grip on Solomon's arm to squeeze his rifle with both hands. He shook the rifle at Solomon, his lips twisting for an adequate expression of his outrage. "I shot, you old bastard, not you! You bastard! We fight your wars and then you come around and preach!"

It was clear that he meant the "you" generically. Solomon revealed his identity with every shrug, with every anecdote, with his intonation, with his liberal use of such notions as Pity and Justice, with his faithful attendance at Saturday services.

Kuhn shared Rodansky's loathing for this old man who presumed to give them lessons in sentiment when he was so little experienced in the passion that proved integrity, the fear of death. The following morning he ordered Solomon back to the rear.

They had come so fast into Germany that they passed through villages still entrucked, leaving the security of the area to the reserve companies that followed. The widely spaced convoy rattled down poor country roads, claiming a new segment of Germany with each turn of the wheels. The Germans who lined the streets cheered the convoy with the enthusiasm of the liberated. When the soldiers dismounted and formed squads to scour a village, they found the Germans more tractable than any ally. *"Nach kirche!"* the GIs shouted. The Germans took up the cry and without further urging streamed to church where they were instructed by the military government. The town was left in the hands of the GIs. These were irreverent hands, not limited by any law. They stripped watches from the grinning Germans. They ransacked the German houses for guns and cameras and silver and food. The Germans yielded their homes to GI boots which trampled their linens and muddied their beds. The women were cheerful offerings to appease the conqueror. Good food, good servants, good plumbing, good women, they were a magnificent fee to conquer. Kuhn despised them. Good cameras, good watches, good pistols, they were as good to Kuhn as any European. Kuhn had a Luger, a Leica, a fine Swiss watch.

Ahead of them, beyond the reach of GI boots, there was law supported by a seemingly death-defying ardor. There was German law and German pride ahead of them. Ahead of them were boasts that the German spirit would endure death rather than humiliation. Behind them they left a disordered mob prepared to sacrifice everything German and human to preserve themselves. Without urging, the Germans denied all that they had been and betrayed any compatriot whose betrayal benefited them.

Kuhn had so far not failed himself. He had not lost himself in the solvent of dread. He had made trembling legs advance. He had made his panicked hands obey him. He had refused to be overwhelmed by fatigue. Whatever beliefs he possessed he was sure of, since they had endured. Yet his victories had not relieved him from oppression. He was more and more oppressed. Instead of being restored by the intervals between hazards, he spent the time anticipating future catastrophes. He didn't know the extent of his endurance. He feared that moment when his courage would fail him and he would act badly.

As the truck bore them across a German valley, he scanned the sky for aircraft. He studied the roadside for cover. He planned his escape from the truck. The sky was too clear, the land too hilly, the opportunities for ambuscade unsettling. He didn't rely on the scouting jeeps to discover snipers. He only trusted his own vision. He tried imagining the city of Helo where they were to dismount and assemble for an assault. He wondered whether the Germans would be supported by tanks and artillery, whether they would be yielding or would resist.

The banter of the GIs irritated him. He considered their ability to forget hazards a kind of amnesia, fortunate if one could settle for something other than truth. The men were crammed on benches that ran the length of the truck on both sides. They squatted on the floor. They pressed together, shoulders and hips joined, knees against backs, rifles held between legs, loosened helmet straps clanging against steel with each toss of the truck.

"—outside of Triers, remember?" Reilly summoned his buddies to hear the anecdote. "That pillbox with the railroad tunnel?" He and Rodansky had left their squad to check a farmhouse. It was a place with an inner court and a ripe compost pile and pigs and chickens and Russian laborers. Rodansky found a book filled with sketches. These showed a man and woman going all out for love. Various attitudes were sketched in provocative detail. The farm wife entered. Rodansky looked at her, then at the sketchbook. "This is you?" He held up the book and tapped his finger on the woman depicted. The farm wife nodded. "This is me!" Rodansky shouted, pointing to the man. He threw off his harness, dropped his rifle on the table, and pursued her into the bedroom.

Rodansky admitted his conquest and in response to their urging detailed it. He was filled with a charge that raised him mile high. "She didn't run no further than that bed. All feathers it was, so she sunk out of sight with her legs poking up. We didn't get past page one. It's lucky for me there was a war on."

What perhaps the men most admired was Rodansky's ability to forget the pillbox where a few hours previously they had lost an entire squad. Rodansky was able to lust when only terror seemed appropriate. He made places and people who were strange to the GIs less intimidating by humbling them. He'd had limey women in England, Frog and Belgian girls, fräuleins—and in circumstances which seemed to rule out any passion but fear. Once he'd disappeared into a cellar with a fräulein while they struggled for a village. Machine guns directed tracers at the GIs from the high ground beyond. They could see Tiger tanks maneuvering on the hillside for a counterattack. And afterwards what they remembered of that village was, not the GI and German dead, not their panic when it seemed that the enemy tanks would assault them, but Rodansky taking a recess from war in order to satisfy an appetite they were delighted had survived.

Kuhn saw in this eagerness to return to manageable passions a betrayal of experience which he attributed not only to GIs, but to allies and enemies everywhere, and above all to those who remained in the rear echelons, never risking death. Instead of being readied for disaster by his relaxing intermissions, Rodansky was becoming untrustworthy. He bitched too much, he talked too much. He failed to tend himself when they were in reserve. And Kuhn believed that if fear hadn't predominated, Rodansky could have taken the German boy prisoner.

The convoy ascended a steep hill. From the crest they looked down upon a valley. The day was clear, and they were able to view a dozen villages, each centered around a church, ringed first with plowed fields and then with forest. The wind came from the east and brought a piney smell and a vague sound which seemed composed of church bells, the lowing of cattle, the barking of dogs, but nothing of war. Across the valley, straggling beneath the distant hills was the city of Helo. No tanks were visible, no Germans, there was no sound of artillery, no machine-gun staccato to presage resistance ahead. On the left, some two miles distant, they observed another column, preceding them toward Helo. The information was passed back that B and C Companies of their battalion would take the city, with small resistance expected, and that their company would follow in reserve.

The men were jubilant. This was a fine big city that had been spared air raids, and they were getting it peacefully. What novelties in bedding, what steals in cameras, what city fräuleins were available? They relished the chickens they would gut; hams, sausages, preserves they would loot; wine from cellars; and finally sleep.

They dismounted six miles from Helo with orders to sweep the area before the city. Kuhn's platoon controlled a sector three hundred yards wide, consisting mainly of open field and farmhouses. He broke the platoon into squads, instructing the squad leaders to keep track of their men. "There's a crossroads about three miles from here. We'll assemble there in two hours. Keep moving. Call me if there's any trouble."

The mission was uneventful. Kuhn reached the assembly point with time to spare. The day had warmed sufficiently to make the march uncomfortable. Chester Grove, the platoon messenger, accompanied Kuhn. Grove was a farmer from Oklahoma, a lumpish man who admired Kuhn. He nervously broached topics which he hoped would interest Kuhn.

"If we get it now, Sarge, when it's almost over, what a joke."

"It's a long way from over."

"It's been a couple weeks since we run into artillery. Everyone's relaxed. I tell you, Sarge, you can be trained for a lot of things. Experience makes you better if you want to be an athlete or a farmer or for screwing. You get smarter reading books. There's a lot of things where practice makes perfect. But, Sarge, when I hear a shell I don't have the nerve I first had. I figure that every time I wasn't killed I was in luck and there's only so much luck a man has before the cards change."

The squads arrived, Reilly's squad reporting last. The men sprawled along the roadside, munching at K-rations and food looted in the course of the march.

"Everybody here?"

"Rodansky ain't showed up," Reilly reported. "Give him a few minutes, Sarge. He'll be along."

"Where is he?"

"You know old Rodansky, Sarge. He could find himself a woman and a bed Sunday morning in church."

"Where is he?"

"Back in that farmhouse." Reilly pointed to a farmhouse

in a grove of trees, half a mile from the assembly point.

"He's got five more minutes." When the five minutes passed, Kuhn nodded. "Okay, Reilly. Let's get him."

Plodding and sour-faced, there were a few buddy indiscretions Reilly wouldn't forgive. He might regret excess in killing, cowardice, gold-bricking, but so long as it was family that was in error he was tolerant. The broadness of his view did not extend beyond the family of buddies.

"Old Rodansky, when he's on tail, it takes a direct hit from a eighty-eight to get him off."

"I'll get him off."

"Take it easy, Sarge. Harry's okay."

"You think this war is a joke, Reilly?"

They walked directly into the kitchen. Rodansky's rifle was on a counter near a tile oven. His field jacket, hung with grenades, lay in a chair.

Kuhn shouted for Rodansky. He walked to the door beside the oven and kicked it. "Rodansky! Come out of there!"

Reilly caught his arm. "Hold on, Sarge. He'll come."

Kuhn shoved the door open. The room was dark. There was a burst of motion from the high bed. Rodansky scrambled from the bed, gripping his pants. He came toward the light, fumbling with his belt, his shirt undone, blinking, stunned, a sweaty smell accompanying him. The woman crouched on the other side of the bed.

"That's a lousy trick, Kuhn. It's no skin off your nose. What are you getting so goddam GI for?"

Kuhn struggled with a murderous impulse he didn't understand. "I catch you again leaving your rifle around like that and I'll bust the hell out of you."

"Bust me. I'm a PFC."

"I can bust you good, Rodansky. You know what I mean? You want to push harder and find out?"

Kuhn hurried back to the platoon without waiting for Reilly and Rodansky.

C Company had the outskirts of Helo. A tank man pissed from a doorway, his free hand gripping a bottle of wine. Chemical mortars had fired the bordering houses, and no efforts were made to stop the burning. B Company had sequestered an entire block, and the men of B Company had already cashed in on the available bounty.

Instead of approaching the heart of town, the reserve company was directed along its periphery. For a moment, peering down a winding street, they glimpsed a sizable plaza that promised the amenities of city life they had long missed. They were marched through a residential area, then to a dirt road, and soon the city was on their left, open field on their right, and it was evident they were not intended to share the fortunes of the other companies in the battalion.

In an open field, two miles beyond the city, they came to barracks enclosed with barbed wire. There were three buildings that formed a *U*-shape. The buildings were mere boxes, with small windows covered with steel mesh. The ground surrounding the buildings was hard clay.

The prospect was barren, and Kuhn shared the general dismay. The battalion jeep was at the entrance to the compound. A group of officers huddled around the jeep while the company halted. The captain and platoon leaders conferred with the major. Solomon was with them. He waved to Kuhn.

Kuhn's platoon was detached from the company and entered the grounds where they assembled around their officer. The rest of the company returned to the city.

"We're only going to be here a few hours. We have to make Brumberg by morning. We go by truck. There'll be hot chow. Get some rest, boys." Lieutenant Gordon was a ruddy-cheeked man of twenty-five, his natural stoutness trimmed down by rigorous living. "Now, about this place—I'm not going to give you the usual crap about looting and fraternizing. I know what goes on. This is a *Lager*. The middle barracks there has thirty women in it—Hungarians. These girls have had a very rough time. Stay away from them. They think the GI is something different, and I want them thinking that way when we leave. Sergeant!" He summoned Kuhn. "Sergeant, I want you to put out a guard detail for the women's barracks. Any man caught fraternizing I'll court-martial."

There were wooden bunks in the long room. A potbellied

stove was in the center of the room, firewood heaped behind it. The men flung down their rifles, helmets, and harness. They sprawled in their bunks on bare springs.

Kuhn waited for them to settle down before assigning details. He felt dizzy and knew the dizziness to precede a blackout. These periods of amnesia had become frequent. Dread
settled on him like a fog and, sometimes for several moments, he couldn't distinguish his place, his role, his purpose. He nerved himself to endure these moments. He took
off his helmet and swabbed his forehead with his wool cap.
Their names tumbled across his tongue, and he scanned the
barracks but couldn't find the faces to fit the names. Then
slowly their faces merged with the fog. He felt as distant
from them as if they had been background to a dream. He
couldn't pluck out the sense of their words. He fumbled for
his detail book and turned the pages. The headings were
senseless, there was no clue in the words recorded. He felt
nauseated but was determined not to reveal his panic
and continued turning the pages. Rebel, Reilly, Rodansky.
Grove, Nelson, Schultz. The words became a rhythm which
was compulsively reiterated.

"Mel, Mel." The blackout lasted a few seconds. He was
not detected. Solomon gripped his sleeve. "Can I talk to you,
Mel? In private? A few seconds? Are you busy?"

The smiling, seamed face was in focus.

"Rebel, your squad takes the first tour of guard duty.
Let's make it till eleven. Nelson, from eleven to three.
Schultz, from three if we need your squad. One post in
front, one in back."

He followed Solomon into the yard. The jeep had left.
The yard was empty. The sun was already low over the
plowed fields. They could hear the distant motors in the
city, the heavy rumble of tanks, a faraway shout.

"They're Jewish girls, Melford. Yesterday, before the Germans left, they cut off their hair and marched them naked
through the streets. They're lucky they are alive. They come
from a village, Mel, where all the Jews are dead except
these girls. The Germans made them whores."

"What do you want from me, Solomon?"

"In two days it's Pesach—Passover—Mel. Tonight, while

we're still here, I want that you and I should help these girls to celebrate their luck. I want we should have a meal which we can pretend is a seder."

The sun was covered by the clouds rolling in from the horizon. Long shadows spread from the forest across the furrows of the encompassing fields. The forest hadn't been cleared of enemies. Germans, by-passed by their column, might now be waiting at the edge of the forest. The road to Helo went through the forest, and Kuhn was to be briefed at company headquarters in Helo. There were rumors that Brumberg, their next objective, was a focus of resistance. He had to get to town before dark to secure the password.

"I want you to meet the girls, Kuhn. It will give them a real pleasure."

"What time is it?"

"It's four o'clock. I have permission from the major to hold a seder, Mel. These poor kids. There are some of them babies yet—fifteen, sixteen."

"I got troubles without you around, Solomon. What do you want? A seder?"

Rebel came out to begin the first tour of duty. "Where shall I dig in, Sarge?"

"In back. Near the wire."

Solomon caught his arm, and Kuhn shoved him away. "Don't touch me, you jerk."

But his single-mindedness brooked no offense. "It's not a question do I annoy you or do you like me or are you worried. The question has to do with these girls. I don't ask any big sacrifice from you, like to give up your life. I only ask you to be a little decent to some girls who, because you are a Jew—even if it annoys you—they would feel some pleasure to meet you."

"You're what annoys me, Solomon."

"Do you so much value yourself, Kuhn, that you can't take a little time for these poor girls?"

"Get off my back." He left Solomon abruptly and returned to the barracks. He told Reilly to take over the platoon while he and Grove went to headquarters for the briefing.

Rodansky lay on his bunk, still harnessed, his knees raised, his arms folded across his chest, his eyes closed.

Reilly accompanied Kuhn to the barbed-wire gate. "How about these gals, Sarge?"

"You heard the lieutenant. They're off-limits."

"What he don't know won't hurt him."

"It'll hurt you, Reilly. It's my orders you listen to. Stay away from them. I hold you responsible, Reilly. You're in charge. Don't get smart."

"What the hell. We're moving out in a few hours."

"I'm telling you straight. I'll break you, Reilly. Don't give me any of that buddy business. No screwing around. Get it?"

Reilly winked. "Got it."

Lately, Kuhn had sensed resistance among the men. He felt eyes following him, averted when he turned. They were handling him as they did officers, accepting orders with sardonic geniality, grins becoming smirks.

"I'll make it a point to check, Reilly."

There was no part of army life which was natural to Kuhn. He had no flair for communal living. He had early discovered that his efforts to establish himself as a buddy made him foolish. He could only pretend sympathy and when the pretense wearied him his antipathy showed.

Forests were strange to him. Initially he had not been able to orient himself in forests. He was not familiar with forest sounds, had poor vision in the murkiness of the forest gloom. There were men who could walk confidently in the dark. They could discriminate sounds and know when to be easy and when to be tense. They could relax vigilance. A snapped twig, a sensed motion, danger felt, and without doing violence to their nerves, they were again prepared. But to Kuhn, all sounds were ominous. He had no sense for danger and was always on guard. He feared the infiltration of enemies and he couldn't take advantage of lulls. Yet Kuhn had mastered his natural disadvantages and by never yielding to terror he had established himself as the equal of any soldier in the company.

The pines leaned together across the road. Kuhn and Grove advanced into pockets of gloom, the only sound being the gravel scattered by their boots. Kuhn held his carbine ready, bracing against panic whenever they approached an area of darkness. He felt himself vulnerable to any violence. If a German should leap from the forest, he would turn and run. He would abandon Grove. If captured, he would beg. He clicked off the safety of his carbine and hunched his shoulders.

He was trembling when finally they were past the forest and had entered the town.

"Maybe we'll get a ride back," Grove suggested.

"They don't run a taxi service."

Cobbled streets twisted up the hill toward the church. Half-timbered houses fronted solidly on the narrow streets, their upper stories cantilevered. The gutters were strewn with wires laid by the Signal Corps. The intersections were placarded with directions indicating the various units in the area. MPs supervised traffic at intersections. Convoys of trucks rolled through. The front which had been at Helo a few hours previously was already several miles beyond.

Company headquarters were located in the main square which centered about the church. Market stalls, shuttered and locked, fringed the square. The area was being used as a motor-pool and was crowded with trucks and jeeps. There were no civilians in sight, and the soldiers who were not attending to their vehicles were rummaging for loot.

The captain briefed them on the coming objective. Brumberg was defended by twelve batteries of German artillery. This was, perhaps, a sizable element of the remaining enemy resistance. Their company was to participate in a task force that included tanks, TDs, and air support. They had earned this privilege by virtue of their great record. The captain was proud. The lieutenants were proud.

Kuhn loathed himself after a session with the officers. A gentlemanly jargon was in common use. The noncoms, as well as the officers, lent themselves to a collegiate view of war. Even Kuhn while in the company of officers was impressed by their vision of combat. They had seen what shell fragments could do. They had smelled blood and knew that it was a fecal smell. They had seen how the perspective of a dying man narrows until it is confined to himself. And yet they could still approach combat with collegiate sentiments. They ate well. They drank the best of Scotch, served from German tumblers. They were established in the mayor's residence and handsomely bedded. Kuhn withdrew from the party spirit that prevailed. He saw them as a spic-and-span hazing crew with a boy-scout ardor for protocol and a sophomoric concern for reputation.

The major, who had joined the briefing, approached Kuhn. "How's my boy Solomon doing, Sergeant? You keep an eye on that old man, hear?" The charge was confided with the easy bonhommie that a master—a decent paternalistic master—has for his underlings. He was a ruddy, bulky, senatorial type, his uniform tailored to fit his bulk, his polished, stiff bearing a mark of his caste. "I love that big-hearted sonofagun. He found himself some Jewish girls who were treated very badly. And Solomon—well he couldn't have been more concerned if it was him the krauts tortured. We could do with more like Solomon." He held Kuhn's elbow and spoke confidentially: "By the way, Sergeant, I've fixed a little surprise for Solomon. Some of the mail has arrived from Division, and the chaplain has sent up some Jewish flat bread—matzos—and I sent it on to your outfit together with the hot chow. The old man will get a kick out of it. See that he's taken care of, Sergeant. Right?" He squeezed Kuhn's elbow.

The password was Easter Bunny.

The twilight was well advanced when they started back toward the platoon. It was chill again, and Kuhn shivered in his woolens which were still damp from sweating. They left the town. The moment they were on the country road the clamor of motors and rummaging GIs diminished. They entered the forest. Grove walked down the center of the road, his rifle clanking against his canteen, the sling of his rifle slapping against the buckles of his harness. Kuhn listened to him chew the chicken leg he had taken from the officer's mess. He used both hands to hold the leg, his head jerking back as he tugged at the meat. He flung the bone away and wiped his hands on his trousers. He belched, then reached into the pocket of his field jacket for a chocolate bar. He stripped the paper, crumpled it into a ball, flung it into the underbrush beside the road. Kuhn was dizzy with expectation of a bullet. He felt like a target.

"You pig!"

"What?"

"Quiet!"

"I was just eating, Sarge."

"They can hear you eating in Berlin. Where did you learn to eat, on your pig farm? You'll bring every kraut in ten miles."

"There're no krauts around."

"You're not getting me killed, Grove. This is enemy territory. How do you know this forest is secure? There are twelve batteries of kraut artillery at Brumberg. Brumberg is only ten miles from here."

"I won't eat then. If my eating is going to lose the war, okay, I won't eat."

"Whisper, Stupid! This isn't an officer's club."

"You're making more noise than me, Sarge."

"Shut up and let's move."

They trudged on opposite sides of the road, less concerned now with possible ambushes than with their hatred of each other. Kuhn listened to Grove's muttering, realized his own childishness, and yet couldn't restrain his loathing for this and all other buddies. He felt himself dying in a stupid war among stupid men whose understanding was confined to what sex and stomach could sense.

"Twelve batteries—they're honored."

Grove steamed with the insult. "You'd think you was General Patton. Who the hell are you to tell me how to eat? I can eat any damn way I please. I was the only friend you had in this platoon. With the friends you got, it ain't kraut shrapnel you have to worry about. Sonofabitch. They better section-eight you before you crack wide open."

They were still far from the barracks when they heard the party. It was night, and the windows hadn't been completely blacked out, and cracks of light sprayed over the plain.

"We move out in three hours and they're screwing up! I warned Reilly!"

The guard was near the door. It was Rebel. He was so

intent upon the sounds from the barracks that he didn't observe their approach.

"*Hands auf,* you jerk! Put down that rifle. If I was a
kraut you'd be a dead man and so would everyone else in
this platoon. This isn't your post, Rebel. I could court-
martial you, Stupid. What the hell's going on?"

"Solomon brought them in, Sarge. He said it was okay.
He said he'd take responsibility. The major give him permission."

"Who's running this outfit, me or Solomon!"

"It ain't my fault, Sarge."

"The password is Easter Bunny. Got it? We're moving out
in three hours. We're joining Task Force Onaway. We've
been volunteered. There's twelve batteries of kraut artillery
at Brumberg. You feel like kicking your heels, Rebel?"

"How come us, Sarge? Why don't they give some other
company the chance?"

"We're honored, Stupid. What's the password?"

"Easter Bunny."

A long table had been constructed from planks fitted over
sawhorses. There were candles on the table. Mess kits had
been placed in front of the seated women. Hot chow was
presented in huge GI pots. The women were shawled. They
wore knee-length smocks, half-sleeved, open-throated. They
were pallid and puffy-faced, an unhealthy taint that was as
much the color of apathy as the consequence of poor food
and imprisonment. Dead men had this color. Bodies molder-
ing in trenches had this smell.

Yet now they could laugh. Now they felt no pain. Now
they were ready to forget the several hundred krauts who
had mounted them. So newly rescued from terror, could
their equilibrium be so quickly restored? Kuhn shrank from
the sight of them. How could they laugh? How could they
respond to the buddy teasing? How could they live after
their complete humiliation? They had given everything
away.

The men stood behind them, helping with the preparations for the feast. They beckoned Kuhn to share the fun.
"Climb in, Sarge. There's room for everybody."

"Grab a matzo, Sarge. Good old Solomon—"

Solomon beamed. Solomon, with his brood of chicks, thought he was among gentlemen.

"Reilly! What did I tell you!"

"Solomon's got orders from the major. I figured you was outranked, Sarge."

"I saw the lights a mile away. Is this what you call a blackout?"

"It ain't hardly dark."

"Clear out these women. I don't want any more screwing around. We move out in three hours."

"That's three hours. That's not now."

"I said, clear them out, Reilly," he slowly advised.

"What's the pitch? We're nice boys. These are friendly gals. What's eating you, Kuhn?"

"Twelve batteries of kraut artillery. That's what's eating me. Come morning we'll be at Brumberg."

"I'll be there, Kuhn, and so will the boys. Meantime, I don't see any artillery. Maybe I'll get kilt in the morning. Right now I'm not getting kilt."

"Melford!" Solomon shouted. "My friend! I want you to meet someone." He beckoned Kuhn with both hands, speaking excitedly to the woman beside him.

"Melford, I want you to meet Leona." In German he told Leona that Kuhn was the Jewish sergeant he had told her about. All the women turned to watch the introduction.

She was the only one not shawled. Her straight black hair was cropped at the neck. Leaning on her elbows, puffing a cigarette, she had seemed a beauty across the room—a dark, slim woman, great-eyed, fine-featured. But up close the ravage was apparent. The skin was jaundiced, and the face was dry and brittle. The swollen cords of her throat traced her gauntness. Her sprawled legs exhibited the welts of lice bites. There was a sore on her lower lip.

"It is a year now since I see a Jewish man," she told him in a rasping voice. She arose to greet him. She didn't bother to find out whether he would accept the identity she imposed on him. She came to him with the stiff gait of a pregnant woman, her arms half raised, and walked up in reach of the embrace she expected.

He was so strongly repelled by her that it required a

physical effort to remain in her presence. She seemed to him fouled by all the abuse she had suffered. Her walk was infirm. The broadness of her hips, the puffy ankles were an unnatural contrast to the bony shoulders and skinny arms. The musty smell which repelled him seemed to have its source in her scabs and her welts. That she was still a young woman made her seem even more repellent. What hadn't she allowed to happen to her? What hadn't she endured in order to avoid death? Dared she claim him as kin? Face him as her equal?

"Everyone's had it tough." He stood his distance.

"Solomon has much praised you to us."

"Solomon is sometimes foolish. Solomon is a big talker. Pardon me, Leona, but now I have to talk to Solomon. I have to speak privately."

He took Solomon outside and when the door was closed, seized him and slammed him against the barrack wall. Solomon's helmet fell across his forehead. He lost his balance and grabbed Kuhn's arm.

"Mel!"

"I hate the way you smile, Solomon! I hate the way you wiggle on your belly to get laughs. I hate you for all the asses you've kissed. I hate you for being so stupid!"

"Because I'm a Jew maybe?" Solomon hissed, gasping under the hand that pinned him to the wall. "You hate me because I'm a Jew, Kuhn?"

"In three hours we go for a ride. At the end of the ride we get out and walk. And while we walk we get killed. The man ahead, the man behind, they get killed. Their bellies open. Their legs tear off. Their heads explode. That's what I concentrate on, Solomon. That's the important thing. And you, Smiley, you Fat-lips, you Big-heart—you drag your ass up here where it doesn't belong and you clap your head and say, 'Poor little kraut who doesn't have a chest—' You come up here and hunt out Jews and you say, 'Okay! Let's stop everything, boys, let's be nice to the Jew girls. They've had it so bad, take pity. Pity the poor Jews who are whores.' And you know what the boys think of you, Solomon? Who is this old jerk with the clean uniform and good food in his belly who comes up here and says, 'Time out, let's take pity.' Pity? What's that word? They use it back in head-quarters? Those gentlemen back there, the ones who tell us we have the honor to get killed? They use words like honor, too, don't they, Solomon?"

He shook Solomon while he spoke. He clutched the lapels of Solomon's field jacket, and the old man gasped and choked, his head wobbling as he submitted to what appeared to him a murderous assault. His lips slackened, white showed in his eyes, his face was gray with shock, he embraced Kuhn's hands with his own.

"You want to kill me?" he hissed.

Kuhn felt the trembling hands on his own and tightened his grip.

"I'm old enough to be your father," Solomon said as if amazed. "Is this the way you treat me?"

"What have you ever learned, you bastard!" But suddenly he couldn't endure the terror in Solomon's eyes. He pushed Solomon against the wall once more and dropped his hands.

"Are you a Hitler or a God you can treat me like this? What gives you the power?"

Kuhn felt drugged in the aftermath of violence. He looked at Solomon as if he could see there the reflection of himself, see his brutishness mirrored there, see reflected in the older man's disillusionment his own deterioration.

"I learned how it is about dying," Kuhn muttered. "I learned what is bullshit. What I learned you have no idea of. Why are you so surprised, Stupid? Don't you know what the world is like?"

Solomon breathed deeply, his seamed face now resolute. "Don't be too proud, Kuhn," he answered hoarsely. "Don't think you only have felt what no one else has felt. There is always someone has had it worse."

"Have your seder, Solomon. But stay away from me. Stay away from me and stay away from this platoon."

He did not respond to the bitter dignity of Solomon's defiance. "It's not only your war, Kuhn."

Toward the east, in the direction of Brumberg, the sky pulsed from dark to lightening white. This was the artillery preparation of Brumberg. The damp chill pinched his toes and shivered his thighs. He raised the collar of his field jacket. It required intense listening to discern the pervasive bass rumble of the distant shelling. The furrows in the field seemed to writhe and twist after steady scanning. Clots of gloom separated from the forest wall and merged with the field. There was laughter in the barracks behind him. They were snug in their lighted room, warmed by the stove, guarded front and rear by entrenched GIs. But what was this one drop of light contrasted with the great puddle of darkness in which they were immersed?

When Solomon left, Kuhn felt the darkness swarm over him. It pressed a bubble of loneliness that rose from his guts to his throat. He despairingly summoned his exhausted pride to suppress this gas of pity.

He was close to tears when Rodansky came around the corner, followed by the girl. She was no more than seventeen. Shawled, her form distorted by the poor-fitting smock, there was still no mistaking her beauty. There was an idiot innocence in her eyes, as though she had preserved herself from further defeat by withdrawing her awareness from all that her body had suffered. She clutched Rodansky's arm when she saw Kuhn. She cowered at the sight of him.

Rodansky was in a fever, tensed from head to toe, his eyes darting in quest of escape. He jerked to a halt and spread out his arms to stop the girl when he saw Kuhn. His fear showed. He stood his ground, nerving himself for punishment. "Okay . . . so what are you going to do about it?"

He was strangely saddened by Rodansky's terror. Was his effort to find release of such pathetic consequence that he could now turn pale at the sight of Kuhn?

"There's kraut artillery waiting for us, Rodansky."

"You can wait for it, Kuhn. I don't ask any favors. At least I got my kicks in."

"Take the girl in, Rodansky. Get some chow. We move out in two hours."

Rodansky guided the girl into the barracks. She followed him docilely, averting her face as she passed Kuhn.

A flare ignited with a hiss, turning the sky greenish-white. It was the first of a series of flares aimed toward Brumberg. Planes flew overhead toward Brumberg. In front of him, the forest appeared in silhouette, the trees as sharply defined as paper cutouts. He remained frozen after the darkness again settled.

He had to clean his carbine, get the ammo distributed, receive the final briefing from the lieutenant. But until his loneliness was relieved, no action was possible.

Solomon was seated at the head of the table. He addressed both the seated girls and the standing GIs. Kuhn went to the opposite end of the table and sat by Leona. He did not reject her hand which gripped his under the table.

Somehow Solomon had made a congregation of his audience. There was pious intensity in their listening.

"—so that is why tonight we talk about the meaning of this day. And to make this meaning clear is why I ask why this night is different from all other nights. It has to do when our people were in Egypt. They were slaves."

THE MAGIC BARREL

Bernard Malamud

BERNARD MALAMUD *was born and educated in Brooklyn,
New York, and then crossed the river for degrees at
CCNY and Columbia. He is married and earns his living as a writer and teacher. He has written two novels:*
THE NATURAL *(1952) and* THE ASSISTANT *(1956). His
book of short stories,* THE MAGIC BARREL *(1958)
received the National Book Award for fiction in 1959.*

Not long ago there lived in uptown New York, in a small,
almost meager room, though crowded with books, Leon
Finkle, a rabbinical student in the Yeshivah University. Finkle, after six years of study, was to be ordained in June
and had been advised by an acquaintance that he might
find it easier to win himself a congregation if he were married. Since he had no present prospects of marriage, after
two tormented days of turning it over in his mind, he called
in Pinye Salzman, a marriage broker, whose two-line advertisement he had read in the *Forward*.

The matchmaker appeared one night out of the dark
fourth-floor hallway of the graystone rooming house, grasping a black, strapped portfolio that had been worn thin with
use. Salzman, who had been long in the business, was of
slight but dignified build, wearing an old hat and an overcoat too short and tight for him. He smelled frankly of fish,
which he loved to eat, and although he was missing a few
teeth, his presence was not displeasing, because of an amiable manner curiously contrasted by mournful eyes. His
voice, his lips, his wisp of beard, his bony fingers were ani-

mated, but give him a moment of repose, and his mild blue
eyes soon revealed a depth of sadness, a characteristic that
put Leo a little at ease although the situation, for him, was
inherently tense.

He at once informed Salzman why he had asked him to
come, explaining that his home was in Cleveland, and that
but for his parents, who had married comparatively late in
life, he was alone in the world. He had for six years devoted
himself entirely to his studies, as a result of which, quite
understandably, he had found himself without time for a
social life and the company of young women. Therefore he
thought it the better part of trial and error—of embarrassing
fumbling—to call in an experienced person to advise him in
these matters. He remarked in passing that the function of
the marriage broker was ancient and honorable, highly approved in the Jewish community, because it made practical
the necessary without hindering joy. Moreover, his own parents had been brought together by a matchmaker. They had
made, if not a financially profitable marriage—since neither
had possessed any worldly goods to speak of—at least a successful one in the sense of their everlasting devotion to one
another. Salzman listened in embarrassed surprise, sensing a
sort of apology. Later, however, he experienced a glow of
pride in his work, an emotion that had left him years ago,
and he heartily approved of Finkle.

The two men went to their business. Leo had led Salzman
to the only clear place in the room, a table near a window
that overlooked the lamplit city. He seated himself at the
matchmaker's side but facing him, attempting by an act of
will to suppress the unpleasant tickle in his throat. Salzman
eagerly unstrapped his portfolio and removed a loose rubber
band from a thin packet of much-handled cards. As he
flipped through them, a gesture and sound that physically
hurt Leo, the student pretended not to see and gazed steadfastly out the window. Although it was still February, winter was on its last legs, signs of which he had for the first
time in years begun to notice. He now observed the round
white moon, moving high in the sky through a cloud-
menagerie, and watched with half-open mouth as it penetrated a huge hen and dropped out of her like an egg laying

itself. Salzman, though pretending through eyeglasses he had just slipped on, to be engaged in scanning the writing on the cards, stole occasional glances at the young man's distinguished face, noting with pleasure the long, severe scholar's nose, brown eyes heavy with learning, sensitive yet ascetic lips, and a certain almost hollow quality of the dark cheeks. He gazed around at shelves upon shelves of books and let out a soft but happy sigh.

When Leo's eyes fell upon the cards, he counted six spread out in Salzman's hand.

"So few?" he said in disappointment.

"You wouldn't believe me how much cards I got in my office," Salzman replied. "The drawers are already filled to the top, so I keep them now in a barrel, but is every girl good for a new rabbi?"

Leo blushed at this, regretting all he had revealed of himself in a curriculum vitae he had sent to Salzman. He had thought it best to acquaint him with his strict standards and specifications, but in having done so now felt he had told the marriage broker more than was absolutely necessary.

He hesitantly inquired, "Do you keep photographs of your clients on file?"

"First comes family, amount of dowry, also what kind promises," Salzman replied, unbuttoning his tight coat and settling himself in the chair. "After comes pictures, rabbi."

"Call me Mr. Finkle. I'm not a rabbi yet."

Salzman said he would, but instead called him doctor, which he changed to rabbi when Leo was not listening too attentively.

Salzman adjusted his horn-rimmed spectacles, gently cleared his throat and read in an eager voice the contents of the top card:

"Sophie P. Twenty-four years. Widow for one year. No children. Educated high school and two years college. Father promises eight thousand dollars. Has wonderful wholesale business. Also real estate. On mother's side comes teachers, also one actor. Well known on Second Avenue."

Leo gazed up in surprise. "Did you say a widow?"

"A widow don't mean spoiled, rabbi. She lived with her

husband maybe four months. He was a sick boy, she made a mistake to marry him."

"Marrying a widow has never entered my mind."

"This is because you have no experience. A widow, specially if she is young and healthy like this girl, is a wonderful person to marry. She will be thankful to you the rest of her life. Believe me, if I was looking now for a bride, I would marry a widow."

Leo reflected, then shook his head.

Salzman hunched his shoulders in an almost imperceptible gesture of disappointment. He placed the card down on the wooden table and began to read another:

"Lily H. High-school teacher. Regular. Not a substitute. Has savings and new Dodge car. Lived in Paris one year. Father is successful dentist thirty-five years. Interested in professional man. Well Americanized family. Wonderful opportunity.

"I know her personally," said Salzman. "I wish you could see this girl. She is a doll. Also very intelligent. All day you could talk to her about books and theater and what not. She also knows current events."

"I don't believe you mentioned her age?"

"Her age?" Salzman said, raising his brows in surprise. "Her age is thirty-two years."

Leo said after a while, "I'm afraid that seems a little too old."

Salzman let out a laugh. "So how old are you, rabbi?"

"Twenty-seven."

"So what is the difference, tell me, between twenty-seven and thirty-two? My own wife is seven years older than me. So what did I suffer?—Nothing. If Rothschild's daughter wants to marry you, would you say on account of her age, no?"

"Yes," Leo said dryly.

Salzman shook off the no in the yes. "Five years don't mean a thing. I give you my word that when you will live with her for one week, you will forget her age. What does it mean five years—that she lived more and knows more than somebody who is younger? On this girl, God bless her, years are not wasted. Each one that it comes makes better the bargain."

"What subject does she teach in high school?"

"Languages. If you heard the way she reads French, you will think it is music. I am in the business twenty-five years, and I recommend her with my whole heart. Believe me, I know what I'm talking, rabbi."

"What's on the next card?" Leo said abruptly.

Salzman reluctantly turned up the third card:

"Ruth K. Nineteen years. Honor student. Father offers thirteen thousand dollars cash to the right bridegroom. He is a medical doctor. Stomach specialist with marvelous practice. Brother-in-law owns own garment business. Particular people."

Salzman looked up as if he had read his trump card.

"Did you say nineteen?" Leo asked with interest.

"On the dot."

"Is she attractive?" He blushed. "Pretty?"

Salzman kissed his fingertips. "A little doll. On this I give you my word. Let me call the father tonight and you will see what means pretty."

But Leo was troubled. "You're sure she's that young?"

"This I am positive. The father will show you the birth certificate."

"Are you positive there isn't something wrong with her?" Leo insisted.

"Who says there is wrong?"

"I don't understand why an American girl her age should go to a marriage broker."

A smile spread over Salzman's face.

"So for the same reason you went, she comes."

Leo flushed. "I am pressed for time."

Salzman, realizing he had been tactless, quickly explained. "The father came, not her. He wants she should have the best, so he looks around himself. When we will locate the right boy, he will introduce him and encourage. This makes a better marriage than if a young girl without experience takes for herself. I don't have to tell you this."

"But don't you think this young girl believes in love?" Leo spoke uneasily.

Salzman was about to guffaw, but caught himself and said soberly, "Love comes with the right person, not before."

Leo parted dry lips but did not speak. Noticing that Salzman had snatched a quick glance at the next card, he cleverly asked, "How is her health?"

"Perfect," Salzman said, breathing with difficulty. "Of course, she is a little lame on her right foot from an auto accident that it happened to her when she was twelve years, but nobody notices on account she is so brilliant and also beautiful."

Leo got up heavily and went to the window. He felt curiously bitter and upbraided himself for having called in the marriage broker. Finally, he shook his head.

"Why not?" Salzman persisted, the pitch of his voice rising.

"Because I hate stomach specialists."

"So what do you care what is his business? After you marry her, do you need him? Who says he must come every Friday night to your house?"

Ashamed of the way the talk was going, Leo dismissed Salzman, who went home with melancholy eyes.

Though he had felt only relief at the marriage broker's departure, Leo was in low spirits the next day. He explained it as arising from Salzman's failure to produce a suitable bride for him. He did not care for his type of clientele. But when Leo found himself hesitating over whether to seek out another matchmaker, one more polished than Pinye, he wondered if it could be—his protestations to the contrary, and although he honored his father and mother—that he did not, in essence, care for the matchmaking institution? This thought he quickly put out of his mind yet found himself still upset. All day he ran around in a fog—missed an important appointment, forgot to give out his laundry, walked out of a Broadway cafeteria without paying and had to run back with the ticket in his hand; had even not recognized his landlady in the street when she passed with a friend and courteously called out, "A good evening to you, Doctor Finkle." By nightfall, however, he had regained sufficient calm to sink his nose into a book and there found peace from his thoughts.

Almost at once there came a knock on the door. Before Leo could say enter, Salzman, commercial cupid, was standing in the room. His face was gray and meager, his expression hungry, and he looked as if he would expire on his feet. Yet the marriage broker managed, by some trick of the muscles, to display a broad smile.

"So good evening. I am invited?"

Leo nodded, disturbed to see him again, yet unwilling to ask him to leave.

Beaming still, Salzman laid his portfolio on the table. "Rabbi, I got for you tonight good news."

"I've asked you not to call me rabbi. I'm still a student."

"Your worries are finished. I have for you a first-class bride."

"Leave me in peace concerning this subject." Leo pretended lack of interest.

"The world will dance at your wedding."

"Please, Mr. Salzman, no more."

"But first must come back my strength," Salzman said weakly. He fumbled with the portfolio straps and took out of the leather case an oily paper bag, from which he extracted a hard seeded roll and a small smoked whitefish. With one motion of his hand he stripped the fish out of its skin and began ravenously to chew. "All day in a rush," he muttered.

Leo watched him eat.

"A sliced tomato you have maybe?" Salzman hesitantly inquired.

"No."

The marriage broker shut his eyes and ate. When he had finished, he carefully cleaned up the crumbs and rolled up the remains of the fish in the paper bag. His spectacled eyes roamed the room until he discovered, amid some piles of books, a one-burner gas stove. Lifting his hat, he humbly asked, "A glass of tea you got, rabbi?"

Conscience-stricken, Leo rose and brewed the tea. He served it with a chunk of lemon and two cubes of lump sugar, delighting Salzman.

After he had drunk his tea, Salzman's strength and good spirits were restored.

"So tell me, rabbi," he said amiably, "you considered any more the three clients I mentioned yesterday?"

"There was no need to consider."

"Why not?"

"None of them suits me."

"What, then, suits you?"

Leo let it pass because he could give only a confused answer.

Without waiting for a reply, Salzman asked, "You remember this girl I talked to you—the high-school teacher?"

"Age thirty-two?"

But, surprisingly, Salzman's face lit in a smile. "Age twenty-nine."

Leo shot him a look. "Reduced from thirty-two?"

"A mistake," Salzman avowed. "I talked today with the dentist. He took me to his safety deposit box and showed me the birth certificate. She was twenty-nine last August. They made her a party in the mountains where she went for her vacation. When her father spoke to me the first time, I forgot to write the age and I told you thirty-two, but now I remember this was a different client, a widow."

"The same one you told me about? I thought she was twenty-four?"

"A different. Am I responsible that the world is filled with widows?"

"No, but I'm not interested in them, nor for that matter, in schoolteachers."

Salzman passionately pulled his clasped hands to his breast. Looking at the ceiling he exclaimed, "Jewish children, what can I say to somebody that he is not interested in high-school teachers? So what then you are interested?"

Leo flushed but controlled himself.

"In who else you will be interested," Salzman went on, "if you not interested in this fine girl that she speaks four languages and has personally in the bank ten thousand dollars? Also her father guarantees further twelve thousand. Also she has a new car, wonderful clothes, talks on all subjects, and she will give you a first-class home and children. How near do we come in our life to paradise?"

"If she's so wonderful, why wasn't she married ten years ago?"

"Why," said Salzman with a heavy laugh. "—Why? Because she is *partikler*. This is why. She wants only the *best*."

Leo was silent, amused at how he had trapped himself. But Salzman had aroused his interest in Lily H., and he began seriously to consider calling on her. When the marriage broker observed how intently Leo's mind was at work on the facts he had supplied, he felt positive they would soon come to an agreement.

Late Saturday afternoon, conscious of Salzman, Leo Finkle walked with Lily Hirschorn along Riverside Drive. He walked briskly and erectly, wearing with distinction the black fedora he had that morning taken with trepidation out of the dusty hatbox on his closet shelf, and the heavy black Saturday coat he had thoroughly whisked clean. Leo also owned a walking stick, a present from a distant relative, but had decided not to use it. Lily, petite and not unpretty, had on something signifying the approach of spring. She was *au courant*, animatedly, with all subjects, and he weighed her words and found her surprisingly sound—score another for Salzman, whom he uneasily sensed to be somewhere around, hiding perhaps high in a tree along the street, flashing the lady signals; or perhaps a cloven-hoofed Pan, piping nuptial ditties as he danced his invisible way before them, strewing wild buds on the walk and purple summer grapes in their path, symbolizing fruit of a union, of which there was yet none.

Lily startled Leo by remarking, "I was thinking of Mr. Salzman, a curious figure, wouldn't you say?"

Not certain what to answer, he nodded.

She bravely went on, blushing, "I for one am grateful for his introducing us. Aren't you?"

He courteously replied, "I am."

"I mean," she said with a little laugh—and it was all in good taste, or at least gave the effect of being not in bad —"do you mind that we came together so?"

He was not afraid of her honesty, recognizing that she meant to set the relationship aright, and understanding that it took a certain amount of experience in life, and courage, to want to do it quite that way. One had to have some sort of past to make that kind of beginning.

He said that he did not mind. Salzman's function was traditional and honorable—valuable for what it might achieve, which, he pointed out, was frequently nothing.

Lily agreed with a sigh. They walked on for a while, and she said after a long silence, again with a nervous laugh, "Would you mind if I asked you something a little bit personal? Frankly, I find the subject fascinating." Although Leo shrugged, she went on half embarrassedly, "How was it that you came to your calling? I mean, was it a sudden passionate inspiration?"

Leo, after a time, slowly replied, "I was always interested in the Law."

"You saw revealed in it the presence of the Highest?"

He nodded and changed the subject. "I understand you spent a little time in Paris, Miss Hirschorn?"

"Oh, did Mr. Salzman tell you, Rabbi Finkle?" Leo winced, but she went on, "It was ages and ages ago and almost forgotten. I remember I had to return for my sister's wedding."

But Lily would not be put off. "When," she asked in a trembly voice, "did you become enamored of God?"

He stared at her. Then it came to him that she was talking not about Leo Finkle, but a total stranger, some mystical figure, perhaps even passionate prophet that Salzman had conjured up for her—no relation to the living or dead. Leo trembled with rage and weakness. The trickster had obviously sold her a bill of goods, just as he had him, who'd expected to become acquainted with a young lady of twenty-nine, only to behold, the moment he laid eyes upon her strained and anxious face, a woman past thirty-five and aging very rapidly. Only his self-control, he thought, had kept him this long in her presence.

"I am not," he said gravely, "a talented religious person," and in seeking words to go on, found himself possessed by fear and shame. "I think," he said in a strained manner, "that I came to God not because I love Him, but because I did not."

This confession he spoke harshly because its unexpectedness shook him.

Lily wilted. Leo saw a profusion of loaves of bread sailing like ducks high over his head, not unlike the loaves by which he had counted himself to sleep last night. Mercifully, then, it snowed, which he would not put past Salzman's machinations.

He was infuriated with the marriage broker and swore he would throw him out of the room the moment he reappeared. But Salzman did not come that night, and when Leo's anger had subsided, an unaccountable despair grew in its place. At first he thought this was caused by his disappointment in Lily, but before long it became evident that he had involved himself with Salzman without a true knowledge of his own intent. He gradually realized—with an emptiness that seized him with six hands—that he had called in the broker to find him a bride because he was incapable of doing it himself. This terrifying insight he had derived as a result of his meeting and conversation with Lily Hirschorn. Her probing questions had somehow irritated him into revealing—to himself more than her—the true nature of his relationship with God, and from that it had come upon him, with shocking force, that apart from his parents, he had never loved anyone. Or perhaps it went the other way, that he did not love God so well as he might, because he had not loved man. It seemed to Leo that his whole life stood starkly revealed and he saw himself, for the first time, as he truly was—unloved and loveless. This bitter but somehow not fully unexpected revelation brought him to a point of panic controlled only by extraordinary effort. He covered his face with his hands and wept.

The week that followed was the worst of his life. He did not eat, and lost weight. His beard darkened and grew ragged. He stopped attending lectures and seminars and almost never opened a book. He seriously considered leaving the Yeshivah, although he was deeply troubled at the thought of the loss of all his years of study—saw them like pages from a book strewn over the city—and at the devastating effect of this decision upon his parents. But he had lived without knowledge of himself, and never in the Five Books and all the Commentaries—*mea culpa*—had the truth been revealed to him. He did not know where to turn, and in all this desolating loneliness there was no *to whom*, although he often thought of Lily but not once could bring himself to go downstairs and make the call. He became touchy and irritable, especially with his landlady, who asked him all manner of questions; on the other hand, sensing his own disagreeableness, he waylaid her on the stairs and apologized abjectly, until mortified, she ran from him. Out of this, however, he drew the consolation that he was yet a Jew and that a Jew suffered. But gradually, as the long and terrible week drew to a close, he regained his composure and some idea of purpose in life: to go on as planned. Although he was imperfect, the ideal was not. As for his quest of a bride, the thought of continuing afflicted him with anxiety and heartburn, yet perhaps with this new knowledge of himself he would be more successful than in the past. Perhaps love would now come to him and a bride to that love. And for this sanctified seeking who needed a Salzman?

The marriage broker, a skeleton with haunted eyes, returned that very night. He looked, withal, the picture of frustrated expectancy—as if he had steadfastly waited the week at Miss Lily Hirschorn's side for a telephone call that never came.

Casually coughing, Salzman came immediately to the point: "So how did you like her?"

Leo's anger rose and he could not refrain from chiding the matchmaker: "Why did you lie to me, Salzman?"

Salzman's pale face went dead white, as if the world had snowed on him.

"Did you not state that she was twenty-nine?" Leo insisted.

"I give you my word——"

"She was thirty-five. *At least* thirty-five."

"Of this I would not be too sure. Her father told me——"

"Never mind. The worst of it was that you lied to her."

"How did I lie to her, tell me?"

"You told her things about me that weren't true. You made me out to be more, consequently less than I am. She had in mind a totally different person, a sort of semimystical Wonder Rabbi."

"All I said, you was a religious man."

"I can imagine."

Salzman sighed. "This is my weakness that I have," he confessed. "My wife says to me I shouldn't be a salesman, but when I have two fine people that they would be wonderful to be married, I am so happy that I talk too much." He smiled wanly. "This is why Salzman is a poor man."

Leo's anger went. "Well, Salzman, I'm afraid that's all."

The marriage broker fastened hungry eyes on him.

"You don't want any more a bride?"

"I do," said Leo, "but I have decided to seek her in a different way. I am no longer interested in an arranged marriage. To be frank, I now admit the necessity of premarital love. That is, I want to be in love with the one I marry."

"Love?" said Salzman, astounded. After a moment he said, "For us, our love is our life, not for the ladies. In the ghetto they—"

"I know, I know," said Leo. "I've thought of it often. Love, I have said to myself, should be a by-product of living and worship rather than its own end. Yet for myself I find it necessary to establish the level of my need and to fulfill it."

Salzman shrugged but answered, "Listen, rabbi, if you want love, this I can find for you also. I have such beautiful clients that you will love them the minute your eyes will see them."

Leo smiled unhappily. "I'm afraid you don't understand."

But Salzman hastily unstrapped his portfolio and withdrew a manila packet from it.

"Pictures," he said, quickly laying the envelope on the table.

Leo called after him to take the pictures away, but as if on the wings of the wind, Salzman had disappeared.

March came. Leo had returned to his regular routine. Although he felt not quite himself yet—lacked energy—he was making plans for a more active social life. Of course it would cost something, but he was an expert in cutting corners; and when there were no corners left he could make circles rounder. All the while Salzman's pictures had lain on the table, gathering dust. Occasionally as Leo sat studying, or enjoying a cup of tea, his eyes fell on the manila envelope, but he never opened it.

The days went by, and no social life to speak of developed with a member of the opposite sex—it was difficult, given the circumstances of his situation. One morning Leo toiled up the stairs to his room and stared out the window at the city. Although the day was bright, his view of it was dark. For some time he watched the people in the street below hurrying along and then turned with a heavy heart to his little room. On the table was the packet. With a sudden relentless gesture he tore it open. For a half-hour he stood there, in a state of excitement, examining the photographs of the ladies Salzman had included. Finally, with a deep sigh he put them down. There were six, of varying degrees of attractiveness, but look at them long enough and they all became Lily Hirschorn: all past their prime, all starved behind bright smiles, not a true personality in the lot. Life, despite their anguished struggles and frantic yoohooings, had passed them by; they were photographs in a brief case that stank of fish. After a while, however, as Leo attempted to return the pictures into the envelope, he found another in it, a small snapshot of the type taken by a machine for a quarter. He gazed at it a moment and let out a cry.

Her face deeply moved him. Why, he could at first not say. It gave him the impression of youth—all spring flowers —yet age—a sense of having been used to the bone, wasted; this all came from the eyes, which were hauntingly familiar, yet absolutely strange. He had a strong impression that he had met her before, but try as he might he could not place her, although he could almost recall her name, as if he had read it written in her own handwriting. No, this couldn't be; he would have remembered her. It was not, he affirmed, that she had an extraordinary beauty—no, although her face was attractive enough; it was that *something* about her moved him. Feature for feature, even some of the ladies of the photographs could do better; but she leaped forth to the heart—had lived, or wanted to—more than just wanted, perhaps regretted it—had somehow deeply suffered: it could be

They entered. Leo fixed tea and a sardine sandwich for Salzman.

As they were drinking, he reached behind him for the packet of pictures and handed them to the marriage broker.

Salzman put down his glass and said expectantly, "You found maybe somebody you like?"

"Not among these."

The marriage broker turned sad eyes away.

"Here's the one I like." Leo held forth the snapshot.

Salzman slipped on his glasses and took the picture into his trembling hand. He turned ghastly and let out a miserable groan.

"What's the matter?" cried Leo.

"Excuse me. Was an accident this picture. She is not for you."

Salzman frantically shoved the manila packet into his portfolio. He thrust the snapshot into his pocket and fled down the stairs.

Leo, after momentary paralysis, gave chase and cornered the marriage broker in the vestibule. The landlady made hysterical outcries, but neither of them listened.

"Give me back the picture, Salzman."

"No." The pain in his eyes was terrible.

"Tell me where she is then."

"This I can't tell you. Excuse me."

He made to depart, but Leo, forgetting himself, seized the matchmaker by his tight coat and shook him frenziedly.

"Please," sighed Salzman. *"Please."*

Leo ashamedly let him go. "Tell me who she is," he begged. "It's very important for me to know."

"She is not for you. She is a wild one—wild, without shame. This is not a bride for a rabbi."

"What do you mean wild?"

"Like an animal. Like a dog. For her to be poor was a sin. This is why she is dead now."

"In God's name, what do you mean?"

"Her I can't introduce to you," Salzman cried.

"Why are you so excited?"

"Why he asks," Salzman said, bursting into tears. "This is my baby, my Stella, she should burn in hell."

Leo hurried up to bed and hid under the covers. Under the covers he thought his whole life through. Although he soon fell asleep he could not sleep her out of his mind. He woke, beating his breast. Though he prayed to be rid of her, his prayers went unanswered. Through days of torment he struggled endlessly not to love her; fearing success, he escaped it. He then concluded to convert her to goodness, himself to God. The idea alternately nauseated and exalted him.

He perhaps did not know that he had come to a final decision until he encountered Salzman in a Broadway cafeteria. He was sitting alone at a rear table, sucking the bony remains of a fish. The marriage broker appeared haggard, and transparent to the point of vanishing.

Salzman looked up at first without recognizing him. Leo had grown a pointed beard, and his eyes were weighted with wisdom.

"Salzman," he said, "love has at last come to my heart."

"Who can love from a picture?" mocked the marriage broker.

"It is not impossible."

"If you can love her, then you can love anybody. Let me show you some new clients that they just sent me their photographs. One is a little doll."

"Just her I want," Leo murmured.

"Don't be a fool, doctor. Don't bother with her."

"Put me in touch with her, Salzman," Leo said humbly. "Perhaps I can do her a service."

Salzman had stopped chewing, and Leo understood with emotion that it was now arranged.

Leaving the cafeteria, he was, however, afflicted by a tormenting suspicion that Salzman had planned it all to happen this way.

Leo was informed by letter that she would meet him on a certain corner, and she was there one spring night, waiting under a street lamp. He appeared, carrying a small bouquet of violets and rosebuds. Stella stood by the lamppost, smoking. She wore white with red shoes, which fitted his expectations, although in a troubled moment he had imagined the dress red, and only the shoes white. She waited uneasily and shyly. From afar he saw that her eyes—clearly her father's —were filled with desperate innocence. He pictured, in hers, his own redemption. Violins and lit candles revolved in the sky. Leo ran forward with the flowers outthrust.

Around the corner, Salzman, leaning against a wall, chanted prayers for the dead.

THE ARTIFICIAL NIGGER

Flannery O'Connor

FLANNERY O'CONNOR *was born in Savannah, Georgia, in 1925. She graduated from Georgia State College for Women and spent two years in Paul Engle's class in creative writing at the State University of Iowa. Her first novel,* WISE BLOOD, *was published in 1952; the latest is* VIOLENT BEAR IT AWAY *(1960). Her short stories have appeared in many magazines and have turned up frequently in the O. Henry Prize selection; a collection of them has appeared in the book* A GOOD MAN IS HARD TO FIND. *She lives in Milledgeville, Georgia, where she is currently at work on a third novel.*

Mr. Head awakened to discover that the room was full of moonlight. He sat up and stared at the floor boards—the color of silver—and then at the ticking on his pillow, which might have been brocade, and after a second, he saw half of the moon five feet away in his shaving mirror. It rolled forward and cast a dignifying light on everything. The straight chair against the wall looked stiff and attentive as if it were waiting an order, and Mr. Head's trousers, hanging to the back of it, had an almost noble air, like the garment some great man had just flung to his servant; but the face on the moon was a grave one. It gazed across the room and out the window where it floated over the horse stall and appeared to contemplate itself with the look of a young man who sees his old age before him.

Mr. Head could have said to it that age was a choice blessing and that only with years does a man enter into that

calm understanding of life that makes him a suitable guide
for the young. This, at least, had been his own experience.

He sat up and grasped the iron posts at the foot of his
bed and raised himself until he could see the face on the
alarm clock which sat on an overturned bucket beside the
chair. The hour was two in the morning. The alarm on the
clock did not work, but he was not dependent on any me-
chanical means to awaken him. Sixty years had not dulled
his responses; his physical reactions, like his moral ones,
were guided by his will and strong character, and these could
be seen plainly in his features. He had a long tube-like face
with a long, rounded open jaw and a long depressed nose.
His eyes were alert but quiet, and in the miraculous moonlight they had a look of composure and of ancient wisdom
as if they belonged to one of the great guides of men. He
might have been Virgil summoned in the middle of the night
to go to Dante; or better, Raphael, awakened by a blast of
God's light to fly to the side of Tobias. The only dark spot
in the room was Nelson's pallet, underneath the shadow of
the window.

Nelson was hunched over on his side, his knees under his
chin and his heels under his bottom. His new suit and hat
were in the boxes that they had been sent in, and these were
on the floor at the foot of the pallet where he could get
his hands on them as soon as he woke up. The slop jar, out
of the shadow and made snow-white in the moonlight, appeared to stand guard over him like a small personal angel.
Mr. Head lay back down, feeling entirely confident that he
could carry out the moral mission of the coming day. He
meant to be up before Nelson and to have the breakfast
cooking by the time he awakened. The boy was always irked
when Mr. Head was the first up. They would have to leave
the house at four to get to the railroad junction by five-
thirty. The train was to stop for them at five-forty-five.

This would be the boy's first trip to the city, though he
claimed it would be his second because he had been born
there. Mr. Head had tried to point out to him that when he
was born he didn't have the intelligence to determine his
whereabouts, but this had made no impression on the child
at all, and he continued to insist that this was to be his second

trip. It would be Mr. Head's third trip. Nelson had said, "I will've already been there twicet and I ain't but ten."

Mr. Head had contradicted him.

"If you ain't been there in fifteen years, how you know you'll be able to find your way about?" Nelson had asked. "How you know it hasn't changed some?"

"Have you ever," Mr. Head had asked, "seen me lost?"

Nelson certainly had not, but he was a child who was never satisfied until he had given an impudent answer and he replied, "It's nowhere around here to get lost at."

"The day is going to come," Mr. Head prophesied, "when you'll find you ain't as smart as you think you are." He had been thinking about this trip for several months, but it was for the most part in moral terms that he conceived it. It was to be a lesson that the boy would never forget. He was to find out from it that he had no cause for pride merely because he had been born in a city. He was to find out that the city is not a great place. Mr. Head meant him to see everything there is to see in a city so that he would be content to stay at home for the rest of his life. He fell asleep thinking how the boy would at last find out that he was not as smart as he thought he was.

He was awakened at three-thirty by the smell of fatback frying and he leapt off his cot. The pallet was empty, and the clothes boxes had been thrown open. He put on his trousers and ran into the other room. The boy had a cornpone on cooking and had fried the meat. He was sitting in the half-dark at the table, drinking cold coffee out of a can. He had on his new suit and his new grey hat pulled low over his eyes. It was too big for him, but they had ordered it a size large because they expected his head to grow. He didn't say anything, but his entire figure suggested satisfaction at having arisen before Mr. Head.

Mr. Head went to the stove and brought the meat to the table in the skillet. "It's no hurry," he said. "You'll get there soon enough and it's no guarantee you'll like it when you do, neither," and he sat down across from the boy whose hat teetered back slowly to reveal a fiercely expressionless face, very much the same shape as the old man's. They were grandfather and grandson but they looked enough alike to be brothers, and brothers not too far apart in age, for Mr. Head had a youthful expression by daylight, while the boy's look was ancient, as if he knew everything already and would be pleased to forget it.

Mr. Head had once had a wife and daughter, and when the wife died, the daughter ran away and returned after an interval with Nelson. Then one morning, without getting out of bed, she died and left Mr. Head with sole care of the year-old child. He had made the mistake of telling Nelson that he had been born in Atlanta. If he hadn't told him that, Nelson couldn't have insisted that this was going to be his second trip.

"You may not like it a bit," Mr. Head continued, "it'll be full of niggers."

The boy made a face as if he could handle a nigger.

"All right," Mr. Head said. "You ain't ever seen a nigger."

"You wasn't up very early," Nelson said.

"You ain't ever seen a nigger," Mr. Head repeated. "There hasn't been a nigger in this county since we run that one out twelve years ago and that was before you were born." He looked at the boy as if daring him to say he had ever seen a Negro.

"How you know I never saw a nigger when I lived there before?" Nelson asked. "I probably saw a lot of niggers."

"If you seen one, you didn't know what he was," Mr. Head said, completely exasperated. "A six-month-old child don't know a nigger from anybody else."

"I reckon I'll know a nigger if I see one," the boy said and got up and straightened his slick, sharply creased grey hat and went outside to the privy.

They reached the junction some time before the train was due to arrive and stood about two feet from the first set of tracks. Mr. Head carried a paper sack with some biscuits and a can of sardines in it for their lunch. A coarse-looking orange sun coming up behind the east range of mountains was making the sky a dull red behind them, but in front of them it was still grey, and they faced a grey transparent moon, hardly stronger than a thumbprint and completely without light. A small tin switch box and a black fuel tank were all there was to mark the place as a junction; the tracks were double and did not converge again until they were hidden behind the bends at either end of the clearing. Trains passing appeared to emerge from a tunnel of trees and, hit for a second by the cold sky, vanish terrified into the woods again. Mr. Head had had to make special arrangements with the ticket agent to have this train stop and he was secretly afraid it would not, in which case he knew Nelson would say, "I never thought no train was going to stop for you." Under the useless morning moon the tracks looked white and fragile. Both the old man and the child stared ahead as if awaiting an apparition.

Then suddenly, before Mr. Head could make up his mind to turn back, there was a deep warning bleat, and the train appeared, gliding very slowly, almost silently around the bend of trees about two hundred yards down the track, with one yellow front light burning. Mr. Head was still not certain it would stop and he felt it would make an even bigger idiot of him if it went by slowly. Both he and Nelson, however, were prepared to ignore the train if it passed them.

The engine charged by, filling their noses with the smell of hot metal, and then the second coach came to a stop exactly where they were standing. A conductor with the face of an ancient bloated bulldog was on the step as if he expected them, though he did not look as if it mattered one way or the other to him if they got on or not. "To the right," he said.

Their entry took only a fraction of a second, and the train was already speeding on as they entered the quiet car. Most of the travelers were still sleeping, some with their heads hanging off the chair arms, some stretched across two seats, and some sprawled out with their feet in the aisle. Mr. Head saw two unoccupied seats and pushed Nelson toward them. "Get in there by the winder," he said in his normal voice which was very loud at this hour of the morning. "Nobody cares if you sit there because it's nobody in it. Sit right there."

"I heard you," the boy muttered. "It's no use in you yelling," and he sat down and turned his head to the glass.

There he saw a pale ghost-like face scowling at him beneath the brim of a pale ghost-like hat. His grandfather,
looking quickly too, saw a different ghost, pale but grinning, under a black hat.

Mr. Head sat down and settled himself and took out his
ticket and started reading aloud everything that was printed
on it. People began to stir. Several woke up and stared at
him. "Take off your hat," he said to Nelson and took off
his own and put it on his knee. He had a small amount of
white hair that had turned tobacco-colored over the years,
and this lay flat across the back of his head. The front of
his head was bald and creased. Nelson took off his hat and
put it on his knee, and they waited for the conductor to
come ask for their tickets.

The man across the aisle from them was spread out over
two seats, one foot propped on the window and the other
jutting into the aisle. He had on a light blue suit and a
yellow shirt unbuttoned at the neck. His eyes had just
opened, and Mr. Head was ready to introduce himself when
the conductor came up from behind and growled, "Tickets."

When the conductor had gone, Mr. Head gave Nelson the
return half of his ticket and said, "Now put that in your
pocket and don't lose it or you'll have to stay in the city."

"Maybe I will," Nelson said as if this were a reasonable
suggestion.

Mr. Head ignored him. "First time this boy has ever been
on a train," he explained to the man across the aisle, who
was sitting up now on the edge of his seat with both feet
on the floor.

Nelson jerked his hat on again and turned angrily to the
window.

"He's never seen anything before," Mr. Head continued.
"Ignorant as the day he was born, but I mean for him to
get his fill once and for all."

The boy leaned forward, across his grandfather and toward the stranger. "I was born in the city," he said. "I was
born there. This is my second trip." He said it in a high
positive voice, but the man across the aisle didn't look as
if he understood. There were heavy purple circles under his
eyes.

Mr. Head reached across the aisle and tapped him on the arm. "The thing to do with a boy," he said sagely, "is to show him all it is to show. Don't hold nothing back."

"Yeah," the man said. He gazed down at his swollen feet and lifted the left one about ten inches from the floor. After a minute he put it down and lifted the other. All through the car people began to get up and move about and yawn and stretch. Separate voices could be heard here and there and then a general hum. Suddenly Mr. Head's serene expression changed. His mouth almost closed, and a light, fierce and cautious both, came into his eyes. He was looking down the length of the car. Without turning he caught Nelson by the arm and pulled him forward. "Look," he said.

A huge coffee-colored man was coming slowly forward. He had on a light suit and a yellow satin tie with a ruby pin in it. One of his hands rested on his stomach which rode majestically under his buttoned coat, and in the other he held the head of a black walking stick that he picked up and set down with a deliberate outward motion each time he took a step. He was proceeding very slowly, his large brown eyes gazing over the heads of the passengers. He had a small white mustache and white crinkly hair. Behind him there were two young women, both coffee-colored, one in a yellow dress and one in a green. Their progress was kept at the rate of his, and they chatted in low throaty voices as they followed him.

Mr. Head's grip was tightening insistently on Nelson's arm. As the procession passed them, the light from a sapphire ring on the brown hand that picked up the cane reflected in Mr. Head's eye, but he did not look up, nor did the tremendous man look at him. The group proceeded up the rest of the aisle and out of the car. Mr. Head's grip on Nelson's arm loosened. "What was that?" he asked.

"A man," the boy said and gave him an indignant look as if he were tired of having his intelligence insulted.

"What kind of a man?" Mr. Head persisted, his voice expressionless.

"A fat man," Nelson said. He was beginning to feel that he had better be cautious.

"You don't know what kind?" Mr. Head said in a final tone.

"An old man," the boy said and had a sudden foreboding that he was not going to enjoy the day.

"That was a nigger," Mr. Head said and sat back.

Nelson jumped up on the seat and stood looking backward to the end of the car, but the Negro had gone.

"I'd of thought you'd know a nigger since you seen so many when you was in the city on your first visit," Mr. Head continued. "That's his first nigger," he said to the man across the aisle.

The boy slid down into the seat. "You said they were black," he said in an angry voice. "You never said they were tan. How do you expect me to know anything when you don't tell me right?"

"You're just ignorant is all," Mr. Head said and he got up and moved over in the vacant seat by the man across the aisle.

Nelson turned backward again and looked where the Negro had disappeared. He felt that the Negro had deliberately walked down the aisle in order to make a fool of him and he hated him with a fierce, raw, fresh hate; and also, he understood now why his grandfather disliked them. He looked toward the window, and the face there seemed to suggest that he might be inadequate to the day's exactions. He wondered if he would even recognize the city when they came to it.

After he had told several stories, Mr. Head realized that the man he was talking to was asleep and he got up and suggested to Nelson that they walk over the train and see the parts of it. He particularly wanted the boy to see the toilet, so they went first to the men's room and examined the plumbing. Mr. Head demonstrated the ice-water cooler as if he had invented it and showed Nelson the bowl with a single spigot where the travelers brushed their teeth. They went through several cars and came to the diner.

This was the most elegant car in the train. It was painted a rich egg-yellow and had a wine-colored carpet on the floor. There were wide windows over the tables, and great spaces of the rolling view were caught in miniature in the sides of the coffeepots and in the glasses. Three very black Negroes in white suits and aprons were running up and down the aisle, swinging trays and bowing and bending over the travelers eating breakfast. One of them rushed up to Mr. Head and Nelson and said, holding up two fingers, "Space for two!" but Mr. Head replied in a loud voice, "We eaten before we left!"

The waiter wore large brown spectacles that increased the size of his eye whites. "Stan' aside then, please," he said with an airy wave of the arm as if he were brushing aside flies.

Neither Nelson nor Mr. Head moved a fraction of an inch. "Look," Mr. Head said.

The near corner of the diner, containing two tables, was set off from the rest by a saffron-colored curtain. One table was set but empty, but at the other, facing them, his back to the drape, sat the tremendous Negro. He was speaking in a soft voice to the two women while he buttered a muffin. He had a heavy sad face, and his neck bulged over his white collar on either side. "They rope them off," Mr. Head explained. Then he said, "Let's go see the kitchen," and they walked the length of the diner, but the black waiter was coming fast behind them.

"Passengers are not allowed in the kitchen!" he said in a haughty voice. "Passengers are *not* allowed in the kitchen!"

Mr. Head stopped where he was and turned. "And there's good reason for that," he shouted into the Negro's chest, "because the cockroaches would run the passengers out!"

All the travelers laughed, and Mr. Head and Nelson walked out, grinning. Mr. Head was known at home for his quick wit, and Nelson felt a sudden keen pride in him. He realized the old man would be his only support in the strange place they were approaching. He would be entirely alone in the world if he were ever lost from his grandfather. A terrible excitement shook him, and he wanted to take hold of Mr. Head's coat and hold on.

As they went back to their seats they could see through the passing windows that the countryside was becoming speckled with small houses and shacks and that a highway ran alongside the train. Cars sped by on it, very small and fast. Nelson felt that there was less breath in the air than there had been thirty minutes ago. The man across the aisle had left, and there was no one near for Mr. Head to hold a conversation with, so he looked out the window, through his own reflection, and read aloud the names of the buildings they were passing. "The Dixie Chemical Corp!" he announced. "Southern Maid Flour! Dixie Doors! Southern Belle Cotton Products! Patty's Peanut Butter! Southern Mammy Cane Syrup!"

"Hush up!" Nelson hissed.

All over the car people were beginning to get up and take their luggage off the overhead racks. Women were putting on their coats and hats. The conductor stuck his head in the car and snarled, "Firstoppppmry," and Nelson lunged out of his sitting position, trembling. Mr. Head pushed him down by the shoulder.

"Keep your seat," he said in dignified tones. "The first stop is on the edge of town. The second stop is at the main railroad station." He had come by this knowledge on his first trip when he had got off at the first stop and had had to pay a man fifteen cents to take him into the heart of town. Nelson sat back down, very pale. For the first time in his life he understood that his grandfather was indispensable to him.

The train stopped and let off a few passengers and glided on as if it had never ceased moving. Outside, behind rows of brown rickety houses, a line of blue buildings stood up, and beyond them a pale rose-grey sky faded away to nothing. The train moved into the railroad yard. Looking down, Nelson saw lines and lines of silver tracks multiplying and crisscrossing. Then before he could start counting them, the face in the window started out at him, grey but distinct, and he looked the other way. The train was in the station. Both he and Mr. Head jumped up and ran to the door. Neither noticed that they had left the paper sack with the lunch in it on the seat.

They walked stiffly through the small station and came out of a heavy door into the squall of traffic. Crowds were hurrying to work. Nelson didn't know where to look. Mr. Head leaned against the side of the building and glared in front of him.

Finally Nelson said, "Well, how do you see what all it is to see?"

Mr. Head didn't answer. Then as if the sight of people passing had given him the clue, he said, "You walk," and started off down the street. Nelson followed, steadying his hat. So many sights and sounds were flooding in on him that for the first block he hardly knew what he was seeing. At the second corner, Mr. Head turned and looked behind him at the station they had left, a putty-colored terminal with a concrete dome on top. He thought that if he could keep the dome always in sight, he would be able to get back in the afternoon to catch the train again.

As they walked along, Nelson began to distinguish details and take note of the store windows, jammed with every kind of equipment—hardware, dry goods, chicken feed, liquor. They passed one that Mr. Head called his particular attention to where you walked in and sat on a chair with your feet upon two rests and let a Negro polish your shoes. They walked slowly and stopped and stood at the entrances so they could see what went on in every place, but they did not go into any of them. Mr. Head was determined not to go into any city store, because on his first trip here he had got lost in a large one and had found his way out only after many people had insulted him.

They came in the middle of the next block to a store that had a weighing machine in front of it and they both in turn stepped up on it and put in a penny and received a ticket. Mr. Head's ticket said, "You weigh 120 pounds. You are upright and brave and all your friends admire you." He put the ticket in his pocket, surprised that the machine should have got his character correct but his weight wrong, for he had weighed on a grain scale not long before and knew he weighed 110. Nelson's ticket said, "You weigh 98 pounds. You have a great destiny ahead of you but beware of dark women." Nelson did not know any women and he weighed only 68 pounds, but Mr. Head pointed out that the machine had probably printed the number upside down, meaning the 9 for a 6.

They walked on, and at the end of five blocks the dome of the terminal sank out of sight, and Mr. Head turned to the left. Nelson could have stood in front of every store window for an hour if there had not been another more interesting one next to it. Suddenly he said, "I was born here!" Mr. Head turned and looked at him with horror. There was a sweaty brightness about his face. "This is where I come from!" he said.

Mr. Head was appalled. He saw the moment had come for drastic action. "Lemme show you one thing you ain't seen yet," he said and took him to the corner where there was a sewer entrance. "Squat down," he said, "and stick your head there," and he held the back of the boy's coat while he got down and put his head in the sewer. He drew it back quickly, hearing a gurgling in the depths under the sidewalk. Then Mr. Head explained the sewer system, how the entire city was underlined with it, how it contained all the drainage and was full of rats and how a man could slide into it and be sucked along down endless pitch-black tunnels. At any minute any man in the city might be sucked into the sewer and never heard from again. He described it so well that Nelson was for some seconds shaken. He connected the sewer passages with the entrance to hell and understood for the first time how the world was put together in its lower parts. He drew away from the curb.

Then he said, "Yes, but you can stay away from the holes," and his face took on that stubborn look that was so exasperating to his grandfather. "This is where I come from!" he said.

Mr. Head was dismayed but he only muttered, "You'll get your fill," and they walked on. At the end of two more blocks he turned to the left, feeling that he was circling the dome; and he was correct, for in a half hour they passed in front of the railroad station again. At first Nelson did not notice that he was seeing the same stores twice, but when they passed the one where you put your feet on the rests while the Negro polished your shoes, he perceived that they were walking in a circle.

"We done been here!" he shouted. "I don't believe you know where you're at!"

"The direction just slipped my mind for a minute," Mr. Head said, and they turned down a different street. He still did not intend to let the dome get too far away, and after two blocks in their new direction he turned to the left. This street contained two- and three-story wooden buildings. Anyone passing on the sidewalk could see into the rooms, but Mr. Head, glancing through one window, saw a woman lying on an iron bed, looking out, with a sheet pulled over her. Her knowing expression shook him. A fierce-looking boy on a bicycle came driving down out of nowhere, and he had to jump to the side to keep from being hit. "It nothing to them if they knock you down," he said. "You better keep closer to me."

They walked on for some time on streets like this before he remembered to turn again. The houses they were passing now were all unpainted, and the wood in them looked rotten; the street between was narrower. Nelson saw a colored man. Then another. Then another. "Niggers live in these houses," he observed.

"Well, come on and we'll go somewheres else," Mr. Head said. "We didn't come to look at niggers," and they turned down another street but they continued to see Negroes everywhere. Nelson's skin began to prickle, and they stepped along at a faster pace in order to leave the neighborhood as soon as possible. There were colored men in their undershirts standing in the doors, and colored women rocking on the sagging porches. Colored children played in the gutters and stopped what they were doing to look at them. Before long they began to pass rows of stores with colored customers in them but they didn't pause at the entrances of these. Black eyes in black faces were watching from every direction. "Yes," Mr. Head said, "this is where you were born—right here with all these niggers."

Nelson scowled. "I think you done got us lost," he said.

Mr. Head swung around sharply and looked for the dome. It was nowhere in sight. "I ain't got us lost either," he said. "You're just tired of walking."

"I ain't tired, I'm hungry," Nelson said. "Give me a biscuit."

They discovered then that they had lost the lunch.

"You were the one holding the sack," Nelson said. "I would have kep aholt of it."

"If you want to direct this trip, I'll go on by myself and leave you right here," Mr. Head said and was pleased to see the boy turn white. However, he realized they were lost and drifting farther every minute from the station. He was hungry himself and beginning to be thirsty, and since they had been in the colored neighborhood, they had both begun to sweat. Nelson had on his shoes and he was unaccustomed to them. The concrete sidewalks were very hard. They both wanted to find a place to sit down, but this was impossible and they kept on walking, the boy muttering under his breath, "First you lost the sack and then you lost the way," and Mr. Head growling from time to time, "Anybody wants to be from this nigger heaven can be from it!"

By now the sun was well forward in the sky. The odor of dinners cooking drifted out to them. The Negroes were all at their doors to see them pass. "Whyn't you ast one of these niggers the way?" Nelson said. "You got us lost."

"This is where you were born," Mr. Head said. "You can ast one yourself if you want to."

Nelson was afraid of the colored men and he didn't want to be laughed at by the colored children. Up ahead he saw a large colored woman leaning in a doorway that opened onto the sidewalk. Her hair stood straight out from her head for about four inches all around, and she was resting on bare brown feet that turned pink at the sides. She had on a pink dress that showed her exact shape. As they came abreast of her, she lazily lifted one hand to her head, and her fingers disappeared into her hair.

Nelson stopped. He felt his breath drawn up by the woman's dark eyes. "How do you get back to town?" he said in a voice that did not sound like his own.

After a minute she said, "You in town now," in a rich low tone that made Nelson feel as if a cool spray had been turned on him.

"How do you get back to the train?" he said in the same reed-like voice.

"You can catch you a car," she said.

He understood she was making fun of him but he was too paralyzed even to scowl. He stood drinking in every detail of her. His eyes traveled up from her great knees to her forehead and then in a triangular path from the glistening sweat on her neck down and across her tremendous bosom and over her bare arm back to where her fingers lay hidden in her hair. He suddenly wanted her to reach down and pick him up and draw him against her and then he wanted to feel her breath on his face. He wanted to look down and down into her eyes while she held him tighter and tighter. He had never had such a feeling before. He felt as if he were reeling down through a pitch-black tunnel.

"You can go a block down yonder and catch you a car take you to the railroad station, Sugarpie," she said.

Nelson would have collapsed at her feet if Mr. Head had not pulled him roughly away. "You act like you don't have any sense!" the old man growled.

They hurried down the street, and Nelson did not look back at the woman. He pushed his hat sharply forward over his face which was already burning with shame. The sneering ghost he had seen in the train window and all the foreboding feelings he had on the way returned to him and he remembered that his ticket from the scale had said to beware of dark women and that his grandfather's had said he was upright and brave. He took the old man's hand, a sign of dependence he seldom showed.

They headed down the street toward the car tracks where a yellow rattling trolley was coming. Mr. Head had never boarded a streetcar and he let that one pass. Nelson was silent. From time to time his mouth trembled slightly, but his grandfather, occupied with his own problems, paid him no attention. They stood on the corner and neither looked at the Negroes who were passing, going about their business just as if they had been white, except that most of them stopped and eyed Mr. Head and Nelson. It occurred to Mr. Head that since the streetcar ran on tracks, they could simply follow the tracks. He gave Nelson a slight push and explained that they would follow the tracks on into the railroad station, walking, and they set off.

Presently to their great relief they began to see white people again, and Nelson sat down on the sidewalk against the wall of a building. "I got to rest myself some," he said.

"You lost the sack and the direction. You can just wait on
me to rest myself."

"There's the tracks in front of us," Mr. Head said. "All
we got to do is keep them in sight and you could have remembered the sack as good as me. This is where you were
born. This is your old home town. This is your second trip.
You ought to know how to do," and he squatted down and
continued in this vein, but the boy was easing his burning
feet out of his shoes.

"And standing there grinning like a chim-pan-zee while
a nigger woman gives you directions. Great Gawd!" Mr.
Head said.

"I never said I was nothing but born here," the boy said
in a shaky voice. "I never said I would or wouldn't like it.
I never said I wanted to come. I only said I was born here
and I never had nothing to do with that. I want to go home.
I never wanted to come in the first place. It was all your
big idea. How you know you ain't following the tracks in
the wrong direction?"

This last had occurred to Mr. Head, too. "All these people are white," he said.

"We ain't passed here before," Nelson said. This was a
neighborhood of brick buildings that might have been lived
in or might not. A few empty automobiles were parked
along the curb and there was an occasional passer-by. The
heat of the pavement came up through Nelson's thin suit.
His eyelids began to droop, and after a few minutes his head
tilted forward. His shoulders twitched once or twice and
then he fell over on his side and lay sprawled in an exhausted fit of sleep.

Mr. Head watched him silently. He was very tired himself but they could not both sleep at the same time and he
could not have slept anyway because he did not know where
he was. In a few minutes Nelson would wake up, refreshed
by his sleep and very cocky, and would begin complaining
that he had lost the sack and the way. You'd have a mighty
sorry time if I wasn't here, Mr. Head thought; and then another idea occurred to him. He looked at the sprawled figure for several minutes; presently he stood up. He justified
what he was going to do on the grounds that it is some-

times necessary to teach a child a lesson he won't forget, particularly when the child is always reasserting his position with some new impudence. He walked without a sound to the corner about twenty feet away and sat down on a covered garbage can in the alley where he could look out and watch Nelson wake up alone.

The boy was dozing fitfully, half conscious of vague noises and black forms moving up from some dark part of him into the light. His face worked in his sleep, and he had pulled his knees up under his chin. The sun shed a dull dry light on the narrow street; everything looked like exactly what it was. After a while Mr. Head, hunched like an old monkey on the garbage-can lid, decided that if Nelson didn't wake up soon, he would make a loud noise by bamming his foot against the can. He looked at his watch and discovered that it was two o'clock. Their train left at six, and the possibility of missing it was too awful for him to think of. He kicked his foot backwards on the can, and a hollow boom reverberated in the alley.

Nelson shot up onto his feet with a shout. He looked where his grandfather should have been and stared. He seemed to whirl several times and then, picking up his feet and throwing his head back, he dashed down the street like a wild maddened pony. Mr. Head jumped off the can and galloped after, but the child was almost out of sight. He saw a streak of grey disappearing diagonally a block ahead. He ran as fast as he could looking both ways down every intersection, but without sight of him again. Then as he passed the third intersection, completely winded, he saw about half a block down the street a scene that stopped him altogether. He crouched behind a trash box to watch and get his bearings.

Nelson was sitting with both legs spread out, and by his side lay an elderly woman, screaming. Groceries were scattered about the sidewalk. A crowd of women had already gathered to see justice done, and Mr. Head distinctly heard the old woman on the pavement shout, "You've broken my ankle and your daddy'll pay for it! Every nickel! Police! Police!" Several of the women were plucking at Nelson's shoulder, but the boy seemed too dazed to get up.

Something forced Mr. Head from behind the trash box and forward, but only at a creeping pace. He had never in his life been accosted by a policeman. The women were milling around Nelson as if they might suddenly all dive on him at once and tear him to pieces, and the old woman continued to scream that her ankle was broken and to call for an officer. Mr. Head came on so slowly that he could have been taking a backward step after each forward one, but when he was about ten feet away, Nelson saw him and sprang. The child caught him around the hips and clung panting against him.

The women all turned on Mr. Head. The injured one sat up and shouted, "You, sir! You'll pay every penny of my doctor's bill that your boy has caused. He's a juve-nile delinquent! Where is an officer? Somebody take this man's name and address!"

Mr. Head was trying to detach Nelson's fingers from the flesh in the back of his legs. The old man's head had lowered itself into his collar like a turtle's; his eyes were glazed with fear and caution.

"Your boy has broken my ankle!" the old woman shouted. "Police!"

Mr. Head sensed the approach of the policeman from behind. He stared straight ahead at the women who were massed in their fury like a solid wall to block his escape. "This is not my boy," he said. "I never seen him before."

He felt Nelson's fingers fall out of his flesh.

The women dropped back, staring at him with horror, as if they were so repulsed by a man who would deny his own image and likeness that they could not bear to lay hands on him. Mr. Head walked on, through a space they silently cleared, and left Nelson behind. Ahead of him he saw nothing but a hollow tunnel that had once been the street.

The boy remained standing where he was, his neck craned forward and his hands hanging by his sides. His hat was jammed on his head so that there were no longer any creases on it. The injured woman got up and shook her fist at him, and the others gave him pitying looks, but he didn't notice any of them. There was no policeman in sight.

In a minute he began to move mechanically, making no effort to catch up with his grandfather but merely following at about twenty paces. They walked on for five blocks in this way. Mr. Head's shoulders were sagging, and his neck hung forward at such an angle that it was not visible from behind. He was afraid to turn his head. Finally he cut a short hopeful glance over his shoulder. Twenty feet behind him, he saw two small eyes piercing into his back like pitchfork prongs.

The boy was not of a forgiving nature, but this was the first time he had ever had anything to forgive. Mr. Head had never disgraced himself before. After two more blocks, he turned and called over his shoulder in a high, desperately gay voice, "Let's us go get us a Co' Cola somewheres!"

Nelson, with a dignity he had never shown before, turned and stood with his back to his grandfather.

Mr. Head began to feel the depth of his denial. His face as they walked on became all hollows and bare ridges. He saw nothing they were passing but he perceived that they had lost the car tracks. There was no dome to be seen anywhere, and the afternoon was advancing. He knew that if dark overtook them in the city, they would be beaten and robbed. The speed of God's justice was only what he expected for himself, but he could not stand to think that his sins would be visited upon Nelson, and that even now he was leading the boy to his doom.

They continued to walk on block after block through an endless section of small brick houses until Mr. Head almost fell over a water spigot sticking up about six inches off the edge of a grass plot. He had not had a drink of water since early morning but he felt he did not deserve it now. Then he thought that Nelson would be thirsty and they would both drink and be brought together. He squatted down and put his mouth to the nozzle and turned a cold stream of water into his throat. Then he called out in the high desperate voice, "Come on and getcher some water!"

This time the child stared through him for nearly sixty seconds. Mr. Head got up and walked on as if he had drunk poison. Nelson, though he had not had water since some he

had drunk out of a paper cup on the train, passed by the
spigot, disdaining to drink where his grandfather had. When
Mr. Head realized this, he lost all hope. His face in the wan-
ing afternoon light looked ravaged and abandoned. He
could feel the boy's steady hate, traveling at an even pace
behind him and he knew that (if by some miracle they escaped being murdered in the city) it would continue just
that way for the rest of his life. He knew that now he was
wandering into a black strange place where nothing was like
it had ever been before, a long old age without respect and
an end that would be welcome because it would be the end.

As for Nelson, his mind had frozen around his grandfather's treachery as if he were trying to preserve it intact
to present at the final judgment. He walked without looking
to one side or the other, but every now and then his mouth
would twitch and this was when he felt, from some remote
place inside himself, a black mysterious form reach up as if
it would melt his frozen vision in one hot grasp.

The sun dropped down behind a row of houses and,
hardly noticing, they passed into an elegant suburban section where mansions were set back from the road by lawns
with birdbaths on them. Here everything was entirely deserted. For blocks they didn't pass even a dog. The big white
houses were like partially submerged icebergs in the distance. There were no sidewalks, only drives, and these
wound around and around in endless ridiculous circles. Nelson made no move to come nearer to Mr. Head. The old
man felt that if he saw a sewer entrance he would drop
down into it and let himself be carried away; and he could
imagine the boy standing by, watching with only a slight
interest, while he disappeared.

A loud bark jarred him to attention, and he looked up to
see a fat man approaching with two bulldogs. He waved
both arms like someone shipwrecked on a desert island.
"I'm lost!" he called. "I'm lost and can't find my way and
me and this boy have got to catch this train and I can't find
the station. Oh Gawd, I'm lost! Oh hep me Gawd, I'm lost!"

The man, who was bald-headed and had on golf knickers,
asked him what train he was trying to catch, and Mr. Head
began to get out his tickets, trembling so violently he could

hardly hold them. Nelson had come up to within fifteen feet and stood watching.

"Well," the fat man said, giving him back the tickets, "you won't have time to get back to town to make this train but you can catch it at the suburb stop. That's three blocks from here," and he began explaining how to get there.

Mr. Head stared as if he were slowly returning from the dead, and when the man had finished and gone off with the dogs jumping at his heels, he turned to Nelson and said breathlessly, "We're going to get home!"

The child was standing about ten feet away, his face bloodless under the grey hat. His eyes were triumphantly cold. There was no light in them, no feeling, no interest. He was merely there, a small figure, waiting. Home was nothing to him.

Mr. Head turned slowly. He felt he knew now what time would be like without seasons and what heat would be like without light and what man would be like without salvation. He didn't care if he never made the train and if it had not been for what suddenly caught his attention, like a cry out of the gathering dusk, he might have forgotten there was a station to go to.

He had not walked five hundred yards down the road when he saw, within reach of him, the plaster figure of a Negro sitting bent over on a low yellow brick fence that curved around a wide lawn. The Negro was about Nelson's size and he was pitched forward at an unsteady angle because the putty that held him to the wall had cracked. One of his eyes was entirely white, and he held a piece of brown watermelon.

Mr. Head stood looking at him silently until Nelson stopped at a little distance. Then as the two of them stood there, Mr. Head breathed, "An artificial nigger!"

It was not possible to tell if the artificial Negro were meant to be young or old; he looked too miserable to be either. He was meant to look happy, because his mouth was stretched up at the corners, but the chipped eye and the angle he was cocked at gave him a wild look of misery instead.

"An artificial nigger!" Nelson repeated in Mr. Head's exact tone.

The two of them stood there with their necks forward at almost the same angle and their shoulders curved in almost exactly the same way and their hands trembling identically in their pockets. Mr. Head looked like an ancient child and Nelson like a miniature old man. They stood gazing at the artificial Negro as if they were faced with some great mystery, some monument to another's victory that brought them together in their common defeat. They could both feel it dissolving their differences like an action of mercy. Mr. Head had never known before what mercy felt like because he had been too good to deserve any, but he felt he knew now. He looked at Nelson and understood that he must say something to the child to show that he was still wise, and in the look the boy returned he saw a hungry need for that assurance. Nelson's eyes seemed to implore him to explain once and for all the mystery of existence.

Mr. Head opened his lips to make a lofty statement and heard himself say, "They ain't got enough real ones here. They got to have an artificial one."

After a second, the boy nodded with a strange shivering about his mouth, and said, "Let's go home before we get ourselves lost again."

Their train glided into the suburb stop just as they reached the station and they boarded it together, and ten minutes before it was due to arrive at the junction, they went to the door and stood ready to jump off if it did not stop; but it did, just as the moon, restored to its full splendor, sprang from a cloud and flooded the clearing with light. As they stepped off, the sage grass was shivering gently in shades of silver, and the clinkers under their feet glittered with a fresh black light. The treetops, fencing the junction like the protecting walls of a garden, were darker than the sky which was hung with gigantic white clouds illuminated like lanterns.

Mr. Head stood very still and felt the action of mercy touch him again, but this time he knew that there were no words in the world that could name it. He understood that it grew out of agony, which is not denied to any man and which is given in strange ways to children. He understood it was all a man could carry into death to give his Maker, and he suddenly burned with shame that he had so little of it to take with him. He stood appalled, judging himself with the thoroughness of God, while the action of mercy covered his pride like a flame and consumed it. He had never thought himself a great sinner before but he saw now that his true depravity had been hidden from him lest it cause him despair. He realized that he was forgiven for sins from the beginning of time, when he had conceived in his own heart the sin of Adam, until the present, when he had denied poor Nelson. He saw that no sin was too monstrous for him to claim as his own, and since God loved in proportion as He forgave, he felt ready at that instant to enter Paradise.

Nelson, composing his expression under the shadow of his hat brim, watched him with a mixture of fatigue and suspicion, and as the train glided past them and disappeared like a frightened serpent into the woods, he muttered, "I'm glad I've went once, but I'll never go back again!"

THE DEVIL WAS THE JOKER

J. F. Powers

J. F. POWERS *lives in St. Cloud, Minnesota. His short stories
have appeared in various magazines, most frequently
in* The New Yorker *and have been collected into two
volumes* THE PRINCE OF DARKNESS (*1948*) *and* THE
PRESENCE OF GRACE (*1956*). *He is now working on a
novel.*

Mr. McMaster, a hernia case convalescing in one of the
four-bed wards, was fat and fifty or so, with a candy-pink
face, sparse orange hair, and popeyes. ("Eyes don't permit
me to read much," he had told Myles Flynn, the night orderly, more than once.) On his last evening in the hospital,
as he lay in his bed smoking, his hands clasped over a box of
Havanas that rested on the soft dais of his stomach, he
called Myles to his bedside. He wanted to thank him, he
said, and, incidentally, he had no use for "that other son of
a bitch"—meaning the other orderly, an engineering student, who had prepped him for surgery. "A hell of a fine
engineer he'll make. You, though, you're different—more
like a doctor than an orderly—and I was surprised to hear
from one of the Sisters today that you're not going into the
medical field." Mr. McMaster said he supposed there must
be other reasons for working in a hospital, but he didn't
sound as though he knew any.

Myles said he'd been four years in a seminary, studying
for the priesthood—until "something happened." There he
stopped.

Mr. McMaster grinned. "To make a long story short,"
he said.

Myles shook his head. He'd told Mr. McMaster all there
was for him to tell—all he knew. He'd simply been asked to
leave, he said, and since that day, three months before, he'd
just been trying to make himself useful to society, here in
the hospital. Mr. McMaster suddenly got serious. He wondered, in a whisper, whether Myles was "a cradle Catholic,"
as if that had something to do with his expulsion, and Myles
said, "Yes. Almost have to be with a name like mine." "Not
a-tall," said Mr. McMaster. "That's the hell of it. The other
day I met a Jew by the name of Buckingham. Some Buckingham!"

Scenting liquor on the patient's breath, Myles supposed
that Mr. McMaster, like so many salesmen or executives on
their last evening, wanted to get a good night's rest, to be
ready for the morrow, when he would ride away in a taxi-
cab to the daily battle of Chicago.

Again Mr. McMaster asked if Myles was a cradle Catholic, and when Myles again told him he was, Mr. McMaster
said, "Call me Mac," and had Myles move the screen over
to his bed. When they were hidden from the others in the
ward, Mac whispered, "We don't know who they may be,
whatever they say." Then he asked Myles if he'd ever heard
of the Clementine Fathers. Myles had. "I'm with them,"
Mac said. "In a good-will capacity." He described the nature of his work, which was meeting the public, lay and
clerical (the emphasis was on the latter), and "building
good will" for the Clementine order and finding more
readers for the *Clementine,* the family-type magazine published by the Fathers.

Myles listened patiently because he considered it part of
his job to do so, but the most he could say for the magazine
was that it was probably good—of its kind. Yes, he'd heard
the Fathers' radio program. The program, "Father Clem
Answers Your Question," was aimed at non-Catholics but
it had many faithful listeners among the nuns at the hospital.
And the pamphlets put out by the Fathers, many of them
written by Father Clem—Myles knew them well. In the hospital waiting rooms, they were read, wrung, and gnawed
upon by their captive audience. "Is Father Clem a real person?" Myles asked. "Yes, and no," Mac said, which struck

Myles as descriptive of the characters created by Father Clem, an author who tackled life's problems through numberless Joans, Jeans, Bobs, and Bills, clear-thinking college kids who, coached from the wings by jolly nuns and priests, invariably got the best of the arguments they had with the poor devils they were always meeting—atheists, euthanasianists, and the like. "Drive a car?" Mac asked. Myles said yes.

Mac then said he wanted it understood he wasn't making Myles any promises, but he thought there might be a job opening up with the Fathers soon, a job such as his own. "Think it over," Mac said, and Myles did—needing only a moment. He thought of his correspondence with the hierarchy, of the nice replies, all offering him nothing. For his purposes, the job with the Fathers, unsuited as he was to it, could be ideal. Traveling around from diocese to diocese, meeting pastors and even bishops face to face in the regular course of the work, he might make the vital connection that would lead him, somehow, to the priesthood. Without a bishop he'd never get into another seminary—a bishop was more necessary than a vocation—but Myles had more than meeting the right bishop to worry about. He had lost his clerical status, and was now 1-A in the draft. The call-up might come any day.

Working with Mac would be action of a positive sort, better than continuing his fruitless correspondence, better than following such advice as he'd had from acquaintances —or even from the confessional, where, too hopefully, he'd taken his problems. There he had been told to go into business or science and get ahead, or into government and make a success of *that,* after which, presumably, he could come —tottering—before the bishops of the land as a man of proved ability and, what was more important, a man of stability. When the wise old confessor realized, however, that Myles not only had been cast aside by the Church but was likely to be wanted soon by the State, there had been no problem at all. His counsel had flowed swift and sure: "Enlist! Don't wait to be drafted!"

"Don't think of it as just a job," Mac said now. "Try

to think of it as the Fathers do, and as I hope I do. Think of it as the Work."

Myles, thinking of it as a steppingstone to ordination, said he'd like to be considered for the job.

Mac said that of course the Fathers would have the last say, but his word would carry some weight with them, since Myles, if accepted, would be working under him—at first, anyway. He then asked Myles to bring a glass of ice water, and easy on the water. Myles, returning with a glass of ice, noted a bottle in bed with Mac, tucked under the sheet at his side like a nursing infant. He left them together, behind the screen.

Two days later Myles was summoned by telegram to an address in the Loop. He found the place, all right—an old building with grillwork elevators affording passengers a view of the cables. Mac was waiting for Myles at the cigar stand downstairs. As they rode up to the Fathers' floor, he advised Myles to forget all about his past as a seminarian, reasoning that if this was mentioned to the Fathers, it might make a bad impression. Myles had to agree with that, if reluctantly.

At the fifth floor, which the Fathers shared with a number of tailors, publishers, and distributors of barbers' supplies, Mac hustled Myles into the washroom. Myles's black overcoat, suit, and tie were all wrong, Mac said. He told Myles to take off his coat and then he suggested that they switch ties. This they did, morosely. Mac's suit, a double-breasted Glen plaid with a precipitous drape and trousers that billowed about his disproportionately thin legs, would "just carry" the black tie, he said, and presumably his tie, with its spheres, coils, and triangles suggesting the spirit of Science and Industry, would carry Myles's black suit. "Don't want 'em to think they're hiring a creep," Mac said.

There was no trouble at all with the Fathers. Mac evidently stood high with them. He told them that Myles had gone to the University of Illinois for a time, which was news to Myles. He let it pass, though, because he remembered a conversation at the hospital during which, assuming Illinois to be Mac's old school, he had said that he'd once attended a football game at Illinois—or almost had. He had been dragooned into joining the Boy Scouts, Myles had explained, and had marched with his troop to the stadium for the season opener, admission free to Scouts, but on reaching the gates, he had remained outside, in a delayed protest against the Scouts and all their pomps. He had spent the afternoon walking under the campus elms. "Then you were there," Mac had said, which Myles had taken to mean that Mac felt as he did about those beautiful old trees.

Mac delivered a little pep talk, chiefly for the benefit of the three Fathers in the office, Myles suspected, although the words were spoken to him. He could think of nothing to say. He was more impressed by the charitable than the catechetical aspects of the Fathers' work. And yet, little as he might value their radio program, their pamphlets, their dim magazine, it would be work with which he could associate himself with some enthusiasm. It would suit his purposes far better than going into business or staying on at the hospital.

"The Work is one hundred per cent apostolic," said one of the Fathers.

Myles remembered that the Fathers ran several institutions for juvenile delinquents. "I know something of your trade schools," he said quickly.

"Would that we had more of them," said the Father sitting behind the desk. He had bloodied his face and neck in shaving. "You have to move with the times." He seemed to be the boss. On the wall behind him hung a metal crucifix, which could have come off a coffin, and a broken airplane propeller, which must have dated from the First World War. "How do you stand in the draft?" he asked Myles.

"All clear," said Mac, answering for him. Myles let that pass, too. He could tell Mac the facts later.

When Myles heard what the salary would be, he was glad he had other reasons for taking the job. The money would be the least important part of it, Mac put in, and Myles could see what he meant. But Myles didn't care about the money; he'd live on bread and water—and pamphlets. The salary made him feel better about not telling Mac and the Fathers that he intended to use his new position, if he could, to meet a bishop. The expense allowance, too, impressed him as decidedly pre-war. Mac, however, seemed to be hinting not at its meanness but at Myles's possible profligacy when, in front of two more Fathers, who had come in to meet Myles, he said, "You'll have to watch your expenses, Flynn. Can't have you asking for reimbursements, you understand." As Myles was leaving, one of the new arrivals whispered to him, "I was on the road myself for a bit and I'd dearly love to go out again. Mr. McMaster, he's a grand companion. You'll make a great team."

Three days later the team was heading north in Mac's car, a lightweight black Cadillac, a '41—a good year for a Cadillac, Mac said, and the right car for the job: impressive but not showy, and old enough not to antagonize people.

Myles was not sorry to be leaving Chicago. The nuns and nurses at the hospital had been happy to see him go—happy, they said, that he'd found a better job. This showed Myles how little they had ever understood him and his reasons for being at the hospital; he'd known all along that they had very little sense of vocation.

Speaking of the nurses, Myles told Mac that the corporal works of mercy had lost all meaning in the modern world, to which Mac replied that he wouldn't touch nursing with a ten-foot pole. Nursing might be a fine career for a girl, he allowed, and added, "A lot of 'em marry above themselves —marry money."

They were like two men in a mine, working at different levels, in different veins, and lost to each other. Mac, who apparently still thought of Myles as a doctor, wanted to know how much the internes and nurses knocked down and what their private lives were like—said he'd heard a few stories. When Myles professed ignorance, Mac seemed to think he was being secretive, as if the question went against the Hippocratic oath. He tried to discuss medicine, with special reference to his diet, but failed to interest Myles. He asked what the hospital did with the stiffs, and received no pertinent information, because the question happened to re-mind Myles of the medieval burial confraternities, and he sailed into a long discussion of their blessed work, advocating its revival in the modern world.

"All free, huh?" Mac commented. "The undertakers would love that!"

Myles strove in vain for understanding, always against the wind. Mac had got the idea that Myles, in praising the burial fraternities, was advocating a form of socialized medicine, and he held on to it. "Use logic," he said. "What's right for the undertakers is right for the doctors."

They rode in silence for a while. Then Mac said, "What you say about the nurses may be true, but you gotta remember they don't have it easy." He knew how Myles felt about hospital work, he said, but instead of letting it prey on his mind, Myles should think of other things—of the better days ahead. Mac implied that Myles's talk about the corporal works was just a cover-up for his failure to get into anything better.

Myles restated his position. Mac, with noticeable patience, said that Myles was too hard on people—too critical of the modern world. "Give it time," he said. When Myles persisted, Mac said, "Let's give it a rest, huh? You wanna take it awhile?" He stopped the car and turned the wheel over to Myles. After watching him pass a Greyhound bus, he appeared to be satisfied that the car was in good hands, and went to sleep.

The first night on the road they stopped in a small town, at the only hotel, which had no bar, and Mac suggested that they go out for a drink. In a tavern, the bartender, when he found out they were from Chicago, showed them his collection of matchbooks with nudes on the cover.

"I have a friend that'll get you all that you want," Mac said to him. "You better avert your eyes, son," he said to Myles. "This is some of that modern world you don't like. He doesn't like our modern world," Mac said to the bartender.

"Maybe he don't know what he's missing."

The bartender seemed anxious to make a deal until Mac asked him to put down a little deposit "as evidence of good faith."

"Do I have to?"

"To me it's immaterial," Mac said. "But I notice it some-times speeds delivery."

"I can wait."

"All right, if you're sure you can. You write your name and address on a slip of paper and how many you want." While the bartender was doing this, Mac called over to him, "Don't forget your zone number."

"We don't have 'em in this town."

"Oh," Mac said. He gave Myles a look, the wise, doped look of a camel.

The bartender brought the slip of paper over to Mac. "They gotta be as good as them I got—or better," he said, and walked away.

Mac, watching him, matched him word for step: "When-you-gonna-get-those-corners-sawed-off-your-head?"

Leaving the tavern with Mac, Myles saw the wind take the slip of paper up the street.

"My friend can do without that kind of business," Mac said.

Mac began operations on a freezing cold day in central Wisconsin, and right away Myles was denied his first oppor-tunity. While Mac went into a chancery office to negotiate with the bishop, who would (or would not) grant permis-sion to canvass the diocese, Myles had to wait outside in the car, with the engine running; Mac said he was worried about the battery. This bishop was one with whom Myles had already corresponded unsuccessfully, but that was small consolation to him, in view of his plan to plead his case before as many bishops as possible, without reference to past failures. How he'd manage it with Mac in attendance, he didn't know. Perhaps he could use the initial interview for analysis only and, attempting to see the bishop as an opponent in a game, try to uncover his weakness, and then call back alone later and play upon it. Myles disapproved of cunning and rather doubted whether he could carry out such a scheme. But he also recalled that puzzling but prac-tical advice, "Be ye therefore wise as serpents and simple as doves," the first part of which the bishops themselves, he believed, were at such pains to follow in their dealings with him.

The next day Mac invited Myles to accompany him indoors when he paid his calls upon the pastors. The day was no warmer, but Mac said nothing about the battery. He said, "You've got a lot to learn, son," and proceeded to give Myles some pointers. In some dioceses, according to Mac, the bishop's permission was all you needed; get that, and the pastors—always excepting a few incorrigibles—would drop like ripe fruit. Unfortunately, in such dioceses the bishop's permission wasn't always easy to obtain. Of course you got in to see bishops personally (this in reply to a question from Myles), but most of the time you were working with pastors. There were two kinds of pastors, Mac said—those who honestly believed they knew everything and those who didn't. With the first, it was best to appear helpless (as, in fact, you were) and try to get them interested in doing your job for you. With the other kind, you had to appear confident, promise them the moon—something they were always looking for anyway—tell them a change might come over their people if they were exposed to the pamphlets and the *Clementine*. Of course, no pastor had a right to expect such a miracle, but many did expect it even so, if the pamphlets and the *Clementine* hadn't been tried in the parish before. You'd meet some, though, Mac said, who would be cold, even opposed, to the Work, and offensive to you, and with them you took a beating—but cheerfully, hoping for a change of heart later. More than one of that kind had come around in the end, he said, and one of them had even written a glowing letter to the Fathers, complimenting them on the high type of layman they had working for them, and had placed an order for a rack of pamphlets on condition that Mac received credit for it. Then there were the others—those who would do everything they could to help you, wanted to feed you and put you up overnight, but they, for some reason, were found more often in the country, or in poor city parishes, where little could be accomplished and where you seldom went.

On the third day out, they came across one of the incorrigibles. He greeted them with a snarl. "You guys're a

breed apart," he said. Myles was offended, but Mac, un-
daunted, went into his routine for cracking hard nuts.
"Don't know much about this job, I'm ashamed to say," he
said, "but it's sure a lot of fun learning." The pastor, instead of going out of his way to help a cheerful soul like
Mac (and a nervous one like Myles), ordered them out of
the rectory, produced a golf club when they didn't go, and,
when they did, stood at the front window, behind a lace
curtain, until they drove off.

Before the end of the first week, Myles discovered that
Mac wasn't really interested in getting permission to canvass
a parish house-to-house. He said he just didn't care that
much about people. What he liked was co-operation; he
liked to have a pastor in the pulpit doing the donkey work
and the ushers in the aisles dispensing pencil stubs and subscription blanks, with him just sitting at a card table in the
vestibule after Mass, smiling at the new subscribers as they
passed out, making change, and croaking, "God love you."
That was what Mac called "a production." He operated
on a sliding scale—a slippery one, Myles thought. In a big,
well-to-do parish, where the take would be high, Mac cut
prices. He was also prepared to make an offering toward
the upkeep of the church, or to the pastor's favorite charity
(the latter was often the former), and to signify his intention beforehand. He had to hustle, he said, in order to meet
the stiff competition of the missionaries; a layman, even if
he represented a recognized religious order, was always at
a disadvantage. Fortunately, he said, there were quite a few
secular pastors who, though they didn't care for the orders,
didn't consider the struggling Clementines a menace. But
there weren't many pastors with flourishing parishes who
would co-operate with Mac or with anybody. They were
sitting pretty, Mac said, and they knew it. If he now and
then succeeded with one of them, it was only because he
was liked personally—or, as it seemed to Myles, because of
what Mac called "the package deal." The package deal
didn't actually involve the Work, Mac was careful to explain, but it sometimes helped it. And, Myles felt, compromised it.

The package deal always began with Mac's opening his

bag of tricks. It was a Gladstone bag, which he had got from a retired cooky salesman. When open, it looked like a little stadium, and where the cookies had once been on display, in their individual plastic sections, ranged in tiers, there were now rosaries, medals, scapulars—religious goods of the usual quality, which didn't catch the eye in many rectories. But there were also playing cards with saints as face cards—in one deck the Devil was the joker—and these were new to some priests, as they were to Myles, and had strong educational appeal. Children could familiarize themselves with the lives of the saints from them, and there were other decks, which taught Christian doctrine. Mac had a new kind of rosary, too. It was made of plastic, to fit the hand, and in function and appearance it was similar to an umpire's ball-and-strike indicator. Each time a little key was punched, the single dial, which showed the Mysteries—Sorrowful, Joyful, and Glorious—revolved a notch, and for the Ave Marias there was a modest tick, for the Pater Nosters an authoritative click. Mac had difficulty explaining the new rosary's purpose to some priests—*not* to replace the old model, the traditional beads on a string, but to facilitate prayer while driving, for the new rosary was easily attached to the steering wheel. "Of course, you still have to say the prayers," Mac would say.

Mac gave freely from his bag. Other things, however, he sold—just as an accommodation, he said, to priests, whose work naturally left them little time for shopping. He seemed to have a friend in every business that a parish priest might have to deal with. Myles saw him take large orders for automatic bingo cards (with built-in simulated corn counters), and the trunk of the car was full of catalogues and of refills for the grab bag. "There's one for you, Father," he'd say, presenting a pastor with one of the new rosaries. Later, speaking earnestly of power lawnmowers, of which he happened to have a prospectus showing pictures and prices, he'd say, "That's practically cost minus, Father. He"—referring to a friend—"can't do better than that, I know."

One day, while they were driving along, Myles, at the wheel, asked about Mac's friends.

"Friends? Who said I had any?" Mac snapped.

"I keep hearing you talking about your friends."

"Is that *so?*" Some miles later, after complete silence, Mac said, "I'm a man of many friends—and I don't make a dime on any of 'em." Still later, "The Fathers know all about it."

This Myles doubted. The Fathers were forbidden to engage in business for profit, he knew, and he believed that Mac, as their representative, was probably subject to the same prohibition. It was a question, though, whether Mac was primarily the Fathers' representative or his friends' or his own. It was hard to believe that *everyone* was only breaking even. And Myles felt sure that if the Fathers knew about the package deal, they'd think they had to act. But a replacement for Mac would be hard to find. The *Clementine,* as Myles was discovering, was not an easy magazine to sell. The pamphlets weren't moving well, either.

Without knowing it at the time, Myles saw a variation of the package deal worked on a pastor who met them in his front yard, baying, "I know all about you! Go!" Myles was more than ready to go, but Mac said, "You know, Monsignor, I believe you do know about me." "Don't call me Monsignor!" "My mistake, Father." Mac's voice was as oil being poured out. "Father, something you said just now makes me want to say something to you, only it's not anything I care to say in front of others." "Whatever you have to say can be said now," the pastor mumbled. "Believe me, Father, I can't say it—not in front of this boy," Mac said, nodding at Myles. Then, in a stage whisper to Myles, "You better go, son." Myles hesitated, expected to hear the pastor overrule Mac, but nothing of the sort happened, and Myles went out and sat in the car. Mac and the pastor, a fierce-looking, beak-nosed Irish type, began to walk slowly around the yard, and presently disappeared behind the rectory. Then, after a bit, there was Mac, coming out the front door and calling to Myles from the porch, "Come on in!" Myles went in and shook hands with the pastor, actually a gentle silver-haired man. He asked them to stay for lunch, but Mac graciously refused, insisting it would be too much trouble for the housekeeper. On the following Sunday morning, this same pastor, a marvelous speaker, preached in behalf of the Work, calling the *Clementine* "that dandy little magazine" at all five Masses. Myles attended them all, while Mac hobnobbed with the ushers in the vestibule. Between Masses, the two of them, sitting at the card table, worked like bookmakers between races. Afterward, when they were driving away, Mac announced that the team had had its most successful day. That evening, in a new town, relaxing in the cocktail lounge of their hotel, Mac gave up his secret. He said he had diagnosed the pastor perfectly and had taken the pledge from him—that was all. Seeing that Myles disapproved, he said, "It so happened I needed it." Myles, who was getting to know Mac, couldn't quarrel with that.

Mac and Myles moved constantly from town to town and diocese to diocese, and almost every night Myles had the problem of locating suitable accommodations. He soon saw that he would not be able to afford the hotels and meals to which Mac was accustomed, and finally he complained. Mac looked hurt. He said, "We don't do the Work for profit, you know." He only got by himself, he said, by attributing part of his living expenses to the car. He wasn't misusing the swindle sheet, though; he was adapting it to circumstances beyond his control. There really *were* expenses. "I don't have to tell you that," he said. "The Fathers, God love 'em, just don't understand how prices have gone up." Myles's predecessor, a fellow named Jack, had put up in "the more reasonable hotels and rooming houses," and Mac suggested that Myles do the same, for a while. "Later, when you're doing better, you could stay in regular hotels."

"Is that what Jack did—later?" Myles asked.

"No. Jack seemed to like the kind of places he stayed in." Jack, in fact, had quit the Work in order to stay on in one of them, and was now engaged to the landlady. "In some ways, Jack wasn't meant for the Work," Mac added. "But we had some fine times together and I hated to see him go. He was a damn fine driver. Not that that's everything."

It had become an important part of Myles's job to do all the driving and put the car away at night and bring it around to the hotel in the morning for Mac and his luggage. More and more, Mac rode in the back seat. (He said he pre-

ferred the ash tray there.) But there was no glass between
the front and back seats, and the arrangement did not inter-
fere with conversation or alter Mac's friendliness. Occasionally, they'd arrive in a town late at night—too late for
Myles to look for one of the more reasonable places—and
Mac would say, mercifully, "Come on. Stay with me." And
on those nights Mac would pick up the tab. This could also
happen even when they arrived in plenty of time for Myles
to look around, provided the drive had been a long one and
Myles had played the good listener.

The association between the two was generally close, and
becoming closer. Mac talked frankly about his ex-friends, of
whom there were many—mostly former associates or rivals
in the general-merchandise field, double-crossers to a man.
The first few times this happened, Myles controlled his desire to tell Mac that by damning others, as he did, he
damned the whole human race—damned himself, in fact.
One day, after Mac had finished with his old friends and
with his wife (who was no good), and was beginning to go to
work on the Jews (who also had given him nothing but
trouble), Myles did tell him. He presented an idea he held
to be even greater than the idea of brotherhood. It was the
doctrine of the Mystical Body of Christ. Humanity was one
great body, Myles explained, all united with Christ, the
Savior. Mac acted as though the doctrine were a new one
on him. "One great body, huh? Sounds like the Mystical
Knights of the Sea," he said, and talked for a while of Amos
and Andy and of the old days when they'd been Sam and
Henry. That was the afternoon that Mac got onto the subject of his dream.

Mac's dream—as he spoke, the snow was going from gray
to ghostly blue, and the lights were coming on in the houses
along the way—was to own a turkey ranch and a church-
goods store. What he really wanted was the ranch, he said,
but he supposed he'd have to play it safe and have the store,
too. Turkeys could be risky. With the general revival of interest in religion, however, a well-run church-goods store
would be sure to succeed. He'd sell by mail, retail and wholesale, and there'd be discounts for everybody—not just for the
clergy, though, of course, he'd have to give them the usual

break. The store would be a regular clearinghouse: everything from holy cards to statues—products of all the leading manufacturers.

"Sort of a supermarket?" Myles asked, thinking of chalices and turkeys roosting all in a row.

"That's the idea."

"It'd be nice if there were one place in this country where you could get an honest piece of ecclesiastical art," Myles said.

"I'd have that, too, later," Mac said. "A custom department."

They were getting along very well, different as they were. Mac *was* a good traveling companion, ready wherever they went with a little quick information about the towns ("Good for business," "All Swedes," "Wide open"), the small change of real knowledge.

One day, when they were passing through Superior, Wisconsin, Mac said that originally the iron-ore interests had planned to develop the town. Property values had been jacked up, however, by operators too smart for their own good, and everything had gone to Duluth, with its relatively inferior harbor. That was how Superior, favored by nature, had become what it was, a small town with the layout of a metropolis.

"It's easier to move mountains than greedy hearts," Myles commented.

"I wouldn't know," Mac said.

Myles found the story of Superior instructive—positively biblical, he said. Another case of man's greed. The country thereabouts also proved interesting to Myles, but difficult for Mac when Myles began to expound on the fished-out lakes (man's greed), the cutover timberland (man's greed), the poor Indians (the *white* man's greed). The high-grade ore pits, Mac foolishly told him, were almost exhausted.

"Exhausted for what?" Myles asked.

"Steel," said Mac, who didn't realize the question had been rhetorical.

"This car!" said Myles, with great contempt. "War!" Looking into the rearview mirror, he saw Mac indulging in what was becoming a habit with him—pulling on his ear lobes.

"What *are* you?" Mac finally demanded. "Some kind of a new damn fool?"

But Myles never gave up on him. He went right on making his points laying the ground for an awakening; it might never come to Mac, but Myles carried on as if it might at any moment. Mac, allied with the modern world for better or worse, defended the indefensible and fought back. And when logic failed him, he spluttered, "You talk like you got holes in your head," or, "Quit moanin'!" or, "Who you think you are, buster—the Pope?"

"This is when you're *really* hard to take!" Mac said one day, when the news from Korea was bad and Myles was most telling. Myles continued obliviously, perceiving moral links between Hiroshima and Korea and worse things to come, and predicting universal retribution, weeping, and gnashing of teeth. "And why?" he said. "Greed!"

"Greed! Greed! Is that all you can think about? No wonder they had to get rid of you!"

A few miles of silence followed, and then a few well-chosen words from Mac, who had most certainly been thinking, which was just what Myles was always trying to get him to do. "Are you sure the place you escaped from was a seminary?" he asked.

But Myles let him see he could take even this, turning the other cheek so gracefully that Mac could never know his words were touching a sore spot.

Later that day, in the middle of a sermon from Myles, they passed a paddy wagon and Mac said, "They're looking for you." Ever after, if Myles discoursed too long or too well on the state of the modern world, there came a tired but amiable croaking from the back seat, "They're looking for you."

At night, however, after the bars closed, it was *Mac* who was looking for Myles. If they were staying at the same hotel, he'd knock at Myles's door and say, "Care to come over to the room for a drink?" At first, Myles, seeing no way out of it, would go along, though not for a drink. He

drank beer when he drank, or wine, and there was never
any of either in Mac's room. It was no fun spending the
last hour of the day with Mac. He had a lot of stories, but
Myles often missed the point of them, and he knew none
himself—none that Mac would appreciate, anyway. What
Cardinal Merry del Val had said to Cardinal Somebody Else
—the usual seminary stuff. But Mac found a subject to interest *him*. He began denying that Myles was a cradle
Catholic. Myles, who had never seen in this accident of birth
the personal achievement that Mac seemed to see, would
counter, "All right. What if I weren't one?"

"You see? You see?" Mac would say, looking very wise
and drunk. Then, as if craving and expecting a confession,
he'd say, "You can tell *me*."

Myles had nothing to tell, and Mac would start over
again, on another tack. Developing his thought about what
he called Myles's "ideas," he would arrive at the only possible conclusion: Myles wasn't a Catholic at all. He was
probably only a smart-aleck convert who had come into the
Church when the coming was good, and only *thought* he
was in.

"Do you deny the possibility of conversion?" Myles would
ask, though there was small pleasure in theologizing with
someone like Mac.

Mac never answered the question. He'd just keep saying,
"You call yourself a *Catholic*—a *cradle* Catholic?"

The first time Myles said no to Mac's invitation to come
over and have one, it worked. The next time, Mac went
back to his room only to return with his bottle, saying,
"Thought you might like to have one in your pajamas."
That was the night Myles told Mac, hopefully, that whiskey
was a Protestant invention; in Ireland, for example, it had
been used, more effectively than the penal laws, to enslave
the faithful. "Who're you kiddin'!" Mac wailed.

Mere admonishment failed with Mac. One day, as they
were driving through primitive country, Myles delivered a
regular sermon on the subject of drink. He said a man possessed by drink was a man possessed by the Devil. He said
that Mac, at night, was very like a devil, going about hotel
corridors "as a roaring lion goeth about seeking whom he

may devour." This must have hit Mac pretty hard, for he
said nothing in his own defense; in fact, he took it very well,
gazing out at the pine trees, which Myles, in the course of his
sermon, had asked him to consider in all their natural
beauty. That afternoon, they met another hard nut—and
Mac took the pledge again, which closed the deal for a
production on the following Sunday, and also, he seemed
to think, put him into Myles's good graces. "I wish I could
find one that could give it to me and make it stick," he said.

"Don't come to me when I'm a priest," said Myles, who
had still to see his first bishop.

That night Mac and the bottle were at the door again.
Myles, in bed, did not respond. This was a mistake. Mac
phoned the office and had them bring up a key and open
Myles's door, all because he thought Myles might be sick.
"I love that boy!" he proclaimed, on his way back to his
room at last. Later that night Myles heard him in the corridor, at a little distance, with another drunk. Mac was roaring, "I'm seein' who I may devour!"

More and more, Myles and Mac were staying together in
the same hotels, and Myles, though saving money by this
arrangement (money, however, that he never saw), wondered if he wasn't paying too much for economy. He felt
slightly kept. Mac only wanted him handy late at night, it
seemed, so as to have someone with whom to take his pleasure, which was haranguing. Myles now understood better
why Jack had liked the places he stayed in. Or was this
thing that Mac was doing to him nightly something new
for Mac? Something that Myles had brought upon himself?
He was someone whom people looking for trouble always
seemed to find. It had happened to him in the hospital, in
the seminary, in the Boy Scouts. If a million people met in
one place, and he was there, he was certain that the worst
of them would rise as a man and make for him.

But Mac wasn't always looking for trouble. One afternoon, for no reason at all, he bought Myles a Hawaiian
sports shirt. "For next summer," Mac said, as if they would
always be together. The shirt was a terrible thing to look at—
soiled merchandise picked up at a sale—but it might mean

something. Was it possible that Mac, in his fashion, liked him?

"A fellow like you might handle that end of it," Mac said one day in the car. He had been talking about the store part of his dream and how he would put out a big catalogue in which it would be wise for manufacturers—and maybe religious orders, too—to buy advertising if they expected to do business with him. "Interested?" he asked.

Myles was definitely not interested, but he was touched by the offer, since it showed that Mac trusted him. It was time to put matters straight between them. Myles spoke then of *his* dream—of the great desire he had to become a priest. Not a punch-drunk seminary professor or a fat cat in a million-dollar parish, he said, but a simple shepherd ministering gently to the poorest of God's poor. He wouldn't mind being a priest-worker, like those already functioning so successfully in France, according to reports reaching him. "That can't happen here," Mac said. Myles, however, saw difficult times ahead for the nation. Here Mac started to open his mouth but grabbed instead for his ears. Myles felt pretty sure that there would soon be priest-workers slaving away in fields and factories by day and tending to the spiritual needs of their poor fellow-workers by night.

"Poor?" Mac asked. "What about the unions? When I think what those boys take home!"

Myles then explored the more immediate problem of finding a bishop to sponsor him.

Mac said he knew several quite well and he might speak to them.

"I wish you would," Myles said. "The two I've seen looked impossible." Then, having said that much—too much —he confessed to Mac his real reason for taking the job: the urgency of his position with regard to Selective Service.

Immediately, Mac, who had not been paying much attention, released an ear for listening. He appeared ill-disposed toward Myles's reluctance to serve in the armed forces, or possibly, toward such frankness.

"I can't serve two masters," Myles said. Mac was silent;

he'd gone absolutely dead. "Are you a veteran?" Myles asked.

"Since you ask," Mac said, "I'll tell you. I served and was wounded—honorably—in both World Wars. If there's another one, I hope to do my part. Does that answer your question?" Myles said that it did, and he could think of nothing to say just then that wouldn't hurt Mac's feelings.

That night, Mac, in his cups, surpassed himself. He got through with the usual accusations early and began threatening Myles with "exposure." "Dodgin' the draft!" Mac howled. "I oughta turn you in."

Myles said he hadn't broken the law *yet*.

"But you *intend* to," Mac said. "I oughta turn you in."

"I'll turn myself in when the times comes," Myles said.

"Like hell you will. You'll go along until they catch up with you. Then they'll clap you in jail—where you belong."

"Maybe you're right," Myles said, thinking of St. Paul and other convicts.

"Then you'll wish you were in the army—where you belong. I'm not sure it's not my duty to report you. Let's see your draft card."

Myles let him see it.

" 'Flynn, Myles'—that you? How do I know you're not somebody else by the same name?"

Myles made no reply. Had prohibition been so wrong, he wondered.

"Don't wanna incriminate yourself, huh? Hey, you're 1-A! Didja see that?"

Myles explained, as he had before, that he was awaiting his induction notice.

"Bet you are! Bet you can hardly wait! I'd better hold onto this." Mac slipped Myles's draft card into his pocket.

In the morning Myles got the card back. Mac, sober, returned it, saying he'd found it in his room, where Myles (who had not been there) must have dropped it. "Better hold on to that," Mac said.

The next night Myles managed to stay in a rooming house, out of reach, but the following night they were together again, and Mac asked to see Myles's draft card again.

Myles wouldn't give it up. "I deny your authority," he said, himself emboldened by drink—two beers.

"Here's my authority!" Mac cried. He loosened his trousers and pulled up his shirt in front, exposing a stomach remarkably round, smooth, veined, and, in places, blue, like a world globe. There was a scar on it. "How d'ya think I got that?"

"Appendicitis," Myles said.

There was no doubt of it. The scar testified to Mac's fraudulence as nothing else had, and for once Mac seemed to know it. He'd strayed into a field in which he believed Myles to be supreme. Putting his stomach away, he managed a tone in which there was misgiving, outrage, and sarcasm. "That's right. That's right. You know everything. You were a bedpan jockey. I forgot about that."

Myles watched him, amused. Mac might have saved himself by telling the truth or by quickly laughing it off, but he lied on. "Shrapnel—some still inside," he said. He coughed and felt his stomach, as if his lungs were there, but he didn't get it out again. "Not asking *you* to believe it," he said. "Won't show *you* my other wound."

"Please don't," said Myles. He retired that night feeling that he had the upper hand.

One week later, leaving a town in Minnesota where they had encountered a difficult bishop, Mac ordered Myles to stop at a large, gabled rectory of forbidding aspect. As it turned out, however, they enjoyed a good dinner there, and afterward the pastor summoned three of his colleagues for a little game of blackjack—in Mac's honor, Myles heard him say as the players trooped upstairs.

Myles spent the evening downstairs with the curate. While they were eating some fudge the curate had made that afternoon, they discovered that they had many of the same enthusiasms and prejudices. The curate wanted Myles to understand that the church was not his idea, loaded up, as it was, with junk. He was working on the pastor to throw out most of the statues and all the vigil lights. It was a free-talking, free-swinging session, the best evening for Myles since leaving the seminary. In a nice but rather futile tribute

to Myles, the curate said that if the two of them were pastors, they might, perhaps, transform the whole diocese. He
in no way indicated that he thought there was anything
wrong with Myles because he had been asked to leave the
seminary. He believed, as Myles did, that there was no *good*
reason for the dismissal. He said he'd had trouble getting
through himself and he thought that the seminary, as an institution, was probably responsible for the way Stalin, another aspirant to the priesthood, had turned out. The curate
also strongly disapproved of Mac, and of Myles's reasons
for continuing in the Work. He said the Clementines were
a corny outfit, and no bishop in his right mind, seeing Myles
with Mac, would ever take a chance on him. The curate
thought that Myles might be playing it too cautious. He'd
do better, perhaps, just to go around the country, hitch-
hiking from see to see, washing dishes if he had to, but calling on bishops personally—as many as he could in the time
that remained before he got his induction notice.

"How many bishops have you actually seen?" the curate
asked.

"Three. But I couldn't say anything with Mac right there.
I would've gone back later, though, if there'd been a chance
at all with those I saw."

The curate sniffed. "How could you tell?" he asked. "I
thought you were desperate. You just *can't* be guided entirely by private revelation. You have a higher injunction:
'Seek, and you shall find.' Perhaps you still haven't thought
this thing *through*. I wonder. Perhaps you don't pray
enough?"

Myles, noticing in the curate a tendency to lecture and
feeling that he'd suffered one "perhaps" too many, defended himself, saying, "The man we met today wouldn't
let us set foot on church property in his diocese. What can
you do with a bishop like that?"

"The very one you should have persevered with! Moses,
you may remember, had to do more than look at the rock.
He had to strike it."

"Twice, unfortunately," murmured Myles, not liking the
analogy. Moses, wavering in his faith, had struck twice and

had not reached the Promised Land; he had only seen it in the distance, and died.

"It may not be too late," the curate said. "I'd try that one again if I were you."

Myles laughed. *"That* one was your own bishop," he said.

"The bishop said that?" The curate showed some alarm and seemed suddenly a lot less friendly. "Is that why you're here, then—why Mac's here, I mean?"

"I couldn't tell you why I'm here," Myles said. In Mac's defense, he said, "I don't think he's mentioned the Work here." It was true. Mac and the pastor had hit it off right away, talking of other things.

"I heard him trying to sell the pastor a new roof—a copper one. Also an oil burner. Does he deal in *those* things?" the curate asked.

"He has friends who do." Myles smiled. He wanted to say more on this subject to amuse the curate, if that was still possible; he wanted to confide in him again; he wanted to say whatever would be necessary to save the evening. But the shadow of the bishop had fallen upon them. There were only crumbs on the fudge plate; the evening had ended. It was bedtime, the curate said. He offered Myles a Coke, which Myles refused, then showed him to a couch in the parlor, gave him a blanket, and went off to bed.

Some time later—it was still night—Mac woke Myles and they left the rectory. Mac was sore; he said he'd lost a bundle. He climbed into the back seat and wrapped himself in the car rug. "A den of thieves. I'm pretty sure I was taken. Turn on the heater." And then he slept while Myles drove away toward the dawn.

The next day, as they were having dinner in another diocese, another town, another hotel—Mac looked fresh; he'd slept all day—Myles told him that he was quitting.

"Soon?" said Mac.

"Right away."

"Give me a little time to think about it."

After dinner, Mac drew one of his good cigars out of its aluminum scabbard. "What is it? Money? Because if it is—" Mac said, puffing on the cigar, and then, looking at the cigar and not at Myles, he outlined his plans. He'd try to get more money for Myles from the Fathers, more take-home dough and more for expenses. He'd sensed that Myles had been unhappy in some of those flea bags; Myles might have noticed that they'd been staying together oftener. Ultimately, if the two of them were still together and everything went right, there might be a junior partnership for Myles in the store. "No," Mac said, looking at Myles. "I can see that's not what you want." He turned to the cigar again and asked, "Well, why not?" He invited Myles up to his room, where, he said, he might have something to say that would be of interest to him.

Upstairs, after making himself a drink, Mac said that he just might be able to help Myles in the only way he wanted to be helped. He was on fairly good terms with a number of bishops, as Myles might have gathered, but an even better bet would be the Clementines. Myles could join the order as a lay brother—*anybody* could do that—swiftly win the confidence of his superiors, then switch to the seminary, and thus complete his studies for the priesthood. "I might be able to give you such a strong recommendation that you could go straight into the seminary," Mac said. "It would mean losing you, of course. Don't like that part. Or *would* it? What's to stop us from going on together, like now, after you get your degree?"

"After *ordination?*" Myles asked.

"There you are!" Mac exclaimed. "Just shows it's a natural—us working as a team. What I don't know, you do."

While Mac strengthened his drink just a little—he was cutting down—Myles thanked him for what he'd done to date and also for what he was prepared to do. He said that he doubted, however, that he was meant for the Clementines or for the community life, and even if he were, there would still be the problem of finding a bishop to sponsor him. "Oh *they'd* do all that," Mac said. Myles shook his head. He was quitting. He had to intensify his efforts. He wasn't getting to see many bishops, was he? Time was of the essence. He had a few ideas he wanted to pursue on his own (meaning he had one—to have another crack at the curate's bishop). The induction notice, his real worry, might come any day.

"How d'ya know you're all right physically?" Mac asked

him. "You don't look very strong to me. I took you for a
born 4-F. For all you know, you might be turned down and
out lookin' for a job. In the circumstances, I couldn't promise to hold this one open forever."

With the usual apprehension, Myles watched Mac pour
another drink. Could Mac want so badly for an underpaid
chauffeur, he wondered. Myles's driving was his only asset.
As a representative of the Fathers, he was a flop, and he
knew it, and so did Mac. Mac, in his own words, was the
baby that delivered the goods. But no layman could be as
influential as Mac claimed to be with the Fathers, hard up
though they were for men and money. Mac wouldn't be able
to help with any bishop in his right mind. But Mac did want
him around, and Myles, who could think of no one else who
did, was almost tempted to stay as long as he could. Maybe
he *was* 4-F.

Later that evening Mac, still drinking, put it another way,
or possibly said what he'd meant to say earlier. "Hell, you'll
never pass the mental test. Never let a character like you in
the army." The Fathers, though, would be glad to have
Myles, if Mac said the word.

Myles thanked him again. Mac wanted him to drive the
car, to do the Work, but what he wanted still more, it was
becoming clear, was to have a boon companion, and Myles
knew he just couldn't stand to be it.

"You're not my type," Mac said. "You haven't got it—the
velocity, I mean—but maybe that's why I like you."

Myles was alone again with his thoughts, walking the
plank of his gloom.

"Don't worry," Mac said. "I'll always have a spot in my
heart for you. A place in my business."

"In the supermarket?"

Mac frowned. Drinking, after a point, made him appear
a little cross-eyed. "I wish you wouldn't use that word," he
said distinctly. "If y'wanna know, your trouble's words.
Make y'self harda take. Don't *have* to be jerk. Looka you.
Young. Looka me. Dead. Not even Catholic. Bloody
Orangeman. 'S truth."

Myles couldn't believe it. And then he could, almost. He'd
never seen Mac at Mass on Sundays, either coming or going,

except when they were working, and then Mac kept to the
vestibule. The bunk that Mac had talked about Myles's
being a cradle Catholic began to make sense.

"Now you're leaving the Work, I tell you," Mac was saying. "Makes no difference now." They were in Minnesota,
staying in a hotel done in the once popular Moorish style,
and the ceiling light and the shades of the bed lamps, and
consequently the walls and Myles's face, were dead orange,
and Mac's face was bloody orange.

Myles got up to leave.

"Don't go," Mac said. He emptied the bottle.

But Myles went, saying it was bedtime. He realized as he
said it that he sounded like the curate the night before.

Ten minutes later Mac was knocking at Myles's door. He
was in his stocking feet, but looked better, like a drunk getting a hold on himself.

"Something to read," he said. "Don't feel like sleeping."

Myles had some books in his suitcase, but he left them
there. "I didn't get a paper," he said.

"Don't want that," Mac said. He saw the Gideon Bible
on the night stand and went over to it. "Mind if I swipe
this?"

"There's probably one in your room."

Mac didn't seem to hear. He picked up the Gideon. "The
Good Book," he said.

"I've got a little Catholic Bible," Myles said. The words
came out of themselves—the words of a diehard proselytizer.

"Have you? Yeah, that's the one I want."

"I can't recommend it," Myles said, on second thought.
"You better take the other one, for reading. It's the King
James."

"Hell with that!" Mac said. He put the King James from
him.

Myles went to the suitcase and got out his portable Bible.
He stood with it at the door, making Mac come for it, and
then, still withholding it, led him outside into the corridor,
where he finally handed it over.

"How you feel now, about that other?" Mac asked.

For a moment, Myles thought he was being asked about
his induction, which Mac ordinarily referred to as "that

other," and not about Mac's dark secret. When he got Mac's meaning, he said, "Don't worry about me. I won't turn you in."

In the light of his activities, Mac's not being a Catholic was in his favor, from Myles's point of view; as an honest faker Mac was more acceptable, though many would not see it that way. There was something else, though, in Mac's favor—something unique; he was somebody who liked Myles just for himself. He had been betrayed by affection—and by the bottle, of course.

Myles watched Mac going down the corridor in his stocking feet toward his room, holding the Bible and swaying just a little, as if he were walking on calm water. He wasn't so drunk.

The next morning Mac returned the Bible to Myles in his room and said, "I don't know if you realize it or not, but I'm sorry about last night. I guess I said a lot of things I shouldn't have. I won't stand in your way any longer." He reached into his pocket and took out his roll. "You'll need some of this," he said.

"No thanks," Myles said.

"You sure?"

Myles was sure.

"Forget anything I might have said." Mac eased over to the window and looked out upon the main street. "I don't know what, but I might have said something." He came back to Myles. He was fingering his roll, holding it in both hands, a fat red squirrel with a nut. "You sure now?"

Myles said yes, he was sure, and Mac reluctantly left him.

Myles was wondering if that had been their good-by when, a few minutes later, Mac came in again. His manner was different. "I'll put it to you like this," he said. "You don't say anything about me and I won't say anything about you. Maybe we both got trouble. You know what I'm talking about?"

Myles said that he thought he knew and that Mac needn't worry.

"They may never catch you," Mac said, and went away again. Myles wondered if *that* had been their good-by.

Presently Mac came in again. "I don't remember if I told

you this last night or not. I know I was going to, but what
with one thing and another last night, and getting all hung
up—"

"Well?"

"Kid"—it was the first time Mac had called him that—
"I'm not a Catholic."

Myles nodded.

"Then I did say something about it?"

Myles nodded again. He didn't know what Mac was trying now, only that he was trying something.

"I don't know what I am," Mac said. "My folks weren't
much good. I lost 'em when I was quite young. And you
know about my wife." Myles knew about her. "No damn
good."

Myles listened and nodded while all those who had ever
failed Mac came in for slaughter. Mac ordinarily did this
dirty work in the car, and it had always seemed to Myles
that they threw out the offending bodies, one by one, making
room for the fresh ones. It was getting close in the room.
Mac stood upright amid a wreckage of carcasses—with
Myles.

"You're the only one I can turn to," he said. "I'd be
afraid to admit to anyone else what I've just admitted to
you—I mean to a priest. As you know, I'm pretty high up
in the Work, respected, well thought of, and all that, and
you can imagine what your average priest is going to think
if *I* come to him—to be baptized!"

The scene rather appealed to Myles, but he looked grave.

"I know what you're thinking," Mac said. "Don't think
I don't know the awful risk I'm taking now, with my immor-
tal soul and all. Gives me a chill to think of it. But I still
can't bring myself to do the right thing. Not if it means
going to a priest. Sure to be embarrassing questions. The
Fathers could easily get wind of it back in Chicago."

Myles was beginning to see what Mac had in mind.

"As I understand it, you don't have to be a priest to bap-
tize people," Mac continued. "*Anybody* can do it in an
emergency. You know that, of course."

Myles, just a step ahead of him, was thinking of the pastors who'd been deceived into giving Mac the pledge. It looked a lot like the old package deal.

"We could go over there," Mac said, glancing at the washbowl in the corner. "Or there's my room, if it'd be more appropriate." He had a bathroom.

Myles hardened. "If you're asking *me* to do it," he said, "the answer's no." Myles was now sure that Mac had been baptized before—perhaps many times, whenever he had need of it. "I couldn't give you a proper certificate anyway," Myles added. "You'd want that."

"You mean if I wanted to go on with it and come into the Catholic Church? All the way in? Is that what you mean?"

Myles didn't mean that at all, but he said, "I suppose so."

"Then you do get me?" Mac demanded.

Myles stiffened, knowing that he was in grave danger of being in on Mac's conversion, and feeling, a moment later, that this—this conversion—like the pledge and baptism, must have happened before. He hastened to say, "No. I don't get you and I don't *want* to."

Mac stood before him, silent, with bowed head, the beaten man, the man who'd asked for bread and received a stone, who'd asked for a fish and got a serpent.

But no, Mac wasn't that at all, Myles saw. He was the serpent, the nice old serpent with Glen-plaid markings, who wasn't *very* poisonous. He'd been expecting tenderness, but he had caught the forked stick just behind the head. The serpent was quiet. Was he dead? "I give you my word that I'll never tell anybody what you've told me," Myles said. "So far as I'm concerned, you're a Catholic—a cradle Catholic if you like. I hold no grudge against you for anything you've said, drunk or sober. I hope you'll do the same for me."

"I will that," Mac said, and began to speak of their "relationship," of the inspiration Myles had been to him from the very first. There was only one person responsible for the change in his outlook, he said, and it might interest Myles to know that *he* was that person.

Myles saw that he'd let up on the stick too soon. The serpent still had plenty left. Myles pressed down on him. "I want out, Mac," he said. "I'm not a priest yet. I don't *have*

to listen to this. If you want me to spill the beans to the
Fathers, just keep it up."

The serpent was very quiet now. Dead?

"You do see what I mean?" Myles said.

"Yeah, now I see," Mac said. He was looking only a little
hurt; the flesh above his snow-white collar was changing
pinks, but he was looking much better, seemingly convinced
that Myles, with an excuse to harm him, and with the power
to do so, would not. Mac was having his remarkable experience after all—almost a conversion. "Had you wrong," he
confessed. "Thought sure you'd squeal. Thought sure you'd
be the type that would. Hope you don't mind me saying that.
Because you got my respect now."

Myles could see, however, that Mac liked him less for
having it. But he had Mac's respect, and it was rare, and it
made the day rare.

"Until I met you, why— Well, *you* know." Mac stopped
short.

Myles, with just a look, had let him feel the stick.

"We'll leave it at that," Mac said.

"If you will, I will," said Myles. He crossed the room to
the washbowl, where he began to collect his razor, his tooth-
brush, and the shaving lotion that Mac had given him. When
he turned around with these things in his hands, he saw
that Mac had gone. He'd left a small deposit of gray ash on
the rug near the spot where he'd coiled and uncoiled.

Later that morning Myles, as a last service and proof of
good will, went to the garage and brought Mac's car around
to the hotel door, and waited there with it until Mac, smoking his second cigar of the day, appeared. Myles helped him
stow his luggage and refused his offer to drive him to the
railroad station, if that was where Myles wanted to go.
Myles had not told Mac that he intended to hitchhike back
to the last town, to confront the difficult bishop and strike
the rock a second time. After shaking hands, Mac began,
"If I hear of anything—" but Myles silenced him with a
look, and then and there the team split up.

Mac got into the Cadillac and drove off. Watching, Myles
saw the car, half a block away, bite at the curb and stop.

And he saw why. Mac, getting on with the Work, was offering a lift to two men all in black, who, to judge by their actions, didn't really want one. In the end, though, the black car consumed them, and slithered out of view.

CYCLISTS' RAID

Frank Rooney

FRANK ROONEY *was born in 1913 in Kansas City, Missouri. Of himself he says: "I came of age during the great depression and so belong to the broke or busted generation." He moved to Los Angeles in 1925, joined the army in 1941, came to New York in 1945. He now lives in Mount Vernon, New York, with a wife and three children. His first two novels were* COURTS OF MEMORY (*1954*) *and* HEEL OF SPRING (*1956*), *his third,* MC GINNIS SPEAKS, *appeared in 1960.*

Joel Bleeker, owner and operator of the Pendleton Hotel, was adjusting the old redwood clock in the lobby when he heard the sound of the motors. At first he thought it might be one of those four-engine planes on the flights from Los Angeles to San Francisco which occasionally got far enough off course to be heard in the valley. And for a moment, braced against the steadily approaching vibrations of the sound, he had the fantastic notion that the plane was going to strike the hotel. He even glanced at his daughter, Cathy, standing a few feet to his right and staring curiously at the street.

Then, with his fingers still on the hour hand of the clock, he realized that the sound was not something coming down from the air but the high, sputtering racket of many vehicles moving along the ground. Cathy, and Bret Timmons, who owned one of the two drugstores in the town, went out onto the veranda, but Bleeker stayed by the clock, consulting the railroad watch he pulled from his vest pocket and moving

the hour hand on the clock forward a minute and a half.
He stepped back deliberately, shut the glass case, and
looked at the huge brass numbers and the two ornate brass
pointers. It was eight minutes after seven, approximately
twenty-two minutes until sundown. He put the railroad
watch back in his pocket and walked slowly and incuriously
through the open doors of the lobby. He was methodical and
orderly, and the small things he did every day—like setting
the clock—were important to him. He was not to be hurried
—especially by something as elusively irritating as a sound,
however unusual.

There were only three people on the veranda when
Bleeker came out of the lobby—his daughter Cathy, Timmons, and Francis LaSalle, co-owner of LaSalle and Fleet,
Hardware. They stood together quietly, looking, without ap-
pearing to stare, at a long stern column of red motorcycles
coming from the south, filling the single main street of the
town with the noise of a multitude of pistons and the crack-
ling of exhaust pipes. They could see now that the column
was led by a single white motorcycle which, when it came
abreast of the hotel, turned abruptly right and stopped. They
saw, too, that the column, without seeming to slow down or
to execute any elaborate movement, had divided itself into
two single files. At the approximate second, having received
a signal from their leader, they also turned right and
stopped.

The whole flanking action, singularly neat and quite like
the various vehicular formations he remembered in the
army, was distasteful to Bleeker. It recalled a little too read-
ily his tenure as a lieutenant colonel overseas in England,
France, and finally Germany.

"Mr. Bleeker?"

Bleeker realized the whole troop—no one in the town either then or after that night was ever agreed on the exact
number of men in the troop—had dismounted and that the
leader was addressing him.

"I'm Bleeker." Although he hadn't intended to, he
stepped forward when he spoke, much as he had stepped
forward in the years when he commanded a battalion.

"I'm Gar Simpson and this is Troop B of the Angeleno

Motorcycle Club," the leader said. He was a tall, spare man, and his voice was coldly courteous to the point of mockery. "We expect to bivouac outside your town tonight and we wondered if we might use the facilities of your hotel. Of course, sir, we'll pay."

"There's a washroom downstairs. If you can put up with that——"

"That will be fine, sir. Is the dining room still open?"

"It is."

"Could you take care of twenty men?"

"What about the others?"

"They can be accommodated elsewhere, sir."

Simpson saluted casually and, turning to the men assembled stiffly in front of the hotel, issued a few quiet orders. Quickly and efficiently, the men in the troop parked their motorcycles at the curb. About a third of the group detached itself and came deferentially but steadily up the hotel steps. They passed Bleeker who found himself maneuvered aside and went into the lobby. As they passed him, Bleeker could see the slight converted movement of their faces— though not their eyes, which were covered by large green goggles—toward his daughter Cathy. Bleeker frowned after them but before he could think of anything to say, Simpson, standing at his left, touched his arm.

"I've divided the others into two groups," he said quietly. "One group will eat at the diner and the other at the Desert Hotel."

"Very good," Bleeker said. "You evidently know the town like a book. The people, too. Have you ever been here before?"

"We have a map of all the towns in this part of California, sir. And of course we know the names of all the principal hotels and their proprietors. Personally, I could use a drink. Would you join me?"

"After you," Bleeker said.

He stood watching Simpson stride into the lobby and without any hesitation go directly to the bar. Then he turned to Cathy, seeing Timmons and LaSalle lounging on the railing behind her, their faces already indistinct in the plummeting California twilight.

"You go help in the kitchen, Cathy," Bleeker said. "I think it'd be better if you didn't wait on tables."

"I wonder what they look like behind those goggles," Cathy said.

"Like anybody else," Timmons said. He was about thirty, somewhat coarse and intolerant and a little embarrassed at being in love with a girl as young as Cathy. "Where did you think they came from? Mars?"

"What did they say the name of their club was?" Cathy said.

"Angeleno," LaSalle said.

"They must be from Los Angeles. Heigh-ho. Shall I wear my very best gingham, citizen colonel?"

"Remember now—you stay in the kitchen," Bleeker said.

He watched her walk into the lobby, a tall slender girl of seventeen, pretty and enigmatic, with something of the brittle independence of her mother. Bleeker remembered suddenly, although he tried not to, the way her mother had walked away from him that frosty January morning two years ago saying, "I'm going for a ride." And then the two-day search in the mountains after the horse had come back alone and the finding of her body—the neck broken—in the stream at the foot of the cliff. During the war he had never really believed that he would live to get back to Cathy's mother, and after the war he hadn't really believed he would be separated from her—not again—not twice in so short a time.

Shaking his head—as if by that motion he could shed his memories as easily as a dog sheds water—Bleeker went in to join Gar Simpson who was sitting at a table in the barroom. Simpson stood politely when Bleeker took the opposite chair.

"How long do you fellows plan to stay?" Bleeker asked. He took the first sip of his drink, looked up, and stared at Simpson.

"Tonight and tomorrow morning," Simpson said.

Like all the others, he was dressed in a brown windbreaker, khaki shirt, khaki pants, and, as Bleeker had previously observed, wore dark calf-length boots. A cloth and leather helmet lay on the table beside Simpson's drink, but he hadn't removed his flat green goggles, an accouterment giving him and the men in his troop the appearance of some tropical tribe with enormous semiprecious eyes, lidless and immovable. That was Bleeker's first impression and, absurd as it was, it didn't seem an exaggeration of fancy but of truth.

"Where do you go after this?"

"North." Simpson took a rolled map from a binocular case slung over his shoulder and spread it on the table. "Roughly we're following the arc of an ellipse with its southern tip based on Los Angeles and its northern end touching Fresno."

"Pretty ambitious for a motorcycle club."

"We have a month," Simpson said. "This is our first week, but we're in no hurry and we're out to see plenty of country."

"What are you interested in mainly?"

"Roads. Naturally, being a motorcycle club—you'd be surprised at the rate we're expanding—we'd like to have as much of California as possible opened up to us."

"I see."

"Keeps the boys fit, too. The youth of America. Our hope for the future." Simpson pulled sternly at his drink, and Bleeker had the impression that Simpson was repressing, openly, and with pride, a vast sparkling ecstasy.

Bleeker sat and watched the young men in the troop file upstairs from the public washroom and stroll casually but nevertheless with discipline into the dining room. They had removed their helmets and strapped them to their belts, each helmet in a prescribed position to the left of the belt-buckle, but—like Simpson—they had retained their goggles. Bleeker wondered if they ever removed the goggles long enough to wash under them and, if they did, what the flesh under them looked like.

"I think I'd better help out at the tables," Bleeker said. He stood up, and Simpson stood with him. "You say you're from Troop B? Is that right?"

"Correct. We're forming Troop G now. Someday——"

"You'll be up to Z," Bleeker said.

"And not only in California."

"Where else for instance?"

"Nevada—Arizona—Colorado—Wyoming."

Simpson smiled, and Bleeker, turning away from him abruptly, went into the dining room where he began to help the two waitresses at the tables. He filled water glasses, set out extra forks, and brought steins of beer from the bar. As he served the troop, their polite thank you's, ornate and insincere, irritated him. It reminded him of tricks taught to animals, the animals only being allowed to perform under certain obvious conditions of security. And he didn't like the cool way they stared at the two waitresses, both older women and fixtures in the town, and then leaned their heads together as if every individual thought had to be pooled and divided equally among them. He admitted, after some covert study, that the twenty men were really only variations of one, the variations, with few exceptions, being too subtle for him to recognize and differentiate. It was the goggles, he decided, covering that part of the face which is most note-worthy and most needful for identification—the eyes and the mask around the eyes.

Bleeker went into the kitchen, pretending to help but really to be near Cathy. The protective father, he thought ironically, watching his daughter cut pie and lay the various colored wedges on the white blue-bordered plates.

"Well, Daddy, what's the verdict?" Cathy looked ex-tremely grave, but he could see that she was amused.

"They're a fine body of men."

"Uh-huh. Have you called the police yet?"

He laughed. "It's a good thing you don't play poker."

"Child's play." She slid the last piece of blueberry pie on a plate. "I saw you through the door. You looked like you were ready to crack the Siegfried line—singlehanded."

"That man Simpson."

"What about him?"

"Why don't you go upstairs and read a book or some-thing?"

"Now, Daddy—you're the only professional here. They're just acting like little tin soldiers out on a spree."

"I wish to God they were made of tin."

"All right. I'll keep away from them. I promise." She made a gesture of crossing her throat with the thin edge of a knife. He leaned over and kissed her forehead, his hand feeling awkward and stern on her back.

After dinner the troop went into the bar, moving with a strange co-ordinated fluency that was both casual and military, and sat jealously together in one corner of the room. Bleeker served them pitchers of beer, and for the most part they talked quietly together, Simpson at their center, their voices guarded and urgent as if they possessed information which couldn't be disseminated safely among the public.

Bleeker left them after a while and went upstairs to his daughter's room. He wasn't used to being severe with Cathy and he was a little embarrassed by what he had said to her in the kitchen. She was turning the collars of some of his old shirts, using a portable sewing machine he had bought her as a present on her last birthday. As he came in, she held one of the shirts comically to the floor lamp, and he could see how thin and transparent the material was. Her mother's economy in small things, almost absurd when compared to her limitless generosity in matters of importance, had been one of the family jokes. It gave him an extraordinary sense of pleasure, so pure it was like a sudden inhalation of oxygen, to see that his daughter had not only inherited this tradition but had considered it meaningful enough to carry on. He went down the hall to his own room without saying anything further to her. Cathy was what he himself was in terms which could mean absolutely nothing to anyone else.

He had been in his room for perhaps an hour, working on the hotel accounts and thinking obliquely of the man Simpson, when he heard, faintly and apparently coming from no one direction, the sound of singing. He got up and walked to the windows overlooking the street. Standing there, he thought he could fix the sound farther up the block toward Cunningham's bar. Except for something harsh and mature in the voices, it was the kind of singing that might be heard around a Boy Scout campfire, more rhythmic than melodic and more stirring than tuneful. And then he could hear it almost under his feet, coming out of the hotel lobby and making three or four people on the street turn and smile foolishly toward the doors of the veranda.

Oppressed by something sternly joyous in the voices, Bleeker went downstairs to the bar, hearing, as he approached, the singing become louder and fuller. Outside of Simpson and the twenty men in the troop there were only three townsmen—including LaSalle—in the bar. Simpson, seeing Bleeker in the door, got up and walked over to him, moving him out into the lobby where they could talk.

"I hope the boys aren't disturbing you," he said.

"It's early," Bleeker said.

"In an organization as large and selective as ours it's absolutely necessary to insist on a measure of discipline. And it's equally necessary to allow a certain amount of relaxation."

"The key word is selective, I suppose."

"We have our standards," Simpson said primly.

"May I ask you what the hell your standards are?"

Simpson smiled. "I don't quite understand your irritation, Mr. Bleeker."

"This is an all-year-round thing, isn't it? This club of yours?"

"Yes."

"And you have an all-year-round job with the club?"

"Of course."

"That's my objection, Simpson. Briefly and simply stated, what you're running is a private army." Bleeker tapped the case slung over Simpson's shoulder. "Complete with maps, all sorts of local information, and of course a lobby in Sacramento."

"For a man who has traveled as widely as you have, Mr. Bleeker, you display an uncommon talent for exaggeration."

"As long as you behave yourselves I don't care what you do. This is a small town and we don't have many means of entertainment. We go to bed at a decent hour and I suggest you take that into consideration. However, have your fun. Nobody here has any objections to that."

"And of course we spend our money."

"Yes," Bleeker said. "You spend your money."

He walked away from Simpson and went out onto the veranda. The singing was now both in front and in back of him. Bleeker stood for a moment on the top steps of the veranda looking at the moon, hung like a slightly soiled but luminous pennant in the sky. He was embarrassed by his outburst to Simpson and he couldn't think why he had said such things. Private army. Perhaps, as Simpson had said, he was exaggerating. He was a small-town man and he had always hated the way men surrendered their individuality to attain perfection as a unit. It had been necessary during the war but it wasn't necessary now. Kid stuff—with an element of growing pains.

He walked down the steps and went up the sidewalk toward Cunningham's bar. They were singing there, too, and he stood outside the big plate-glass window peering in at them and listening to the harsh, pounding voices colored here and there with the sentimentalism of strong beer. Without thinking further he went into the bar. It was dim and cool and alien to his eyes, and at first he didn't notice the boy sitting by himself in a booth near the front. When he did, he was surprised—more than surprised, shocked—to see that the boy wasn't wearing his goggles but had placed them on the table by a bottle of Coca-Cola. Impulsively, he walked over to the booth and sat across from the boy.

"This seat taken?"

He had to shout over the noise of the singing. The boy leaned forward over the table and smiled.

"Hope we're not disturbing you."

Bleeker caught the word "disturbing" and shook his head negatively. He pointed to his mouth, then to the boy and to the rest of the group. The boy, too, shook his head. Bleeker could see that he was young, possibly twenty-five, and that he had dark straight hair cut short and parted neatly at the side. The face was square but delicate, the nose short, the mouth wide. The best thing about the boy, Bleeker decided, were his eyes, brown, perhaps, or dark gray, set in two distorted ovals of white flesh which contrasted sharply with the heavily tanned skin on the cheeks, forehead and jaws. With his goggles on he would have looked like the rest. Without them he was a pleasant young man, altogether human and approachable.

Bleeker pointed to the Coca-Cola bottle. "You're not drinking."

"Beer makes me sick."

Bleeker got the word "beer" and the humorous ulping motion the boy made. They sat exchanging words and sometimes phrases, illustrated always with a series of clumsy, groping gestures until the singing became less coherent and spirited and ended finally in a few isolated coughs. The men in the troop were moving about individually now, some leaning over the bar and talking in hoarse whispers to the bartender, others walking unsteadily from group to group and detaching themselves immediately to go over to another group, the groups, usually two or three men, constantly edging away from themselves and colliding with and being held briefly by others. Some simply stood in the center of the room and brayed dolorously at the ceiling.

Several of the troop walked out of the bar, and Bleeker could see them standing on the wide sidewalk looking up and down the street—as contemptuous of one another's company as they had been glad of it earlier. Or not so much contemptuous as unwilling to be coerced too easily by any authority outside themselves. Bleeker smiled as he thought of Simpson and the man's talk of discipline.

"They're looking for women," the boy said.

Bleeker had forgotten the boy temporarily, and the sudden words spoken in a normal voice startled and confused him. He thought quickly of Cathy—but then Cathy was safe in her room—probably in bed. He took the watch from his vest pocket and looked at it carefully.

"Five minutes after ten," he said.

"Why do they do that?" the boy demanded. "Why do they have to be so damned indecent about things like that? They haven't got the nerve to do anything but stare at waitresses. And then they get a few beers in them and go around pinching and slapping—they——"

Bleeker shivered with embarrassment. He was looking directly into the boy's eyes and seeing the color run under the tears and the jerky pinching movement of the lids as against something injurious and baleful. It was an emotion too rawly infantile to be seen without being hurt by it, and he felt both pity and contempt for a man who would allow

himself to display such a feeling—without any provocation
—so nakedly to a stranger.

"Sorry," the boy said.

He picked up the green goggles and fitted them awkwardly over his eyes. Bleeker stood up and looked toward
the center of the room. Several of the men turned their
eyes and then moved their heads away without seeming to
notice the boy in the booth. Bleeker understood them. This
was the one who could be approached. The reason for that
was clear, too. He didn't belong. Why and wherefore he
would probably never know.

He walked out of the bar and started down the street
toward the hotel. The night was clear and cool and smelled
faintly of the desert, of sand, of heated rock, of the sweetly-
sour plants growing without water and even of the sun which
burned itself into the earth and never completely withdrew.
There were only a few townsmen on the sidewalk wandering up and down, lured by the presence of something unusual in the town and masking, Bleeker thought, a ruthless
and menacing curiosity behind a tolerant grin. He shrugged
his shoulders distastefully. He was like a cat staring into a
shadow the shape of its fears.

He was no more than a hundred feet from the hotel when
he heard—or thought he heard—the sound of automatic firing. It was a well-remembered sound but always new and
frightening.

Then he saw the motorcycle moving down the middle of
the street, the exhaust sputtering loudly against the human
resonance of laughter, catcalls, and epithets. He exhaled
gently, the pain in his lungs subsiding with his breath. Another motorcycle speeded after the first, and he could see
four or five machines being wheeled out and the figures of
their riders leaping into the air and bringing their weight
down on the starting pedals. He was aware, too, that the
lead motorcycles, having traversed the length of the street,
had turned and were speeding back to the hotel. He had
the sensation of moving—even when he stood still—in the
relation to the objects heading toward each other. He heard
the high unendurable sound of metal squeezing metal and
saw the front wheel of a motorcycle twist and wobble and

its rider roll along the asphalt toward the gutter where he sat up finally and moved his goggled head feebly from side to side.

As Bleeker looked around him, he saw the third group of men which had divided earlier from the other two coming out of the bar across the street from Cunningham's, waving their arms in recognizable motions of cheering. The boy who had been thrown from the motorcycle vomited quietly into the gutter. Bleeker walked very fast toward the hotel. When he reached the top step of the veranda, he was caught and jostled by some five or six cyclists running out of the lobby, one of whom fell and was kicked rudely down the steps. Bleeker staggered against one of the pillars and broke a fingernail catching it. He stood there for a moment, fighting his temper, and then went into the lobby.

A table had been overthrown and lay on its top, and wooden legs stiffly and foolishly exposed, its magazines scattered around it, some with their pages spread face down so that the bindings rose along the back. He stepped on glass and realized one of the panels in the lobby door had been smashed. One of the troop walked stupidly out of the bar, his body sagging against the impetus propelling him forward until without actually falling he lay stretched on the floor, beer gushing from his mouth and nose and making a green and yellow pool before it sank into the carpet.

As Bleeker walked toward the bar, thinking of Simpson and of what he could say to him, he saw two men going up the stairs toward the second floor. He ran over to intercept them. Recognizing the authority in his voice, they came obediently down the stairs and walked across the lobby to the veranda, one of them saying over his shoulder, "Okay, Pop, okay—keep your lid on." The smiles they exchanged enraged him. After they were out of sight, he ran swiftly up the stairs, panting a little, and along the hall to his daughter's room.

It was quiet and there was no strip of light beneath the door. He stood listening for a moment with his ear to the panels and then turned back toward the stairs.

A man or boy, any of twenty or forty or sixty identical figures, goggled and in khaki, came around the corner of

the second-floor corridor and put his hand on the knob of
the door nearest the stairs. He squeezed the knob gently and
then moved on to the next door, apparently unaware of
Bleeker. Bleeker, remembering not to run or shout or knock
the man down, walked over to him, took his arm and led
him down the stairs, the arm unresisting, even flaccid, in his
grip.

Bleeker stood indecisively at the foot of the stairs, watching the man walk automatically away from him. He thought
he should go back upstairs and search the hall. And he
thought, too, he had to reach Simpson. Over the noise of
the motorcycles moving rapidly up and down the street, he
heard a crash in the bar, a series of drunken elongated
curses, ending abruptly in a small sound like a man's hand
laid flatly and sharply on a table.

His head was beginning to ache badly and his stomach
to sour under the impact of a slow and steady anger. He
walked into the bar and stood staring at Francis LaSalle—
LaSalle and Fleet, Hardware—who lay sprawled on the floor,
his shoulders touching the brass rail under the bar and his
head turned so that his cheek rubbed the black polished
wood above the rail. The bartender had his hands below
the top of the bar and he was watching Simpson and a half
a dozen men arranged in a loose semicircle above and beyond LaSalle.

Bleeker lifted LaSalle, who was a little dazed but not really
hurt, and set him on a chair. After he was sure LaSalle was
all right, he walked up to Simpson.

"Get your men together," he said. "And get them out of
here."

Simpson took a long yellow wallet folded like a book and
laid some money on the bar.

"That should take care of the damages," he said. His
tongue was a little thick, and his mouth didn't quite shut
after the words were spoken, but Bleeker didn't think he
was drunk. Bleeker saw, too—or thought he saw—the little
cold eyes behind the glasses as bright and as sterile as a
painted floor. Bleeker raised his arm slightly and lifted his
heels off the floor, but Simpson turned abruptly and walked
away from him, the men in the troop swaying at his heels

like a pack of lolling hounds. Bleeker stood looking foolishly after them. He had expected a fight, and his body was still poised for one. He grunted heavily.

"Who hit him?" Bleeker motioned toward LaSalle.

"Damned if I know," the bartender said. "They all look alike to me."

That was true, of course. He went back into the lobby, hearing LaSalle say, weakly and tearfully, "Goddamn them —the bastards." He met Campbell, the deputy sheriff, a tall man with the arms and shoulders of a child beneath a foggy, bloated face.

"Can you do anything?" Bleeker asked. The motorcycles were racing up and down the street, alternately whining and backfiring, and one had jumped the curb and was cruising on the sidewalk.

"What do you want me to do?" Campbell demanded. "Put 'em all in jail?"

The motorcycle on the sidewalk speeded up and skidded obliquely into a plate-glass window, the front wheel bucking and climbing the brick base beneath the window. A single large section of glass slipped edge-down to the sidewalk and fell slowly toward the cyclist who, with his feet spread and kicking at the cement, backed clumsily away from it. Bleeker could feel the crash in his teeth.

Now there were other motorcycles on the sidewalk. One of them hit a parked car at the edge of the walk. The rider standing astride his machine beat the window out of the car with his gloved fists. Campbell started down the steps toward him but was driven back by a motorcycle coming from his left. Bleeker could hear the squeal of the tires against the wooden riser at the base of the steps. Campbell's hand was on his gun when Bleeker reached him.

"That's no good," he yelled. "Get the state police. Ask for a half dozen squad cars."

Campbell, angry but somewhat relieved, went up the steps and into the lobby. Bleeker couldn't know how long he stood on the veranda watching the mounting devastation on the street—the cyclists racing past store windows and hurling, presumably, beer bottles at the glass fronts; the two, working as a team, knocking down weighing machines and the signs in front of the motion-picture theater; the innumerable mounted men running the angry townspeople, alerted and aroused by the awful sounds of damage to their property, back into their suddenly lighted homes again or up the steps of his hotel or into niches along the main street, into doorways, and occasionally into the ledges and bays of glassless windows.

He saw Simpson—or rather a figure on the white motorcycle, helmeted and goggled—stationed calmly in the middle of the street under a hanging lamp. Presumably, he had been there for some time but Bleeker hadn't seen him, the many rapid movements on the street making any static object unimportant and even, in a sense, invisible. Bleeker saw him now and he felt again that spasm of anger which was like another life inside his body. He could have strangled Simpson then, slowly and with infinite pride. He knew without any effort of reason that Simpson was making no attempt to control his men but waiting rather for that moment when their minds, subdued but never actually helpless, would again take possession of their bodies.

Bleeker turned suddenly and went back into the lobby as if by that gesture of moving away he could pin his thoughts to Simpson, who, hereafter, would be responsible for them. He walked over to the desk where Timmons and Campbell, the deputy, were talking.

"You've got the authority," Timmons was saying angrily. "Fire over their heads. And if that doesn't stop them—"

Campbell looked uneasily at Bleeker. "Maybe if we could get their leader—"

"Did you get the police?" Bleeker asked.

"They're on their way," Campbell said. He avoided looking at Timmons and continued to stare hopefully and miserably at Bleeker.

"You've had your say," Timmons said abruptly. "Now I'll have mine."

He started for the lobby doors, but Campbell, suddenly incensed, grabbed his arm.

"You leave this to me," he said. "You start firing a gun——"

Campbell's mouth dropped, and Bleeker, turning his

head, saw the two motorcycles coming through the lobby
doors. They circled leisurely around for a moment and then
one of them shot suddenly toward them, the goggled rider
looming enormously above the wide handlebars. They scattered, Bleeker diving behind a pillar, and Campbell and Timmons jumping behind the desk. The noise of the two machines assaulted them with as much effect as the sight of the
speeding metal itself.

Bleeker didn't know why, in course of watching the two
riders, he looked into the hall toward the foot of the stairway. Nor did it seem at all unreasonable that when he
looked he should see Cathy standing there. Deeply, underneath the outward preoccupation of his mind, he must have
been thinking of her. Now there she was. She wore the familiar green robe, belted and pulled in at the waist, and
beneath its hem he could see the white slippers and the pink
edge of her nightgown. Her hair was down, and he had
the impression her eyes were not quite open, although, obviously, they were. She looked, he thought, as if she had
waked, frowned at the clock, and come downstairs to scold
him for staying up too late. He had no idea what time it was.

He saw—and of course Cathy saw—the motorcycle speeding toward her. He was aware that he screamed at her, too.
She did take a slight backward step and raise her arms in a
pathetic warding gesture toward the inhuman figure on
the motorcycle, but neither could have changed—in that
dwarfed period of time and in that short, unmaneuverable
space—the course of their actions.

She lay finally across the lower steps, her body clinging
to and equally arching away from the base of the newel
post. And there was the sudden, shocking exposure of her
flesh, the robe and the gown torn away from the leg as if
pushed aside by the blood welling from her thigh. When he
reached her, there was blood in her hair, too, and someone
—not Cathy—was screaming into his ears.

After a while the doctor came, and Cathy, her head bandaged and her leg in splints, could be carried into his office
and laid on the couch. Bleeker sat on the edge of the couch,
his hand over Cathy's, watching the still white face whose
eyes were closed and would not, he knew, open again. The

doctor, after his first examination, had looked up quickly, and since Bleeker, too, had been bent over Cathy, their heads had been very close together for a moment. The doctor had assumed, almost immediately, his expression of professional austerity, but Bleeker had seen him in that moment when he had been thinking as a man, fortified of course by a doctor's knowledge, and Bleeker had known then that Cathy would die but that there would be also this interval of time.

Bleeker turned from watching Cathy and saw Timmons standing across the room. The man was—or had been—crying, but his face wasn't set for it, and the tears, points of colorless, sparkling water on his jaws, were unexpectedly delicate against the coarse texture of his skin. Timmons waved a bandaged hand awkwardly, and Bleeker remembered, abruptly and jarringly, seeing Timmons diving for the motorcycle which had reversed itself, along with the other, and raced out of the lobby.

There was no sound now either from the street or the lobby. It was incredible, thinking of the racket a moment ago, that there should be this utter quietude, not only the lack of noise but the lack of the vibration of movement. The doctor came and went, coming to bend over Cathy and then going away again. Timmons stayed. Beyond shifting his feet occasionally, he didn't move at all but stood patiently across the room, his face toward Cathy and Bleeker but not, Bleeker thought once when he looked up, actually seeing them.

"The police," Bleeker said sometime later.

"They're gone," Timmons said in a hoarse whisper. And then after a while, "They'll get 'em—don't worry."

Bleeker saw that the man blushed helplessly and looked away from him. The police were no good. They would catch Simpson. Simpson would pay damages. And that would be the end of it. Who could identify Cathy's assailant? Not himself, certainly—not Timmons nor Campbell. They were all alike. They were standardized figurines, seeking in each other a willful loss of identity, dividing themselves equally among one another until there was only a single mythical figure, unspeakably sterile and furnishing the norm for hundreds of others. He could not accuse something which didn't actually exist.

He wasn't sure of the exact moment when Cathy died. It might have been when he heard the motorcycle, unbelievably solitary in the quiet night, approaching the town. He knew only that the doctor came for the last time and that there was now a coarse, heavy blanket laid mercifully over Cathy. He stood looking down at the blanket for a moment, whatever he was feeling repressed and delayed inside him, and then went back to the lobby and out onto the veranda. There were a dozen men standing there looking up the street toward the sound of the motorcycle, steadily but slowly coming nearer. He saw that when they glanced at each other their faces were hard and angry but when they looked at him they were respectful and a little abashed.

Bleeker could see from the veranda a number of people moving among the smashed store-fronts, moving, stopping, bending over and then straightening up to move somewhere else, all dressed somewhat extemporaneously and therefore seeming without purpose. What they picked up they put down. What they put down they stared at grimly and then picked up again. They were like a dispossessed minority brutally but lawfully discriminated against. When the motorcycle appeared at the north end of the street, they looked at it and then looked away again, dully and seemingly without resentment.

It was only after some moments that they looked up again, this time purposefully, and began to move slowly toward the hotel where the motorcycle had now stopped, the rider standing on the sidewalk, his face raised to the veranda.

No one on the veranda moved until Bleeker, after a visible effort, walked down the steps and stood facing the rider. It was the boy Bleeker had talked to in the bar. The goggles and helmet were hanging at his belt.

"I couldn't stand it any longer," the boy said. "I had to come back."

He looked at Bleeker as if he didn't dare look anywhere else. His face was adolescently shiny and damp, the marks, Bleeker thought, of a proud and articulate fear. He should

have been heroic in his willingness to come back to the town
after what had been done to it, but to Bleeker he was only
a dirty little boy returning to a back fence his friends had
defaced with pornographic writing and calling attention to
the fact that he was afraid to erase the writing but was determined nevertheless to do it. Bleeker was revolted. He
hated the boy far more than he could have hated Simpson
for bringing this to his attention when he did not want to
think of anything or anyone but Cathy.

"I wasn't one of them," the boy said. "You remember,
Mr. Bleeker. I wasn't drinking."

This declaration of innocence—this willingness to take
blame for acts which he hadn't committed—enraged Bleeker.

"You were one of them," he said.

"Yes. But after tonight——"

"Why didn't you stop them?" Bleeker demanded loudly.
He felt the murmur of the townspeople at his back and
someone breathed harshly on his neck. "You were one of
them. You could have done something. Why in God's name
didn't you do it?"

"What could I do?" the boy said. He spread his hands
and stepped back as if to appeal to the men beyond Bleeker.

Bleeker couldn't remember, either shortly after or much
later, exactly what he did then. If the boy hadn't stepped
back like that—if he hadn't raised his hand. . . . Bleeker
was in the middle of a group of bodies and he was striking
with his fists and being struck. And then he was kneeling
on the sidewalk, holding the boy's head in his lap and trying
to protect him from the heavy shoes of the men around
him. He was crying out, protesting, exhorting, and after a
time the men moved away from him and someone helped
him carry the boy up the steps and lay him on the veranda.
When he looked up finally, only Timmons and the doctor
were there. Up and down the street there were now only
shadows and the diminishing sounds of invisible bodies. The
night was still again as abruptly as it had been confounded
with noise.

Some time later Timmons and the doctor carried the boy,
alive but terribly hurt, into the hotel. Bleeker sat on the top
step of the veranda, staring at the moon which had shifted

in the sky and was now nearer the mountains in the west. It was not in any sense romantic or inflamed but coldly clear and sane. And the light it sent was cold and sane and lit in himself what he could have liked to hide.

He could have said that having lost Cathy he was not afraid any longer of losing himself. No one would blame him. Cathy's death was his excuse for striking the boy, hammering him to the sidewalk, and stamping on him as he had never believed he could have stamped on any living thing. No one would say he should have lost Cathy lightly—without anger and without that appalling desire to avenge her. It was utterly natural—as natural as a man drinking a few beers and riding a motorcycle insanely through a town like this. Bleeker shuddered. It might have been all right for a man like Timmons who was and would always be incapable of thinking what he—Joel Bleeker—was thinking. It was not—and would never be—all right for him.

Bleeker got up and stood for a moment on the top step of the veranda. He wanted, abruptly and madly, to scream his agony into the night with no more restraint than that of an animal seeing his guts beneath him on the ground. He wanted to smash something—anything—glass, wood, stone— his own body. He could feel his fists going into the boy's flesh. And there was that bloody but living thing on the sidewalk and himself stooping over to shield it.

After a while, aware that he was leaning against one of the wooden pillars supporting the porch and aware, too, that his flesh was numb from being pressed against it, he straightened up slowly and turned to go back into the hotel.

There would always be time to make his peace with the dead. There was little if any time to make his peace with the living.

THE DANCER

Harvey Swados

HARVEY SWADOS *is the author of three books of fiction:*
OUT WENT THE CANDLE *(1955)*, ON THE LINE *(1957)*
and FALSE COIN *(1960)*. *His stories and articles have
appeared in most of the leading American periodicals
in the last decade and have been widely anthologized.
He has taught at the Writer's Workshop of the State
University of Iowa, at New York University, and most
recently at Sarah Lawrence College. In 1957–58 he
was* Hudson Review *Fellow in fiction.*

When Peter Chifley left Elyria, Ohio, for New York City, he
was twenty-one years old. He took with him all the money
he had saved while serving in the occupation forces in Japan, where something had happened which changed the
course of his life.

One day Peter had wandered into a movie where one of
the early Fred Astaire pictures was being shown. He sat
through it three times, and he began to follow the Astaire
movies from one section of Tokyo to another: he was no
longer the same person. Peter felt that the lightness and
grace of Fred Astaire and Ginger Rogers corresponded to
something in the daily life of the Japanese of which he had
been vaguely aware before; and he recognized that Astaire's
trim and airy leaps had released a great creative force
within himself.

He decided to become a dancer.

Peter had never learned to suppress his true feelings, and
when he stepped into the cool winter twilight after a rap-

turous afternoon watching *Top Hat,* he was overcome with
a breathless buoyancy, and he began to dance at once. The
two military policemen who elbowed their way through the
crowd of smiling Japanese leaped to the grotesque conclusion that Peter was drunk; and Peter tried to explain without much success that his movements were wobbly simply
because he had never danced before.

This incident, and several others, may have influenced
the army authorities to return Peter to the United States
somewhat early. He hurried home to Elyria, worried about
what his parents would think of his new ambition; but they
were reasonable people, and when customers gathered in
droves at their lunchroom to watch Peter dancing alone in
the empty lot next door, they could actually measure their
pride and happiness in the ringing of the cash register. However, when they saw that the curious customers never
bought anything except coffee, and that Peter was growing
restless and unhappy, they reluctantly consented to his desire to go to New York to study dancing.

It was a cool sunny day, very early in spring, when Peter's
bus crossed the bridge into Manhattan, and as he craned his
neck to the rear he could see the glowing rays of the de-
clining sun striking sharply against the iron girders of the
bridge, like a vision of his bridges burning behind him.

"Look," he cried without thinking, "look, the bridge is
burning!"

Everyone turned and gaped. Some of the passengers were
disgruntled at seeing only the sunset. A fat man who had
been dozing in the seat directly in front of Peter's muttered
audibly, "Damned yokel! Man can't even take a nap."

"I'm sorry," Peter said tentatively, "I didn't mean to
bother anybody." But no one paid any attention, now that
their goal was so near.

Peter alighted from the bus on Eighth Avenue, in the middle of the city, and found himself surrounded by an even
greater throng than he had ever seen in Tokyo, which was
the only other large city that he knew. These people were
carrying briefcases and newspapers, and some even pushed
wagons filled with Hershey bars and Chiclets. He decided

to approach a shabby smiling man who wore a cardboard hat bearing the words SIGHTSEEING TOURS perched rakishly on his curly gray head.

"Excuse me." Peter spoke, without thinking, in Japanese. "Do you know where I can find a nice clean room?"

"Got much money?" the guide asked coolly.

"No, I don't," Peter admitted, in English. "But how did you understand me?"

"Fortunately you came to the right party, son. I used to coach baseball in Kobe—ran a sex shop on the side." He drew forth a grimy calling card. "Mrs. Blight, who runs this rooming house in Chelsea, went to P.S. 127 with my bookie's sister-in-law. Caters to theatrical people. Tell her Shanker sent you."

"What does P.S. 127 mean?" Peter asked, but the man had already turned away and was calling out softly, as though he hoped no one would hear: "See the secrets of Chinatown, the world-famous Bowery, the tallest building in the world . . ."

Peter picked up his valise and walked slowly downtown in the pale glow of the late afternoon twilight. At 17th Street he took out the card that the guide had given him and surveyed the old red brick houses, some latticed with tough old ivy branches like protruding veins, some with flowerpots on their window ledges. Almost every house bore a small sign: *Furnished Rooms, Rooms for Men,* or *Light Housekeeping Rooms.*

He rang the doorbell of the house that had been recommended to him and was greeted by a small worried-looking woman, who stuck out her tongue at him.

"I'm looking for a room." Peter held out the card. "But if—"

"Oh, Shanker sent you! I thought you were a meter reader. I've been having a feud with the Consolidated Edison Company. Your eyes are going to pop right out of your head when you see the lovely room just waiting for a nice boy like you. At seven dollars a week it's a steal."

Peter followed Mrs. Blight, who was wiping her hands furtively on her meager hips, into a long narrow room that was dark and not lovely at all.

"I'll take it, ma'am. Should I pay you now?"

Mrs. Blight nodded in a motherly way and pocketed the money. "I'll give you a hand-painted receipt tomorrow, Mr.—"

"Chifley. My name is Peter Chifley. I'm going to be a dancer."

"Thrilling! My late husband Benito was an accomplished soap carver—"

She was interrupted by a stout young man who suddenly appeared in the doorway. "An addition to the personnel, Mama?"

"Oh, you startled me! This is Mr. Chifley. I'll leave you two alone now. Angus, you'll explain about the lavatory and the rules, won't you?" She slipped out beneath his outstretched arm and disappeared down the hall.

"Are you Mrs. Blight's son?" Peter asked.

"Oh no! My name is Angus Mondschein. Like yourself, I am a paying guest. I reside directly across the hall, and I entered to ascertain whether I might possibly be of assistance while you were getting acclimated."

"That's very kind of you." Peter surveyed Angus more closely. He was perhaps twenty-five, with an extraordinarily large, fleshy, powerful-looking nose, and a pair of thick, well-nourished ears that grew out of either side of his head like cabbages. His eyes were surprisingly large and soft, and his long white teeth were clamped around a fragrant calabash pipe.

"Where do you hie from?"

"I come from Ohio," Peter replied, "if that's what you mean. My father has a lunchroom in Elyria."

"Ah, a native of the Buckeye State. Have your parents, too, been unable to comprehend your desire for the higher things?"

"I want to go to school. But my parents are being very helpful."

Angus nodded cynically. "A false front. You must make a clean break. May I assist your cogitations, as an older student?"

"That's very nice of you, Mr. Mondschein."

"Call me Angus."

"Do you know of a school where I could study dancing?"

"One must avoid a stereotyped curriculum. I myself have explored the offerings of—" He extended his sturdy fingers under Peter's nose and flexed them at the first joint, one by one, "—the New School for Social Research, the Henry George School, the Ethical Culture School, Cooper Union, and at the moment of speaking I am enrolled in several fascinating courses at the Paul Revere School. If you accelerate your unpacking, you'll be enabled to accompany me to said institution. It's within perambulating distance."

"Do they have dancing courses?" Peter asked dubiously.

"They offer a broad schedule of progressive classes. For a dancer it is essential to grasp the Marxist approach to the arts."

So Peter became a student at the Revere School. . . . It struck him at once as odd that the dance should be known as The People's Dance Group.

"After all," he asked at the first session, "how can you dance without people? I took it for granted that dancing was for people."

This statement created consternation. Almost immediately Peter was characterized as a cynic and a confused aesthete. By the time the class broke up, Peter, who had not even slept one night in New York City, was beginning to think that perhaps he might have done better to stay in the empty lot in Elyria.

"I never would have thought," he said to Angus as they walked home, "that you have to have opinons about the atom bomb. I only want to dance to make myself happy."

"And what about the rest of humanity?" Angus asked severely, escorting him up the steps of Mrs. Blight's house.

"Well, them, too," replied Peter, abashed.

The first thing that struck Peter's eye in Angus' room was a charcoal portrait of Joseph Stalin with a pipe parting his mustache in the middle. Below it on the bureau lay an incredible collection of pipes: narghiles, chibouks, meerschaums, skull pipes, South African gourds. On the desk was a jumble of reamers, after-pipe mints, bushy-tail pipe

cleaners, moistening pellets, initialed pouches, and back is-
sues of *Pipe Lore*.

Peter looked up at a framed letter that hung above the
bed. It was on official United States Senate stationery, and
it read: *Dear Mr. Mondschein, While I agree with you on
the virtues of pipe smoking, as one pipe smoker to another
I must dissociate myself from your unique interpretation of
recent history. I have instructed my secretary to send you
under separate cover the Department of Agriculture pamphlet on The Care of Pipes. Very truly yours, I. Angelo
Sanes.*

"I received that epistle," Angus stated modestly, "in response to a missive that I dispatched to the Senator containing my views on why we should press for closer relations with our former Russian ally."

"You certainly have a wonderful pipe collection."

"I am in correspondence with myriads of individuals in
connection with my collection. And I would not hesitate to
asseverate, as I did to Senator Sanes, that Prime Minister
Stalin's statesmanship, *and* his military genius, can be attributed to his choice of a curved-shank pipe."

"I promised my father I wouldn't smoke until I was
twenty-one," Peter said apologetically, and added, "I certainly appreciate your thoughtfulness, Angus. If you'll excuse me now, I think I'll turn in, because I want to make an
early start tomorrow."

At the door, as if it were an afterthought, Angus reached
out to his bookcase and pulled out a handful of pamphlets.
"You may find it worthwhile to peruse this literature at your
leisure, especially if you are addicted to reading nocturnally
in bed."

"Thank you." Peter was about to cross the hall into his
own room when a group of young men came bounding
along the hallway, giggling and chattering among themselves as they mounted the steps to the floor above.

"They certainly look like they're having fun," Peter said.

"Parties, parties." Angus pursed his lips. "They're very
shallow, Piotr, very shallow indeed. If progressives had to
rely on people of *their* ilk . . ."

Just then one of the young men looked back from the

head of the stairs, raised his fist merrily in a mock salute, turned, and disappeared.

"Well," Peter said, "good night, Angus."

"Good night, Piotr."

When Peter was comfortably settled in bed at last, he picked up one of Angus' pamphlets. *Peace, Plenty, Progress and Prosperity,* written by somebody named Joe Worker, was a dialogue between a very uneducated man and another man who was completely illiterate. Peter read one paragraph, turned out the light, and fell into a deep dreamless sleep.

The next morning Peter arose early and made his way directly to the Veterans Administration office, where he explained his problem to the Vocational Counselor. The office was enormous. It was a nearly bare loft in which several dozen young men milled about, smoking, swearing, arguing, or merely reading the morning papers listlessly and sleepily, as though they were still resentful at their mothers for having routed them out of bed at such an hour. The floor was littered with hundreds of ground-out cigarette butts, and the walls were placarded every few feet with large red and white NO SMOKING signs.

The Vocational Counselor, who had one piercing eye and one wandering eye, sat with his fists clenched angrily on the glass top of his desk, as though he could barely restrain himself from punching Peter in the nose.

"The tests," he said in a hard, quiet voice, "will take two or three days. Then we will know definitely whether you have terpsichorean talent."

"What does that mean?"

"Whether you have the ability to become a dancer. If you don't, we'll recommend another line of work."

"But what good will that do?" Peter asked. "I *know* that I'm a dancer."

"You may be wrong." The Counselor smiled bleakly, fixing Peter with his good eye, while his wandering eye gazed wearily about the room.

"Supposing I am wrong? Then you won't even let me

dance at all, even though that's what I want to do most. Is that fair?"

"I'm here to help you," the Counselor replied threateningly. "If you persist in being willful, you'll only cut your own throat."

"That's cruel!" Peter burst out, so loudly that one fellow nearby started nervously and broke the point of the pencil with which he was doing a crossword puzzle. "That's like killing a baby before it has a chance to learn to walk!"

"You're being a little harsh, Cheaply. Remember that you're talking to a representative of your Uncle Sammy."

"What's that got to do with my dancing?"

The Counselor unclenched his fist and snapped his fingers smartly as though he were calling for a bouncer. Peter took this for a signal that the interview was over and left the office hastily.

He returned home and was about to enter his room when he was once again greeted by the young men whom he had seen the night before. There were actually only two of them this time, but their high-pitched noisy chattering made them sound like a larger company.

"Hul-lo there," said the first, who was exceedingly tall and fair, with two spots of color high on his cheekbones.

His bald-headed companion was plump and moist. He made Peter think of a peeled peach.

"So you're Mama Blight's new boy," said the tall one brightly. "Bert and I thought you were one of the comrades."

"I'm Bert," his moist friend added, "and this is Freddy. We're your upstairs neighbors. If we'd known that you'd moved in, we would have been down for a chat, but we assumed that you were a buddy of Moonshine's."

"Of who?"

Freddy tilted his head at Angus Mondschein's door. "Anxious Moonshine. He tried to convert *us* at first—just imagine!—and he keeps his hand in by propagandizing everyone who moves in."

"He's been very nice to me."

"That's a sure sign he wants to convert you. Has he given you any reading material?"

"Well . . ."

"Oh, let's not stand out here discussing Anxious," Freddy murmured, passing his hand over his pale yellow hair. "We've just come from a fatiguing session at the Unemployment Insurance office. Won't you come up to our digs and have a glass of wine?"

"Thank you, but I've never tasted wine."

"We'll brew some lovely Chinese tea. *Do* come!"

"All right then."

Peter stepped gingerly forward at Freddy's insistence onto a worn oriental rug, and found himself sitting presently on a studio couch, half smothered in little pillows and a fur throw of some sort which Freddy tossed across his lap.

"Now Bert," Freddy said, "do hurry and brew the tea, that's a dear. I'm sure that Mr.—"

"Oh, I'm sorry." Peter struggled to sit erect in the midst of the little pillows. "My name is Peter Chifley. It's just an ordinary name, but everybody seems to get it mixed up."

"That's probably because you're an extraordinary person. I'm going to call you Pierre, if I may," said Freddy. "As for us, Bert is a very promising young poet. His grandfather was a merchant prince of San Diego, and *No Quarter* magazine has already printed one of his poems. And I—" He paused to light an Egyptian cigarette, "—I'm trying for a career on the Broadway stage."

"Are you an actor?"

Freddy began to comb his yellow hair rhythmically with a small gold comb. "I've done one or two small things at the Cherry Lane Theater in summer stock, but I've been forced to clerk from time to time in one of the Doubleday Book Shops. At present Bert and I have to get along on our unemployment checks, plus what Bert receives from his filthy-rich aunt in San Diego."

"Now tell us all about yourself, starting with what brought you to 17th Street," said Bert, who had come in with a flowered tray and was pouring tea into three small oriental cups.

"I came to New York because I wanted to learn how to dance, but I haven't got very far as yet."

"What kind of a dancer are you?"

"I don't know yet."

"It strikes me," Bert said nasally, "that you're not beautiful enough."

"I didn't know you have to be beautiful."

"It's the soul that I'm thinking of. Your face is too pastoral. I think you lack the *spirituel* quality of our truly great mimes."

Peter did not know what a mime was, but he was too cast down by Bert's words to inquire its meaning. Freddy said, with some asperity, "Sometimes you don't know when to stop talking, Bert. Pierre is just on the threshold of a career. In fact I want him to meet the right people and possibly make a few contacts."

Bert leaped to his feet with a snort and began to prowl agitatedly about the room.

"Oh, do sit down, Bert!" cried Freddy. "Someone has to see that Pierre isn't taken in by nuisances like Anxious Moonshine." In the next breath he continued, "While you're at work composing verse I'm going to take Pierre to meet our crowd, and to a few shows, and most important of all he must join a dance group in the Sevenfold School of Theatrical Arts."

Bert remarked coldly, "The only thing you've left out is that we should throw a party for Chipmunk."

"Chifley," Peter said.

"That's a wonderful idea, Bert!" cried Freddy. "Do you have any money, Pierre?"

"A little."

"That's all we need. But we can talk about that later—we'll need to buy wine, pretzels, apples, cigarettes, and soya sticks."

Peter looked up at a painting of a greenish girl seated on a yellow burro. The word "Blight" was lettered on the girl's buttock, like a tattoo. "Isn't that the landlady's name on that girl?"

"Didn't you know?" muttered Bert. "Mama Blight is a painter. Imagine, she gave it to us for a Christmas present!"

"It's kind of funny-looking, isn't it?"

"Ever since she read about Grandma Moses in a picture

magazine," said Freddy, "she made up her mind that she's a great primitive. She makes everybody call her Mama Blight, and she paints only naked ladies with burros."

Peter answered suspiciously, "I never heard of a landlady before who was a painter too."

"Well, you have now," remarked Bert.

"You've been very hospitable," Peter said, his hands sinking into several appliqued pillows as he pushed himself erect, "and I hope you'll come down to visit me in my room soon."

Bert looked at him with renewed belligerence. "Together or separately?"

"Oh gosh," Peter replied, "I don't know. Whichever you want."

Freddy threw back his long fair head and laughed so that Peter could see nearly all his teeth. "Suppose I call for you early in the evening, Pierre, on my way to the Sevenfold School?"

"That'll be all right, I guess. And thanks again."

Peter took the steps two at a time going down to his room. He was restrained from leaping down the entire flight when he caught sight of Angus Mondschein and Mrs. Blight on the landing.

"Hello Angus," he said. "Hello, Mrs. Blight."

"If it isn't the prodigal!" said Angus, puffing furiously on a short stubby pipe. "Have you been killing a fatted calf with the girls upstairs?"

"Did you happen to notice," asked Mrs. Blight, "the painting that I gave Freddy and Bert?"

"I couldn't help but notice it, it's so big."

Angus yanked his pipe out of his mouth and glared at Peter expectantly. "And what was your reaction?"

"I thought it was kind of crazy."

Mama Blight was not put out at all by Peter's judgment. "You'd better watch out," she chuckled, "or I may not give you a primitive for your room!"

"Fortunately," said Angus acidly, "Mom won't request you to pose, inasmuch as she only portrays naked *femmes*."

Peter blushed. "I have to go in and clean up now." As he closed the door behind him, he heard Angus saying to the landlady, "You fail to recognize that the oppressed multitudes will look to your pictures for a clearer understanding . . ."

Peter felt a thrill of excitement that evening when Freddy led him through the corridors of the Sevenfold School building to a gymnasium where many young men and women were leaning forward at strange angles from bars attached to the wall, and cavorting about like young animals. Peter began to tremble with anticipation; but it seemed to be one of the rules of the school that they register first for a classroom course in the Theater of Tomorrow.

When Freddy and Peter entered the classroom, the students were just settling themselves to listen to a guest lecturer, a huge red-haired man with a voice like a foghorn. An enormous metal ring on his index finger glittered every time his fist flashed through the air. "That's Gripping Rotheart, the big producer," whispered Freddy. "He flirts with the avant-garde."

When the class was over, Freddy took Peter by the hand and led him to the front of the room. "Gripping," he said confidently, "I'd like you to meet a new friend of mine, Pierre Chiffon."

Peter was about to correct this when he felt his hand being grasped in a vise of steel. Rotheart squeezed Peter's fingers in his powerful hand as though they were so many grapes. The hand of his skull and crossbones ring cut into Peter's flesh so cruelly that he felt the tears start to his eyes.

"Ah, a nonprofessional," Rotheart boomed, in a kindly tone. "I don't meet many of them."

"We're throwing a little party for Pierre next Friday," smiled Freddy. "Could you drop in for a while—after the show, of course?"

"Love to."

On the way home Freddy spoke excitedly to Peter. "You see? Grip is a force in the theater. Next time he casts a musical, he'll remember you."

"I don't know how to thank you."

Freddy smiled down at him. "Don't worry. I'll show you."

During the next week Peter was truly caught up in the whirlpool of New York theatrical life. It seemed to him at times that he would have drowned if not for the helping arms of Angus Mondschein and Freddy, for he was still not really dancing, and with every passing day he seemed to be further away from his goal. But to tell the truth Angus seemed to be losing interest in him, and indeed to be actually hostile.

This came about as a result of Angus' insistence that Peter invite a homely but progressive Negro girl to go to the Stanley Theater to see a Russian technicolor movie about spores and algae in the Soviet Arctic. "I'd ask her," Peter assured his friend, "except that she doesn't like me, and besides she's so homely. Couldn't I take a nice-looking girl?" "Sometimes," Angus said patiently, "I think that you simply aren't interested in the fight for peace and civil rights." Peter made the mistake of laughing heartily, and replying, "You think I ought to like colored people because they're colored. But I like people because they're people. Isn't that *more* radical? You know, I think you're not radical at all, Angus." To his astonishment Angus was infuriated with this statement, and refused to argue calmly, as he had done on numerous occasions when he had explained that Peter was confused or backward. Peter tried to make amends, but Angus would not yield.

As for Freddy, he took an immense pleasure in escorting Peter to those plays for which Peter could afford to buy them seats, and in introducing him to the members of his set—until the night of the party.

The party was a staggering surprise to Peter, even though he was by now familiar with the habits of Freddy and Bert. When he entered their room, he was stunned by the babbling of voices (some of which were singing a kind of church music) and the thick gray fog of tobacco smoke. He felt quite forlorn, even after Freddy caught sight of him with a gay cry and proceeded to lead him about, introducing him to a collection of strange faces.

In one corner of the room four people were gathered intently about an elderly drunken gentleman wearing suede shoes without stockings, seated in Freddy's sling chair and

reciting very rapidly in French with his eyes closed. A few
feet away, a young lady with long black hair and a flowing
velvet skirt, who looked a little like a witch, was sitting on
the oriental rug, piping sadly on a little wooden recorder.
Her knees were drawn up so close to her chin that Peter
could see clear up to her crotch before he averted his eyes.

Nearby, under Mama Blight's painting, Bert was de-
claiming nasally, "*Tex*tual critics, *tex*tual critics," to a knot
of intensely angry young men.

None of these people paid the slightest attention to Peter,
even when Freddy introduced him as the guest of honor;
and Peter was beginning to wonder how he could steal back
down to his room unobserved, when Freddy deposited him
on the couch in the midst of the little pillows, next to Gripping Rotheart and a beautiful girl.

"Introduce Pierre, won't you, Grip?" Freddy requested.

The producer smiled at Peter in a most friendly way, and
for one tense moment Peter feared that Rotheart was going
to shake his hand in another crushing grip; but the producer
was merely pointing at him with his index finger, on which
the skull and crossbones ring glinted grimly. He wore a
tuxedo, and a stiff white shirt, on which an enormous enameled yellow stone glinted as he swung around.

"Hello again, son," he shouted. "Have you met Imago
Parson? Mag, this is Pedro Chieftain. A nonprofessional."

"How utterly interesting," the girl murmured. She had the
roundest face that Peter had ever seen, and the prettiest little nose, and the roundest eyes, which were a wonderful
orange-brown shade that made him think of Hallowe'en.
They looked at him so intently—in contrast to the supercili-
ous glances everyone else had flung at him—that he felt his
face grow hot. Reluctantly he removed his gaze from her
smooth face, only to find himself staring at her equally
round and luscious bosom, and then at her warm bare little
arms.

"Grip," she said, without turning her eyes away from
Peter, "be a gem and get me a glass of wine."

"Of course."

"Are you a friend of Freddy's, Miss Parson?" Peter
asked.

"You must call me Imago." She smiled, and displayed a number of magnificently even, white teeth. "I went to Bennington College with Bert's sister Electra, a repellent virgin from San Diego. But I'm here tonight because I was eager to meet you."

Imago had leaned forward as she spoke, and now it seemed that she was suspended before him, ready to fall against his chest if she were so much as touched. A spring-like fragrance drifted up to his nostrils from the mysterious valley between her bell-like breasts. Peter felt himself growing dizzy, and as he leaned back among the little pillows, Imago swung about on the couch so that there should be no room for Gripping Rotheart when he returned.

The rest of the evening was a blur. Thinking back on it later, Peter could remember little except the smoke, Imago whispering flattering words, and the angry frustrated expressions of Freddy and Gripping when he and Imago left together.

Nor could he remember his first view of Imago's little apartment, or even how he managed to remove his clothes in the dark without knocking anything over or otherwise making a fool of himself. But he would always be able to recall his halting reference to his total lack of experience, and Imago's clear-eyed, immediate reply.

"How shockingly refreshing!" she had cried. "I'll be the envy of my colleagues!" And then, "Don't just stand there like Dionysus. Come to bed at once, do you hear? At once!"

In the ensuing hours Peter experienced a portion of that soaring delight that he had first previsioned months before in Japan. Intoxicated by Imago's elastic flesh, he began to appreciate simultaneously the pure pleasure of the selfless spirit, and the benefactions that his dancer's body was able to dispense.

So in the early hours of the morning Imago sat up in bed, the faint rays of dawn glowing on her enchanting breasts, and cradled Peter's weary head in her arms. Pressing his damp tousled hair against her smooth belly, she rocked back and forth, crooning contentedly, "You're a little dear, that's what. A dear, do you hear? A dear, a dear!"

In the following weeks Imago Parson consumed Peter as though she were a flame and he a candle, melting slowly under the fierce heat of her ardor. Her dark warm bed was a temple wherein he performed the mystic rites required of him as dancer and lover. For now he was persuaded that he who danced, loved, and he who loved, danced; and it was the assurance that he was realizing his dream, even if in an unexpected way, that sustained Peter in the more difficult daylight hours with his beloved.

Imago was Lotions Editor of *Chic* magazine. It amused her to demand that Peter call for her, for she liked to have a cab waiting on Madison Avenue, and she enjoyed flaunting Peter at the Hormones Editor, an elderly debutante with whom she was continually feuding. Peter even learned to shop in the drugstores for Imago's personal requisites. He was saddened when he discovered that she took the most elaborate precautions in order to keep from becoming a mother; and it was with the greatest reluctance that he purchased those items which seemed so important to Imago. When he had to wait at the rear of the Boring Pharmacy ("Nothing Ever Happens To Our Customers") until everyone else had left so that he could whisper his order, Peter felt that his love for Imago was stretched to its uttermost point.

Yet he was willing to go on, and indeed he was led to recognize the justness of Imago's criticism of the way he lived. She resented the time that he spent with Mama Blight, Angus Mondschein, and Freddy; and Peter had to admit that his outside life was irrelevant to the act of creation that he performed repeatedly for her delectation.

Furthermore, Imago was unutterably annoyed, as she put it, when she learned that Peter had answered an advertisement in the *Journal-American* and gotten a job. In fact she became so angry that her Hallowe'en eyes grew bloodshot and inflamed—and Peter could seek refuge from her accusing voice only in his work.

The ad had read: *Wide-awake livewires needed by Market Analysis and Tip Sheet Organization. Big commissions positively guaranteed to young veteran go-getters fast on their feet. L.A.F. earned $185.72 LAST WEEK!*

The President and Managing Director of Matso was a cadaverous, seedy young man named Moe Spleenwell who wore a sweater coat sprinkled with moth holes and who formed bubbles at the corners of his mouth when he spoke. His office was an incredibly small hutch in a rabbit warren on lower Broadway. Peter was astonished to find that the entire building was broken up into hundreds of tiny wallboard cubicles, each fitted with a desk, two chairs, and a telephone. In most of those into which Peter could see, men with dark blue beards were shouting into telephones, scraping the breakfast egg from their flies, or adding up columns of figures in the margins of their morning newspapers. The open glass doors were inscribed with names calculated to bowl over the casual visitor: GLOBAL FINDINGS CORP., INTERNATIONAL UNION OF PUBLIC OPINION RESEARCH INTERVIEWERS, HEMISPHERIC FEDERATION OF JUTE, HEMP, AND TWEED IMPORTERS, and one more modestly lettered, CHALEH MANUFACTURERS' ASSOCIATION OF GREATER NEW YORK.

"You'll do!" shouted Spleenwell, when Peter had done no more than introduce himself. "Pronounce your name clearly—names are basic, Shifty—and extend your hand in a manly grip. I'm going to teach you how to *swing* into action." He broke off abruptly and commenced staring out his tiny dusty window at the street scene below.

He stared so long that Peter grew uncomfortable and began to think that perhaps Spleenwell had forgotten all about him, half hidden as he was behind high stacks of Matso literature. But in a moment Spleenwell leaped to his feet, flinging his lank black hair out of his eyes and crying, "Plans, dreams, plans! Come, Shifty, let's repair to the ready room. There's money to be made!"

He hustled Peter out of the cubicle and down to the street, where he began to march uptown at a great rate of speed.

"Are we going to take a bus, Mr. Spleenwell?"

"No, no, call me a cab!"

Inside the taxi Moe Spleenwell said to the driver, "To the Hotel Splendide, just as fast as you can." When the taxi careened to a stop at their destination, he leaped out and ran indoors with his head lowered, as if it were raining; Peter paid the driver and hurried after his new employer.

The Hotel Splendide was a furtive-looking structure on
the ragged fringe of Times Square; the Turquoise Room
of the Hotel Splendide was rented by Spleenwell, it appeared, as a classroom for his salesmen.

Matso was a regular bulletin offering inside information
on stock market fluctuations, advice on evading federal
trade regulations, and suggestions on dumping the surplus
war materials of the last three conflicts in which the United
States had been involved. It was mimeographed on butcher
paper and delivered once a month, wrapped in a plain envelope, by messenger. Peter nudged his right-hand neighbor
and whispered, "Why don't they mail it out?"

"Messenger boys are more impressive. Besides," hissed
the young man, "don't you know of the penalties for using
the mails to defraud? You should—they're listed in Matso."

Peter also learned that Moe Spleenwell put out every issue of Matso singlehanded in his Broadway cubbyhole. This
took him about a day and a half each month; the rest of
the time he spent at the race tracks, grimly losing the money
that his salesmen had earned for him. Peter was somewhat
surprised to observe that the *Matso* Master Salesmen, far
from resenting Mr. Spleenwell's deep interest in the horses,
admired the skill with which he managed to keep their working hours at a maximum and his own at a minimum.

At the close of the session all of the salesmen arose,
linked arms, and chanted the company anthem. Moe Spleenwell blew harshly on a pitchpipe, dropping spittle as he
shook his hair out of his eyes, while his agents sang happily, "Matso is tops, it never stops, it never flops! When
Moe's got the dope, why should we mope?"

Peter was issued a Matso Minute Man's kit. It included
a pearl-gray Homburg two sizes too large (for which he was
billed $11.23), a zipper briefcase initialed Z.B.—"for Zip-
per Briefcase," Moe Spleenwell explained with a chuckle
($6.57), a set of three thousand Matso calling cards ($1.74)
on each of which Spleenwell insisted that Peter print his
name with a ball-point pen, and a supply of give-away reminder pads ($9.18) containing useful information for po-
tential subscribers, such as the signs of the Zodiac, the date
of Bruno Richard Hauptmann's execution, and the finish-

ing times in the track and field events of the 1912 Olympic Games. If the pages of the reminder pad were riffled rapidly, one could catch glimpses on the paper's edge of an unclothed girl engaged in an unmentionable activity.

"Gosh," Peter muttered, "I'll have to sell millions of subscriptions before I break even on what I owe already."

"Good boy!" shouted Spleenwell, who had overheard this remark. "Sourpusses starve, Shifty, but you'll ring the bell."

Peter felt a little ridiculous when he set out, his initialed briefcase sagging with Matso material; and when his oversize Homburg fell over his eyes, he was almost run over by a crosstown bus.

For the first few days Peter was unhappy with his work. He would have been extremely lonely, meeting so many people, if it had not been for Imago. And yet something about the city was congruent with his mood: a sense of loss, of something once sought for but long since forgotten, in the faces of all the people, corresponded with his own temper.

One day, while he was hot on the trail of a jobber who was interested in learning how he could legally export to South Africa twenty thousand silk ties hand-painted with obscene pictures, Peter felt something clammy against the back of his hand. He looked down nervously. A little boy of five or six, clutching the remains of an ice-cream sucker, was trying to slip his sticky little fingers into Peter's free hand. He looked straight up at Peter with his grimy earnest face and said, "Cross me, Mister?"

Peter felt his heart turn over. "What's that?"

"Cross me, Mister?" the little boy repeated impatiently.

Peter walked slowly across Seventh Avenue with the child's hand firmly enclosed in his own. At the far side of the street the boy pulled his fingers free as soon as his feet touched the curb. He raised his hand in farewell and ran off without another word, leaving Peter standing on the corner staring after him.

Turning the incident over in his mind, Peter finally decided that he had been so moved because never before had anyone shown such complete faith and trust in him. He could not keep from contrasting the image of the little boy skipping down Seventh Avenue with the memory of himself only the night before, cavorting elatedly before his shadow on Imago's stippled wall. Imago, clapping her hands with delight, had bedecked her glowing nude form with metallic bracelets and, shaking a pair of gaily painted gourds (souvenirs of a Mexican vacation), had rattled out a frenzied accompaniment to his gyrations.

Peter could not wait to speak to Imago about the little boy. At the last minute he decided to visit her that evening instead of going to ballet class.

He inserted the key that Imago had given him in her door and stepped noiselessly into the foyer, intending to surprise her. But there on the love seat only a few feet from him lay a boiled dress shirt, white, rumpled, and shaggy, like a polar bear, with a yellow enameled jewel gleaming dully on its surface, like a polar bear's eye.

Peter recoiled. He bumped into a plaster of Paris forearm splint which Imago had gotten from a lovesick interne so that she could wire it into a lamp, it smashed into smithereens at his feet—and instantly the apartment was ablaze with light.

"How dare you!" growled Gripping Rotheart, sitting erect on the bed, his thick red hair flaming fiercely on his head and chest.

"You've broken my lamp!" wailed Imago, real tears flowing into her fingers as she pressed her hands to her hot cheeks.

Peter picked up the pieces and placed them on the love seat. Then he turned and left Imago's apartment for the last time.

For the first time in his life, Peter was afflicted with insomnia. Night after night he lay in his little room, staring up at the dark ceiling. The disappointments he had suffered were of the kind, he supposed, that people got used to as they grew older—but he didn't *want* to get used to them.

In desperation Peter tried to put himself to sleep by reading the pamphlets that Angus Mondschein had given him; but they only reminded him of Angus (who now avoided him in the hallway), and when they did succeed in putting him to sleep, he only had nightmares and awoke sweating and unhappy.

His waking life, selling for Moe Spleenwell, seemed to grow steadily more unpleasant, but for some days Peter could not bring himself to admit that it was anything more than his own depressed state of mind which made so many people appear cruel, acquisitive, and coldhearted.

The crisis came one day while he was wandering through the shiny overheated catacombs beneath Radio City. Turning a bend in the corridor, so that suddenly he could see the rich people, the Europeans, and the tourists lunching under the awnings in Rockefeller Plaza, he came upon a group of sightseers listening to a blue-uniformed girl.

"Three hundred million tons of solid rock," she was saying briskly, "were blasted through, solely that you might stand here and marvel at modern science and American civilization."

"That's ridiculous!" Peter cried. "Even Angus Mondschein——"

Everyone turned to look at him. The guide compressed her lips and folded her arms as though she were waiting for Peter to disappear; but her listeners pounced on him as though he were a sneak thief. One little beady-eyed man pointed his rolled-up umbrella at Peter and said, "Where's your button, Mr. Wise Guy?"

It was true that everyone else wore a large button pinned over the heart. But Peter replied indignantly, "I don't see what that's got to do. I've got a right——"

"Oh no you don't, smarty. You didn't pay, and you've got no right, none at all."

"But I——"

Someone shouted, "Go on back to 14th Street, you troublemaker!"

Disheartened and puzzled, Peter escalated up from the cavern. He mounted a downtown bus that would take him to 14th Street, as they had suggested, and seated himself in the rear.

At Union Square Peter arose and walked to the front, but the entrance was blocked. The driver was engaged in

an altercation with a fat Negro woman who had attempted
to pay her fare with a five-dollar bill.

"You got a hell of a nerve, lady!" the driver yelled.

"I got nothing smaller."

"I never saw nothing bigger, either. You ought to pay
double."

"Don't get smart."

"All right then, here's your change!" He emptied the
pennies from his change-maker and hurled them angrily at
the woman. Soon the floor was carpeted with coppers which
she stooped to pick up, muttering curses while the driver
continued to fling pennies at her. At last she could stand it
no longer and began to belabor the driver about the head
with a heavy handbag.

The passengers sat quietly. Some watched the fight
openly, grinning uneasily, but most shoved their faces into
their afternoon papers, or simply gazed languidly out the
windows at the sweating crowd waiting to board the bus.

"Isn't anybody going to do anything?" Peter asked in a
loud trembling voice. He remembered how he had cried
out, seeing the fiery sun behind the bus that had brought
him to New York so recently. How different his excitement
had been then! "People can't live like this. There isn't time!"

"The kid's right," a husky laborer spoke up to the driver.
"We haven't got time to horse around. Give her the change
and let's get going."

"Come on, lady," another man said to the Negro woman.
"My boss is waiting for me. Take the pennies and let's go."

"That's not what I meant!" cried Peter. He stepped between the driver and the Negro woman, holding them apart
with his arms. "Why don't you make up? Don't you want to
do anything better than this with your lives?"

The bus driver looked up with his arm still extended over
his head. "If you don't like it, buster, you can always get
off."

"That's right, boy," the woman chimed in, glaring at
Peter. "Go on, get lost."

Peter stumbled from the bus. If only he could have explained!

Patches of tar were bubbling in the broiling streets.

Women raised their bare arms to push back damp strands
of hair, exposing wet bristly armpits. A hot wind blew the
sticky wrappers of ice-cream suckers against Peter's legs.
He shuddered with a sudden chill and tried to walk faster,
but his feet were clinging to the melting tar. On an impulse
he turned and passed a Good Humor man who sagged
limply at the curb, wailing softly like a muezzin at prayer
time, and entered the lobby of an office building at the far
end of Union Square.

Listlessly Peter surveyed the glassed-in board which carried the alphabetical listing of the building's tenants. His eye
was caught by the firm of Ginsburg and Gainsborough.

"Fifteen, please," Peter said wearily to the elevator
operator.

Ginsburg and Gainsborough, Converters, occupied the
entire fifteenth floor. The first thing that Peter saw as he
stepped from the elevator was a rotogravure blowup, covering one entire wall, of a modernistic factory. Above its
smoking streamlined chimneys was a sign: OUR WOON-
SOCKET FACTORY. At the far end of the reception room, in
front of the long window, a girl with shoulder-length yellow
hair was seated behind a kidney-shaped desk, reading a
novel and sucking her thumb.

The book was called *Queen of the Seize,* and its dust
jacket displayed a listing frigate and a big sullen girl whose
bust was bursting upwards from its sheath like two ripe
onions. The receptionist's hand was curled tensely around
the corners of the book; her fingernails were tinted an
emerald green.

"Pardon me," Peter said dully, looked down at her
model's hostess gown and her gold platform shoes.

"You'll have to wait until I finish this chapter," she replied, without looking up. She had removed her thumb from
her mouth: she looked at it carefully, observing how the
green nail polish had worn off, shook her head sadly so that
her yellow hair swung slowly across her face, put the thumb
back in her mouth, and resumed reading.

Peter dropped his zipper briefcase on a chair. What am
I doing here? he thought. What shall I ask this girl? Actually

he had only desired to escape for a little while from the heat and crush outside.

There was a steady humming coming from someplace outside his head. Peter walked cautiously to the far end of the reception room and peered through a small glass peephole set into a leather-padded door. He found himself looking into a large workroom where four rows of elderly women, fagged and worn, were drooping over sewing machines, stitching slowly on large bolts of a glittering fabric similar to the gown that the receptionist was wearing. To the right of the workroom an arched open doorway led into the private office of Ginsburg and Gainsborough, where the two owners sat facing each other across a wide green desk before an open window.

One of them was a tall corpselike blond, with a monocle screwed tightly into his face and the longest, saddest jaw in the world. The other was a ferocious little bald man whose ears stuck out like handles and whose mashed nose spread out across his face like a pancake. They were both chewing bubble gum energetically—Peter could hear it snap above the whirring of the sewing machines—and they had handkerchiefs tucked around their necks to keep their collars from becoming soiled. They were playing gin rummy with the largest deck of cards that Peter had ever seen. The cards were bigger than seafood menus, so that when they were held up fanwise Mr. Ginsburg and Mr. Gainsborough could not see each other's faces. The blond one peered suspiciously through his monocle around the edge of his cards at his bald little partner, who was keeping score with a piece of red chalk on a tall blackboard that stood against the wall. All around their desk the floor was littered with what looked like little snowballs; but then, as Peter observed them mopping their necks and foreheads, he saw that the little snowballs were wadded-up pieces of Kleenex which the partners flung to the floor each time they wiped the perspiration from their faces.

"My God," sighed the receptionist. Peter started guiltily. "A hundred and two pages and she hasn't even got her feet wet. Although it's true," she added magnanimously, "that four different guys have stripped her clear down to *here*."

And she pointed to her navel, the indentation of which Peter could see quite clearly through the thin sheath of her gown. "It's enough to drive you crazy. What can I do for you?"

"Why . . ." Peter hesitated. "Maybe you can tell me what Mr. Ginsburg and Mr. Gainsborough convert."

"Mostly each other." The girl uttered a short metallic laugh. "Little baldy is Gainsborough, and the tall one with the monocle is Ginsburg. Life is full of surprises. . . . What you selling, kiddo?"

"An invaluable periodical for forward-looking business-men published by Moe Spleenwell of Matso," replied Peter automatically. "Every issue is guaranteed to double the profits of any shrewd operator, including converters."

"There's no profits to double. You're wasting your time here—unless you want to pick me up later and take me to an air-cooled show."

"But what about the Woonsocket factory?"

"That just shows to go you. G and G wouldn't know how to get to Woonsocket if you put them on the train. They borrowed that picture from *Fortune* magazine—it's the new-est Finnish suppository factory, in Helsinki."

"But . . ." Peter shuddered as a drop of perspiration freed itself from his collar and crawled slowly down his back. ". . . But what about all those old women working on the sewing machines?"

"They work for a guy named Bulldozer. G and G rent office space from him. They share my services with Bull-dozer, too, if you know what I mean." The girl yawned, arched her feline back, scratched her shoulder blade with a green fingertip, and crossed her silken legs smoothly, with a soft hissing sound. "What about that movie—didn't you ever play with a girl in the dark, or what?"

"If you'd let me see them for a minute, maybe I—"

"Impossible. They're in conference."

"But I just saw them playing cards."

"They're not seeing anyone for at least two more months. It's too hot right now. As far as that movie is concerned, I'll have to consult my engagement book. Just wait a min-ute." She uncrossed her legs with the same hissing sound and swung open the door of the typewriter cabinet at the side of the kidney-shaped desk.

A dead baby was lying on its back in the drawer. The little body rested on several sheets of carbon paper; its wrinkled thighs were smudged with ink, its tiny feet tangled in a snarl of paper clips and rubber bands.

A scream rose like a bubble of blood in Peter's throat. He backed away from the desk, unable to look at the receptionist, turned, and ran noiselessly on the broadloom carpet to the door at the far end of the room. He rushed into the workroom where the old women labored at their machines.

"Help!" he croaked. He grasped the nearest woman by the arm. "A baby . . . there's a dead baby in that room!"

The old lady showed him the bloodshot whites of her eyes. She shook off his hand. "I can't quit work. Got to meet my quota." She nodded toward the office. "See them in there."

Peter ran ahead into the office, crushing the little balls of Kleenex under his feet. Before he could say anything, the blond man threw down his giant cards and exclaimed happily, "I knock with five!"

"There's a baby . . ." Peter sobbed.

The bald man cracked his bubble gum and pulled on his jug-handle ear. "Ophelia," he shouted angrily, "who is this interloper?"

"A nut," answered the receptionist, who had followed Peter into the office.

"I'm Peter Chifley," Peter cried. "I'm a man. She has a dead baby in her desk!"

"You're overwrought, old boy," said the bald little man, rubbing his flat nose.

"You've got a bad case of sunstroke," said the blond man, blowing on his monocle and polishing it with a piece of Kleenex.

"He's hard up," said the receptionist.

"You're both guilty," Peter said imploringly, "if you don't do anything about this."

"I seen once a man at Brighton Beach," the blond man said, "was affected just like this. A vision he said he had, right by where they rent the beach umbrellas. And then he started to jump around like crazy."

"You're the ones that are crazy. All of you."

"You're right, Mr. G," the receptionist nodded, tugging at her garter. "First thing you know he'll start to dance around the office like Fred Astaire."

"What's wrong with that?" sobbed Peter. "Isn't that better than killing a baby that hasn't even had a chance to walk?"

"You got maybe a point there." Mr. Ginsburg smiled around his monocle. "Let's sit down a minute and talk about it."

Mr. Gainsborough took a small black leather case from the top drawer of his desk, opened it with his thumbs, and displayed the three joints of a fine silver flute and blew one or two experimental notes. "Charms to soothe the savage breast, you know."

Peter stared at the little man in horror. "How can you play at a time like this?"

"The same way you can dance. You *can* dance, can't you, old chap?"

Peter could find no words with which to answer. Ophelia the receptionist stood in the doorway, blocking his path with her aggressive hips; Mr. Ginsburg smoothed down his hair and fanned his long thin face with a jack of spades. Mr. Gainsborough dug a piece of wax from the depths of his brawny ear and pointed the embouchure of his flute at Peter.

"Suppose I attempt a few notes of Ravel's *Pavane for a Dead Princess?*"

"No! No!"

But Gainsborough put the flute to his lips and began to play. While Peter held his breath, he could only hear Gainsborough breathing through his silver flute, and Ophelia breathing through her pores; but as soon as he himself began to breathe once again, the grave melodic line sank slowly, like a baited silver thread dropping down through clear water, into the depths of his soul.

"All right," he whispered, feeling his feet moving slowly along the hot dusty floor. "I'll dance again . . . but not for you!" And with a bound he cleared the distance to the open window and gained the granite ledge that overhung the street, fifteen stories below.

"Holy Jesus," muttered Ophelia, "did you see him go?"

"Come back, sonny!" screamed Mr. Ginsburg, leaning out the window and reaching gingerly for Peter's twinkling foot.

"Should I stop playing?" Gainsborough asked fearfully. "Perhaps I should notify the super, or the cops."

"Call Bellevue," said Ophelia. She moved jerkily toward the telephone.

"Don't stop!" Peter called in. "Keep on playing!"

As Gainsborough blew frantically on his flute, Peter moved easily along the ledge until he was out of anyone's reach. In the clear blaze of the afternoon sun he was sharply outlined against the face of the building, and in a few minutes, while he wheeled, dipped, and spun on the narrow stone, the heads of stenographers and their bosses began to pop out of windows all around him. Peter could even hear their exclamations and their gasps. Far below a crowd began to gather. They collected on the far side of the street, as though they were afraid that Peter might plummet to the ground in their midst.

It was the greatest audience that Peter had ever had, and it increased with every step that he took. He wanted desperately to express the elemental things he had learned in a way that everyone could understand. But it was no use. He could not look at the hundreds of gaping faces, watching him as though he were a chef frying eggs behind a plate-glass window.

And so Peter closed his eyes. As he glided slowly along the protruding lip of the building, the figures of the people he had known rose before him in the darkness like crying statues: Mama Blight and Anxious Moonshine, Freddy and Bert, Imago Parson and Gripping Rotheart, Moe Spleenwell and Ophelia the receptionist.

"Easy now," a startlingly near voice murmured. "Just a few feet more."

Peter opened his eyes. Just a few steps ahead an elderly man in a Palm Beach suit was leaning toward him from a corner window, his bifocal glasses glittering in the sunlight.

"Don't be nervous," the man said, gesturing to Peter with his fingers crooked. "Take it easy."

"But I'm not nervous," Peter replied in some exasperation. "You look a lot more nervous than me. Besides, I have no intention of coming in."

"Wouldn't you like one of these to keep?" The man held out a gaudy pamphlet entitled *Jungle Comics*.

"What for?"

"How about this?" In his other hand the man held an Esquire Girl Calendar which he waved so that it flapped in the wind.

"I'm sorry," Peter said patiently. "I don't know why you think I'd be interested in that. Maybe you ought to see a doctor."

"Now see here—"

Peter turned away and walked back toward the faint sound of Gainsborough's flute; but he had not gone more than a few steps when he saw a blood-red face dangling upside down just above his head. The face belonged to a policeman who seemed to be hanging by his toes from a sixteenth-floor window.

"Look out!" Peter cried.

"It's all right," said a voice from above. A fireman was holding the policeman by the ankles. "We're going to save you."

"That's right," gasped the policeman in a strangled voice. "Just take my hands and hang on. We'll haul you up."

"I don't want to be hauled up."

"Don't you want to be helped?" asked the policeman angrily.

"No!" Peter backed away from his dangling arms. "Help yourself! Save yourself first."

From the other corner of the building the elderly man was making his way slowly toward Peter, a stout rope tied about his waist. He was waving a long railroad ticket in one hand; in the other he brandished a melting ice-cream sucker.

"Look at the nice things I have for you," he said menacingly.

"Go back. Please."

"How would your parents feel if they knew all the trouble you're causing?"

"That's cruel! How could you say anything so cruel?"

The music had stopped. But Peter could not have danced any more even if Gainsborough had continued playing, because the elderly man and the policeman were closing in on him. He took a step forward on the granite ledge and looked up at the heavens, at the sky, last free space in all the world.

Two airplanes were gamboling through the cool blue air, swooping and darting as gaily as two young birds. But then Peter saw that they were not merely frisking: they were engaged in a hawklike duel to the death, streaming trails of white spume as they ferociously intertwined the words PEPSI COLA and I J FOX in a frenzied tangle of melting loops of smoke.

Peter silently asked forgiveness of his parents, of all the people he had met, and of the crowd waiting tensely for his next movement. Then he opened his arms and dove slowly through space, his hair streaming back in the summer sky, his eyes flashing silver tears, as the stone curtain of the sidewalk rose triumphantly on his final dance.

ANCHOR BOOKS

AMERICAN HISTORY AND STUDIES

LITTELL, FRANKLIN H.   From State Church to Pluralism, A294
LUBELL, SAMUEL   The Future of American Politics, A71
LUKACS, JOHN   A History of the Cold War, A322
LYNN, KENNETH S., ed.   The Comic Tradition in America, A187
MC GEE, REECE J., & CAPLOW, THEODORE   The Academic Marketplace, A440
MARTINEAU, HARRIET   Society in America, ed. Lipset, A302
MASSEL, MARK S.   Competition and Monopoly, A386
MAYER, MARTIN   The Schools, A331
MELVILLE, HERMAN   Selected Poems of Herman Melville, ed. Cohen, A375
MILLER, PERRY, ed.   The American Puritans, A80
—— The American Transcendentalists, A119
—— The Legal Mind in America, A313
—— Margaret Fuller: American Romantic—A Selection from Her Writings and Correspondence, A356
PEEL, ROBERT   Christian Science: Its Encounter with American Culture, A446
PETERSEN, WILLIAM, ed.   American Social Patterns, A86
PIERSON, GEORGE W.   Tocqueville in America (Abridged), A189
POWELL, SUMNER CHILTON   Puritan Village: The Formation of a New England Town, A441
RAAB, EARL   American Race Relations Today, A318
—— Religious Conflict in America: Studies of the Problem Beyond Bigotry, A392
RANSOM, HARRY HOWE   Can American Democracy Survive Cold War?, A402
RIESMAN, DAVID   Constraint and Variety in American Education, A135
—— Selected Essays from Individualism Reconsidered, A58
ROURKE, CONSTANCE   American Humor, A12
ROZWENC, EDWIN C., ed.   Ideology and Power in the Age of Jackson, AD1
SANFORD, CHARLES, ed.   Quest for America, 1810–1824, AD3
SMITH, LILLIAN   Killers of the Dream, A339
TAYLOR, WILLIAM R.   Cavalier and Yankee: The Old South and American National Character, A351
VERNON, RAYMOND   Metropolis 1985, A341
VIDICH, ARTHUR, & BENSMAN, JOSEPH   Small Town in Mass Society, A216
WARSHOW, ROBERT   The Immediate Experience—Movies, Comics, Theatre and Other Aspects of Popular Culture, A410
WASHBURN, WILCOMB, ed.   The Indian and the White Man, AD2
WHYTE, WILLIAM H., JR.   The Organization Man, A117
WILLIAMS, JOHN A.   White Man, Listen!, A414
WILSON, EDMUND   The American Earthquake: A Documentary of the Jazz Age, the Great Depression and the New Deal, A382
WOODWARD, C. VANN   Reunion and Reaction, A83

AMERICAN FICTION

BARTHELME, DONALD   Come Back, Dr. Caligari, A470
HARRIS, MARK   Bang the Drum Slowly, A324
JAMES, HENRY   What Maisie Knew, A43
JEWETT, SARAH ORNE   The Country of the Pointed Firs, A26
MELVILLE, HERMAN   Redburn, A118
WILDER, THORNTON   Heaven's My Destination, A209

ANCHOR BOOKS

BRITISH FICTION

CONRAD, JOSEPH   The Secret Agent, A8
—— The Shadow-Line, Typhoon *and* The Secret Sharer, A178
—— Under Western Eyes, ed. Zabel, A323
—— Victory, A106
—— Youth, Heart of Darkness *and* The End of the Tether, A173
KIPLING, RUDYARD   The English in England: Short Stories by Rudyard
   Kipling, ed. Jarrell, A362
—— In the Vernacular: The English in India, ed. Jarrell, A363
MISH, CHARLES C., ed.   Anchor Anthology of Short Fiction of the Seven-
   teenth Century, AC1
SNOW, C. P.   The Masters, A162
WEINTRAUB, STANLEY, ed.   The Yellow Book: Quintessence of the Nineties,
   A421

CONTINENTAL FICTION

ALAIN-FOURNIER, HENRI   The Wanderer, A14
CHEKHOV, ANTON   Ward No. 6 *Six Russian Short Novels,* ed. Jarrell, A348
COLETTE   My Mother's House *and* The Vagabond, A62
DOSTOEVSKY   Three Short Novels of Dostoevsky, A193
FLORES, ANGEL, ed.   Nineteenth Century German Tales, A184
GOGOL, NIKOLAI   The Overcoat *Six Russian Short Novels,* ed. Jarrell, A348
JARRELL, RANDALL, ed.   Six Russian Short Novels, A348
LERMONTOV, MIHAIL   A Hero of Our Time, A133
LESKOV, NIKOLAI   The Lady Macbeth of the Mtsensk District *Six Russian
   Short Novels,* ed. Jarrell, A348
MERWIN, W. S., trans.   The Life of Lazarillo de Tormes, A316
SERGE, VICTOR   The Case of Comrade Tulayev, A349
TOLSTOY, LEO   The Death of Ivan Ilych *and* Master and Man *Six Russian
   Short Novels,* ed. Jarrell, A348
TURGENEV, IVAN   A Lear of the Steppes *Six Russian Short Novels,* ed.
   Jarrell, A348

ORIENTAL LITERATURE

KAI-YU, HSU, trans. & ed.   Twentieth Century Chinese Poetry—An Anthol-
   ogy, A413
KANG-HU, KIANG   The Jade Mountain—Being Three Hundred Poems of the
   T'ang Dynasty 618–906, trans. Bynner, A411
MURASAKI, LADY   The Tale of Genji, trans. Waley
   Vol. I—A55
SCOTT, A. C.   Literature and the Arts in Twentieth Century China, A343
TSAO HSUEH-CHIN   Dream of the Red Chamber, trans. Wang, A159

A 2a

ANCHOR BOOKS

DOLPHIN BOOKS

AMERICAN FICTION

DOLPHIN BOOKS

BRITISH FICTION

CONTINENTAL AND OTHER FICTION